Whitstead Harvestide

Enjoy the
Hantastical
adventures!
Ronnell Rae
Smith

Whitstead Harvestide

A Speculative Anthology

For all those who have struggled in this last year.
'All shall be well, all shall be well,
and all manner of things shall be well.'

Although the fig tree shall not blossom, neither shall fruit be in the vines; the labour of the olive shall fail, and the fields shall yield no meat; the flock shall be cut off from the fold, and there shall be no herd in the stalls: Yet I will rejoice in the LORD, I will joy in the God of my salvation. ~Habakkuk 3:17-18

Contents

Introduction

In the autumn of 2020, we went mad. What began whimsically soon turned into the strange, magnificent, quirky, sublime thing that is Whitstead and the *Whitstead Christmastide* anthology. It turned out far more successful than we ever anticipated, bringing together a community of writers and readers. So, of course, we had to put together a follow-up collection.

These stories take place the year after the events of the first anthology, and many feature characters we met there and grew to love (or hate). While it isn't necessary to read Christmastide first to enjoy these stories, many refer to previous events and you might find more depth and richness when you have read them all.

The stories ahead contain characters that appear and reappear, events that shape or explain other tales, and hold many crossover easter eggs that are a delight to spot. Whitstead is a small, quiet farming village where little happens and everyone knows everyone else, so it's natural that they drop in on each other's lives—even when faeries happen to be involved too!

Harvest-time has come to the Whitstead countryside and with it, struggle and difficulty. 1845 has been a cold, damp year, and the autumn is no balmier. Darkness threatens to take advantage of the hard-worn village, as All Hallows' Eve nears and with it the thinning of barriers between worlds...

Along with the wonder and bounty of autumn, this anthology explores the true meaning behind All Hallows' Eve and the darkness that often touches it. But evil is confronted in these pages. Sometimes, the battle is hard and the cost is high, but it is always worth it—faith, hope, and love conquer, light overcomes the darkness, and the battle is always our Lord's. If you come to this book amidst difficult times of your own, we hope you find encouragement as well as escape, tears of laughter as well as joy, thrills of mystery and adventure as well as romance. And the reminder that all shall be very well.

Abigail Falanga and Sarah Falanga

Map

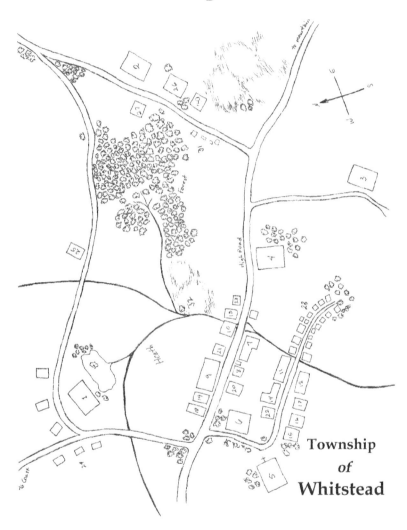

Township
of
Whitstead

Map Legend

The Mirror, Whitstead, All Hallows' Eve
by David Wayne Landrum *(ghost story/historical)*

enelope hugged Samantha Clark, gave her a kiss on the cheek, and saw her to the door. Reverend Hollybrook heard it close and heard his wife's footfalls as she came up the stairs. Once she entered the parlour, he took her hands.

'How is Samantha?'

Penelope shook her head. 'Not good. She's still very upset at what happened — upset and heartbroken.'

Samantha was enduring the aftermath of a broken engagement. The young man's dismissal of his bride-to-be two weeks ago, only one month before the planned wedding, had been abrupt and rude. He had visited her, given her the news that he had found someone new, and departed, leaving Samantha behind, hurt and stricken.

Reverend Hollybrook headed to his study, located in a small building a short way from his house and on the same plot as Saint Nicholas' Church. All Hallows' Eve was near. The weather had been cold, rainy, and nasty. He pulled his collar up and shivered as he walked the distance, went inside, and closed the door behind him. He stoked a fire in the hearth and lit a lamp. The tiny, cosy room where he wrote sermons, studied, and sometimes counselled warmed up. He took out a sheet of paper, dipped his pen, and began to write some notes for his next sermon.

He sensed something, turned, and saw Sister Elisabeth.

Sister Elisabeth was a ghost. Usually, he encountered her at the ruins of Saint Etheldreda's Convent, which lay a mile or so beyond the town (it had been closed in 1540). He had never seen her here, in the study, before.

'Welcome,' he said. 'You're in unfamiliar territory.'

'I've been here once or twice,' Elisabeth replied. 'It used to be an auxiliary site for the convent — only used for storage — mostly books.'

Elisabeth wore a white habit and wimple. Tall, straight, and beautiful, she cut a striking figure — not in the least ghostly. When he first met her, he had doubted his sanity. But years of her visitations had convinced him she was real and not a creation of his mind.

'Are any of the convent's books still here?' Hollybrook asked.

'Maybe a few stuck in nooks and crannies,' Elisabeth said. 'But that isn't why I came here. I'm concerned about the girl who just visited your home.'

'Miss Clark?'

1

'Yes. She's a relative—distant, but she carries my family's blood in her veins—my blood as well.' Elisabeth had left the convent after it closed in the dissolution of such establishments under Henry VIII. Now, her descendants walked the streets of the village.

"The girl is in great danger,' Elisabeth said.

'How?'

'All Hallows Eve is approaching. It's a night when lost spirits roam—spirits who only know evil and, like their master, come for no other reason than to steal and kill and destroy. In her melancholy state, she is a prime target for their attacks.'

'They might try to possess her?'

'No. She is a believer. But they will strike at her heart, play upon her emotions, and use the sorrow she feels to lead her into a desperate act.'

'Suicide?'

'Yes. She is quite low; and they are very potent with such spirits,' she answered.

By 'such spirits' she meant people who were, in their spirits, suffering as Samantha Clark was suffering. He wondered if Elisabeth's word usage was simply from the era in which she had lived or if she were referring to Shakespeare's play *Hamlet* that made use of that particular phrase (she might have seen the play when Shakespeare was still alive).

'That's sobering news,' he said.

'I've come here with a plan to keep her safe during the assaults on her spirit—which will undoubtedly come with some strength on All Hallows.'

'We can pray for her protection.'

'Pray, as always. But I've a plan that will make the ordeal much easier. However, I will need your help.'

He gave her a quizzical look. She only smiled. Her smiles always presaged some sly and brazen scheme.

•◇•◇•◇•◇•◇•◇•◇•

The next day Roland Simmons came to Matins. Only a handful of people attended the morning prayer service, especially in late October weather. Rain poured outside. Worshippers wore oilcloth coats and cloaks and carried umbrellas. Mr Simmons came in last, took off his cloak, placed his umbrella in the holder and joined the other eight worshippers.

Samantha Clark was one of them.

They did not sit near each other. Yet Reverend Hollybrook knew that when Elisabeth worked her spells, she performed them efficiently and with hardly any delay. That the two of them were here together was probably her doing. He finished reading the service of prayer and wondered if Samantha and Roland would speak, but they did not. Samantha smiled at Hollybrook and left quickly, not joining the knot of worshippers who always gathered after the service to chat and exchange pleasantries. Hollybrook spoke with Roland Simmons.

'Good to see you back, Mr Simmons,' he said.

The young man smiled. He worked for his father's business at the London branch and was absent from the village most of the year.

'Yes, Reverend. I'm back in town. I thought I would attend Matins this morning.'

'Welcome home, and I trust we'll be seeing more of you.'

The young man took leave. The church had emptied out by now.

Hollybrook took off his surplice. He knew Roland Simmons had some part in whatever Elisabeth planned to do.

He returned home. Rain lashed the windows as he sat down in the parlour. Penelope brought him tea. The children were at school.

'Collin asked if he could join a group of children who plan to go revelling on All Hallows Eve,' she said when she sat down.

'Revelling?'

'Lighting bonfires, calling up spirits, using divination to see who will marry whom. Those sorts of things. No doubt it will be only harmless fun, but a few people are objecting to the idea.'

Penelope said this because some of the more pious people in the church had encouraged her husband to denounce the things that went on during All Hallows'. Those objecting to the practices complained that bonfires originally were 'bone fires' from human sacrifices held in ancient times on that day of evil customs and the pagan celebration of Samhain. Hollybrook intended to spend some time reading up on the issue but, the next day, as he leafed through his library looking for books that might address the subject of the debate, he came upon an ancient, leather-bound volume he did not remember seeing before. He took it out of its place and, opening it, saw it was not printed but written in the beautiful, ornate calligraphy of the Middle Ages. His pulse quickened to think he might have unearthed a hitherto unknown book from ancient days. His heart fluttered when he saw the title. He had discovered a hand-written copy of Julian of Norwich's *Revelations*, composed around 1410.

He ran back and burst into the house to share the joyous news of his find. Penelope was there with Samantha. Hollybrook muted his excitement to respect the presence of their guest, but both Penelope and Samantha had seen his elation. They smiled and asked him what was afoot. He explained.

'Saint Julian,' Samantha said. 'Oh, yes. Her most famous quotation has always been a comfort to me.'

Though called a saint, Julian had never been canonized. The nun from the 1400s was famous for the 'revelation' given to her by Jesus Christ that 'all shall be well, and all manner of things shall be well.' It was to this quotation that Samantha had undoubtedly referred.

3

Hollybrook smiled. 'I am excited about stumbling across this, as both of you can see. It's a marvellous discovery – right under my nose and I didn't ever know it, even as much as I use the library.'

As he spoke, he realised the book had been placed there for him to find. He also knew who had placed it there.

'I've never read the book in its entirety,' Samantha said. 'I would love to possess a copy like this one.'

'It's valuable' Hollybrook said, 'and so old that a library might be a better custodian of it than I would be. At any rate, we'll find out.' Then an idea sparked into his mind. 'Perhaps,' he added, 'before I pass it on to better caretakers, I might organise a read-through of the text – open to the public.'

'That would be wonderful,' Samantha said.

'We'll see about it.'

He took leave of Penelope and Samantha and returned to his study. Undoubtedly, Elisabeth had left the book there for him. He could not fathom why.

•◇•◇•◇•◇•◇•◇•◇•◇•

'All we're going to do is to re-enact some old customs – things from local legends. We're doing these enactments for the Whitstead Folk Society.'

Anita – Samantha's older (and married) sister – addressed a group of people who had gathered at the village meeting hall.

'These are simply re-enactments of old folk customs,' she continued. 'They have nothing to do with the occult. We are enacting them to build a sense of community and an appreciation of our village's past. All of it is wholesome, silly and educational fun.'

Anita had deliberately emphasised the word 'educational.'

Hollybrook had seen enough debates over theological issues to know when one side had got the better of the other. And in this case, those suggesting that the old customs the Folk Society meant to re-enact were harmless and purely educational were winning the debate. The Folk Society was popular in Whitstead and included many prominent, well-educated, and wealthy citizens.

'Besides,' Anita Garrick added, 'They are all related to marriage and how someone can get a vision of who might be their spouse. I don't see how *that* can endanger anyone's immortal soul.'

This brought a smattering of laughter. The people who had objected were defeated and they knew it. Rather than taking a vote, the mayor of Whitstead asked if anyone now objected to the young people of the village engaging in these re-enactments. No one answered. After a long silence the project was approved. They asked Reverend Hollybrook to close in prayer.

Hollybrook wanted to say something to Samantha, who had come to listen (and, if necessary, vote). He had seen her flinch painfully at the mention of marriage and getting a vision of one's future spouse. But when he saw her head for the doors, he found himself suddenly surrounded by well-wishers congratulating him on finding the manuscript by Julian, the news of his discovery having already spread through town. They plied him with questions on what he planned to do with it. By the time he got free, Samantha had left.

•◇•◇•◇•◇•◇•◇•◇•◇•

After Matins the next morning, Roland and Hollybrook spoke. Roland asked if the Reverend put any stock in the visions to which mystics like Julian often made claim. 'Some of my more modern friends say it was simply a case of female hysteria.' He looked around to see if anyone was near enough to hear him, lowered his voice and added, 'From unrequited desire.'

Hollybrook had heard such statements questioning mystical visions. He had his own doubts about the validity of Julian's 'revelations,' but he held to a broad view of things. 'My ideas on the matter are complicated,' Hollybrook said. 'They're too complicated to share here. But the Clark family has asked me to come to their house and discuss the whole thing—it was originally just for wine and conversation; we visit every year around this time. But tomorrow night will be a discussion on mysticism, visions, and revelations. You should join us. I'll check with them to make certain they don't mind you coming along—which I'm sure they will not.'

Roland smiled. 'Yes. And it will be another chance to see Samantha.'

Hollybrook returned the smile. 'She is a fine young woman.'

'I think so too—not that she has equivalent thoughts about me.'

'What do you mean by that?'

'She seems distant and lost in her own musings; her own melancholy.'

Hollybrook remembered what Sister Elisabeth had said about the spirits that went abroad on All Hallows' Eve and their propensity to tempt the depressed and the melancholic. 'She's sad over a broken engagement. You knew that, didn't you?'

'Her mother and father told me of it, yes. Pity.'

Hollybrook heard a noise and glanced up. 'Well, there they are,' he said, seeing the couple and their daughter walk into the church. He then remembered they had said something about a donation to the benevolent fund—a donation they wanted to deliver in person.

Hollybrook and Roland walked over to the trio. Hollybrook noted how sad and tired Samantha looked. She gave Roland a small but weary smile. The reverend asked if the young man might join their discussion tonight. The Clarks happily consented.

After everyone in the church departed, Hollybrook knew he had to go to the convent. He felt summoned. That afternoon, telling his wife he had to run an errand, he took the path that led to the convent. Fog had rolled in. Soon he could not see the countryside around him, though the path, well-marked, kept him heading in the right direction.

Disturbing thoughts began to fill his head. What if he lost his way and wandered until he died of cold? What if someone came to his house whilst he was gone, assaulted his wife and murdered her and the children? Someone who had been on the losing side of the debate last night might retaliate against him for giving his opinion that the folk practices on All Hallows Eve were harmless. Such a person might burn down his house.

He tried to shake off these imaginings, which on one hand seemed absurd but, for some reason, also oddly possible. The thick fog made him deeply uneasy. He heard a noise, cried out in fear, and jumped back. A dog wearing a collar stepped out from behind a large rock, looked up, wagged its tail, and came towards him. He petted the creature and hurried on his way, coming at last to the spot when Elisabeth usually appeared. He saw her and felt relief.

'So, you made it,' she said. 'Was it bad?'

He stared a moment then recovered his focus. 'Yes, it was. It was hideous. How did you know?'

'The spirits I spoke of don't want you talking with me. They filled your head with frightening thoughts to stop you from coming here, made you want to return home to protect your family. You have experienced their evil influence.'

'Yes, I think I did. But why?'

'Father Hollybrook, you are a shepherd of the church and have the duty of securing the spiritual safety of your congregation. Doesn't our faith teach you that we are in a spiritual battle? That we fight against principalities and the dark forces of evil?'

Her chastening words helped him recover his emotional equilibrium. 'Yes, you're right, Elisabeth.'

'Our faith is not a list of doctrines you persuade people to believe. It's a struggle against evil.'

He could only gaze at her.

'I'm sorry for being harsh with you,' she said. 'I am greatly concerned for Samantha.'

'As I am. You said you had a plan.'

She smiled her sly smile. 'I do. The citizens of Whitstead who were against re-enacting the folklore of All Hallows' won't like what I mean to do, but the evil forces will like it even less.'

'And you think this—whatever it is—will work?'

'Evil,' she said, 'is often depicted as powerful, magnificent, and sophisticated. It is none of these things. Evil is stupid, crude, and unimaginative. The Devil and his minions thought they had pulled off a feat of triumph when they crucified our Saviour. They had no idea that the thing they did was not their supreme triumph but rather their doom — their ultimate destruction, and the destruction of their kingdom.'

He quoted a Bible verse: "Which none of the princes of this world knew; for if they had known it, they would not have crucified the Lord of Glory."

'Exactly. They were too stupid to know what was happening.' Again, she displayed her sly smile. 'It's the reason I left the copy of Julian's book in your library. No more questions now, Reverend. Just be certain you go to the Clarks' house at the appointed time; and make certain Roland comes along with you.'

•◇•◇•◇•◇•◇•◇•◇•

Reverend Hollybrook invited Roland over for whisky just before the meeting with the Clark family. He showed him the handwritten copy of Julian's book and told the young man that he had posted an invitation for a representative from Oxford's Bodleian Library to come to town to negotiate on the sale of it.

'I debated the matter in my mind,' Hollybrook said, 'and decided that, as much as I would love to keep the text, more people would see it and a greater number of scholars could study it if it were located at a world-renowned library. Have you ever read Julian's book?'

'No,' Roland answered. 'Samantha quoted the line, "all shall be well, and all manner of things shall be well" to me when we were talking the other day. She said she hoped things would be well. I wasn't sure what she meant by that.'

Hollybrook only said it was about time to go to the Clarks' house.

When they arrived, Mr and Mrs Clark received them and invited them into the parlour. Hollybrook asked where Samantha was.

'She's upstairs,' Mrs Clark said. 'I'll send Ella to fetch her down here.' Ella was their serving maid.

Roland stood. 'Mrs Clark, would you allow me to fetch her?'

She smiled. She considered Roland a fine young man. 'Of course. She will be interested in a discussion about Saint Julian.'

Roland went up the stairs. Hollybrook felt a surge of evil similar to what he had felt walking to the convent last night. It coursed through his body. Then he felt it dissipate. Samantha and Roland appeared. Ella, the serving maid, walked behind them. She carried a plate. On it, Hollybrook saw an apple core, parings, and a very sharp knife.

'I was having a little snack,' Samantha said when she noticed Hollybrook had seen the plate Ella carried. She smiled. 'I felt hungry, so I peeled an apple and ate it at my vanity table. I'm sorry I was late for the discussion.'

The five of them sat down in the parlour and began to talk. Hollybrook gave his theory on mystical revelations. He did not believe Julian's visions were real in the way she herself thought, but had Christ spoken to her? 'Yes,' he said. In some manner what she wrote was true. No doubt those truths had come from her devotion to God. Her visions were not exactly 'real' in the scientific sense, but in the spiritual sense they *were* real and true.

'People have found guidance and comfort from Julian's writings through four hundred years. Such a thing could not have happened if the source of her revelations was some sort of neurosis. The revelations were revealed through her imagination, which framed them. That does not mean they did not come from a divine source or that they are to be disregarded. They are meditations inspired by valid Christian truth and given form by Julian's imagination. Ultimately, they come from Heaven. The degree to which they have ministered to people through the centuries is ample evidence both of their truth and divine origin.'

Much conversation followed. The people agreed with him and complimented him on his understanding of the matter. Ella brought them wine and cakes. They drank and ate and celebrated. Hollybrook noted that Samantha and Roland sat together and seemed to enjoy each other's company. When Hollybrook and she were together in private for a moment, Samantha asked if she could speak to him tomorrow.

'That would be fine,' Hollybrook said. 'Can you come by my house at ten? Penelope and I will both be there.'

The group visited, drank, and talked until just past midnight. A little tipsy, the Reverend headed home, noting that All Hallows' Eve had just ended.

•◊•◊•◊•◊•◊•◊•◊•◊•

When Samantha next came to the Hollybrook home, she said she wanted to confess.

The Reverend knew she meant she wanted to confess in the sacramental manner, not just to reveal a truth. He took her to his study. Penelope went along for the sake of seemliness and waited in the next room by the open door.

The Anglican communion saw confession not so much as absolution from sin as to give assurance of forgiveness and counsel for a person who had realised an error or transgression for which they had repented.

'My sin is that I was going to kill myself last night,' Samantha told him. She quickly assured him that she had discarded the idea. She hesitated a long moment then continued. 'This is going to sound ridiculous — you might even think me mad or deluded for doing it. But last month I read a feature in *Graham's Magazine* about customs related to All Hallows' Eve.'

Graham's Magazine was an American periodical to which Samantha subscribed because it often published the stories of Mr Edgar Allan Poe, an author she enjoyed reading. He knew this because when she had finished an issue of the magazine, she passed it on to Penelope, who also liked Poe's stories.

8

'One of the legends said that a girl could see a vision of her husband-to-be if she performed certain rituals in front of a mirror on that night. The one I chose was to eat an apple. I took the knife you saw Ella carry off to the kitchen with the apple core and the parings. One reason I took it was to peel the apple, slice it, and eat it. According to the superstition, I would see the face of the man I would marry in the mirror; if I saw nothing, it meant I would never marry. I was so melancholic and sad, and I felt so overwhelmed with sorrow, despair, and… I guess I'd have to call it *evil*, that I meant to cut my wrists with the knife if I saw no vision.'

She paused. He waited for her to go on.

'I know that sounds as if I am insane, but for some reason I felt this. I really meant to do it; I really meant to cut my wrists so I would bleed to death. Then –' She had to wait a moment before she could continue. 'The door opened. I saw Roland's reflection in the mirror behind my reflection – just as the legends said. He was there to fetch me so I could join the discussion downstairs.'

She stopped, looked down, and then up at him. 'Have I gone mad, Reverend? Should I have my parents commit me to an asylum?'

His mind worked rapidly. Not at all, he told her. She had been saved by the providential appearance of Roland. God had intervened for her – a thing at which she could rejoice and be most thankful. He played the role of the moralist and said superstition could be dangerous and the desire to take one's own life needed to be healed. 'But,' he added, 'God intervened in a strange and wonderful way to preserve your life, child. We will thank him for that. And I think Penelope should continue to counsel you – though you seem to be getting past your melancholy.'

Samantha actually smiled. 'I do feel better. In fact, what I did and what happened seems now – well, almost funny. The whole thing snapped me out of the oppression and sense of evil I felt that night. I feel like I've left all of that behind and am more my old self again. I really do want to get on with life now. I think the thing with the mirror is absurd, but at least it snapped me out of all that had burdened me up until last night. Now I have a new perspective on life.'

He returned her smile. 'So, to an extent, the little ceremony you performed did some good for you.'

'It did. It would be nice if it also worked for the result it claimed it would bring about.'

They shared a laugh.

•◇•◇•◇•◇•◇•◇•◇•◇•

Hollybrook did not see Sister Elisabeth again until just short of a year later, the day after Samantha and Roland were married. She appeared to him in the parlour of his home.

'The words of Julian came true yesterday,' he said when he saw her.

'They did,' Elisabeth answered. 'I went to the church in my spiritual, invisible form and watched Samantha and Roland's wedding ceremony. I was married in that same spot in 1540. After I had been taken out of the convent my parents immediately arranged a marriage for me. I think they were afraid I would run away to a convent in France. I was probably the most unhappy bride in all of England.'

'You once told me you liked being married and that it was a blessing. What changed the way you felt on your wedding day?'

Her sly smile came. 'What changed the way I felt on my wedding day was my wedding night,' she answered.

They laughed. She went on to tell him she had given him the book and put it in a place where he would find it. She knew the Clarks would be interested in it and that talking about the book would be a way to get Samantha and Roland together. Hollybrook told her about how almost the entire village had turned out to listen to his public readings of Julian's book.

'The foul spirits wanted to drive Samantha to take her own life,' Elisabeth said. 'We were able to save her through God's intervention.'

'And through Julian of Norwich's.'

Again, they laughed. He glanced away. When he looked back, Elisabeth was gone.

The Faerie Queene of Autumn's Death
by Beka Gremikova (*fantasy/thriller*)

'The faerie queene of autumn's death
Carries with her mourning's wreath
If you see her on the heath
Flee before she takes your breath.'

So the mortals sing of me, when they think I do not hear. Little do they realise that the autumn leaves repeat their words as I pass—the tiny, gossiping things.

Today, as I step through the portal from Faerie into the forest of the human realm, the leaves whisper of death.

Edith Smith of the Orchards is on her sickbed. She was healthy last week. And so young, too. So beautiful. Not as beautiful as her stepdaughter Sylvie, though the girl's been sickly of late.

The leaves shudder in a sudden blast of chill wind, and a flurry of them flutter from the branches to swirl around my bare feet. I step over them gingerly. The grass is wet and shining with dew, brushing against my toes.

I suck in a deep breath. Though mortals fear me as a sign of summer's end, of autumn's deathly thrall, this time of year brings me life. Usually, I would revel in the crisp, hazy autumn morning, take joy in the crackling grass and changing colours.

But not today, for I go to the Orchards to bring what comfort I can to the dying. I have not been there since Sylvie's mother, Fanny, died four years ago. Fanny's husband never liked me, and I know to avoid where I'm unwelcome.

But I cannot avoid the song of death, the cry for consolation.

Humans believe me an ill omen, a harbinger of death. To them, I bring the frost that kills their gardens and the wind that drives into their bones. As if I have any real power. I'm merely a signal, a sign.

Most mortals do not understand that I was borne from the season itself, not the other way round.

Yet, because autumn's damp cold seeps into their bones and kills them, they believe I cause it. And they think that, in my visits to the dying, I steal their souls.

Such vivid imaginations, those mortals.

I do wonder—what must Fanny's little Sylvie think of me? It's been so long—too long. I always forget how quickly mortal years pass…

My footsteps quicken. The woods' fiery beauty blurs around me as I focus on the sprawling heath peeking between the trees. I break out into open land, where the ground appears on fire—the plants boasting vibrant brown, crimson, and purple hues. Below me, Whitstead's cottages nestle together as though for warmth.

Autumn was Fanny's favourite season. She loved to pick leaves and weave wreaths with them. Once she wove a crown for my hair. She was among the handful of mortals who did not fear me—who understood my true nature. Perhaps because she was part wilderness herself.

'If I ever have a daughter,' she'd say, 'I want her lips to be as red as crimson leaves, and her hair as black as an autumn night.'

I snorted. 'Why not wish for her to have long life? To be merry always?'

Fanny shook her head. 'I wish for her to be beautiful, so she might catch the eye of a faerie prince and be whisked away from this world.' Then she plucked more leaves from the ground to braid together.

I tried my best to help Fanny find a way out of her life. Before she married, she joined me in Faerie, dancing for the High King's court. Yet she never found the love she sought amongst the fae. Instead, a brave young tailor rescued her one day from a giant and whisked her back into the mortal world. After that, she could no longer leave; like any well-bred English wife, she devoted herself to her house and husband.

And, later, her little Sylvie.

'Lady Morgana!' The harsh cry trills across the heath. A woman runs up the hill, skirts flapping around her legs. Her heart-shaped face is pale, her lips thin, pursed, and deep crimson. She shivers in a threadbare dress and scraggly shawl. Holes pepper her worn boots, whilst thick strands of black hair escape her braided twists.

Realisation strikes me like a sudden searing ray of sunshine.

Sylvie is no longer a child.

She reaches the hilltop and flings out her arms, blocking my path. 'Go back!' she cries. 'You can't have her!' Her lips tremble.

It feels like someone's stabbed me with an iron poker.

'Oh, Sylvie… You believe all that nonsense, too?' I thought Fanny taught her better.

Her shoulders quiver as I step forward. Perspiration streaks her forehead. There's a frenzied light in her eyes reminiscent of panicked squirrels racing to forage before winter.

Poor child. Her mother looked that way four years ago when I last entered Whitstead. When we learnt that I, too, am nothing but a child of the earth, that I hold no power over life and death.

No matter how much I might wish to.

Sylvie's jaw clenches. She raises her head, eyes flashing. She resembles a tombstone in her sombre grey wool. 'I saw you,' she spits. 'You came to our house,

12

and then Mama died! You stole her!' She covers her face in her hands. 'Just like you'll steal Edith,' she whispers.

My fingers clench as the image of Fanny on her deathbed wavers in my mind: her hollowed-out eyes, her thin lips, her wispy hair. Nothing I said or did could stop her crumbling away like an autumn leaf underfoot. Yet she'd still thanked me for being there. 'You're a welcome distraction,' she'd quipped.

Death cares not about beauty or power. Death snares at any and every hour. The Faerie proverb rattles through my mind. Despite what humans may believe, we are not immortal. We merely have longer to anticipate the awful end.

'You—you have no idea.' My voice crackles. 'You have no notion, silly child, of what I'd have given to leave her alive and well in this world. If I stole her, don't you think she'd be here with me now?'

Sylvie blinks. Her cheeks flush.

I continue to advance. Her stance wavers, but she does not retreat. 'I'm not here to steal. I'm here to distract. To comfort.' For all the Fannies, longing to hold onto beauty even as the darkness wrests it from them. For the Fannies who pass on from this lovely-yet-withering world into one eternally lovely.

And for someone like Edith Smith, a woman renowned in Whitstead for her looks, I suppose she might appreciate a reminder of her own youthful days. Perhaps I might act as a mirror, help her mind latch onto those memories as a solace.

Just as I reach her, Sylvie straightens like someone has poked her viciously in the back. 'That's what you say!' she hisses. 'But you—poison things, just like—' She bites her lip and rubs her arms, shivering.

Chills skitter down my spine.

Poison. I shut my eyes against another vision: the Spring Queene, her face contorted in agony after her mortal lover unknowingly wrapped her in a poisoned shawl. Spring has had no queen since. 'Who's poisoning?' I ask sharply.

Sylvie's hands tremble violently. Her lips open and shut.

She's stalling. Neither I nor the dying have patience for such things. I will wrest the truth from her after I visit her stepmother. I press past her.

She latches onto my elbow, dragging her heels into the earth. 'You cannot take her!' She scrabbles against the wet grass. I continue striding down the heath, Sylvie hanging from my arm.

I almost want to laugh at her pathetic attempts to stop me. But she's Fanny's daughter, and the amusement turns rancid in my stomach. I pry her fingers from my skin. 'Have some dignity,' I snap. 'If I were here to kill her, I'd kill you for being so unwelcoming.'

Her grip on me loosens. 'So… with Mama…'

'Coincidence.' The word catches in my throat. How many times must I go over this? Why do mortals assume no other being feels pain? 'Cannot a faerie visit a friend on their deathbed? Surely Fanny told you about the days she visited Faerie to dance for the High King? That we were as close as sisters?'

Sylvie's eyelashes flicker like an autumn leaf about to drop from its branch. 'She did,' she whispers. 'But... Papa said...' She fiddles with the hem of her shawl. 'Papa claimed you took Mama, and someday you'd come after Edith, too. I didn't realise...' She wrings her hands. 'Papa hated your friendship with Mama. Oh, she'd be ashamed of me.' Her voice breaks. 'I've become so—scared. I cannot tell foe from friend anymore.' Her gaze flicks to Whitstead's cottages clustered along the heath, as though even they might contain enemies.

We reach the bottom of the hill. A wide dirt road opens before us, and I cross briskly, Sylvie lagging behind. On the other side, an orchard of bursting trees stretches towards a tiny stone cottage. Bright red apples hang low on the branches. I reach up, plucking one like a flower.

Despite her illness, Fanny's sweet tooth enjoyed apples to the very end. Perhaps Edith might as well. I glance at Sylvie. 'Of what are you afraid? Is it to do with the poisoning you mentioned?'

Sylvie stares at the apple as though it's made of iron. A strangled noise escapes her throat. 'Have you... ever been poisoned?' she asks at last.

'No.' I rub my fingers over the apple's smooth, cold skin.

Sylvie bows her head. 'It's awful,' she whispers. Her eyes well. 'Edith... she's nearly killed me a few times.' She raises trembling hands to clasp her head. 'With a comb, and laces... gifts from Faerie, she said. But they nearly killed me!'

I whirl, gossamer skirts hissing against my legs. 'How did I not hear of this?'

Sylvie won't look at me. 'Edith kept me in the house. If Widow Larkin hadn't knocked on the door to check on me...' She shudders. 'I don't understand why, but Edith hates me! So, I...' She swallows, and her words turn breathy. 'I made her ill, so she might never hurt me again. I thought she would die, and you might steal her soul. But—it's so wrong!' She sinks to the ground, weeping. 'I cannot let her die,' she wails. 'I called Widow Larkin to tend her, and I swore I wouldn't let you claim her soul.'

I stroke Sylvie's sleek black hair. Wrapping her arms around my legs, she buries her face in my skirts.

A different kind of rage is building in me. Not the spitting anger of an aunt scolding a silly child, but the blinding wrath of a queen on behalf of those who should be under her care. 'Did your father never protect you?' Had I but known...

'He... passed on last year. And even before then, he saw her as the...' Her arms tighten around my legs. 'The prime example of a woman Queen Victoria might approve.' Her voice quivers. 'He didn't see her jealous nature.'

My lips thin. He may not have comprehended it, but he'd felt it. His envy and possessiveness kept me from my dear friend's company for years. He'd called me a bad influence for encouraging Fanny to neglect her household duties for a while to have time for herself.

Then, to add to the insult, he married a woman who made his daughter miserable? *He should count himself blessed that I did not visit him on his sickbed.*

I glance at the apple in my hand. 'Come,' I say crisply and stride across the grass. Sylvie stumbles to her feet, staggering after me. As we draw nearer, the cottage's light grey stones glow like fog, and Sylvie slows. She clasps her shawl tighter around her shoulders.

To her, this house is nothing but a coffin.

'Wait here,' I murmur and slip through the door.

'What are you going to do —?' But her words are lost as I shut the door behind me. I step into a narrow entry, a chamber on either side.

'Hullo?' I call. There's no answer. Widow Larkin must be gone on an errand, then. All the better.

Coughing echoes from the back of the house, and I creep down the hallway into a large airy chamber that was once the parlour. A woman lies in the bed set against the wall. This is the only room in the entire place that boasts curtains, and they are drawn.

Despite the gloom, I recognise Edith from my many wanders through Whitstead. Her auburn hair now straggles across her shoulders. Her rosy cheeks are wan, her lips pasty.

The chamber suddenly feels nauseating. Images swarm my mind, as pesky as flies: Fanny's gaunt face, hollowed eyes, pasty lips.

The heat spreading through me bubbles. *Death cares not about beauty or power. Death snares at any and every hour.* This woman tried to send Sylvie her mother's way.

My lips twist. Autumn's frost seeps from my fingertips into the fruit I carry. With one bite, this vile woman will wither from the inside out. I can protect Sylvie from her enemies, as I failed to do before.

'Good morrow, Edith,' I murmur, perching on her bed.

Edith blinks at me, her gaze unfocused. 'You —'

'Shhh. Eat this. It will help you feel better.' I offer the apple. 'It's from your very own orchard.'

Gnarled, shaking fingers brush the apple's skin. 'Is it… poisoned?' she whispers.

'Why should it be?' I lean forward. 'Aren't apples meant to bring health?'

A cold hand catches my wrist. Edith and I both turn to Sylvie, whose grasp on my arm is like iron—strong, determined. Sylvie's gaze snags mine. 'It's poisoned, isn't it?' she hisses.

Edith gasps. 'You! You brought her here to finish me off!' Her voice rises. 'Widow Larkin!' she screams.

I try to wrench myself free from Sylvie's grip, but it only tightens. 'Isn't it?' Sylvie snaps.

'How did you know?'

'Because I understand the feeling.' She bows her head. Her pulse beats rapidly in her fingertips, thrumming against my skin. 'I've wanted to kill her for years. Just as she's wanted to kill me. But…' Her lips press together. 'I couldn't bear it! Widow Larkin says she will live, and I intend to see that happen.'

Edith's wails fade to whimpers, and she sits back weakly. But her eyes blaze. I realise that in her weakened state, more mercy would be shown to her than to her victim. 'She shouldn't,' I say. I want to cram the apple down Edith's throat, but Sylvie's hold on me will not loosen. 'She tried to kill you!'

With her other hand, Sylvie pries the apple from my fingers. A strand of hair falls into her face, and she blows it aside. 'Let that be on *her* conscience. Why should I suffer more because of her?' She glares at Edith, who glowers back. 'If Edith has her way, I'll be hanged.'

I clench my fingers into fists. My power may be little, but what little I have, I will use. Though I could not save my friend, perhaps I can save her daughter. 'You needn't be.'

Sylvie turns her head, staring at me.

'It's been far too long since a friend has joined me in the High King's court,' I murmur.

Edith utters a gurgled protest, but we both ignore her.

'The faerie dances?' Sylvie whispers, awestruck. 'Like Mama used to…?'

I nod. 'No one will come after you there. When autumn arrives, and I walk in the human world, the High King will keep you safe until I return. Faerie is not dangerous if you have the proper friends.' I nearly add, for Edith's benefit, 'Friends of which, perhaps, Queen Victoria would *not* approve.'

Edith's spluttering floats out after us as we depart the cottage. Sylvie brushes off the apple, now thawed of its autumnal poison, and takes a bite. She chews thoughtfully as we cross the heath together, towards the forest with its towering trees that guard the entrance to Faerie. With each mile, Sylvie's steps grow lighter… until it almost looks like she's dancing.

•◊•◊•◊•◊•◊•◊•◊•◊•

The next year, Autumn arrives as usual, but unlike before, I'm loth to leave Faerie. Sylvie walks me to the portal and sees me off with a hug. 'Give Whitstead my greetings, Auntie Morgana,' she murmurs, kissing my cheek.

'Oh hush, you make me feel old.'

She snorts and gives me a cheeky grin. She's become far more devious of late, keeping company with seven of the most mischievous faeries in Court. But it cheers me to know that human envy can no longer touch her.

16

I pass through the Faerie portal into the bright, cooling sunlight of Whitstead's forest. From their perches in the trees, the leaves greet me. *The mortals have a new song of you.*

'How intriguing. Let me hear it.'

The little leaves recite the ditty, and I keel over in laughter. Indeed, mortals are so very creative — with such vivid imaginations.

> 'The faerie queene of autumn's death
> Carries with her mourning's wreath
> Sylvie Smith saw her on the heath
> So the queene stole her very breath.'

Junior's Arrow
by Ronnell Kay Gibson (*fantasy/mythology*)

I take the tainted arrow and slice through the barrier between my world and the human world. As the only child of Cupid and Daonie, the goddess of The Hallows, I am the only one who can slip in and out at will. And right now, I have no choice. My father is hunting me—he has no choice. He needs my heart to break the curse I triggered.

When I poisoned Cupid's arrows.

As I step forwards to assess my surroundings, the veil between worlds seals behind me. I'm in a forest—temperate woodlands with ancient trees. Their trunks so high, even without their leaves, they cast dark shadows everywhere. Through their knotted limbs looms a darkened sky. Smells like autumn rain.

I plop down on a weathered log, place my elbows on my knees, and rest my head on clenched fists, trying to figure out just where to go next. There's nowhere in either world—nor time itself—where I am safe.

My whole life I'd been taught human lives were expendable. So, I had no remorse when after Cupid released his arrows, the humans—instead of falling deeply in love—fell deathly ill. I even chortled. The sacrifice of two human lives would be worth it to reunite my parents.

And it worked. Cupid flew to The Hallows to confront my mother. It was only then I learnt my actions demanded the ultimate cost: My life.

I hold the arrow up to my lips and breathe. When I do, the silver tip sparkles, revealing the remnants of the poison. I've tried millions of different antidotes, sought the best apothecaries across multiple realms, but so far nothing.

Lingering here isn't an option. I need to figure out where and when I am. I fold my wings in and choose to use my feet to explore, stepping over brush and downed tree limbs. Discovering a barely visible path, I follow it till the foliage starts to thin and a clearing appears.

A man hobbles towards the woods. From his clothes and his hat, it seems I've stumbled into the Victorian era. My guess—England, mid-1800s.

Though I used to despise all humans, along my journey I've discovered they are not the savages I'd been led to believe. They have a great capacity for compassion; but then again, they have great capacity for violence as well. I never know which I'll encounter.

With a basket in one hand and pruning shears in the other, the man mumbles to himself. 'Darn rabbits. Gonna eat my nice herb garden. Well, when I'm through with you…'

I can't help but snort.

'Who's there?' He jumps back, his shears raised in defence.

Oops.

But I can tell this man isn't the evil sort. With a blink, I alter my clothes to match the era, and make sure my wings are hidden. Though in reality I'm much older, my appearance is similar to their young people.

No sense in hiding. I step from the shadows. 'Sorry, sir, if I startled you.'

The gardener puts his hand to his chest and sighs. 'You sure did, lad.' His eyes scrunch as he looks me over. 'Where did you come from? You're not from around here?'

'No, sir. Neighbouring town.' I hope my vagueness is sufficient.

He tilts his head. 'You look kinda familiar. Do I know your papa?'

I notice a wedding ring on his left hand. 'Maybe.' I smile. But then I catch myself. 'Probably not, though. He's a… travelling pedlar.'

The man nods. 'Well, what you doin' in Whitstead?'

I pinch my lips, trying to craft another lie.

'Don't tell me you ran away from home.'

'Yeah, kinda.' That isn't a lie.

'Well, as a father myself, I want you to turn yourself around and march straight back. Your papa's probably worried sick.'

'No. No, he isn't.' Again, not a lie.

The man pauses, his eyes softening. 'Family sometimes hard to get along with, eh?'

'Complicated, that's for sure.'

The wind swells and whips the man's hat from his head, lifting it swirling up into the air. I use my lightning reflexes to leap and catch it.

'Good show, lad.' He sets the cap back on his head and pulls it down tight. 'Looks like there's a storm brewin'. Do you have somewhere safe to stay?'

I'm sad to admit I don't.

He must read it on my face. 'C'mon. You can ride out the storm with the missus and me.'

His lips curl into a large grin, his smile emanating kindness. My insides are overwhelmed by an instant kinship to this man.

He holds out his hand to shake. 'Douglas Green, Master Gardener for the Fentiman family.'

I grip firmly. 'Junior.'

He waits for more of an explanation, but there's nothing more I can offer him.

A howling rises through the trees behind us.

'Well, Junior, we better get movin'.'

Clusters of leaves chase us down the dirt road. The sky grows ominous. Thunder and lightning start, followed by a heavy downpour.

We pick up the pace.

Around the next bend, Mr Green shouts through the storm. 'Here we are.' He points to a simple dwelling with mums planted in the front and a cornucopia of gourds and fruits on the front stoop. Towering over the house is a stately elm. The wooden swing hanging from its branches sways frantically in the storm.

Another boom of thunder followed closely by a clap of lightning. Too close.

The door to the cottage swings open and a woman dressed as a lady's maid steps out. She holds her hands over her eyebrows scanning the horizon. Though she calls out, her words are lost to the rain.

'Viola, get back in the house,' Douglas shouts.

When Viola spots us, she takes a step into the rain. At the same time, another crack of lightning strikes the elm sending the branch with the swing crashing towards their house. Right above Mrs Green.

I don't think, I just react. My wings pop and I'm in the air before the sparks on the tree have a chance to evaporate. Hovering underneath, adrenaline racing, I catch the tree limb before it touches the cottage.

Next to me, Viola Green has her eyes closed, screaming.

With rain streaming down my face, into my eyes, down my back, I strain my muscles, give the branch one large umpf and toss it away from the house.

The crash silences Mrs Green's screams, and she opens her eyes.

Mr Green is there and runs into her outstretched arms. He gives his wife a long, tight squeeze, then, still holding her close, he looks over at me.

I realise I'm still floating, wings exposed.

I'm expecting horror. Bulging eyes. Incredulous pinched brows. Instead, I get a grin.

He motions me towards him. When I get close enough, he pulls me into their hug. The warmth of their love ravages my soul. The bitterness of the past, my parents, the mess I made of my life, melt away. In its place, peace settles.

And so does the storm.

Douglas is the first to pull away. Reaches for my hand and squeezes. 'Thank you, Junior.'

I still don't understand how he's not fleeing in terror. 'You're not surprised?'

'You were right. I do know your father.'

Footsteps come up from behind me. 'Hello, Junior.'

My feathers bristle. I turn. 'Hello, Father.'

I steady my legs, preparing to soar.

Cupid puts out a hand. 'Just wait, son.'

I look over at the Greens. They're still holding each other, still smiling like they know something I don't. Now I'm the one confused.

My father opens his other hand, revealing the tainted arrow I had been carrying with me. He slowly takes a couple steps forward.

Again, I brace myself to flee if I must.

Cupid blows on the silver tip of the arrow. Nothing. No sparkles. No remnants of poison.

My words stutter. 'H…How?'

'A life for a life. This time restoring, not taking.'

'But I only saved one, what about the other?'

Mr Green shakes his head. 'In saving my wife, lad, you saved me too.' He peers over at Mrs Green. 'I don't know how I could live without my dear heart.'

Viola kisses her husband's lips.

The beating of my heart quickens. 'Does this mean the curse is broken?'

My father nods. 'Yes.'

Cupid winks at Mr Green. 'Douglas, Viola, so good to see you again.'

They both bow their heads.

'Douglas, thanks for looking out for my boy.'

'Of course.'

I turn to Mr Green. 'And you're not the least shocked or surprised by all this?'

The gardener shakes his head no and winks at my father. 'You're not the only god I've found wandering in the woods.'

The Clockwork Study, Part II
by Sara Francis (*Gothic/steampunk/suspense/fantasy*)

The Readfuss family still was not trusted.

Theodore Readfuss had tried to make amends since the New Year, but nothing was sufficient. The peculiar man frequented the town he used to avoid, speaking with the inhabitants that ostracized him. All Theodore wanted was to make peace for himself and his family.

But the past clung to him.

Were some villagers open minded? Did some believe he had changed? Of course. But the fear that hung in the empty poorhouses after most of their people didn't return lingered throughout Whitstead.

Theodore wished he could tell them it wasn't his fault. For the sake of his children's safety, he suffered in silence.

Until his sons unearthed the secret on their own.

●◇●◇●◇●◇●◇●◇●◇●◇●

Terrence and Thaddeus Readfuss were up to no good.

As the days grew shorter, so did their attention span. The twins raced about Readfuss Grange with sheets around their necks. The fabric flapped in the wind as they chased one another down the halls.

Thaddeus was the slimmer of the two and his quick reflexes outmatched his brother's. He dove to the side whenever he felt Terrence's thick fingers snatch at his make-shift cape. Tables were pushed aside, trinkets knocked over.

Sweat dripped into Thaddeus' eyes but he could see his goal: the back door. Heart hammering, Thaddeus wouldn't stop until he made it to the end.

A figure stepped through the doorway.

Thaddeus stopped short and Terrence bumped into his back. The latter was about to comment until he noticed the sour expression on the figure before them.

'What 'ave I told you boys about runnin' inside?' Willow the housemaid stated. Her dark eyes glanced over their shoulders. 'And are those the fresh linens?'

The twins gulped and quickly tore off their homemade capes. 'Sorry, Willow,' Thaddeus apologised. 'We were just playin'.'

The older woman harrumphed. 'You two 'ave been in the Grange all week. Why don't you go play with the Westons or that curious Davey Micklewright?'

Terrence crossed his arms and wrinkled his nose. 'Because Father said we needed to stay away for a bit.'

'That's right—All Hallows' Eve,' Willow said softly. The wrinkles in her face deepened. She sucked in a breath and shook off the thought. 'All right, but no more mess makin'. Fold those sheets and clean up the hall,' she ordered and returned to the kitchen.

Grumbling, the two stomped down the corridor, picking up their toys. As Thaddeus was piling his possessions into his arms, his foot caught on the sheet over his shoulder. He slid and crashed to the floor. Wooden soldiers clattered and marbles scattered. Several clay spheres rolled across the smooth mahogany floor and slid underneath a door.

The boy gasped as he scrambled to snatch them before they disappeared. He wasn't fast enough. His favourite toys were in the forbidden room.

The Clockwork Study.

Their father abandoned his beloved room after the previous New Year when the poor folk visited Readfuss Grange for a blessed evening, never to be seen again.

The twins developed their own theories, but neither were satisfied with their conclusions. Thaddeus was the only one to see the last old man before he disappeared. The boy remembered the clock he took in his wrinkled hands and the kind eyes that never blinked.

Thaddeus tried not to think about that night. He was overjoyed that his father began to revert back to the man he once was. No more quirks. However, he couldn't shake the feeling that *something* happened that night.

Something no one was allowed to speak about.

Thaddeus peered under the door. The room was dark and empty. The Clockwork Study no longer had clocks; another peculiar result of New Year's. Father's leather chair sat alone in the centre of the room.

A breeze tickled Thaddeus' nose, and his body jumped when a shadow crossed the study.

He yelped and pushed himself away from the door. 'Terrence! Terrence!' he cried.

His brother rushed over and exclaimed, 'What 'appened?'

Thaddeus pointed a shaky finger towards the study. Colour faded from his cheeks as he stammered, 'S-someone was-was in there.'

Terrence rolled his eyes. 'You and your wild imagination. Nothing is in there.' He made his way towards the study but paused, not as brave as he claimed. He swallowed hard, put his hand on the knob, and flung the door open.

No one was there.

Thaddeus sat shaking on the ground, watching through the door frame as his brother examined the room. Terrence was about to speak when something caught his eye. He crossed the study and returned with his findings.

It was a pocket watch.

'W-where did that come from?' Thaddeus asked.

Terrence shrugged. 'Perhaps it was left behind.'

'O-or it was put there by that *thing* I saw before!' Thaddeus swiped at his brother's hand, which yanked the watch away. 'Terrence, it's not safe.'

'It's a watch, Thaddeus.' The boy rubbed the nickel cover. Swirls and accents were etched into the metal. On the back the letters *O* and *X* were enveloped by the intricate design. He clicked the top.

Tick. Tick. Tick.

Terrence stared at its face longingly as if it brought back an old memory. His pupils dilated as he watched the second-hand travel in a circle. Every second that passed, Terrence's facial muscles slowly relaxed.

Thaddeus gripped Terrence's arm. 'Father told us no, so put it back,' he commanded.

Blinking three times, Terrence locked eyes with his brother. 'Y-yes.' He was in and out of the study; no watch in his hand. 'Let's finish our chores, I suppose.' Without another word, he proceeded to clean up.

Thaddeus latched onto the study door and pulled it shut, leaving his marbles inside. A knot formed in his stomach as he watched his brother complete a task *without* complaint.

Something Terrence would *never* do.

•◊•◊•◊•◊•◊•◊•◊•◊•◊•

Theodore Readfuss walked to the church. On his way, he interrupted some villagers' daily routines to offer them bundles of wheat. Every week he would distribute some of the harvest from Readfuss Grange as a way to make amends with the townsfolk. All the villagers accepted, but not all did it warmly. Cold glares and abrupt snatches were more common than not.

But Theodore was grateful for any progress.

After handing out the last of the wheat, a sharp pain formed behind his eyes. His brain throbbed and his skin crawled. He stood in the road, pinching the bridge of his nose with his forefinger and thumb.

No more, please, he begged. It's over. It's been over for months. I'm free. My family is free.

But the pain worsened.

Gritting his teeth, he squeezed his eyes shut. He would not succumb. Not anymore. He failed once before, and his wife suffered.

The pain faded a few moments later. Theodore opened his eyes and blinked rapidly. He glanced around at the town. He felt warmth, he saw colour, and joy emanated from many of the faces.

But an eerie feeling lingered.

He picked up his feet and darted to the church, eager to speak with Reverend Hollybrook.

The day was approaching, and for the first time, Theodore would beg for help.

•◊•◊•◊•◊•◊•◊•◊•◊•

Terrence's body sat at the table, but his mind was elsewhere. The delicious aroma of fresh bread and sweet cooked vegetables could not bring him back to reality. With every passing second, he would see something different.

Words. Phrases. Images. Repeat.

Terrence was slightly illiterate, not having gone to school since his mother disappeared. He couldn't make sense of what went through his head.

Regardless, it captivated him.

He heard a voice. It was muffled but familiar. It called to him like a mother to her child. He thought perhaps it was *his* mother. Had she returned? At least to say goodbye?

'Terrence!' the voice cried the third time.

It cut through his muddled mind and Terrence was yanked back into the present.

Thaddeus shouted across the table; his face burning and his eyes wet.

Terrence blinked twice. 'What's wrong?'

'You haven't been listening to me,' his twin rebuked. 'What were you thinking about?'

He shrugged. 'Nothin',' he lied. He sank his teeth into his bread, tearing it in half like an animal. The warmth should've brought him comfort and satisfaction.

But he felt nothing but the quiet ticks of the pocket watch in his coat.

•◊•◊•◊•◊•◊•◊•◊•◊•

Coloured leaves scattered across the Church grounds. Theodore Readfuss had not been there since the Christmas his wife disappeared. He requested a funeral service for her despite not having any remains.

If she wasn't dead when she was Chosen, then she must be now.

The pain behind his eyes worsened. He feared it wasn't over. He needed advice, but he needed it kept secret. A holy man of God would surely grant him this request.

Reverend Hollybrook stood in the graveyard, praying over new headstones. White and black garments flapped in the crisp autumn wind. It was a symbol of being dead to the world but alive in Christ.

Death was all Theodore could focus on.

He shook his head hard and forced himself to blink three times. Never again would he succumb. His sons needed him.

25

Reverently, he walked across the graveyard and up to the minister. 'Reverend Hollybrook,' he greeted with a bow. 'Pardon my interruption, but I was wondering if I could have a moment.'

The reverend put his hands together and finished his prayer. 'Theodore Readfuss,' he began. 'It has been some time, has it not?'

'Yessir, it has,' he replied in an even tone. 'I need your guidance.'

Reverend Hollybrook turned. Surprise in his eyes. He extended a hand and guided Theodore across the grounds. 'What troubles you?'

'What doesn't trouble me?' Theodore's eyes darted back and forth.

The reverend nodded. 'It seems we have a lot to talk about.'

Together they walked back to Reverend Hollybrook's home.

Theodore was ready to tell someone everything.

•◇•◇•◇•◇•◇•◇•◇•◇•

Chaos. Order.

A strange voice whispered into Terrence's mind. It drove him mad yet brought him comfort all at the same time.

He stood alone in the hallway, gripping the watch in his pocket. Something behind the unlocked Clockwork Study door called to him. Its warbled voice intermingled with the two words replaying in his mind.

His chubby hand gripped the handle, turned, and pushed. He slipped through and disappeared in the black room.

The door shut behind him.

•◇•◇•◇•◇•◇•◇•◇•◇•

'I have changed,' Theodore began. He sat beside the man of God who listened intently. The room in Reverend's home dedicated for counselling was warm, but a cold feeling chilled Theodore to the bone. 'If I harmed others of Whitstead, I beg for their forgiveness. I am struggling to make amends, but my sins are chasing me.'

Reverend Hollybrook tilted his head to the side. 'What sins?'

Theodore's mouth formed a straight line. Sharp pain resumed behind his eyes. He blinked hard, wishing it away. 'I know why my wife disappeared,' he started softly. 'She wasn't supposed to go.' A fiery lump formed in his throat. 'I was Chosen, not her.'

'Chosen?' Reverend Hollybrook repeated inquisitively. 'For what.'

His eyes throbbed as the pain worsened.

They knew.

They knew he was speaking of them. Would he die if he continued?

He accepted the risk.

'For generations, the Readfuss family has been involved with some,' he paused, 'revolutionaries, if you will. A group that desired to change the world even if their ways were unethical.'

Reverend Hollybrook nodded. 'And you were born into such a tradition, yes?'

'Born into, but accepted,' Theodore replied. 'I thought it was a beautiful, noble cause. Giving back the world to the purest ones, but...' He sucked in a deep breath. '...it came with a price I was afraid to pay.'

'So your wife paid it for you,' the reverend concluded.

Tears welled in Theodore's eyes. 'I wasn't strong enough,' he croaked. 'They asked for my life to serve, but I was a coward. I desired the comfort of the Grange. Waking up to my sons every morning, enjoying meals, and taking care of my fields. But if I didn't heed, it was death to my family.' His cheeks dampened. 'My wife accepted the call and joined the fight, but my cowardice led to more consequences.' Shifting in his chair, Theodore wiped his face with the back of his hand. 'To keep my comfort *and* prevent my sons from suffering, I had to surrender my will until I could find twelve to take my place. Thus, the past New Year.' His shoulders slumped and he dropped his head in his hands. 'Forgive me,' he begged.

Reverend Hollybrook was quiet. Theodore feared the reprimand and the damnation to hell. He truly was a coward.

However, there was no reproach. The reverend leaned forwards and whispered, 'The Lord's mercy is unending. Seek to make amends and you will be blessed.' Kindness and sincerity were woven into each word.

The pain behind his eyes was unbearable, but his spirit grew lighter. There was hope. Theodore could be redeemed. His family could be saved.

Whilst Reverend Hollybrook continued to provide counsel, there was a buzzing in Theodore's ear. It started as barely audible until it gradually crescendoed, making it hard to hear.

The joy in Theodore's soul faded as the noise overpowered his thoughts. In the past, he would experience this sensation at the end of every two months.

But he was free. His family was free. He did his due diligence. Why were they calling to him again?

There were only two possible explanations.

The first: his duty was not fulfilled.

The second: the Readfuss line had heeded the call once more.

This revelation was like a jolt, and he shot up in his seat. Reverend Hollybrook stopped speaking and asked if he was all right. Theodore shook his head. 'My sons, my sons,' he repeated. His body shook as he rose. 'They may be in grave danger.'

The reverend stood with him. 'Why do you say that?'

Theodore's eyes met the holy man's. 'I feel them.' He didn't blink.

•◇•◇•◇•◇•◇•◇•◇•

'Terrence!' Thaddeus shouted, his voice echoing down the Grange hall. A knot formed in his stomach. Something wasn't right.

He prayed Terrence would jump out of his usual hiding place. He prayed Terrence would be sleeping away in the field, avoiding chores.

But every instinct directed Thaddeus to the Clockwork Study.

Sweat dripped down his face as Thaddeus gripped the door handle. He was the only one to see the peculiar events of the previous Christmas. His heart told him something unholy went on behind that study door. Something that Thaddeus never wanted to entangle himself with.

But his brother was in trouble. Thaddeus needed to be strong.

Taking a shaky breath, the boy entered the room.

The walls were barren, and all was still. Long shadows formed as Thaddeus searched by candlelight. He prayed Terrence was hiding in the corner, ready to pounce as a joke.

But the room was empty.

Heart hammering, Thaddeus went around Father's chair and examined the wall. Nails stuck out of the wallpaper where clocks should have been. One of them stuck out so far it scraped the boy's arm as he walked past.

Thaddeus let out a quiet yelp and rubbed his raw skin. He eyed the nail with discontent. It was a reminder of the horrible events that occurred in the study. He slid the shoe off his right foot and gripped it tight. Teeth gritted and eyes watering, he slammed the heel into the nail, driving it further into the wall.

Agitated, he proceeded to hammer every nail on the wall. Angered thoughts poured out with every bang. He wanted answers but received none. He wanted a normal life but was denied. Now, all he wanted was his family.

But something in the Clockwork Study would not allow it.

'Give him back,' he panted as he smashed another nail. 'Give him back.' Another strike. One final nail was above his head, taunting him. He inhaled, jumped, and screamed, 'Give him back!' as he hammered the final nail into the wall.

There was a click and Thaddeus did not feel the ground beneath his feet.

His shoe and candle flew out of his grasp as his body plummeted into darkness.

•◊•◊•◊•◊•◊•◊•◊•◊•◊•

Voices hummed in Thaddeus' ears as he lay unmoving on the ground. Pain shot from his feet to his back. To his relief, nothing was broken, but his body refused to move.

He remained still as he listened to two phrases over and over: '*We are Order. We are Chaos.*'

The voices overlapped and intertwined like a chorus of discord. No tone was the same and yet they were unified. In the dim light, the boy could make out twelve familiar figures standing in a circle, facing one another. On the backs of their necks were black numbers from one to twelve. Their eyes remained open, never blinking. Each one held a different clock against their chest.

All from the Clockwork Study.

Feeling returned to Thaddeus' feet and he mustered the courage to move. He needed to find his brother and escape. How? He was unsure, but he was determined to succeed, nonetheless.

With a quiet grunt, he pushed his torso up and got into a squat. Legs shaking, he rose to his feet. A burning sensation overpowered him, and he fell to the ground with a thud.

All twelve heads turned in unison.

'Thaddeusss,' Number Four hissed. 'We are pleased you have joined us, but there was no need.'

'The Chosen has accepted his role,' Number Nine said in a drone. 'Your father's failures will be undone. You will be freed.' They all turned back and faced something in the centre of their circle.

Thaddeus crawled forward, trying to get a glimpse of what they were watching. He dragged his body across the ground, taking laboured breaths, until he was between two of the poor folk.

His heart sank.

Terrence sat in a leather chair with his head tilted back. His eyes stared straight ahead at the pocket watch which dangled from the low damp ceiling.

He didn't blink.

Tears welled in Thaddeus' eyes as he whimpered, 'Terrence?'

No response.

'Terrence!' he called louder.

The boy tilted his head to the left but said nothing. His eyes were fixated on the blasted pocket watch that Thaddeus had begged him to get rid of.

Enraged, Thaddeus pushed his body off the ground and snatched at the watch. His slender fingers swatted it, causing it to spin in a circle.

Terrence's eyes twitched, but he didn't blink.

Thaddeus tried to grab it again, but a wrinkled hand gripped his wrist. He tried to yank himself away but could not escape.

'I told you, my boy, all will be well,' an old man with a Number One on his neck said in a monotonous tone.

Thaddeus froze and looked up. He recognised those glazed eyes. They belonged to the poor man who was kind to the Readfuss twins the previous Christmas. The one Thaddeus invited into his home. The one who became cursed by the Clockwork Study.

He was the one who promised that the Readfuss family would be free.

'Sir, what happened?' Thaddeus cried, trying to wriggle away.

Number One pulled the boy to his feet but did not let go. 'We were selected to wreak chaos upon Whitstead.'

'B-but why?' the boy asked. His feet slid under him as he tried to run towards his brother.

Yanking Thaddeus back, Number One continued, 'The Order will continue to return the world to the worthy ones. It will take hundreds of years, but every step taken is another step forward.' He nodded to two other men who grabbed Thaddeus beneath the armpits and hoisted him up. 'All will be well.'

'No!' the boy screamed as he writhed in their grasp. Fingers tightened around his arms. Thaddeus' feet dangled as he was lifted into the air. He kicked and screamed, but his blows were weak. Darkness enveloped him as the men took him away from his brother.

Tears streamed down Thaddeus' face as he kicked and screamed. 'Terrence! Terrence!'

But the Readfuss twin kept his eyes fixed on the watch. The poor folk clutched their clocks tighter as they murmured around him. Their overlapping voices were a swarm of bees buzzing about their queen.

As Thaddeus was about to scream again, the two men shoved him down into a dark corner, securing him by a rope that felt like thick thread.

Thaddeus thrashed as they tightened the knot around his torso. He threw his legs out to kick his captors. The first man jumped and scurried back to his place in the circle. The other was not as quick. The Readfuss boy drove his foot into the side of the cuckoo clock tucked under his arm. The man's possession crashed to the ground; a crack shot like lightning down the side.

The man staggered, struggling to stand upright. Beads of sweat dripped down his bald head. Glazed eyes frantically searched for the clock that was no longer in his grip.

His eyelids fluttered.

Thaddeus writhed and threw his leg out again. He brought his foot down upon the clock. His ankles bled as he repeated the process. Springs shot out through the broken wood. Thaddeus smashed the clock until it no longer ticked.

The perpetrator's knees buckled, and he dropped to the ground. His frail body was soaked and his eyes, bloodshot. Tremors spread up and down his arms. Thaddeus thought he would start convulsing, but the man pulled through. His quaking ceased and his breathing grew heavy. With his head tilted back, he met Thaddeus' gaze.

Slowly, he blinked.

Thaddeus stared, mouth agape, as the man fell on his face. He lay beside his broken clock, breathing slowly.

'Oh no,' a voice said. 'You've made us incomplete.'

Thaddeus looked up to see Number One approach. He hid his clock behind his back.

'Looks like we may need you after all,' he hissed. He grabbed the thread which entangled Thaddeus and dragged him back to the circle where Terrence continued to stare at the pocket watch. 'The first is complete. On to the second,' Number One ordered.

The rest of the poor folk nodded as they called for Terrence in unison.

Terrence's eyes were glazed over, and his breathing was shallow. Colour drained from his cheeks. Thaddeus thought he was dead until Terrence's lips parted and three words escaped: 'Ready to heed.'

Number One smiled and nodded to the others who gently removed Terrence from the chair. Abruptly, the men shoved Thaddeus into it.

'We need twelve to follow,' the older man stated as he rewound the pocket watch.

It started to tick, and Thaddeus pinched his eyes shut. He was not going to look.

Frail fingers squeezed his cheeks so tight Thaddeus felt bruises forming.

'The Order likes obedience,' Number One said. 'Open of your own accord.'

Thaddeus refused.

Number One sighed. 'We wanted you to be free, Thaddeus. Now you leave us no choice but to force a new freedom upon you.'

Two other hands grabbed the boy's head. Dirty fingers pressed against Thaddeus' eyelids, pulling them back.

The Readfuss boy's eyes were forced to look upon the dangling watch.

The ticks of the second hand echoed in his head as the poor folk murmured around him. Thaddeus tried to tear his eyes away, but they were fixated upon the clock face. The beautiful design, its peaceful clicks, all of it captivated him.

Then, it started to speak to him.

Words, numbers, phrases, and images slowly flickered to life in his mind.

He felt it taking him away.

Muddled voices floated around him. Figures moved quickly in and out of view. Angry faces flashed as fists rose, coming down on something to his right. The ground rumbled beneath his feet. Thaddeus needed to move but could not. The watch engrossed his entire being. He sat helpless among an unknown chaos erupting around him.

His mind was about to succumb when he heard someone calling to him. The throaty voice was familiar. One he had grown to love and trust.

It was his father.

'Thaddeus!' Father screamed. His cry was clear, and the boy could now hear the commotion.

Following deep screams was the sound of shattering glass which rang through the room like a bell. Then, the thud of a body hitting the floor.

In an instant, Theodore Readfuss jumped in front of Thaddeus. Red hair unkempt, shirt torn, blood streaking down his cheek. He snatched at the pocket watch that dangled in front of his son, but Number One grabbed it first.

'You made your choice, Theodore,' Number One said in a stern tone. 'Your sons will take your place.'

Theodore shook his head. 'No Readfuss will lead Whitstead to its destruction.' He jabbed himself with his finger and declared, 'Not whilst I yet live!' He lunged for Number One, tackling the old man to the ground. Both landed on top of the round wall clock decorated with an *O* and *X*.

Number One's clock.

Wood snapped and glass shattered as it was crushed beneath the men's weight. Number One gasped for air as Theodore shoved his shoulders against the pavement.

Theodore's eyes watered. 'I am sorry for what happened to you, but...' Through gritted teeth, he spat: 'Don't take my son.'

Number One's muscles tightened. 'I told you...' His face relaxed and he let out a deep breath. 'All will be well.' The old man slowly blinked twice and then shut his eyes.

Theodore panted as he stood. He composed himself and turned to Thaddeus who watched with amazement. Gently, Theodore unbound his son and embraced him.

'Thaddeus, I am sorry,' Theodore wept. 'Never again will I fail you.' He pressed his lips to Thaddeus' forehead.

'Father,' Thaddeus sobbed. 'W-where's Terrence?'

Theodore cupped the boy's face with his hands. 'He is quite well,' he whispered with a smile. He rose, took his son by the hand, and brought him over to the corner of the room where Terrence lay curled up, snoring softly.

Theodore sat on the ground and scooped Terrence up, resting the boy's head against his chest. Terrence groaned and mumbled that he wanted to go back to sleep. A weight lifted off Thaddeus' shoulders, knowing his brother was all right.

'What happened?' Thaddeus asked as he knelt beside his brother.

'A wretched family legacy,' Theodore stated. 'A responsibility to serve a cause we want no part in.'

Thaddeus' head spun. The images and phrases were but shadows in the back of his mind. However, he felt no peace. Something was nagging at him. Calling to him. He shook his head hard and blinked.

Theodore put an arm around Thaddeus and pulled him in close. 'Son, I am sorry for everything.' He pressed his son's head to his chest. 'I thought we could cut ties but not quite. I was told to replace myself with Twelve, and now there are none. All these folks are freed of the burdens I gave them.'

'What about us?' Thaddeus asked. Tears dripped down his face as he looked at all the broken clocks. Glass twinkled in the dim candlelight. Springs rolled across the ground. These clocks once hung in the Readfuss' beautiful home. Thaddeus only saw them as decoration.

Now, they signified destruction.

'We, unfortunately, have more clocks to break,' Theodore said in a low voice. 'They know we refused to be Chosen.' He took a deep breath. 'They'll come back to silence us.'

Thaddeus swallowed the fiery lump in his throat. 'Will we be able to fight back?'

Theodore smirked. He picked up the pocket watch connected to Thaddeus' mind. 'We are the Readfuss family.' In a swift motion, he slammed it against the ground, destroying it. 'Of course, we will fight back.'

Tea and Shadows
by Sarah Falanga *(historical/spiritual warfare)*

Jacob Needsworth, that worthy gentleman of Whitstead, walked home soaked. A heavy fog was settling, hiding every house he passed from its neighbouring house.

Needsworth came to his own home and walked slowly up the path.

A low howl or moan, carried through the fog, stopped him where he stood. It was a strange sound—impossible to tell whether beast or man.

Needsworth shuddered and walked on at a quicker pace.

Every minute the fog grew thicker.

Before he could try the handle, the door was opened to him by his housekeeper. 'Oh, Mr Needsworth, just look at you.'

He grunted. 'It's a dim day. Makes everything dim, even tea,' he added in a lower voice. 'And I am weary of it.'

'Aye, sir, you're right there,' the woman said, taking his overcoat and hat. 'The house is dim, no matter how many fires John keeps up and candles I light, and it's downright depressing to the spirits!'

Needsworth looked around at the big hall where they stood with its dark wood walls and heavy curtains. 'It's a gloomy house, especially on days like today. Not a good house for a young child. How is Dickon, Mrs Mallory?'

'He keeps to himself, as he's done since he arrived after…' Her voice faded and, with a shake of her head, she went on. 'It's better on days when he can go out and play, but today has not been one of those days.'

'Is he in the nursery?'

'No, he's in your study, sir,' Mrs Mallory answered.

'I will go and see him after I've changed.'

Turning to go, Needsworth stopped mid-step as the same moan rose in the fog outside. Still as statues, they listened.

Slowly, the moan faded.

'A strange sound,' Needsworth said.

'I don't like it at all, sir. The sounds one hears on the heath…' She shuddered.

'Put a lamp outside by the door,' Needsworth said.

Mrs Mallory stared at him.

He went on; 'Perhaps someone is in trouble. The only way we can help them is if they come to us out of the fog.'

'I'm not sure I'd want it in the house if it's dangerous, sir.'

'Nevertheless, I don't like the idea of someone – or something – being hurt, and not doing anything to help them.'

'Yes, sir,' Mrs Mallory muttered, and then went on quickly, 'Would you like dinner today, sir?'

Needsworth shook his head. 'I'll take tea in my study. Bring something for Dickon, though.'

He turned and went up the stairs but stopped and stared at the long hallway before him. He made a face, muttering, 'Everything is dim – and this is no ordinary fog.'

After putting on a warm smoking jacket and slippers, Needsworth descended into the hall and went into the study. The dark of the foggy evening had crept into that room as well, even though there was a roaring fire.

The tea things had already arrived, with a rustic cake, bread, cheese and cold ham.

A small boy stood with his back to the door, staring out the window. He turned when Needsworth shut the door.

'I think a ghost just left, Uncle Jake,' he said in a small voice. 'You can see it sitting out there, next to the door.'

Needsworth looked out the window and then smiled.

'That's just the lamp I asked Mrs Mallory to put outside, in case anyone's lost in the fog.'

Needsworth closed the curtain, then turned and went to the tea things, pouring himself a cup.

He handed Dickon a teacup and a plate with the ham and toast on it and sat down in the chair next to the fire. Dickon sat down in the chair opposite.

'Have you gone exploring the house yet, Dickon?' Needsworth asked, sipping his tea. 'It's a capital house for exploring.'

'I thought of exploring… but the library was cold. I – I went there first, to look at books.'

Needsworth raised an eyebrow. 'Really, I've never known that room to be cold. Good thing too – who'd want to read in a cold library?' He laughed.

'It was *very* cold,' Dickon went on, quicker. 'And… and I heard a voice. And the house is so dark, Uncle Jake!'

'That it is, and I don't like it either,' Needsworth said.

'Mrs Mallory says it's the rain and fog,' Dickon said, taking a huge bite of toast.

'Yes. Cloudy, cold weather often makes one sad.'

Dickon nodded, chewing again, saying, 'It's not happy, like sunshine is.'

'We belong to light… to joy and love. Perhaps that's why we don't like dark.'

'But… sometimes I like it when it rains,' the boy said. 'Not like today, but other times.'

'There's nothing wrong with rain or clouds. It's darkness, a particular kind of darkness, that one doesn't like, and which we don't belong to. It's an unnatural darkness.'

'Are there ghosts… or ghouls, Uncle Jake?' Dickon whispered, his mouth full of ham.

Needsworth laughed. 'I've never seen or heard a ghost and seems I ought to have by now. What's more likely is that this is a very old place — England, Whitstead itself, is old with much tumultuous history, some of which we know little about. With so much trouble, a place is bound to be affected by it, and sometimes the darkness tries to sneak through and take over.'

Dickon stared at him.

Needsworth looked at him a minute, and finally said, 'Am I scaring you?'

The boy nodded.

'It's all right, Dickon,' Needsworth said. 'The darkness can't get us, no matter how much it seems it can. Now, you say you heard a voice in the library?'

Dickon nodded.

'It's been a long time since I heard a voice,' Needsworth said, standing. 'Would you like to accompany me to the library?'

The boy stared at him. 'But, what if…'

He didn't finish.

Needsworth shrugged. 'If there's someone in my home, Lord make me a toad if I don't make them welcome. Bring the cake, will you, Dickon?'

Dickon carefully picked up the cake and followed his uncle out the room. 'Will the Lord *really* make you a toad, Uncle Jake?'

'Pardon me, I was being absurd.'

•◊•◊•◊•◊•◊•◊•◊•◊•

The moan drifted past Jane as she stood frozen in the heavy fog. Her eyes were wide as she looked around, but nothing but shifting shadow was visible.

'Will,' she whispered. No answer.

Jane walked forwards and then suddenly fell, landing amid brush and mud.

'Clumsy,' a voice said out of the fog, as Jane pulled herself up.

'Will, where were you? I've been waiting *hours*,' she said, crying.

'It's not been *hours*,' the boy answered. 'It's the dark, that's all.'

'I don't like it, Will,' Jane said, wiping what mud would come off.

'Did you find any food?' she asked presently. 'I'm so hungry.'

An icy breeze shifted the fog somewhat, revealing a form in front of her, and she walked carefully towards it.

'No, no food,' Will answered. Jane groaned.

She reached the form, slipping in mud, and catching the hand that was put out to her. She screamed, wrenching her hand away.

'Shut up, Jane!' Will said hoarsely, colliding into the girl. They hugged. 'I'm right here, there's no need to scream.'

'There's someone in the fog with us,' Jane said in a shaken voice. 'His — his hands were cold.'

'You're imagining things. Who would be stupid enough to be out on the heath in this weather?'

'Let's go home, Will. I don't like running away.'

'I thought you didn't like that old hag father got us for a nurse.'

'I don't, but anything is better than this!'

'Even without Mother?'

A low moan, caught on the dying breeze, hovered around them. Jane gasped.

'Please, Will, let's go home.'

'All right,' he said, pulling himself away from the girl, but holding her hand tight. 'Follow right behind me, and with some luck we won't fall into *every* ditch.'

They went on, trudging through mud and brush. Suddenly, something in the bushes next to them took flight. Jane screamed.

'Do shut up, Jane!' the boy said. 'We just scared a wild animal.'

'I'm so tired, Will,' she answered, stopping. 'Hadn't we better stop and wait for the….' Her voice stopped suddenly. She went on in a breathless, terrified voice. 'Will, do you know which way is home?'

He didn't answer at once. 'Yes, it's that way.'

'No! I can always tell when you're lying.'

'That's not true.'

'You're lying,' Jane yelled. 'You don't know where home is — we're lost!'

'Jane, do be quiet!' he answered in a hushed voice. 'All right, I don't know where we are.'

They were silent for a minute.

'What do we do?' the girl asked.

'If we could only find somewhere dry and wait until morning. It's so cold — and dark.'

•◊•◊•◊•◊•◊•◊•◊•◊•◊•◊•

Needsworth shivered, pulling his smoking jacket collar up. 'It is cold in here,' he laughed. 'I hope you brought your fur coat, Dickon.'

He advanced into the dark library, ringing the bell by the door and putting the teapot on the table. Dickon, looking around the room with wide eyes, carefully went to his uncle, grasping his hand as soon as he stood next to him.

In a moment, a servant appeared. He shivered, looking around the library with narrowed eyes.

'John, it's evidently winter in the library,' Needsworth said. 'We will be needing a blazing fire and candles everywhere.'

'Immediately, sir,' John said. 'But… pardon me for asking, will you be *staying* in here?'

'No, there is a noticeably distasteful atmosphere here tonight,' he said. 'We will be going back to the study.

'Yes, sir,' John said. 'I can't think why a fire wasn't started already.'

He turned, and, with great alacrity, built up a fire in the grate.

Needsworth turned and lit the candles on the desk behind him.

The whole of his house was neat and comfortable, but the desk in the library remained crowded and disorganised with the many subjects the master of the house found interesting. Needsworth's eyes fell on a map that lay open on top of a pile of books. 'Here's something you may find interesting, Dickon. You seem like the sort of lad that would like maps.'

Dickon went around the desk and, kneeling on the big armchair, stared at the map in front of him.

'This is an old map of Whitstead,' Needsworth said, 'when it was little more than a few manors and the abbey was still occupied.'

He pulled out another map and laid it on top of the first. 'Here is a more recent map.'

'Where are all the houses?' Dickon asked, pointing to the older map.

'They weren't built yet.'

'Everyone in those houses…' Dickon pointed vaguely to the manors. '…must have been very lonely.'

'Yes, I imagine they were.'

'Where's *your* house?'

'It wasn't built yet either,' Needsworth said. 'Not for another fifty years, perhaps.'

'It's a *very* old map, then.'

'And here…' Needsworth pointed to another house. '…is your old house, where you lived with your dear father.'

Dickon stared at the house he'd pointed to, carefully running his fingers over it.

John came over to the desk.

Needsworth looked up. 'Ah, that is an excellent, comfortable fire, John,' he said. 'Thank you.'

'Will you be needing anything else, sir?' He eyed the tea cake that Dickon had put on the corner of the desk next to an old breviary.

'What do you say, Dickon? Shall we finish our tea in here and continue looking at the maps?'

Dickon looked around at the library. It was much brighter now than when they'd first come in. Already, the fire was making a difference, but a strange chill still hung in the air and the darkness was heavier than ever.

Dickon shook his head.

'That will be all, John,' Needsworth said. 'We'll be needing another pot of tea in the study.'

With another bow, John turned and left the room.

'Are we going to leave the teapot and cake here, Uncle Jake?' Dickon asked, looking up at him.

Needsworth nodded.

'But there's no one here.'

'That's all right.'

Needsworth quickly went to one of the many bookshelves and glanced over the books. He grinned suddenly, pulling out a large volume. 'When it's too cold outside to explore, and too gloomy inside, there are *always* books. Come along, Dickon—I've found an excellent book with beautiful illustrations that will have you dreaming of adventurers and hidden treasure.'

•◊•◊•◊•◊•◊•◊•◊•◊•

Jane and Will sat huddled with their back to an old tree. The fog was so thick that even the body of the tree was hardly visible.

'I wish we'd never left,' Jane said in a whisper.

'Oh, do stop saying that.'

A low moan started. The children stiffened, staring around them.

The moan slowly drew nearer. They backed up against the tree, holding their breath and clinging to each other. Something large and dark stood before them.

Without saying a word, they stood and ran headlong in the opposite direction, Will holding fast to Jane's hand. Jane stumbled, falling over a fallen tree branch. Quickly, Will pulled her up, and they ran on.

The strange cry followed them and then suddenly stopped. Presently, they stopped, breathless.

'Look, Will!' Jane breathed. 'A light!'

Far ahead, a tiny twinkling could be seen through the darkness.

'Oh, God, thank You,' he said, walking on and dragging Jane with him.

'I'm so tired, Will.'

'I can't carry you. And you don't want to stay out here with… *that*… no more than I do! Come on!'

The girl groaned, and followed, crying quietly. They walked towards the tiny light.

They were silent for a long time. Then, suddenly, the light disappeared.

'Where did it go?' Jane asked.

They stopped.

'It must be the fog — getting thicker.'

'Are we lost again?'

Suddenly, the light reappeared, and Will breathed a sigh of relief. 'There it is again. Come on, we should hurry if the fog is getting thicker.'

The moaning started up again. Jane jumped and started forward sat a stumbling pace.

'Jane, stop!' Will's voice was distant.

Jane froze where she was, putting her hands out. 'Oh, Will — where are you?'

Something touched her shoulder. She screamed, falling to the ground.

'It's me,' Will's voice said. 'It's me, Jane, don't worry.'

Carefully Jane reached out. Her hands touched something, and Will's hand clasped hers, and they hugged.

'I can't go on, Billy — I'm so tired.'

'The light's still there, Jane,' he said. 'It's just a little further.'

'No, it's not. That might be the light from a house, and it's tiny. It might be miles away. I *can't* go on. Just let me rest for a minute.'

Will sighed and sat down next to her. They were silent for a minute.

'Is it just me…' He paused, sitting up straighter. 'It's warm — *I'm warm!*'

'So am I,' she said with a sigh. 'Oh, it feels marvellous. I'm starting to feel my toes again.'

'It's very odd, though,' Will said.

'Maybe it's magic.'

Will snorted.

'Don't be rude. Come on, perhaps there's a faerie hole where we'll find food and a bed!'

'The faerie mightn't like us eating its food,' Will muttered, standing. He added, 'If you're feeling well enough to look for faerie holes, hadn't we better go on now?'

'Oh! Oh, Will, I found…'

'What?'

He followed her voice and, following her hand, found something warm. 'What is it?'

'I don't know,' Will said, picking up the lid and smelling it. 'It's warm, though!'

He took a long sip and then handed it to Jane, who also took a long drink. They both breathed a long sigh.

'My tummy feels warm,' Jane said. 'I hope the faerie doesn't mind us taking its food.'

'We've only taken its drink so far,' the boy muttered. 'Where did you find it?'

'Right here on the ground, on this stump.'

Will felt the stump, and presently he straightened. 'Look, it's a whole, enormous cake!'

They sat down on the stump and started to eat the cake and drink more of the warm liquid. Neither of them said anything for a long time.

Presently, as the last chunk of cake was being eaten by Will, he said, 'Is that all? Feel around the stump in case there's more food.'

They both felt around the stump.

'I found something,' Jane said, and her voice stopped suddenly.

'What's wrong?'

'Will,' she said, her voice choked. 'It's — it's our breviary.'

His hands reached out, touching the familiar leather cover. He took the book from Jane, laying it carefully on his lap and opening it. His hand ran down the first page.

Their names — his own and Jane's, Father's and Mother's. He could almost feel the writing.

'I suppose…' His voice was low. '…we do belong. I mean, our names are here…'

'Of course, we belong,' Jane's voice said. She hugged him and added, 'What are you talking about?'

'Father's been so different, since…' He didn't finish. Jane's hand squeezed his.

'Come on,' he said. 'Let's go home.'

They stood up and again started for the tiny light in the distance, one of Will's hands clasping Jane's, and his other holding the breviary tight.

They went on only a little while, with the light sometimes being hidden by the fog. Suddenly, they came to the source of the light — a lamp sitting on a large stone. It stood alone, with no signs of houses nearby.

Jane and Will stood staring at the light. Neither said anything. Suddenly, a second, wavering light appeared some distance from them.

A voice cried out. 'Jane! Will!'

'Father!'

The light stopped a moment, and then suddenly, with leaps and bounds, drew nearer. A figure appeared and, in a moment, wrapped its arms around the two smaller figures.

'My children,' the man half-sobbed. 'Am I fortuned to find my children return, or are you phantoms of shadows?'

'We return, father,' Will said, quietly.

'But why leave at all, little ones…' His voice caught. 'And — how have you our breviary?'

'I — I thought…' Will's voice was distant. 'I thought there was no place for me.'

'Would the Good Lord know every star's place in the sky, but pay no heed to the place He has for you? Nay, for you are His own, and mine to care for. Now, take my hand, that we will be together.

'And you, Jane, I think, would risk winter and darkness to be your brother's comrade, even when he would treat you ill—am I right, or do I not know my own daughter?'

'It is as you say, father,' she answered through tears.

'Oh, my children, you are dear to me—though you do give me fright. Come, let us be home.'

'But how shall we find our way in this fog?'

'Listen, for though we're blind in this dark, the blessed nuns are not mute—say you can hear them singing.'

They were silent for a minute. 'Yes, I can hear them—but only just now,' Will said.

'When on the heath, between the river and forest, their singing will bring you home. Let me carry you, Jane, and you, Will, take the lantern—let us return.'

•◊•◊•◊•◊•◊•◊•◊•◊•◊•

The next morning, Jacob Needsworth stood in the entrance to the library, staring at the desk with eyes wide and mouth open. Mrs Mallory came down the hall, walking quickly, with a brief curtsy and a good morning.

Needsworth turned abruptly. 'Mrs Mallory, did you take away the teapot and cake that were in the library?'

The woman's eyes opened wider. She glanced into the library with a shake of her head. 'No, indeed, sir. I did not even know you had tea and cake in this room, or I would have had it cleared away.'

'And none of the other servants came in here?'

Mrs Mallory looked at him again. 'No, sir. Your instructions have always been to not disturb the library in the morning, in case you are studying, sir. Only John goes in to start a fire, and he would certainly not take the teapot or cake…'

'Or the old Cobbett breviary?'

Mrs Mallory's eyes opened wider still. 'No, indeed, sir.'

'Good, good,' Needsworth said, staring at the floor.

'Will that be all, sir?'

'Yes,' he said, adding in a low voice, 'Only if anyone should ask where that teapot went, say it broke… and Dickon and I finished the cake. It was quite delicious, by the way.'

Mrs Mallory laughed, saying, 'Cook will be pleased—and baffled—to hear you've changed your opinion of candied citrus.'

Needsworth made a face. 'Better not mention the cake, then.'

Wishing her a good morning, Needsworth turned to enter the library. Just then, running down the hall, Dickon appeared.

'Uncle Jake!' he shouted, breathless. 'It's sunny and—and the library is warm! It's all right after all!'

Needsworth chuckled. 'It is indeed! No number of shadows and chill can capture us, can it?'

They entered the library, Dickon glancing at the corner of the desk. 'It looks so different. There was nothing to be afraid of.'

'Not to say there was nothing there, though,' Needsworth muttered as he sat down. 'This is a different room from the one we entered yesterday.'

He looked at Dickon, who was eagerly looking in a picture book, and smiled. 'It's been a difficult year,' he went on to himself, 'But we'll be all right in the end.'

'Were you saying something, Uncle Jake?' the boy asked, looking at him.

'Only talking to myself, Dickon—a silly habit.' He leaned forward. 'And now the sun is shining at last—though it looks like a chilly day—what will you be doing?'

'Exploring!'

'Excellent, but only on the grounds, I hope,' Needsworth said. 'Many children have got lost on the heath—though thankfully been returned safely to home.'

Dickon shook his head. 'No, definitely not the heath! I will explore the gardens.'

'And you'll find them muddy.'

'What will you be doing, Uncle Jake?' the boy asked, as he hopped towards the door.

'Visiting the Charitable School for children,' Needsworth answered.

Dickon, hand on the doorknob, frowned. 'I don't like that place—that lady was nasty,' he scowled.

With a brief, thoughtful smile, Needsworth murmured to himself; 'Never underestimate the power of light, Dickon.'

Absolution
by Sondra Bateman *(ghost story/historical)*

It is said that the closer to three a.m., the thinner reality becomes between the living and the dead.

Bradford Matlock looked out the window of his small cottage on the edge of Whitstead and into the growing darkness of eventide. Compared to previous weeks, this day broke clear and cool. Clouds weren't exactly rolling in but had built enough to drift across the moon. It had been a cold summer and one that he was glad that was at its end. The crops struggled throughout the growing season, which seemed like it was hardly anything this year. It was just odd, he mused as he stepped away from the window and let the curtains drop back into place. Tomorrow was his first All Saints' Day in this small town, and he was looking forward to Reverend Hollybrook's sermon on forgiving oneself. At least this would be one of the last holy days separated from his wife, Anne.

The fire flickered in the hearth, making shadows dance on the walls. A piece of wood snapped, showering sparks out onto the stones. Images of his brother popped unexpectedly into his mind. The same brother with whom he'd had a bitter argument last year, then left. Maybe it was his brother's obsession with liquor that brought the emotions to the surface.

Taking a deep breath, he tried to push the images from his mind. Most of the time it worked, and he hoped one again that he would be successful.

When he'd first arrived at Whitstead, he wanted to make a new start. He was welcomed with open arms. No one knew of his family, for which he was thankful.

Bradford went back over to the lone chair in the parlour and sat down, letting out a mixture between a sigh and a groan. By this time there should have been more furniture, but he just didn't feel like hiring a carpenter. Anne would fuss at him for his lack of initiative, but he just didn't feel like doing anything at this point.

The warmth of the fire and the flickering flames either put him into a light sleep, or something entirely different. When Bradford opened his eyes, he found he was back in the home where he grew up, or so it seemed. He blinked and rubbed the back of his hands over his eyes, to clear out the sleep. 'Where am I?'

'In a place you should not remain,' an oddly familiar voice came from behind.

Bradford froze, then slowly looked over his shoulder. At the back of the room stood what he thought was a man wearing breeches and a waistcoat, the same clothing that men wore in earlier times. 'Who are you?'

The spectre cocked his head. 'Don't you rem…? Wait, I don't think you had been born yet before I fell off that horse.'

It took a moment for Bradford to decide whether to believe this apparition or not. It was unnerving. All he wanted was to be back home. As of its own volition, his right hand came up and he crossed himself.

'Crossing yourself doesn't work here.' The image let out an amused chuckle that echoed across the room.

Bradford took a deep breath and stood up. He folded his arms so that it wouldn't show them shaking. 'Then why am I here since you stated that I cannot remain?'

'Your brother is looking for you,' the voice echoed as his surroundings began to swirl, blurring the colours.

'Wait,' Bradford reached out as a dark maw opened before him, and he felt as if he were being sucked down into the —

Bradford's eyes opened with a start. He looked around the dark room, breathing hard. The fire had died down to almost nothing, yet the coals still glowed red. 'What was that?' He rubbed his eyes with the back of his hand, then squeezed them shut.

As if in answer the door shook in its frame, making him jump. Muffled voices came through the solid construction.

Knowing the person outside wouldn't be going away any time soon, Bradford pushed himself to his feet. After lighting a lamp, he went back to the entrance. The window he'd looked through earlier was at such an angle that he couldn't see anyone standing outside. 'I'm here,' he muttered as he pushed open the door.

Three figures shrouded in the darkness stood before him. He raised the lamp and took a step back as the one in front pushed the hood back, revealing Anne.

'It took you long enough.' Her level of annoyance was in proportion to how he was addressed. With no honorific, Bradford knew it would be a while before she calmed down.

Anne pushed her way past him and into the parlour. 'Did you fall asleep in front of the fire again?' She pulled off her gloves whilst giving him a critical look.

Bradford looked down to his clean, albeit rumpled, clothing. 'I was waiting for you.'

A smile brightened her face, then fell as she looked over his shoulder. 'There's someone here who wishes to speak with you.'

Bradford shook his head. He had heard that before, but he couldn't recall where. He turned to see who had come with Anne. William his brother, and his wife Margaret, stood before him, both with uncertain looks on their faces.

45

'What are you doing here?' Bradford frowned then turned his back on the two as he went back over to his chair.

'To apologise, brother. You know what happens when I drink liquor.'

Bradford set the lamp down near the hearth. The stonework helped to reflect the light so that it was now easier to see across the room. 'And it always happens, brother. It never changes.'

'Things are different this time.'

Bradford snorted. 'Why should I believe you?'

'Because I had a dream.'

Dream? The word triggered something in his memories and the images that refused to come earlier came flooding back, especially the man dressed in clothing from the previous century.

'Yes, a dream,' William started. It was obvious he was still unsure of the whole situation. 'I believe it was our grandfather who came to me the last time I slept. All I hope is that you will understand that things have changed.'

'Please give him a chance,' Anne came towards him, her hands clasped before her.

'I have many times, why should I now?'

'Because we are commanded to forgive even if the number of wrongs committed against us is seventy times seven.'

The Haunted Huntsman
by Deborah Kelty *(fantasy/action/horror)*

Rain poured down in torrents, making the perfect cover for ghost hunting. Intending to pass through Whitstead, the silent traveller rode first through rural fields towards the forest, where signs of wandering souls might be found. And in turn, an easier place to capture them without anyone's notice. *Perfect timing indeed,* Jeremy Carlisle thought with satisfaction.

Finding the right spot to catch forbidden, mischievous spirits who would start terrorizing the living was no easy task. Whether it was young children's nightmares, or older men and women wakeful in the late evening alone or with loved ones — they always found a way to leave behind a terror that would scar thoughts for days, months, or years afterward. And of course, during the night of All Hallows' Eve, when their appearances were most frequent. Jeremy dismounted at the forest opening, dark brown branches with wilting leaves stretching out to welcome him. He sighed deeply, sensing the heaviness of his breath as a cough parted with it.

The horse Colby snorted, making him chuckle.

'Old age is catching up to me, friend, even if I may look young.'

A breeze blew through the trees behind him as those few persistent words returned once more: *A bang. A pain. A scream.* Trying to forget them had never really worked, and at this point, they were a warning to remember dangers he'd come to expect. From the two panniers on Colby's back, he pulled out a silver jar which was secured to his belt and a small lantern whose wick he turned alight by a thin pointed match. With one hand holding the lantern, a flintlock in the other, and a musket over the shoulder, the hunter walked into the canopy, gaze alert for movement.

His black cloak clung to him, and his boots trudged through mud and leaves. An owl hooted far above. The wind grew stronger with the rain, hushing the night animals that scuttled on the soil. Then the lantern blew out. Instantly the ghost hunter placed it down before standing up once more to listen for a change in the undergrowth. From behind came hollow breathing. It crept up behind and past him, wandering away lightly in its own direction without much sound. A smaller creature, an easy catch.

Jeremy didn't fully bring this into thought; the spirits could hear the living, both in mind and body, as they walked on the physical plane. But with his unnatural senses in knowing their whereabouts, he knew where it moved near his position.

He froze to let it go by, quieting his breath whilst making the smallest of movements, ready in perfect position to capture his prey.

One minute became two, and two became three, as the wispy blue mist slowly wandered around him. Before it could completely vanish, Jeremy pounced on the ghost with the open cased jar. In doing so, he fell onto the forest floor, covered in autumn leaves that sprang into the air and floated onto his back as he struggled to hang on to the jar, both hands covering where the lid was opened. Its cries and whimpering screams morphed into strange shapes, which crackled in streaks of light as it spun around faster in the mist. Suddenly the orb burst open the jar and the shattered glass split into tiny fragments, leaving little in Jeremy's hands. He hid his face from the impact with his cloak, hearing the pieces shimmer near his ears before scattering onto the ground.

Out of the corner of his eye, he saw the swirling orb disappear into the forest. Swearing, Jeremy Carlisle got to his feet and ran after its trail. This evening had already not started in his favour, and that made his chances of success even slimmer.

To capture and return escapees from the underworld was no easy task. Most were easily transported to their final resting place and never returned, whilst others found either extreme luck or cleverness in discovering an easy route out from their eternal sentence. Which only made this situation stranger, for the ghost had no name or distinct appearance that was recognisable to Jeremy. *I hope this isn't as dangerous as I think it might be.*

He halted in his stride to catch his breath, and once recovered, whistled for Colby to follow and join him on the other side of the forest. Outside the trees, torrents of rain came upon him, making his dark clothes, brown hair, and hat soaking wet.

Jeremy shook his head in weary frustration, only to notice flashes of white light blink and fade towards a large building in the distance. *Thank the heavens, I haven't completely lost it.*

After a short walk, Jeremy and Colby found shelter at the manor as the storm worsened. Stabling Colby in a small barn, Jeremy crept inside to find any sign of the strange ghost, as well as a chance to get some food in his belly. Only a few servants passed in opposite corridors by the main passageway, unaware of the man who walked through the shadows to reach the food store. Once he quietly went down the steps, Jeremy calmed easily, as he saw what contents were kept inside. There were massive wine barrels and sacks of food, some opened to show a vast array of ingredients, particularly more exotic fruits from other countries.

But a small few were from plants of English soil, like apples, plums, nuts from acorns, walnuts, raspberries — even pine nuts of a European variety made an appearance.

He found a loosened sack of apples to take one to eat, browsing the larder to view what other supplies were set up. So far, so good. Eyeing the larder's shelves and the scarce provisions that each held, he sat on one of the cold steps and waited. He kept an ear out for occasional footsteps and chatter above, but the closest were small sounds not even close to the door. But Jeremy, with other senses through the mind, was searching around the manor for any sound or movement from the ghoul itself. He pondered on the previous ghouls he'd captured (including some that escaped multiple times), and how some were very foolish and obstinate, even prior to their eventual ends. Whether it involved an attempt to steal a slice of black pudding, vandalising the walls of a building, or worse, playing a prank for some callous humour, they were terrible and silly ways to be a cause of death. Then again, there were others who had it much worse, as he knew only too well himself.

By the time he had reached the thin apple core, Jeremy slowly climbed back up the stairs, noticing how quiet it had become above him. He walked the way he'd come towards the small kitchen passage, when a cold darkness chilled his spine.

Nearby light from candelabras was dimmed to nothing, and the night swarmed through the stone walls. From there came a strange feeling, one that almost hit him from behind with a powerful, intimidating force. Jeremy stopped himself in time before falling to the floor, sensing something big and threatening behind this dark presence. He wasn't alone.

'Hello, Jeremy Carlisle.'

He'd heard that voice before and felt a twinge of pain in his heart that he hadn't felt in years. He didn't want to see its face; that face held the very memories he'd tried to escape for so long. But that was why he came to Whitstead, to stand against it once more, after all this time.

'I sense your fear, soldier. What are you waiting for?'

What occurred next was a conscious choice of quick thinking by Carlisle. In one swift move, he pulled out his pistol, spun around, and aimed at his enemy, eyes half closed as he pressed the trigger. For an instant he saw him, irises dark red as blood. But as the bullet took the ghoul's attention, Jeremy Carlisle started to run, through the corridor and into the kitchen, before making for the barn where Colby grazed.

Freeing his horse, the ghost hunter rode away from the estate, sensing the ghoul close behind. Jeremy tried to lead the chase further from the village, to keep it from coming to harm and avoid the attention of the living. The ghoul appeared again, this time coming directly towards him and his horse.

'Don't try to run from me, Carlisle!' it called out in a furious tone. 'You are a fool to do so!' But Jeremy didn't look back at it again, nor answer its rage.

He stopped in time to turn into a village backstreet, half paralyzed at seeing part of its countenance. That fixed stare, those cold eyes, desiring to pull him away again forever. Seeing a door leading into a large cottage, which appeared to be empty, he decided to do the unthinkable.

'Time to be the distraction now,' Jeremy quickly whispered to Colby, before attaching his cloak to the reins, jumping off the saddle, and aiming himself into the ditch hidden by crates. A few minutes passed as the horse's hooves faded away before Jeremy picked himself up from the mud, brushed dirt off his shoes and clothes, and went inside the small house to hide.

●◇●◇●◇●◇●◇●◇●◇●

Sheltering inside this cottage was not as comfortable as he expected it to be.

In a small study room on the upper floor, Jeremy curled up inside a boxed corner between a table and bookshelf, where his enemy would less strongly detect his hiding spot than in a more open space. In flickering images that split in and out of vision, he sensed its trail almost go into the lower floor, only to change its mind and disappear into the village itself. Colby also appeared in these, keeping the ghoul's attention averted by the illusion his cloak gave.

'Don't be stupid now, Colby,' he muttered silently, 'and don't get hurt.'

The ghost-hunter slowly recovered from his fright, questioning what exactly had attacked him from his expansive knowledge on this type of creature. And from previous experience.

Jeremy considered the possibility that it may not be fully in form, perhaps even half possessed by either a demon or madness. The only certain answer he had was that it clearly held some connection to the spirit orb he'd found in the forest. Perhaps that, he considered, was also a distraction. *Maybe a way to lead me into its trap? No wonder I nearly lost focus there.*

His gloves dug into his palms, making them sore and hot, and small beads of sweat trickled down his forehead and beard. He stayed in that room for some time as the sound of raindrops gradually lessened. Through a small gap in the curtains, the clouds started to part away with the mist. Jeremy leaned his head to glance closer, when he noticed the moon shining through an inky blue sky. His eyes started to squint as he saw how high it was above him. *It's nearly an hour to midnight. More spirits will be running amok here soon, and that monster is becoming more powerful. I need to work faster before –*

The bang. The pain. The scream.

He flinched a little at those three images returning from his long distant memory, and by habit, clutched at the rosary beads that were attached near the centre of his belt.

It was one of the few heirlooms Jeremy had managed to keep intact from his early life, despite the stern disapproval of his father when he first took it from a cold, lifeless hand. Grieving over his mother's death had kept them from any further strife, at least for a short while.

Now he wondered if the rosary brought comfort anymore, like he thought it once did during later times of civil war. A war he had never desired to fight in, and one that scarred his memories. *Like Mother could ever rise from the dead to help me here. Let alone any saints.*

Sounds of laughing chatter bubbled in through the window, soon joined with walking feet out on cobblestones as tired villagers headed home for the night.

'Time to move,' Jeremy reminded himself, when the sound of an opening door came from below, with a second creak after a brief pause. Someone else had come inside, and he had little choice but to move or be caught. Jeremy crept carefully out of the small room, fingers tight on his pistol. He blended into the shadows near the staircase, peeking over the bars to see what the door had allowed inside.

It appeared to be an older couple, who were still quite awake and alert.

The husband, who yawned behind a raised hand in the politest manner he could manage despite showing his sleepiness, called out to his wife, 'I'm heading to my bed early, love. Do bring up a cup of tea though, will you?'

'Of course, my dear Mr Winterhaven! I need one especially so to calm myself for sleep.'

The man started to climb the stairs, each creak a warning to Jeremy that discovery neared. One step, two steps, three steps. A fire started to crackle and pop into life, its flames leaving glints of orange light on the walls. Four, five, six….

'Jeremy…' The voice sent a chill up his spine. It was another voice he knew, but a different kind that he almost didn't recognise, coming from the second room further in. Except he knew it from somewhere, but from another time than the one before.

A confused mutter from Mr Winterhaven made him turn back down the stairs, which gave Jeremy a chance to move. He started to walk within the shadows towards the beckoning call.

Quietly pulling out his gun, he continued around the corner to open the door to the second room. Another face from the past confronted him, one with a greater hold on his heart than the last he had encountered.

She wore a pale blue dress, which he recognised from one of their last times together. Her glowing figure floated, head cradled on her right shoulder as if she slept, raven black hair cascading over her shoulders towards her elbows. He noticed the shredded tears in her skirts, which hung to the floor, which her feet just touched.

'Avis?' he called, voice quivering whilst he kept his gun aimed steadily.

'Jeremy? Where have you been all this time? Why have you only found me now?'

Jeremy, in his moment of entranced awe, was taken aback by this question. 'Avis, my love. I did try to look for you when we separated… I really did!'

'I know, dear. But why give up when you were so close?'

51

Then he noticed the two beds that were beside her: a young boy and girl were tucked in, deeply slumbering and completely unaware of the ghostly form hovering close by. Jeremy realised he must keep them safe from what could happen next.

'Avis, tell me what happened to you,' he said calmly, starting to circle around her to stand in front of the beds.

'O Jeremy, do you really want to know of my poor, tragic demise?' she added in a light, frigid tone.

'Yes, all of it.'

'Once you left to fight, I was taken away to a terrible place, a dungeon, dark and cold with little light from the outside world. They claimed I was a madwoman, entranced with knowledge and ideas too foreign for them to understand.'

Her eyes rolled to the ceiling as Jeremy reached the foot of the beds, listening to her story with one eye on the children and the other on Avis. He tried to stifle both his rage and sobs. Hearing such horrific details from the only person he'd hoped had a happy ending, even without him, made his heart heavy.

'Tell me, dear Jeremy, what happened to you? Surely you remember it all? Every last detail?' In those final words, Avis's voice lowered to a deadly threat.

Jeremy was pulled from its illusion as a separate poltergeist. This was not Avis. She would never say such a thing to him. She'd normally been sweet-tempered in her manners.

A small squeak from his right made him notice the boy move in his blankets, and Jeremy realised he was close to waking from the change of temperature in the air.

'Avis, I'm sorry for everything,' Jeremy apologised in a whisper, fearful of waking the children. 'I wish I had been there to stop it all from happening.'

The boy's eyes opened, and Jeremy clasped a hand over his mouth before his gasp could turn to a scream. He looked into the boy's gaze, imploring silence.

'If you really were sorry, you never would have refused to marry me,' the apparition accused.

'I had no choice. Our families never would have approved.'

'None of that matters anymore, Jeremy. I have chosen my new path to find purpose…'

'—Please, whatever this is, don't do it—'

'…Where I, Avis Garland, shall have my revenge!' With that final word, she let out an ear-piercing scream. The glass from the mirrors around him shattered into pieces.

Jeremy was flung back by the force of her cry, the impact breaking the wall on the other side, sending him out and down into a large muddy pool of rainwater below.

It took him a moment to recover from the dizzy impact, when he saw the sneering ghoul looking out the window from above.

'Well, Jeremy, look what I have,' it called, holding up the terrified boy and his sister by the scruffs of their necks. 'It's time to pay your long due debts. Meet me near the village forest at the stroke of midnight, or I will terrorize this village for the remainder of All Hallows' Eve and beyond its early morning!'

She vanished in scattered mist before Jeremy could even stand up to give chase.

'What on Earth was that noise, and where are the children?' he heard the elderly woman's voice cry out.

'I don't know, Katy, but I'm sure it's of no worry —' There was a pause before the man cried out, 'Merciful heavens!' which was all Jeremy heard before he ran into the shadows of a quieter street.

Mr and Mrs Winterhaven were not going to have a peaceful night's sleep, and it was all Jeremy's fault. The house vanished behind as he moved further into the growing mist of the night.

He needed to plan how to get the children back. And also Colby, wherever he had gone to. Most of all, he needed to be ready to face his long-avoided past.

•◇•◇•◇•◇•◇•◇•◇•◇•◇•

The towering church loomed over him with its ancient stones and large wooden doors standing ominously in the centre. Jeremy shivered from the fear of someone following close behind, his head leaning on one of the doors to rest.

He was hesitant, but where else could he go for decent shelter? Slowly he opened the right door, trying to avoid a creak and groan, and entered. As far as he could see, no one was there. Thin candles lit a table by the end of its wide hall, surrounded by other candles on its metal supporters and large white pillars reflecting their dim light.

The arriving moon permeated the stained-glass circle above the table. To the eyes of Jeremy, this setup was akin to both the Catholic and Protestant services he'd attended at a young age. In one way, it almost felt like a return to a home he once had, and one he'd almost forgotten.

Two smaller doors were positioned in the right and left corners of the church nave, leading to chambers elsewhere — which made Jeremy a little fearful of what might come from them.

He tried to keep himself from casting an outline that would be noticed by any passers-by outside. For a moment, the cold world outside was nothing but a blur, and only the holy place remained, warm and welcoming.

'Hello, is anyone here?' The quizzical voice stopped Jeremy in his tracks by a pillar, which he just managed to hide behind. The parish's vicar was peeking out from the right door.

Of course, he'd be here, Jeremy pondered as the man walked out into the centre of the nave. *Maybe I'll be safe — maybe I will escape his notice.*

'My name is Reverend Hollybrook, and I am no stranger to apparitions. If you wish to show yourself, you may do so freely. I mean you no harm.'

Carlisle's chest tightened as he kept his back to the pillar. The fact Hollybrook wasn't unnerved by his presence both relieved and frightened him.

As much as he didn't want to, replying to this stranger was the only way he wouldn't cause a fright. 'Do you really wish to see me in full form?'

'I'll try not to call out in fear if that's where you hold concern.'

Jeremy didn't know how to introduce himself. But he couldn't avoid this embarrassment here, let alone the worry of what would happen afterwards. Slowly and tentatively, the hunter stepped out of the shadows, showing his truest form to the reverend: a half bone, half flesh skeleton, holding cobwebs as old as time past. He walked into the moonlight towards Hollybrook, lost in overwhelming sadness and pain. His eyes closed into drenching tears, and he clattered onto the floor, weeping as he knelt. A shadow fell across him as the reverend's hand touched his grey-boned shoulder.

'Why are you so distraught?' Hollybrook asked.

Jeremy looked up into the reverend's eyes, surprised by how little the man was afraid. 'Because no one can sympathise. I have no wish to be a man half dead and half alive!'

'Perhaps… but I am not that case.' Hollybrook added. 'The Word says, "Let not your heart be troubled." After all, if you believe in our Father and His Son, surely you could believe in their power in this world?'

'I have long been distant from those assurances, Reverend,' Jeremy confessed, 'when faith divided my life and this land more than it brought them together.'

'Well, those were different times. And much has changed since then; peace has slowly returned. A second chance might be a help to whatever troubles are behind your fears. Like this curse that befalls you.'

Jeremy was quiet. He didn't know what to say further on this advice but knew the reverend meant well in his statements. 'I suppose I could try.'

'The past has come and gone. Whatever it once was, you shouldn't keep hiding from the memories you try to bury —' A child's scream halted the conversation. It came from the direction from which Jeremy came but was cut short before he got a clearer idea of its location.

'That might be your signal to leave,' said Hollybrook. Jeremy started to get up, until Hollybrook stopped him. 'May He go before you, from tonight and forever more.'

With that final parting, Jeremy Carlisle left the church borders, whistling for Colby in the hopes of him appearing, and less heavy and anxious in heart for the task at hand.

●◇●◇●◇●◇●◇●◇●◇●◇●

The hunter found himself near the woods once again. Around him the wind had grown quieter—still present but less ferocious. He saw the monster staring back at him, with a countenance of whirling shadows. In one clasped hand was the boy, and the girl in the other: The Winterhaven children. They showed no expression of further shock besides recognition at the sight of the hunter, as his true appearance didn't appear to those of younger age.

Good thing that still works, he recalled in relief. *They are already scared enough as it is.*

The church bells far behind him chimed the arrival of midnight.

'I have come at the time you asked of me!' he called out. 'And if you plan to commit further crime in the physical realm, you will have to deal with me first. Now what more do you want?'

'That's a ludicrous question to ask, Master Carlisle, when you already know the answer too well.' The ghost's face became more visible, revealing the first haunted figure he had seen at the manor house earlier that night.

The memory of death hit him with a bang:

Wind brushing on leaves reflecting sunlight, walking towards the well to quench his thirst from a long, fast ride, wearing a rather dishevelled uniform as an attempt at disguise. Sensing the bullet that hit his shoulder and the images of the charging soldier striking him next with a tipped sword. A half complete scream came from his mouth, hearing another scream—a neighing—as another bullet pierced the body of another living creature. His own horse, his Colby.

And then his fall backwards into a final daze before turning unconscious.

This was the last face he'd seen before everything had changed: the man that had killed him.

'Hello again, David Islington.'

'And greetings to you, Jeremy Carlisle. Fascinating how our paths cross again, yes?'

'I suppose. Answer my question: What do you want?'

The soldier didn't respond. Instead, he pointed to the pistol in Jeremy's hand.

'I remember that weapon of yours, when you tried to shoot me before I got you first. And what you tried again earlier this evening.'

'Did you take pride in killing me then and there?'

David Islington chuckled with a cynical smile. 'If I did, it was only because my duty was done so I could retire for the rest of my days.'

'The same fate I could have also shared, had you spared me.'

'I doubt you would have survived, regardless of whether I killed or spared you. And what did you have to live for?' You still have to join the underworld like all the others you find and capture every night. As for the rest of your life—' His countenance changed to another face from Jeremy's past, his father, which terrified him even more. 'You were a terrible son.'

In his horror, Jeremy wondered what was going on. Then it made sense; it wasn't David Islington after all. These different forms he'd seen—from his killer, his lover, and then his father—were the ghoul's way of frightening him with the remainder of his lost life. And in turn, manipulating him into a greater vulnerability and weakness.

Jeremy had no other choice in handling this twisted creature than to confront it head on. 'What is your real name, monster?'

'How dare you speak to me like that, Jeremy! I am your father!'

The children shivered, whimpering as the arms and hands squeezed tighter.

'Silence your illusion! What is your true name?'

'I am Ealdeth,' screamed the changing faces, 'a ghost of all forms, and I am here to make all suffer from their sins, from past, present, and future forever!

'Except you're no ghost at all. You're a dangerous demon!'

'Whatever you say, then. Come and face me, boy.'

'Very well, then, Ealdeth, I'll face you.'

Ealdeth rose into a morphing cloud, wrapping around the children and screaming in many voices as it spread out towards Jeremy. In the distance, Jeremy saw Colby galloping to join him, his cloak still attached and in full skeletal structure. He mounted and rode straight towards Ealdeth.

The cloud enveloped its prisoners and the hunter. With the Reverend's words echoing in his mind, he fought his way through to where only a twisted face appeared.

Jeremy stabbed through it with his sword, crying triumphantly, 'Go back whence you came!' It howled and shrieked as its cloud exploded into bright light.

Only four things could Jeremy remember from then on: landing onto the grass on his back; staring into a world that spun around him in a blur; the boy and his sister briefly glancing at him before disappearing entirely. It seemed they said a word of thanks to him and something else, but it was hard to hear them clearly. And finally, the night sky that became ever brighter with twinkling stars.

Jeremy smiled. It was over for another night. He was still around, but content in knowing that, although there were still unanswered questions, he had found redemption. Perhaps.

•◊•◊•◊•◊•◊•◊•◊•◊•◊•

Whitstead was left in quite a hubbub after the Winterhaven children were found. Although neither at first spoke a word on where they had been or what had occurred, due to a strange state of shock, word soon spread about sightings of a mysterious figure and a horse riding away into the trees. Other claims of seeing the same figure earlier that night only added to the confusion when no physical evidence could prove it. Only days later, when Mrs Winterhaven casually asked her children what happened, did she and her husband get any answer.

'Very little, Mother, but God was always with us.'

The Miller's Daughter
by A.D. Uhlar *(fantasy/time travel)*

dventure. Fiddlesticks!' her mother, Abigail, had said whilst plaiting Addie's hair into the fiery rope that hung down her back. 'You don't need adventure, you need stability.' She rested her chin on Addie's shoulder and whispered, 'Philip is a wonderful young man, and your father approves.'

Addie shifted as best she could on the edge of her bed. 'I don't want to run the mill and I don't want Philip.'

'Silly girl, you think you have a choice?'

'Yes.'

Her mother only shook her head. 'Rest, child. We will speak more in the morning.' She blew out the candle and closed the bedroom door behind her.

Addie had punched the bed before changing clothes and escaping through the back door with the satchel Widow Larkin had given her. The only thing testifying she was a girl and not a boy were her boots. No one looked twice at a boy lurking in the shadows. The unrelenting rains forced the cemetery ground to swallow the heel of her boot with every step. She started walking on her tiptoes and heard her mother's 'Adventure. Fiddlesticks!' float on the wind. She stomped her heel into the muck and stood a little taller. Her mother would have to clean Addie's evening adventure off the boots before church.

With shoulders back and satchel gripped tight, she aimed her steps towards the massive ash tree at the west edge of the cemetery. Tonight was the beginning of the small window of time when she could collect the petals as payment for Widow Larkin's lessons.

Addie reviewed the instructions in her mind as she neared the grave at the base of the tree. 'Only pluck the inner petals of eight blooms — no more, no less.' At that point, she had leaned in and squeezed Addie's arm. 'Be sure not to touch them. It will pull you towards the grave from which it grows.'

The gravestone the vine wrapped around was essentially unmarked, or at least for anyone in Whitstead. It had strange markings that looked more like a toddler's first efforts to scrawl with chalk than any language that could convey meaning. Most townspeople avoided the cemetery unless attending a burial, but everyone avoided the ash tree and its unidentifiable grave except Widow Larkin and now Addie. Stories circulated about who was buried beneath the tree and what the markings meant.

Addie's favourite was the tale of a cursed wizard buried alive, which told that the ash tree sprang from his magic and the Devil's Trumpet was the angels' warning not to disturb the spot. As her mother said, it was all fiddlesticks, but the idea of magic and angels always made her smile.

Lightning jumped from one cloud to the next and thunder shook the air. Addie placed her hand on the trunk of the ash tree. She was one of the only people to come to this spot and she wanted to mark it. Walking to the back side, she retrieved the small knife she brought to cut the petals if needed and carved an AH in the bark. Translucent sap caught the moon light as it seeped from the fresh scar leaving a blue line around each letter. Widow Larkin's voice echoed again: 'Pluck the inner petals. Be sure not to touch them.' Addie bit the handle of the knife and put on the leather gloves she had tucked into the satchel.

Her eyes darted up as she retrieved the knife.

What was that? she thought, squinting at the forest's edge nearly fifteen metres beyond her.

Was she being watched? No, she couldn't be. It must be a deer or some other animal.

She took a step away from the tree and paused, deliberately returning the knife to the satchel.

'It's nothing. You're imagining things, Addie,' she said to herself and fumbled for her collecting jar.

A glow deep in the forest halted her search. She looked back over her shoulder. No one else was there. No one to ask what they thought the glow was or to talk her out of getting closer, so she tucked her head under the satchel's strap. It was easier to run with it across her body instead of bouncing from her hip. In a minute she crossed the threshold of the trees, heart racing. She slowed her steps a short distance into the wood.

A flash of light accompanied almost simultaneously by the crash of thunder shook the ground, sending Addie face-down in the mud. She pushed herself to her knees and searched for the glow, but it was gone.

Addie jumped to her feet, eyes searching for Widow Larkin.

'No, it must be my imagination,' Addie thought and stepped out of the woods in time to see a smoking branch fall from the ash tree.

'Devil's Trumpet!' she exclaimed and ran to the vine, slowing as she neared it. The gravestone had been cleaved in two.

There, at the base, lay an unsinged vine reaching towards the tree's trunk. How many blooms? She needed eight—'no more, no less.' Addie dropped to her knees, retrieved the large collection jar, and began plucking the inner purple petals just beginning to unfurl themselves. She avoided the outer white petals. This section of vine only had five blooms—five was not eight. More lightning flashed and she cradled the jar beneath her and dove between the stone and tree. The thunder followed soon after, but not immediately. Farther away. She stood and saw, lying just across the top of the broken headstone, a single remaining bloom.

Addie stepped on uneven ground. A young man sat up, yelled, and yanked his ankle from beneath her boot sending her back against the tree. Her chest tightened, and she reached into her satchel for the knife. Finding it, she held it in front of her. 'What do you want?'

The young man wore curious loose trousers folded at the ankle, which he rubbed with an arm covered in a light shirt that caught what little light there was.

Addie stepped closer. 'Who are you? What do you want?' He looked up at her and their eyes locked. She thought about averting her eyes, but she wanted answers.

He moved to stand.

She stepped closer, stabbing the air between them.

He held his hands up. 'I'm Cumberland. Who wants to know?'

'The person with the knife.'

Cumberland grabbed onto the headstone for leverage, thoroughly crushing the remaining bloom.

'You dolt! You mustn't touch the blooms.'

He looked down and lifted his hand. 'Sorry. It's only a flower.'

Addie put the knife away and screwed the lid on the jar before putting it back in the satchel. 'It pulls you towards the grave.'

'Oh.' Cumberland's eyes widened and he rubbed his hand on his trouser leg.

'We need to get you to Widow Larkin. She will know what to do. Follow me.'

Addie turned towards High Road and Cumberland fell in step next to her. He stood a head taller than she with strong square shoulders and easily matched her stride for stride.

'Who is Widow Larkin? I don't remember any Larkins in Whitstead — and you still haven't told me who you are.'

They passed the Winterhaven home. 'There will be time for that once Widow Larkin sees you,' Addie said as someone emerged from the alley. '…and before anyone else sees you.'

'I feel killer diller, except for my ankle.'

Addie stopped. 'Killer diller? You are strange, Cumberland.' She turned and kept walking.

'No stranger than a cold fish like you.' He stumbled and grabbed onto Addie's shoulder to steady himself.

'I am not a fish!' She pushed him off and he swayed like a milk bottle about to topple.

Philip stepped under Cumberland's arm and wrapped his own around Cumberland's chest. 'Your friend looks a bit unsure. Addie? What are you —'

'Ah, Addie. That's a strange name for a boy.' Cumberland interjected.

'A boy?' Philip pulled back and quickly braced himself against Cumberland again. 'Addie is a girl. Although she does resemble a boy in my clothing and her father's jacket.' He leaned forward. 'I was wondering where those knickers had got to.'

Addie rolled her eyes. 'We have to get him to Widow Larkin's before he dies.'

'Dies? What did you do to the poor boy?' Philip teased.

'The dolt crushed a Devil's Trumpet bloom with his bare hands.'

'A flower? You're fretting over a flower?'

Addie held her leather-clad hands up to Philip's face. 'Why do you think I have gloves on? The flowers pull you towards the grave. Just help me get him to Widow Larkin's.' Addie took a few steps and stopped. 'Where were you anyway? It's a little late to be lurking about High Street.'

'You were,' Philip countered.

She scowled and led them between the mill and the smithy.

'I was behind the Fentiman Arms,' Philip responded.

'You were playing dice again, weren't you?'

Philip shrugged, sending Cumberland's head back. 'Whoooo—we best get to Widow Larkin's. Your friend is about to be my luggage.'

Addie glanced back at them. Cumberland's head bounced off Philip's shoulder and his right arm lay limp at his side.

They followed the river until it forked around the part of the forest shrouding Widow Larkin's cottage. Addie pounded on Widow Larkin's door until it swung open, and she nearly wrapped her knuckles on Widow Larkin's forehead.

'Dear, you needn't bring the bloom… who's this now?' Widow Larkin looked past Addie to Philip and the crumpled mass of Cumberland.

'He crushed a bloom with his bare hand,' Addie exclaimed.

Widow Larkin moved with dexterity and cleared the table with one sweep of her arm. 'Put him here, child. Addie, put the chair beneath his feet.'

She and Philip obeyed, and Widow Larkin disappeared behind another door to emerge moments later with a dish of powder and a glass of water. She added enough water to make a paste.

'Hold his mouth open.'

Addie did and Widow Larkin painted the back of Cumberland's tongue with the paste. 'You,' she pointed at Philip, 'sit him up.' Addie backed away. 'Keep his mouth open, dear.' Addie pulled his bottom jaw down again and Widow Larkin poured the glass of water into his mouth. 'Now hold his mouth closed and pinch his nose.' She did and Cumberland swallowed. 'Now let go, dear, or you will suffocate the poor boy.'

Addie jumped back, Philip set him back down on the table, and both watched in silence.

'Dear? Addie!' Widow Larkin called impatiently. 'Do you have my petals?'

Addie slid her eyes from Cumberland, and her hand shot to the satchel. 'Oh. Yes, well all there were. The lightning singed part of the vine.' She fumbled with the top flap of her satchel. 'I would have plucked six, but Cumberland smashed one, so...' She held up the jar of purple petals and saw Widow Larkin's steely grey eyes glaring at her through the curvature of the glass.

Widow Larkin snatched the jar. 'Eight blooms, girl. No more, no less.'

'But there weren't any left!'

Widow Larkin squinted her eyes. 'Did you look near the tree and the headstone?'

'Well, no. The lightning and Cumberland, then Philip—'

Philip held up his hands. 'Don't bring me into this. I just helped carry your friend.'

Addie exhaled loudly and dropped her shoulders. 'I don't even know him.'

'Off with you now. Take the jar. Collect more and return tomorrow. He will either be awake or dead by then.' Widow Larkin pushed them through the doorway.

The next day, the whole town seemed to be talking about the storm, but no one mentioned the burnt tree or split headstone; but they wouldn't—their superstition and fear weren't limited to physically avoiding the spot.

Philip only asked how she slept on his way to the spout floor where he bagged the finished flour once Mr Hawke checked it for quality.

'Fitfully,' she said on her way to the bin floor to pour grain into the hopper.

There had been a time when she and her father worked side by side on the spout floor. He had taught her how to use her thumb and forefinger to determine the distance of the stone nut and the speed with which to feed the hopper. When Philip came to work at the mill three years earlier, he had started on the bin floor, but in the last year, her father replaced her with him. Initially, Addie skulked around. It was not that she wanted to run a mill; she wanted to be near her father. Her skulking led to her mother sending her on most of the flour deliveries, but it became so obnoxious her mother's annoyance outweighed her fear of a hag meddling in natural remedies, and she sent Addie to deliver flour to Widow Larkin.

Normally, Addie would pass the time between bags by studying her notes from Widow Larkin, but today she paced. Once the last bag had been poured, she flew down the spiral stairs, grabbed her satchel, and scurried out the door before either parent could inquire where she was heading.

The night before, she had returned to the ash tree and collected the remaining petals from a vine around the base of the trunk. She hadn't remembered it being there before, but she shrugged it off and returned home in time to get a few hours of sleep. At least she tried to sleep.

Now she ran along the creek to the fork and Widow Larkin.

This time she did not knock but pushed through the door yelling, 'Widow Larkin! I have them!'

Cumberland sat facing the door and looked over the edge of a steaming cup of tea.

'Oh!' Addie stopped and quickly smoothed her windblown hair.

Cumberland raised his eyebrows and Widow Larkin scurried from behind him with hand outstretched and grasping at the air. 'Give them here, girl.'

Addie quickly produced the jar and the bony fingers snatched it. Widow Larkin licked her lips and without looking up, said, 'Eight blooms — no more, no less?'

'Yes.'

Without another word, she disappeared within.

Addie stared after her and shifted her weight as she became aware of Cumberland watching her. He stood and pulled out the chair opposite him. 'Sit. Have some tea.'

She looked at her hands and slid into the seat. He poured tea into one of the empty cups on the table. 'Thank you.'

He smiled and returned to his seat. 'I must apologise. Last night, I was confused and nearly left this world. I am Cumberland Fitzroy. Formerly of South London but evacuated to Whitstead five years ago.'

Addie wrinkled her forehead. 'Evacuated? I have lived here all my days and I have never seen you.'

'I was twelve when they brought a group of thirty of us to the country.' He watched her reaction.

'The only children brought here go to the Charitable School, and I have never seen more than two or three come at a time.' She sipped her tea but kept her eyes on him.

'They brought us to keep us safe from the Nazis —'

'You are still confused. The poison must have altered your mind. What is a Nazis?'

Cumberland leaned forward. 'The ones bombing the country. Haven't you heard the bombs?'

'What's a bomb?'

'She won't know what you are talking about, dear.' Widow Larkin reappeared and filled another cup of tea as she sat between the two. 'What year do you think it is?'

Addie looked at Widow Larkin and back to Cumberland.

He paused and said, '1945.'

Addie spit her tea back into her cup. '1945? It's 1845.'

Cumberland sat up straight and filled his lungs before looking at Widow Larkin. 'Am I dreaming? How can this be?'

'What is the last thing you remember?' Larkin said and took a sip from her cup.

'Well...' He leaned back. 'There was a group of us running to the trees. I was faster and reached the ash tree, but they must have dropped a bomb because I woke up at night with someone standing on my ankle.'

Without moving the cup from her lips, Widow Larkin asked, 'Was the headstone whole or cracked?'

'It's always been cracked. Why?'

She set her cup down. 'My dear, you fell through the crack.'

'He did what?' Addie asked, setting her cup down.

'He fell through a crack and ended up one hundred years in the past.'

Addie shook her head. 'You are a crazy old hag like they say. That can't happen.'

'Oh, but it can, and it has more than once. I too fell through a crack forty years ago.' Widow Larkin grabbed a small biscuit from the table and took a bite before finishing her cup.

Cumberland leaned forward. 'So how do I get back?'

'You can't.'

'What do you mean, I can't?' His voice broke. 'I have to help protect the others. In a year I can fight.'

She poured herself another cup. 'I have been searching for a way back, or forwards, since I arrived. If it makes you feel any better, I can tell you that the Nazis are defeated.' She took another bite of biscuit.

Addie whispered, 'How do you know?'

'Because I fell through a crack in 2005. The war was—is—part of my history. My crack was near yours.' She tipped her cup towards Cumberland. 'We were renovating St. Nicholas Church. It was a night in September and there was a storm then too. We ran to the crypt because water was coming in the roof. I too was the first one down. I tripped on the last step and fell through a crack in the foundation. When I woke up, I was so disoriented the poor reverend didn't know what to do with me. Eventually I figured out what had happened, but people already thought I was crazy.'

'Who else has fallen through a crack?' Addie asked.

'Only me and now Cumberland as far as I know.' She finished the biscuit and took another sip.

'Maybe Cumberland can help you figure out how to get back? You know for sure it's cracks now, and you both fell through on the church grounds.'

Widow Larkin stood up. 'You may be right, dear.' She turned and patted Cumberland on the shoulder. 'Don't get your hopes up. There may be no way back.' She disappeared behind the door again.

Cumberland stared at Addie and his tea crashed to the floor as he crumpled into a heap on the table. His shoulders rose and fell sporadically. Addie stood. The sound of her boots on the wood planks echoed through his muffled sobs. Her hand hovered over him, and with a deep breath, she rested it on his back. 'I'm sure we can find a way back.'

Cumberland sat up. His cheeks wet with tears. 'What if we can't?'

'Then I will help you find your way here.'

Cumberland sprang to his feet and embraced her. She froze momentarily and pulled her shoulders in before wrapping her own arms around his back. 'We will both find our way.'

An Autumn Night's Dream
by Joanna Bair *(fantasy/romance)*

'You're going to be the most beautiful bride.' Jemima admired the lace on her sister Martha's dress. Mother had spent hours stitching intricate detailing for the bodice.

Aromas of mince pies and apple crumble wafted upstairs from the bakery. 'Jeremiah is working hard down there.'

'I told him to allow someone else to bake for his own wedding, but he insisted.'

'Well, he is the best in Whitstead. His gingerbread cake was the talk of the town at Christmas.'

'And he's been busy ever since.' Martha twirled, ready for the evening's festivities. Bonfire night would be her last unmarried night. 'I'm almost ready.'

Someone banged on the door. Martha raced to open it. 'Hide the dress. It's probably him.'

Jemima threw the dress over a chair and covered it with a blanket before Martha opened the door. The pounding continued.

A tall dark-haired man stood in the doorway, a bundle of blood-covered clothing in his arms, his muscles tight and clenched.

'What in heaven's name?' Jemima snatched up an empty basket. She recognised the man from somewhere, but with blood caked on his face she couldn't place him. 'You need Widow Larkin, not me.'

'It's not my blood, but there was an accident at the mill.' His voice shook as he spoke, and he refused to make eye contact with either one of them. 'The miller needs them back tonight.'

'Oh. You do realise clothing takes time to dry?'

He stared at the floor as if a bug crawled there.

'I'm sorry, I don't even know your name.'

He wiped his forehead and chin with one of the cloths. 'Philip.'

'Goodness, the miller's apprentice, I didn't recognise you with all the — well — is everyone all right?'

'Hard to say. Mr Hawke sent me off before I could see. One of the boys from the Charitable School snuck away exploring down river and tripped, injuring himself.' He gasped for breath as if that sentence had taken a huge effort. Jemima winced. Such an awkward man.

'I can bring it to Mrs Pettleston.' He tripped as he turned to go.

'No,' Jemima hated the thought of that lady taking away their customers. 'We'll manage.'

'The mill is closed for the day and I've the afternoon off, if you need any help making the soap,' he stuttered, wiping his face with a wet rag Martha tossed him.

Jemima caught her sister's eyes. Martha nodded. 'You go on, I'm almost done with the wedding flowers. I'll meet you at the bonfires?'

•◊•◊•◊•◊•◊•◊•◊•◊•◊•

Atala swirled in a frenzy. Sun on her face, scent of autumn leaves in the air, and earth between her toes. She stomped her feet harder than ever on a calendula as it dropped pollen, pirouetting, all her senses lost. She shook the ground beneath her as her feet spun her body. The other faeries joined. Some sat back, playing instruments. A flute, a drum, and even wings created a rhythm. A swirl of fabric and dust clouded the twilight air until a man appeared in the centre. The faeries froze and stared. They couldn't decipher details on his body, which, like an apparition, appeared to float through space, until the blur became clearer. Now he stood, a young sprite, perpetually on the brink of adulthood, bronzed body, flowing hair, and the picture of a god.

'A human boy Tatiana seeks, one courageous, wild, yet often meek.' His words flowed like nectar, and Atala's dancing stopped. The others paused, a circle of colours amongst the leafed and muddy forest floor.

The sprite continued talking. 'Cupid's arrow failed this past September. She sent a man through time if you remember.'

'But the miller's daughter discovered him on her own; do you mean to tell me, he wasn't to be known?' Atala asked.

'It's done now, but no.' The Faerie King leaned forward. 'Noctiluca?'

'Here.' Noctiluca flitted and bowed her glowing wings in front of her king.

'Go find the boy, his plight will make these wrongs right. The miller's assistant suffers from a broken heart. Bring him to Tatiana. It's time to play out our part.'

Noctiluca floated away.

'Lampyris, Swallowtail, Fritillary, be on your way with her. Atala—'

'Here.' Atala danced before him.

'Keep watch in this clearing for the girl. To the calendula you must lure. Centred in the clearing place a lone Helianthus flower. When she breathes it in, true love for the next man will overpower.'

'And the boy?'

'Tatiana will use for her next muse. Away.'

•◊•◊•◊•◊•◊•◊•◊•◊•◊•

Crisp autumn air allowed Jemima to take clear deep breaths as she half walked, half ran through the leaf strewn streets along the river footpath to Widow Larkin's . Her family hadn't visited the widow since her mother had miraculously been healed at Christmastide. The widow kept lye and oils Jemima used in soaps, so this was the one time she returned to the lady's dungeon, as her sister had dubbed it. She slowed as she neared the ramshackle dwelling. Smoke billowed from the chimney. Jemima peeked around the corner of the open door and tapped on the door frame. The widow hunched over a black pot in the fireplace, a mix of burning wood and something strange, almost mushroom-like filled the air.

'Come in, Mima, looking for lye? I'm about done. If you come back in a few hours, it'll be ready.' The widow didn't even turn.

'Have you not got any left?'

'It's all used up, but I had a hunch you'd be coming. I heard about the mill.'

'Ah. Well, have you got lavender or calendula?' Jemima searched the walls for the flowers she desired. Every spare inch that didn't support shelving held a nail with herbs or flowers dried and ready for healing. She scanned the jars for potions, oils, anything with the flowers she needed for her soap.

'I have plenty of lavender, but I need to collect more calendula flowers. My bones are aching today; perhaps you might go find me some.'

'Haven't they died for the winter?'

'There's a large patch of them growing in a clearing in the forest outside the village.'

'Where is it?'

'Tarry 'til the moon like silver bow will bend in the heavens. Make haste through holly bush, through brier, past the park, past the woodpiles, wander the trail swifter than the moon's sphere. Before the frost or dew falls on the green, before the golden leaves of autumn, in the middle of those ruby trees, the clearing freckled with calendula lies. Hurry child.'

'I'll be back before moonrise.' Jemima shook her head at the lady's puzzling words. She meant the clearing in the forest, didn't she? Past the rows of holly trees, to the trail, the only trail there was. The leaves had already turned and fallen from the trees, so she wasn't sure what the widow's words implied, but she'd find them in the middle of the red oaks? Is that what she meant by ruby trees? She carried the lye in one arm and hurried past the green where some men were tossing trees into piles for tonight's bonfires.

Coming to the edge of the forest, she discovered a new path alongside the one she often used. Would it lead to the clearing? It went the right direction, so she followed it. The sunlight sparkled off leaves falling with each breeze like golden snow. A magpie squawked from its perch then flew off as Jemima cracked a branch with her foot, so she'd be sure she found her way back.

Philip had been kind to offer his help. He'd be waiting for her with the lard for soap by now. Perhaps Martha would tell him what he needed to do. His awkwardness repulsed her; she understood why the miller's daughter Addie had rejected him. He'd barely spoken a word to her. How could someone marry a man who refused to carry on a conversation? She spun around to absorb her surroundings. A glimmer of light through the trees led her on, twinkling like fireflies except it was too late in the year for them, and the sun still shone. Strange. Jemima picked up her pace, chasing after it.

The light flitted and wove its way around some silver birches, under branches, over mushrooms, until they came to a clearing. Calendula. Jemima gasped. Never had she witnessed such brilliance of colour in the simple flowers. Ruby red, amber, lemon yellow, and orange not quite as bright as the fruit, the flowers filled the clearing as if waiting to see who came first, human or frost. Rain had fallen in this part of the forest and each flower sat like jewellery encrusted with precious stones. She unwrapped her cloak, laid it on the ground and picked until her cloak was filled with sweet-smelling flowers. She'd save the seeds for their own garden, then she wouldn't have to come so far again.

One golden flower sat in the middle of the clearing taller than the rest, the twinkling firefly glistening on it like real gold. An unusual flower. She leaned forwards and poked a petal with her hand, soft as if touching a caterpillar she wanted to ensure would transform into a butterfly. But would the flower grow? She breathed in its scent; it had a repulsive odour that made her jump back. What an awful flower. So beautiful yet deceiving. She picked it, determined to not let it overtake the lovely marigolds. Jemima took one more whiff just to make sure she hated the smell, then tossed it aside.

As she studied her cloak full of flowers to determine how she'd lift it, sleepiness overcame her and she decided to have a short rest. Glorying in the sun and flowers, she settled on the driest spot, closed her eyes for a short moment, and slept.

Jemima rolled over onto her back brushing away a firefly. A firefly? Her eyes fluttered into nothing but darkness. Opening them wide she sat with a start. Black. Except one lantern.

'Jemima, I found you.' Someone breathed a mere inch away.

Had that been a firefly or a kiss? In the shadows she could distinguish details of the most beautiful face she'd ever laid eyes on. 'Philip?'

'You never came back to the laundry, so your sister sent me after you,' he stuttered, yet his voice sang in a beautiful harmony. His fingers touched hers and, fumbling, he pulled her to her feet. She brushed flowers off her dress but couldn't keep her eyes off his face in the lantern light.

'How did you ever find me?'

'Widow Larkin gave me the strangest directions, though why she didn't come after you herself I don't know.' Philip peeled his fingers away, but Jemima clung to them.

'Wait, Philip? Or Paris? Like a Greek warrior you come to rescue me from the perils of these woods. The light is muddy, yet how bright your eyes…' She brushed a hand up to his cheek, unable to help herself. 'Your lips—'

He took her hand and lowered it. 'Stop. Did Addie put you up to this? Please don't injure my heart any more than it already is. I've been through enough, watching her fall for that strange man. Must you mock me as well?'

'It is not so.'

'It's dark, the bonfires…' He handed her the lantern then gathered the corners of her cloak, tying up the flowers.

'I mean every word I say. I never saw until now.' Jemima stumbled after him as he marched into the woods. She struggled to keep up. 'Do you know the way?'

'I do. Now please, leave me be.'

'I didn't mean… I just woke up. I'm sorry I don't always think before I speak, and that's what came out. I never meant to offend. Quite the opposite in fact.' She softened her voice. 'Has no one told you, you have beautiful eyes?'

'No.' He slowed.

'Well, you do.'

He said nothing but let her walk next to him when the path widened.

'I didn't mean to scare you. The forest is bad enough.' Jemima froze as a howl sounded off in the distance. 'Is that wolves?'

'Dogs, I should hope.'

'We must hurry. I am so sorry I fell asleep. I found the most beautiful flower; it shone like gold, real gold. But when I sniffed it, it let off the most hideous odour. Like manure or worse. The next thing I knew, there you were.'

'Did you pick the flower?'

'I did and tossed it, because it reeked something awful.'

'Widow Larkin sent you only for calendula.'

'She did, but I wonder if she knows about that flower.'

'I wonder.'

Though she held the lantern, she nearly walked into a branch. The waxing crescent provided only a sliver of light through the dense forest. Not enough to see Philip ahead of her. 'Tell me more about the accident. Did you discover anything more?'

'Not a thing.' They moved through the dark forest at a snail's pace. How much faster she'd run chasing the firefly. Where were the fireflies now? The moon hung so high in the sky it had to be nearly midnight. Then a flicker of light glimmered through the trees.

'Look.' Jemima ran to a small clearing, or was it the edge of the forest?

A bonfire. Where were the people? Soft voices rose above the crackling of the fire, not so large as they drew close.

'Hello?' Jemima called out. The voices stopped. 'Hello?'

A boy came around from the other side of the fire followed by a man and a woman. In the darkness, she couldn't make out their faces until they stood right in front of her. But Philip recognised them. 'Addie? Cumberland? Who's this?'

'We found this boy running from the mill,' Cumberland said. 'Finally caught him, sat him down, and demanded an explanation. The sky grew dark, and we made our own bonfire. I have no idea where we are. These woods are so different from, well, from what I know.'

Philip said nothing, so Jemima spoke. 'We are heading back. At least I think we're going in the right direction. Widow Larkin sent me for calendula, I fell asleep, and Philip was dear enough to come find me.'

'Philip?' Addie stepped into the light.

Jemima slipped her hand around his elbow for moral support. It had to be hard to watch someone you thought you would marry announce their plan to wed another.

'Shall we rest a moment?' Jemima peered up at Philip and took his slight raise of shoulders as a yes.

'It was a dare,' the boy said when they'd all sat around the fire. 'We bet Danny he couldn't make it across the river.'

'So he swam across?'

'But we were upstream, not downstream of the mill — less waves — and we thought he'd make it in time, but the current from the wheel —' the orphan stopped.

'And then you ran,' Cumberland said.

'That's about it. Am I gonna get hanged? What if they decide to burn me in the bonfires tonight? Like the Guy?'

'Is that why you ran? You won't get hanged, but you will be in serious trouble. Your friend could have died.'

The boy burst into tears. Jemima held her hands out and he curled up in her arms. She patted his back to calm him, and before she could say another word, he'd fallen asleep.

Cumberland rose. 'Now what? I'll carry him and we'll try to find our way back in this darkness?'

'There will be a huge bonfire, we should be able to see it soon.' Addie stood as he helped her up. Cumberland took the sleeping boy from Jemima as if he were a lightweight newborn.

'I'm not so sure. We should have found it already,' Jemima scooped up dirt to put out the fire. 'Which direction did we come from?'

Philip pointed behind him.

'Then we go that way.' Jemima gestured to the other side of the fire.

'But that's where we came from,' Addie said.

'And you came from the mill.'

'No. We had turned around with the boy, so the mill is that way, and we need to go there.' Addie raised her hand in the one direction no one had indicated.

'That doesn't seem right.' Jemima searched the glow of firelight for Philip's face. He gave her a brief nod.

Cumberland nodded towards the boy in his arms. 'I say we spend the night here in the clearing and in the morning we can see more.'

'The moon will guide us,' Philip said.

'Besides, we can't stay out here all night. Can you imagine the scandal that would cause? They'd make us all marry in the morning,' Addie said.

'My sister is getting married in the morning — I have to be back.' Jemima tugged on Philip's free hand; he held her flowers in the other. She gazed up at him. 'Your laundry won't be done.'

'Nothing we need to worry about until after the wedding.' Philip held her gaze and her chest pounded as if she'd been running. He pulled her hand and led her back into the forest. She heard Addie and Cumberland talking, then leaves crackled behind her.

'It's safer if we stay together,' Addie said.

The group pressed on through the forest. Branches pushed in their faces, the trees grew denser, and a sinking feeling fell into Jemima's stomach.

'Do you think we should have found the village by now?' Cumberland shifted the boy in his arms. No one answered. 'I thought so.'

Philip pushed more branches away, and Jemima lifted her head to the sky. The moon stayed hidden by the ghostly sea of clouds overhead. There was no real way to tell which direction they headed.

But then she caught sight of a broken branch on the ground. Was that one she had broken earlier to mark her path? 'I think I found my trail.'

'You made a trail?' Philip asked.

'I did, but I forgot about it since I was so sure you knew the way back. I only marked a few trees by breaking branches. That's no help in the dark.' Jemima grabbed his elbow to avoid tripping over a rock. Philip froze. They'd reached a break in the trees. The clouds parted just enough so they could see. The calendula clearing. 'Oh no.'

'What?' Cumberland set the boy down on the ground when they paused. His arms had to be sore at this point.

'This is where I found my flowers.' Jemima sat down. It must be midnight by now; they'd been wandering for hours. How could they have gotten so lost in their woods?

'Oh.' Addie plopped down next to her. 'I'm exhausted.'

Cumberland lowered himself next to them. 'I say we call it a night, set up camp, and find the village in the morning.'

'At this point, I agree with you.' Addie flopped back into a bed of flowers and Cumberland lay back with her. 'You can't sleep with me, in case anyone finds us.'

'No one is finding us in these woods. I'm going to put the boy in the middle, you ladies on either side of him and us men on the outside, for protection.' Cumberland had it all figured out. Jemima wanted to avoid a scandal, but safety won.

Philip seemed to be weighing the options as well, and sat down next to her. 'He's right, it's safest.'

•◇•◇•◇•◇•◇•◇•◇•◇•◇•

Atala flitted down from the treetops as the Faerie King made his way back to her. 'Well done.'

The Faerie Queen pushed them away, holding the golden flower the girl had tossed to the ground over the sleeping boy. 'The boy is mine.'

'Did you cause that accident?' Noctiluca floated to the ground crossing her arms.

The queen slinked around the boy with a sly grin. 'Why?'

Atala stared down her queen. 'These humans haven't got a clue what to do with children who need the love and care of a family. Now they shall know.'

With that, their mission for the day ended: Bringing happiness and spontaneity to people suffering, like Philip, or the orphan boy.

Atala leapt onto the sleeping miller's assistant. She stomped her feet, one, two, three times, and spun in a circle. She shook pollen from the calendula on him and tossed more on the girl to ensure the love would last. Her hair undone, fabric flowing all around in a swirl like the autumn leaves flying in the wind, she was one of them. Freedom. Noctiluca strummed a lyre, but Fritillary drowned out the sound with drumming. The Queen sat observing, picking yellow flowers from the ground. Yes, Atala had informed the widow they were the only kind that grew this time of year. She was pretty sure the widow, so close to the afterlife, heard her whispers in the breeze. The Queen wove calendula into crowns for each one who stepped in to join Atala in the dance. A celebration of love.

Atala laid a crown of the golden flowers on the girl next to the miller's assistant's head; the other girl got calendulas. The best flowers came from the faeries. They'd learn that now, and some day when the Widow left earth this young laundress would take her place.

•◇•◇•◇•◇•◇•◇•◇•◇•◇•

Jemima fluttered her eyes open as loud voices called to her from her dreams. She jolted upright, clutching her cloak around her, startling Philip awake in the process. Somehow, he'd fallen asleep with his arm around her, but she rectified that quickly. Addie and Cumberland opened their eyes, sitting up, but the boy slept on.

'We've found them,' a man on horseback called. Jeremiah. His wedding. He should have been preparing for his wedding, not searching for them. They would have found their way back.

'Thank God.' Martha rode on horseback into the clearing, her eyes taking in the scene before her. 'Widow Larkin said she sent you for flowers yesterday.'

'We searched for bonfire light but circled round the wood 'til we came upon these two. They caught up with the boy from the mill. Then we wandered until we happened upon the clearing where I first discovered your sister. It was too dark to find our way, and we were worn out, so we rested with plans to find our way back in time for you to wed.' Philip rose, his eyes darting between the riders.

Jemima's heart melted at his ability to clarify nothing had happened. Yet so much had happened in the woods.

'Well, fair lovers, it's fortunate I came upon you, and no one else. I'll hear no more and we shall all head to the church.' Jeremiah pulled on the reins to turn his horse around.

'That's a way to solve things.' Cumberland gently shook the boy awake.

'I had a strange dream,' the boy said.

'As did I,' Cumberland said.

'And what was your dream?' the boy asked.

'That dreamers often lie,' Cumberland snickered. Jemima didn't find any humour in his response.

'In bed asleep whilst they do dream things true,' Philip responded.

'I see Queen Mab hath been with you,' Cumberland said.

The Faerie Queen? Did Cumberland believe in faeries? He certainly had some unique qualities; of course, Addie had fallen for him fast enough for her to believe a faerie had been involved. But Jemima's interest in Philip, that was no work of the faeries. She reached up to brush a flower stem from her head and pulled down an entire flower crown. The golden flower. Hundreds of new blossoms encompassed the intricately woven wreath. She glanced over at Addie; her head held a circle of calendulas. Could it be?

'Shakespeare.' Philip turned to the confused girls. He held out his hand to Jemima and they followed.

Glimmers of Hope

by Becky Ann Little *(spiritual warfare/historical)*

laborately scrolled gates guarded a meandering drive that led to the grand estate at its end. The name Whitmore Park spiralled across the gate's top. Tianna and her young son stood gazing, knowing they would never be invited in the front door.

Tenant farmers' row houses along the back and side, languished under the Big House's luxurious shadow. They stared hungrily at Tianna.

Visions of her past flashed through her mind. Trembling, she pulled little Drew closer. Never again. She must provide for Drew, but she never wanted any of her family to work a big house or its land again. And her love, Andrew, promised her that she never would. But Andrew was gone.

The overwhelming sense that brought her here—almost as if an invisible hand had pushed her—had faded, and she questioned why she felt so drawn to this village.

A violent shudder pulled her mind back to the present. Her modest brown dress, designed to breathe in the hot, humid weather of her native country, let in the chill of the English countryside. She pulled her ragged shawl tighter.

There must be another way. She had her needles and threads in her crocus bag. She would look for more genteel work like Andrew wanted.

The pair trudged back to the main road to search further. This time the gentle hand nudged her to turn left upon High Road, then to stop at Church Street. A dark cloud coalesced over the entrance of the road, slinking to hover over her head. The pressure she felt reminded her of the Obeah rituals of home. She recited an incantation and threw in a prayer for good measure, then pulled Drew away from the uneven track. 'There is nothing for us there, mi love. I trusted once, but what did God ever do for us?'

'But the teacher at the mission school say He good.'

'I thought so, child, but not anymore. He din' do any more than the Obeah priestess to keep your papa safe.' Tianna's eyes misted.

'But God… He good.'

She knew this in her heart, even firmly believed it at one time, but her loss clouded her mind.

Tianna stumbled her way up High Road. Just as she reached the point where she felt she could go no further, a placard on the face of a building grabbed her attention.

It advertised a line of various shops. A card in one of the windows announced, 'Help Wanted'.

'Come, mi love, mebbe the gods are on our side after all.'

•◇•◇•◇•◇•◇•◇•◇•◇•◇•◇•

Tianna did her hair, tucking her braids under a white kerchief. Andrew used to delight in helping her. When she feared this culture would not accept them, he'd gather her to his heart and whisper it didn't matter what others thought—their love was a gift from God. A pang of sorrow sliced through her at the memory. She shook her skirts adjusting them to hang just so, shaking the memory away also.

Tianna checked her reflection as best she could in the sliver of mirror positioned on the box she used to hold their belongings. She was told her new customer, Lady Fentiman, was a stickler for proper attire.

Drew watched with solemn eyes. She hated to leave him alone in the draughty hut nobody else wanted at the end of Poor House Road. But she knew taking him with her on the delivery would be frowned on. Missus Esther, the dress shop owner, was gracious, but there were limits. And Tianna needed the jobs the woman gave her to keep them from starving.

'Drew, you be good now. I be back soon. Leave the fire 'til I return.' She wrapped a tattered quilt around his shoulders. The coals would keep the rain's chill from the room for a while, but she knew there wasn't enough to chase it away all day. She prayed for a good commission today to buy more.

Tianna gathered the project Missus Esther had given her to finish, folded it neatly, and carefully placed it in her bag. She took one last look at her son and closed the door snug, stopping on the stoop to draw in a deep breath.

'Good morning!' Tianna startled at the greeting. A simply dressed woman stood before her. 'My name is Edith. My brother, Bennet, and I let the cottage down the way. I'm very pleased to make your acquaintance.'

'Good mornin', miss. My name is Tianna.'

'I know.' Edith smiled enigmatically. 'I won't keep you; I pray you have a prosperous day!'

'Thank you, miss.' A peace that seemed to radiate from the young woman washed over Tianna, calming her soul, even as she puzzled over how she knew her name.

The unseen angelic being standing at attention by the corner of Tianna's hut communed with his fellow angel, signalling he would guard Tianna's son. Edith was free to follow her charge.

•◇•◇•◇•◇•◇•◇•◇•◇•◇•◇•

'Mama, there's a strange person in the hall.' Miss Caroline hugged the wall, pulling her skirts close. Lord and Lady Fentiman's daughter edged into her mother's morning room.

'Yes, dear, I know. She has brought your new gown for Guy Fawkes Day.'

'I thought the seamstress was doing it.' The young woman peered around the half-shut door. 'This person has my gown?'

'That is what I just said, dear.'

'But, she's a …'

'I have it on good authority from Miss Esther that she is an excellent seamstress.'

Lady Fentiman rose from her desk and preceded her daughter into the hall. Tianna straightened and passed a hand over her kerchief.

'I'm sorry, I don't know what to call you?' Mrs Fentiman said by way of greeting.

'It's Tianna, Missus.' Tianna's grip tightened on her bag. The daughter's look of disdain caused beads of sweat to form on the back of her neck.

'Cheen… Chain… Mama, I can't say that!' The young woman's face scrunched in disdain.

'Very well, how about we call you Anna? That's a lovely name, isn't it? So much easier.'

Tianna bit the inside of her cheek. Picturing little Drew in the draughty hut prompted her to agree. 'Yes, Missus, Anna is a nice name.'

'Good!' Mrs Fentiman pulled a cord, and a maid appeared. 'Millicent, please escort Anna to the first-floor guest room.' She turned to Tianna. 'You may set up there. We'll be along shortly.'

Caroline's whines followed Tianna as she climbed the stairs after the disgruntled maid. *It's for Drew,* she repeated to herself.

•◇•◇•◇•◇•◇•◇•◇•◇•◇•

'Look at what you did! I can't wear this. You must fix it. Mama, look!' Miss Caroline's strident voice pierced the room. The girl collapsed into her mother's arms.

There was nothing wrong with Tianna's work. The selfish debutante had stepped on her own hem trying to exact a dance twirl in front of the mirror. The torn hem dragged on the floor.

Tianna stood rigid, waiting to see what the mother would do. She could not afford to lose the income from this project.

'There, there, dearest. I'm sure this can be repaired. Anna, can you fix this?'

'Yes, Missus, I can fix where she tore it.' Tianna knew she shouldn't have pointed out the girl's fault in the matter, but she couldn't help it.

'I didn't do it, you cow! You didn't make it right!'

'Caroline, that is enough! Remove the dress and go to your room.'

'But Mama…'

'Now, Caroline.'

The girl flounced away, muttering about how stupid Tianna was. Tianna cleaned up the mess and neatly folded the dress into her bag again. Whilst she worked, Lady Fentiman spoke. 'I apologise for my daughter's behaviour, Anna. I dare say she is a bit high-strung. I trust you will be able to repair the damage quickly?'

'Yes, Missus, I'll get at it right away.'

'Good. I can see you have done a beautiful job so will look forward to its completion. I'll have Millicent show you out.'

'Missus?' Tianna clasped her hands tightly. 'I know it is not finished, but… could you… my boy, it's gettin' colder and I need to buy coal…'

'Oh, yes, of course. I can give you an advancement until you make it right.' Tianna bit her tongue. Lady Fentiman pulled another cord by the door and waited until a woman bustled into the room.

'Mrs Ballard, please see that the seamstress gets a half payment for Miss Caroline's dress. Thank you. That is all.' The lady of the house swept out of the room and Tianna was left with the housekeeper.

'Come with me then. I'll get your money.' Her face did nothing to soothe Tianna's nerves.

•◇•◇•◇•◇•◇•◇•◇•◇•◇•

The week continued as it began. People were leery of Tianna. The scant payments for her work were never enough. She was tired of the same gruel for every meal. So was Drew, though he never complained. The rain was a constant curtain of bleak coldness. At their home they wore most of their clothing to keep warm.

She longed for her country where the rain was like a soothing caress from above. Here she couldn't seem to drive the biting cold from her bones. Drew was developing a cough, too. Daily, Tianna fought her demons of despair.

The only bright spot was the day she met Miss Maisie Bloom. The precious gift of her cheerful spirit lifted Tianna's for a moment in time. Maisie was a sympathetic listener to her plight and her interest helped ease Tianna's distress.

However, because the love she and Andrew shared would never be understood, Tianna disclosed only that Andrew was gone. Drew was her priority, and this would keep him safe from more maltreatment than what he already experienced.

That bright spot was long gone, though—and still it rained.

•◇•◇•◇•◇•◇•◇•◇•◇•◇•

Tianna, or Anna, as she was now known, sloshed her way to Missus Emma's house with a dress for her little girl. As always, she hoped her work would be found satisfactory.

Her eyes widened when Missus Emma, not a maid, opened the door. 'Come in, come in. You must be frozen! This rain is dreadful. It is a bit much, even for our standards.'

Tianna stiffened when the lady helped her remove her shawl and hung it over a chair in front of the fire. She waited for the snubs and insults that she knew were coming. Servants were never treated this way—it just wasn't done. And Tianna knew she was thought of as far less than any of England's servants. She pondered this whilst the lady chatted away.

However, the woman said not a disparaging word. She only asked her to follow her into her daughter's nursery, speaking all the while how grateful she was that Anna was able to finish the gown so quickly. Her daughter was so excited to try it on.

How was it Missus Emma spoke to her as if... No, something wasn't right. She waited for the expected treatment to be dealt out.

Climbing the stairs, Tianna ran her eyes over the balustrade and caught a glimmering flicker of something. It was there and then gone. Her heritage affirmed the existence of spiritual beings. Could there be one in this home? If there was, it was benevolent. Her heart felt the same calm as she had with Edith.

'Here we are,' the woman said. 'Darling, Miss Anna brought your dress!'

A lovely little girl ran up to her mother squealing. 'Let me see it! Let me see it!'

'Now, sweetheart, mind your manners. Say hello to Miss Anna first.'

'Sorry, mama. Pleased to meet you, Miss Anna.' She sketched a sweet little curtsy, her red curls bouncing merrily.

Tianna found herself smiling at the delightful child. 'Good mornin', little one.'

The girl giggled. 'She talks funny, Mama. But I like it!'

'Oh, dear. I'm sorry, Anna.'

'It is all right, Missus. I do talk differen', don' I?' She smiled at the child again.

'I'm special! My mama got me from the Charitable School. She picked me! Didn't you, Mama?'

'Yes, I did dear. But again, you need to remember your manners. Miss Anna is very busy. Don't you want to try your dress now?'

The little girl quickly whipped off her day dress and let Tianna lower the new garment over her head. She stood perfectly still whilst Tianna made adjustments and waited until the dress was removed before showing her enthusiasm for it. Quite a difference from the Fentimans' daughter.

On her way home Tianna carried her bag that held the payment for her work, plus a loaf of bread that Missus Emma said had been dropped off for her.

'A gift, from Edith, the new woman on your row,' Emma said. 'How she knew you would be here today, I don't know!'

Tianna smiled at the thought of the feast Drew would have this evening. Before she could bring it to him, though, she had to stop in to pay her rent. She didn't know how the hovel she and Drew lived in could be deemed worthy of the amount she paid. But it was better than living in the forest. They were already too close to that dark vegetation for her comfort. She was positive it held a duppy man or any manner of bad spirits. Strange lights and moans confirmed it.

'There she is! That's the person who made a mess of my dress.' The exaggerated whisper struck her from behind. Miss Caroline and her friend tittered and whispered some more. Maybe the forest wasn't the only place monsters dwelled. She was certain of it when a clod of dirt was kicked up, knocking her bag out of her hand and into a puddle. The priceless bread was ruined. Her heart fell at the loss of Drew's special surprise.

Squeals erupted from the young women as a carriage rumbled past, splashing their feet with mucky water. Tianna glimpsed the same glimmer from Missus Emma's house float around a corner.

Unfortunately, though the women's misfortune made her smirk, it didn't replace the soggy mess in the bottom of her bag. Resigned, she scooped up her money before it, too, became water-logged.

Fear licking her spine like the sandy tongue of a lizard, she entered the office of the landowner. Clutching coins she knew were not enough, she stammered her name and why she was there. The clerk looked her up and down, pausing at the dripping tangle of cloth grasped in her hand.

'Give me your payment, then.' The scrawny clerk held out his hand.

'Yes, sir. If you please, I don' have all of it. I need to buy supper for my boy.' The man's countenance darkened. 'But I can get it for you by the end of the week, sir.'

The man stared. 'I'm sorry, but we do not accept partial payments. If you can't pay for it today, you'll have to vacate the premises.' He didn't look sorry.

Tianna sagged. 'Yes, sir.' She scrounged for the remainder and handed it over to him. Not bothering to look at her, he slid the confirmation of her payment across the desk.

Tianna's mind grappled with her situation as she trudged home. The dark despair of loneliness and hopelessness pressed her down.

She looked up when Missus Emma and her charming girl passed, calling out a greeting and thanks for the dress. A thought began to form. Lurching down the path leading to her house, she never saw the figures along the side of the road — one glimmering, one roiling in darkness. Her mission filled her vision.

•◇•◇•◇•◇•◇•◇•◇•◇•

'Momma, did you do good today?' Drew sat curled near the waning heat of the coals. A cough racked his body giving certitude to her plan. She must keep him safe.

'Ya, mi love,' she said, holding her tears for later. 'And I have a surprise for you.'

'For sure?' His brown eyes brightened some.

'Yes, we are taking a visit for you to play with other children.'

'Oh. Do I have to? The childrens, they don' like me.'

'I don' think you have met these, mi love. These children are like you. They don' have a papa, just like you.'

'Oh. Then I guess it's all right. When do we go?'

'Now, love. Get your things because you are going to stay for a little while.'

'With you?'

'No, jus you for right now. Momma needs to do something first.'

She gathered Drew's pitiful belongings and set out for the Charitable School. She prayed Andrew and any powers that be would understand this was the only way to take care of her baby.

•◊•◊•◊•◊•◊•◊•◊•◊•◊•

'You are asking to leave your son here? Why?' The orphanage's matron glared down her nose at Tianna. Drew's voice, playing with the other children, floated through the open door.

'Missus Rossiter, my husband, he is dead. And I'm sick, so I canna care for him no more.'

'But this is a charitable organisation for orphaned children. Your boy still has a parent.'

'Yes, I do know that. But I... I have a wastin' disease and will be dead soon, so I want to make sure he is taken care of before I...' Tianna swallowed a sob.

Miss Rossiter sat with hands folded and mouth pursed. She sighed and said, 'Well, I suppose in light of your circumstances we can take him in now.' She extracted a red ledger from the drawer and placed it on the desk. 'What is the child's full name?' Tianna hesitated. 'Madam? The boy's name?'

Tianna pulled in a breath. 'Andrew Charles Alston,' she said quietly.

Miss Rossiter put her pen down. 'Are you saying his father is English?'

'Yes, Missus. His father and I were joined in holy matrimony in my country.' She twisted her bag around her fingers, tightening it into a knot.

'I see,' said the matron. She looked like she just bit into a lemon. 'This does change things somewhat. It will be difficult to place a child like that.' Miss Rossiter shuffled papers on her desk then picked up her pen once more. 'But, not impossible, I suppose. Perhaps he could stay here until he ages out, as a help to the local man who does odd jobs here.'

Tianna released a breath. That solution would be an answer to her prayers.

Miss Rossiter slid a sheet towards her. 'Sign your name here on this line. You do know how to write your name?'

'Yes, Missus.' Hand shaking, Tianna wrote her name. As soon as she finished the last letter, a sense of dread came to nest in her stomach.

Miss Rossiter picked up the paper and filed it in her ledger. She stood, indicating the meeting was over. Tianna didn't know what to do.

'I suggest you depart now before your son comes back in. I think it is best he does not see you leave.'

An icy cold hand seized Tianna's heart. What had she done?

What is best for the child, a silken voice whispered in her mind.

Tianna placed one foot ahead of the other. She hadn't lied to the matron. She did have a wasting disease. Hopelessness. It threatened to swallow her into a deep, dark hole. She wasn't dead yet, but she might as well be. Without her love, Andrew, and now her precious Drew, she might as well be.

•◇•◇•◇•◇•◇•◇•◇•◇•◇•

The town was busy with preparations for the Autumn festivities coming up, so Tianna could act on her plan uninterrupted.

Andrew had told her what mushrooms to stay away from, and those were the ones she searched for behind her hut. Shivering from the frosty air, a portent of the coming winter, she almost ran in to fetch another shawl. Then she laughed wildly at herself. In a few moments it wouldn't matter.

'Miss Tianna, what are you doing? Are you all right?' Tianna whirled to see Edith standing a few feet from her. Her face was filled with concern and care far beyond her years.

'Ya, I'm well.' Tianna placed her basket on the ground. Her fingers were numb from more than the cold of the misting rain. 'But is it wise for you to be out in this cold?' Tianna was desperate for her to leave.

'You know much truth, Miss Tianna. "The older the moon, the brighter it shines".'

Tianna stumbled back. How did Edith know this expression?

'But Miss Tianna, is it wise to do what you are doing? Isn't there anything else you can do?' Edith touched Tianna's arm and warmth radiated through her body. 'Miss Maisie is looking for you. I think you should talk to her before you have your meal.'

The girl removed her hand and stepped back. An ageless look shone from her eyes.

Tianna breathed deeply. Could this be a sign from above? A warning that she should not act on her plan? A sob escaped from the bottom of her heart. 'Lord, what have I done?'

•◇•◇•◇•◇•◇•◇•◇•◇•◇•

She heard Maisie's song wafting on the night air. It reminded her of a song from the mission house back home. She began to hum along. How she wished her Andrew was beside her again with his rich bass voice. She'd forgotten how he loved to sing songs about God.

'Miss Anna, I'm right happy to see you tonight,' said the old woman.

Tianna covered her mouth with a trembling hand. 'Miss Maisie, I've done a terrible thing.'

'Somebody is here to help, lass.' Maisie pointed past her.

Tianna turned to see Edith and her brother. 'Hurry, now, we'll help you get your son back,' said Bennet.

'God speed!' called Maisie.

The three hurried to the Charitable School, Tianna's heart in her throat with worry. Soon, soon she would hold her Drew.

Tianna was the first to reach the school. She pounded up the steps and beat on the door. A stony-faced Miss Rossiter greeted them. 'What tomfoolery is this? You are interrupting my tea.'

'Please, Missus, I need to see mi boy,' said Tianna. 'I've made a terrible mistake.'

'This is outrageous. Go to the back and we can discuss it.'

Edith stepped to the woman and quietly said, 'You should let us in here now.' Miss Rossiter obediently moved aside to allow the threesome entry.

'Where is he? Where is mi boy?'

'I'm afraid you are too late. I found a position for him in a city the next county over, to apprentice as a chimney sweep.' The woman pulled on her watch pin. 'They left a half-hour ago.'

'No, no, no!' Tianna's grief flooded over her. She didn't see Bennet slip out the door.

'Come my dear, sit here. It will be all right.' Edith guided her to a bench. 'Just trust in the Holy One.'

•◇•◇•◇•◇•◇•◇•◇•◇•

Tianna felt like she was drowning. Like the time the tide along the beach at home almost pulled her under. She had been terrified then, and she was now.

It seemed a lifetime, but only an hour had passed since they stormed into the school. With a look from Edith, Miss Rossiter stopped her complaints about her missed tea and sat down.

Tianna jumped up when the door flew open and Drew charged in. 'Momma!' He dashed into her arms. 'I told you God is good!'

'Oh, Drew. Oh, mi love. Yes, I know He is.' She covered his face with her tears and kisses.

Just then, Bennet and the local odd jobs man walked in.

'Aengus, what is the meaning of this?' Miss Rossiter glared at him.

'Och, I'm sorry, Miss Rossiter.' He twirled his cap in his hands. 'The thing is, the horses... weel, I cannae explain it. We got over the main road and they refused to go any further.'

'What are you saying? Couldn't you whip them or something?'

'Aye, mum. I tried, but they just sat in the middle of the road. I never seen anythin' like it! And then…'

'What? What happened man!' said Miss Rossiter furiously.

'Weel, mum, I swear I heard them talk. Something like, "You can whip us all you want, but we were told not to budge".' The man took out his handkerchief and mopped his brow.

'Absurd!' Miss Rossiter stormed away muttering something about brandy.

Whilst Tianna and her beloved son clung to one another, Bennet and Edith shared conspirative smiles. They knew the horses obeyed the message Bennet gave from The Holy One.

•◊•◊•◊•◊•◊•◊•◊•◊•◊•

The odd jobs man told the story of the sitting horses over many a cup. And when folks asked Drew for the details, he gladly shared Who saved him that day. And Tianna's faith was restored a hundredfold.

For the most part, the people of Whitstead finally accepted Tianna and her young son. And, for the most part, Tianna and Drew grew to love them back.

Harvestide Excerpts from the 1845 Logbook of Matthew Rossiter, Midshipman of HMS *Dovecott*
by Sarah Levesque *(epistolary/historical)*

To Miss Rossiter, Charitable School, High Road, Whitstead
HMS *Dovecott,* Bristol
16 October 1845

My dear sister,

It is my pleasure to inform you that you may expect me within the week, for a blunder by a buffoon has rendered my leg unsound, and I am no longer able to fulfil my duties as a midshipman. What I shall do without this post that has defined my life, I cannot say further than I will return to you until my leg is more sound.

Your brother,
Mattie

•◇•◇•◇•◇•◇•◇•◇•◇•◇•

21 October 1845

Arrived in Whitstead. The children who I met on my last visit were pleased to see me. Fanny was not so pleased, but no worse than expected. I wonder if her opinion of me will fall further when I reveal the fireworks I managed to purchase on the journey. It has been quite some time since I celebrated Guy Fawkes Day on land, but I look forward to it, and to carving turnip heads for All Hallows' Eve.

My sister continues to look after — I cannot in good conscience write 'care for' — many children. I remember John, Charles, Jim, Claire, Martha, Eliza, and little Freddie from my last visit. Freddie seems to have put more swagger into his step now that I have two crutches to his one. The bigger boys are working with the farmers getting in the harvest, though already I have heard that the harvest will not be plenteous. There are also some new children — Catherine, Mel, and Will, as well as Ollie and Frank Dobbins, who strike me as a mischievous twosome. The reunion with Robbie and Margie was joyous, and they appear to be doing well with the Winterhavens.

•◇•◇•◇•◇•◇•◇•◇•◇•◇•

22 October 1845

The children asked for a story. Having nothing to do, I cheerfully obliged. The first story that sprung to mind was Medusa, that old Greek tale. What child doesn't like the excitement of Perseus battling the monster whose very face turns people to stone? I must admit that my description of her may have had some similarities with my sister....

•◇•◇•◇•◇•◇•◇•◇•◇•◇•

23 October 1845

Turnips acquired. Still need candles. Arranged to go to doctor's tomorrow; there's none in the village, but a few miles to Westford by cart isn't far.

•◇•◇•◇•◇•◇•◇•◇•◇•◇•

24 October 1845

Today the groundskeeper drove me to Westford to have the doctor check my leg. Of course, it was broken nigh on four weeks ago, and I told him so. He hemmed and hawed and told me to stay off it for another two weeks, and then he'd see me again. It was quite a large fee for such little information. He did tell me I was lucky it had not become infected and gangrenous, but I already knew that.

The children and I drew charcoal faces on the turnips. Tomorrow we'll carve them. Jack McLantern is an Irish tradition I heard of; should be interesting to see people's reactions. The boys drew the most grotesque faces, of course, whilst the girls' are rather more genteel.

•◇•◇•◇•◇•◇•◇•◇•◇•◇•

26 October 1845

Turnip carving went well. Told the children the Irish story of Stingy Jack and his turnip head. It may not have been the best idea, for Eliza got quite frightened, and even stout-hearted Frank seemed a mite put off. I may have to tone down my stories... they are only children, after all. I didn't think an immortal man with a turnip head was all that frightening, but Ollie's eyes were as big as saucers. I wouldn't be surprised if Frank embellished the story a bit more after lights out. I shall have to talk to him about how he treats the others. It's not their fault he's the biggest, aside from the three working the fields.

•◇•◇•◇•◇•◇•◇•◇•◇•

27 October 1845

Took a walk—well, a hobble—around town. Saw some of the turnip heads leering. Might be able to get a job as a shop clerk. Not sure I'd be suited for it, nor it for me, as I dislike the idea of being enclosed in a dark shop all day, but I do need the money and something to do besides tell the children stories. Today's was Hansel and Gretel. Some of the children—Frank especially—are bloodthirsty mites and enjoyed every minute of it. Others—like Ollie—seemed nigh scared stiff. But perhaps it will keep him and his brother from wandering off. It's twice since I've arrived that they stayed out all night, and sleeping in a straight-backed kitchen chair is not as comfortable as it used to be.

•◇•◇•◇•◇•◇•◇•◇•◇•

28 October 1845

Spoke with Mr Phillips about employment as a clerk. He will take me on for a day to see if it will work out. Already I have my doubts; the shop is dark and close, and Phillips himself is more grumpy than Captain Toomy! Also spoke with a few people about Guy Fawkes Day.

Approached by Mr Winterhaven today; he told me my stories were scaring Margie. Shamed, I promised to be more careful when she's around. Apparently ghost stories and small girls do not mix.

•◇•◇•◇•◇•◇•◇•◇•◇•

29 October 1845

Job with Phillips will not work out. Not only is he incredibly sullen, he will not allow a breath of fresh air in the shop, he won't allow me to whistle or even hum, and the dust would get someone the bosun's lash if found on any ship. He paid me reluctantly and poorly. Must find other work.

•◇•◇•◇•◇•◇•◇•◇•◇•

30 October 1845

Fanny's upset I didn't work with Phillips today; wouldn't listen to explanations. Children excited and scared for tomorrow. I recited to them parts of the Rime of the Ancient Mariner, but not the more frightening parts.

•◇•◇•◇•◇•◇•◇•◇•◇•

1 November 1845

All Hallows' Eve left me with a crick in my neck, as Ollie and Frank did not return. So much for Hansel and Gretel keeping them sleeping in their own beds. Otherwise, the evening was quite enjoyable, despite the rain. Ollie did return some time after midnight, thankfully, but Frank did not. Ollie mentioned that Frank had said he wouldn't come back, but nearly all boys who run away say that and return anyway. I know I did.

•◇•◇•◇•◇•◇•◇•◇•◇•

2 November 1845

Marked out a place for the bonfire in the town square for Guy Fawkes. Met a man named Arthur Cobbett today who knew nothing of Guy Fawkes at all. How anyone could be English and make it to adulthood without knowing about the Gunpowder Plot is beyond me, but I told him the story and he offered to help me with the bonfire.

•◇•◇•◇•◇•◇•◇•◇•◇•

4 November 1845

I've decided Frank Dobbins is not coming back. I've slept in the kitchen these last few nights and I'm quite looking forward to my bed again. Fanny scoffs at me for staying up at all, but that doesn't bother me nearly as much as the fact that she is in correspondence with chimney sweeps in other towns, in order to put boys into apprenticeships. The butchers, bakers, and such I can agree with, but sending the poor little chaps up chimneys is appalling. Thankfully I've managed to convince her that even Ollie is too big for the job, and of course Freddie would never manage to climb a chimney. I think he takes pride in his crutch now that I have two. Quite endearing.

•◇•◇•◇•◇•◇•◇•◇•◇•

6 November 1845

Last night Ollie was a great help with the bonfire, as was Cobbett. Not sure where the bigger boys were; probably making mischief somewhere. I shall have to give them a talk about being a good example to the smaller children. The woodpile was high long before sundown despite their absence. Coaxed it into flame easily enough. Our Guy was burnt to ashes startlingly fast, but it was a good show. And the fireworks and crackers were a great hit. Cobbett did quite well setting off the larger ones, though he needed quite a lot of direction. But I couldn't do it with this bum leg of mine. At one point I thought he'd singe off his eyebrows, but he managed to dodge that.

There was an odd number of butterflies around the fire, and a strange woman among the fire-watchers. She was dancing in a way that made me think of another butterfly, and she was there one minute and gone the next. Odd. I know most of the people in this town by now, but I didn't recognise her.

I discovered today that whilst I was preparing for the fire yesterday, my sister took in a new boy and shipped him off immediately to that chimney sweep she had been in correspondence with! A horrid trick, particularly as his mother was only ill. Somehow, he was rescued from that cruel fate, and is now back with his mother. I shall have to look in on them and make apologies for Fanny… Perhaps I should speak to the trustees. Fanny does her best, but the children need so much more than a roof and food and clothes. They need love, and that she seems unable to provide for them.

•◇•◇•◇•◇•◇•◇•◇•◇•

7 November 1845

I took it upon myself to find and meet Mrs Alston, whose son Drew was nearly chimney fodder. She received me more cordially than I had anticipated, given the circumstances. Her accent put me off — she seemed to be from the West Indies, I would guess — but I apologised as handsomely as I could.

Ran into Reverend Hollybrook on the way back and voiced my concerns over the children under my sister's roof. He remarked that the children appeared to be well fed and clothed, so I hastened to tell him that my sister was certainly not misspending the money entrusted to her, but simply that she had no love of children at all and was not averse to subjecting them to dangerous occupations such as chimney cleaning. He said he'd been hearing things as well, and that he would speak to the earl and the other trustees.

Rode to the doctor's in the cart. Paid another too-large sum for him to tell me what I already expected — I can begin putting my weight on my leg and, in time, I can build it back to nearly full strength, but it will likely never be sound enough for me to return to sea.

•◇•◇•◇•◇•◇•◇•◇•◇•

To Mr Matthew Rossiter, Charitable School, High Road, Whitstead
The Trustees of Whitstead Charitable House
Whitstead Rectory,
17 November 1845

Dear Mr Rossiter,
It is our intention to instate you as the caretaker of the orphans of the Charitable House of Whitstead. Should you choose to accept the position, your status as caretaker

87

shall be effective on Friday the twenty-first of November 1845. Please notify us in writing of your decision as soon as possible.

Sincerely,
The Trustees of Whitstead Charitable House
Reverend Diggory Hollybrook (Whitstead)
Reverend Frederick Bates (Westford)
Reverend Christopher Moore (Rollingsford)
Arthur Fentiman, Earl of Whitmore
Jacob Needsworth (Whitstead)
Frederick Chapman (Westford)
Charles Smith (Rollingsford)

•◇•◇•◇•◇•◇•◇•◇•◇•

To Mr John Bradshaw, HMS *Dovecott*
Charitable School, Whitstead
18 November 1845
Bradshaw,

You will never guess what has happened. I have accepted the charge of caretaker of the Charitable School of Whitstead, supplanting my sister Fanny. Whilst I am not wild about the idea of turning her life upside down—for she has nothing but her job and reputation—it is best for the children, and I hope she will not hold it against me but stay on as housekeeper. I am quite honoured by the appointment and delighted to be guardian of these children who are so dear to me. It came as quite a surprise, of course, for I never had a thought of running the House myself.

But I have been remiss in telling you the latest news rather than starting at the beginning. First, I ought to tell you of the turnip heads....

(The End... for now)

Fiddler's Ruse
by Nathan Peterson (*fantasy*)

And then they stole my tarts!' Ada's voice went shrill. 'Oh, Mother, Frank and Ollie are beasts!'

'Now, Ada.' I summoned my most matronly tone, a blend of concern and authority I had yet to master. 'That certainly wasn't kind of them, but name-calling will not do.'

Ada's lip jutted out so far, I was surprised she didn't catch raindrops from the afternoon's steady drizzle. 'The next time I see them, I'll do more than name-calling,' she muttered.

I suppressed a sigh. Truth be told, I half-wished Ada would give those boys a taste of their own medicine. But that would only start a row. 'None of that, young lady,' I struggled to emulate my old governess, Mrs Weatherby. 'Imagine what your father would say, hearing you.'

Ada's pout melted into a crooked smile so like Mortimer's it was uncanny. 'You're right! Father would think of some scheme, maybe soaking their socks in syrup or –'

'Ada Roebuck!' I raised my voice. 'I will speak to Miss Rossiter about this. But I will not allow any more talk of getting even.'

'Yes, Mother.' Ada wilted.

We continued down the path near the Ramsden Farm in silence. The breeze made the golden rows of hay sway in a gentle dance, and I almost thought I could hear snatches of some tune weaving through the trees.

'When will Father return?' Ada's question was almost lost to the wind. 'He's been gone so long.'

Once more, I had to hold in a sigh whilst trying to ignore the knot in my stomach. Mortimer's absence was… troubling. Since Christmas, his demeanour had grown brighter; his abstractions, staring out over the heath not hearing a word either Ada or I said, had become rarities. It was a welcome change. When he did leave for business, it was only for a day or two at most. Truly, he and I had never been happier.

But he'd been gone for nearly a week now. There had been no sign, no hint that he had grown restive as some men are wont to do. I hadn't reported it to the constable. He would only think me a nit-picking wife.

'Mother?'

Ada was staring at me, her curly hair refusing to be tamed. I couldn't help but smile. 'All will be well, love.' I gave her a quick hug. 'He'll be back before you know it. Maybe even sooner.'

Ada chewed her bottom lip. But at last, she nodded. We hadn't gone much further when the hayfield beside us began to ripple and quiver like a pond disturbed by a stone. There was a sound too, a high whistling hiss that rose and fell in unsteady bursts.

'Momma!' Ada cried as she clung to my skirts. I knelt, sheltering her in my arms as rain and bits of hay pelted us.

Just as quickly as it began, the commotion ended with a thud. The wind dwindled to nothing. I rose slowly, glancing around to make sense of it all.

'Great Aunt Nelly's knickers!' Ada exclaimed.

Distracted by the sight before me, I barely heard her. A miniature top hat had appeared, bobbing back and forth among the hay. It made its way towards us till the most curious figure stepped into view.

Decked out in a well-cut suit, he stood little over a yard high, leaning on a cane with a handle shaped into a dragon's head. He was barefoot and had a scar over his left eye and a gold hoop earring in his right ear. All in all, he looked like a child who couldn't decide between masquerading as a sailor or law clerk.

'Afternoon, ladies.' He raised his hat, revealing a thicket of red hair. 'Could you point me in the direction of the nearest haberdashery? I'm afraid my jacket's seen its final days.' He made a show of brushing dust from his sleeves.

My mouth hung open. I had seen more than my fair share of sights, but this…

'It's—it's that way.' Ada recovered first, though her voice shook even worse than her trembling finger.

'Much obliged!' He made a sweeping bow and set off down the path towards the village.

I still hadn't moved. I couldn't. The appearance of this… creature and Mortimer's absence seemed too obtrusive to be a coincidence.

'Momma,' Ada pulled my hand. 'Do let's go home. Please.'

'Yes, love,' I answered, my eyes still on the little man's disappearing figure. 'But let's take the long way, shall we?'

• ◇ • ◇ • ◇ • ◇ • ◇ • ◇ • ◇ •

Three weeks. Three weeks Mortimer had been gone!

I'd long ago swallowed my pride and reported it. At first, the constable took the news with a patronizing smirk and a dismissive remark about the many demands on a man's time. But with each passing day, his smirk faded.

'Mother? Is something wrong?'

I shook myself out of my daze. I was standing in the parlour, holding the satin the visiting Lady Ylva had offered earlier this morning as payment for her new dress. 'I— I still cannot believe Lady Ylva's generosity. This material must easily be worth three month's wages. I'm not sure how best to use it.'

Ada drew closer. 'Is that all you were thinking of?'

For a moment, the words, the worry, the fear all threatened to burst from my lips. But a picture of Governess Weatherby towering over me, hands on ponderous hips, came unbidden to mind, lecturing, *An adult should never confide in a child.*

'Heavens, Ada, you grow bolder by the day.' I forced out a chuckle.

'Well, I am nearly eight and four fifths,' she countered.

'Indeed. Were you saying something when I became… distracted?'

'May I play outside? Please?'

'Off you go. Just don't wander,' I said. We hadn't seen so much as a glimpse of the bizarre little man from the field.

Yet townsfolk had begun to talk: strange snatches of music drifting from the woods; the town's only herd of goats disappearing one Thursday eve; and not only them, but people as well, close to a dozen, just gone. The constable had no clue. I hoped against hope that Mortimer hadn't been caught up in this.

I took a deep breath, closed my eyes in silent prayer, and then did my best to return to matters at hand. I'd done everything in my power to find Mortimer. The rest I had to entrust to the Lord, as Reverend Hollybrook often reminded us.

The morning passed slowly. Trousers for mending, dresses for hemming, and all the rest—they did little to distract me. I passed the parlour window and expected to glimpse Ada hard at play at pirates or knights or fairies. And saw nothing. I rushed over to the window. Ada was nowhere to be seen.

My heart thudded. 'Merciful God, no!'

I was already throwing on my jacket and rushing for the stairs. At the last moment, I hesitated long enough to retrieve Mortimer's spare pistol. I stowed it in my pocket and hurried down to the grassy space behind our home. A closer inspection revealed nothing.

I cried aloud. Where could she have gone? First Mortimer and now Ada? I couldn't—

'You!' I caught sight of a small figure weaving across the heath. Even over that distance, I recognised his ambling swagger.

Racing through prickly heather and gorse, I grabbed his elbow. 'Where is my daughter?' I roared.

The man's round face, dominated by a bulbous nose and merry eyes, showed no sign of concern. 'Slow down. What's wrong?'

Bearing too much semblance to the constable's snide mockery, his voice unhinged something within me. I grabbed his shoulders and shook him hard. 'Do not patronise me, little… troll! Where is my daughter? Ada was outside playing, and then she was gone.'

The man's features remained placid. 'I have no idea, ma'am. I was just…' he trailed off as his head tilted to the side.

I was about to shake him again when a strange sound reached my ears. At first, it seemed but a gentle gust of wind, but blended with it were snatches of something more haunting. My heart began to stir, yearning to follow the sound. But I quelled the impulse.

'So that's where he is!' The little man beamed as he casually slipped out of my grip and resumed his trek across the heath.

'Wait!' I hurried after him. 'You must tell me where my daughter is!'

'I told you, I don't know,' he called over his shoulder. 'If circumstances were different, I'd help, but there's something I have to do. Good luck.'

He seemed to be telling the truth. This fact struck me almost like a physical blow. I shuffled to a stop. My only clue to Ada had come to nothing.

'Sir, please,' I called. 'If there's anything you can do, please.'

For a few moments, he kept walking, further and further, and my hopes sank.

But then he hesitated, pounding the dragon head on his cane. 'Fine,' he grunted. 'Tell me about your daughter. When did you see her last?'

Relief sent my words tumbling one over another. 'Thank you, thank you, sir! Her name's Ada. She's about eight and a half years old. I believe you saw her before when you, er… when you appeared in the field. She was playing behind our home. She's never wandered off before.'

The little man crouched on his haunches to poke at the damp earth. 'It looks like she's come this way, nearly running, which isn't a good sign.' His brow furrowed. 'We have to hurry.'

Without another word, he set off at a quick jog. Despite the thick clusters of heather tugging at my skirts, I kept pace. Each step brought me closer to Ada, and judging by the man's expression, not a moment too soon.

'Sir, if I may,' I managed between breaths, 'who, or what, are you?'

'You can call me Hans.' He gave me a sidelong look. 'And you already said what I am. Incidentally, how'd you know?'

'Pardon me?'

'Well, I'm a troll. From Norway. I assumed it was obvious. You've met others like me before, I'm guessing.'

'A troll?' I asked. Immediately, a picture of a hulking behemoth filled my mind. A wart-covered creature with arms the size of tree trunks, spiked cudgel in one hand and a screaming human in the other. 'No, no, I don't think I've ever met another troll. I wouldn't place your accent as Norwegian either.'

'Well, maybe you did meet one of us unawares. We can shapeshift, you know. And as far as the accent goes, I've been a lot of places.'

'I see,' I said, even though I did not, in fact, see at all.

We soon reached the edge of the woods. As Hans paused, picking at a clump of ferns, I caught a glimpse of pale blue amongst the trees and plunged after it.

'Ada, love, is that you?'

Within moments, I'd overtaken her, suppressing a sob of relief as I wrapped her in my arms. Ada didn't respond. Her limbs kept moving, as though she were walking in place, her eyes settled on something far away.

'Ada, what is it?'

'She's under his enchantment.' Hans appeared beside me. He took a large handkerchief and wrapped it tight around her head, covering her ears.

Almost immediately, Ada's eyes sparked with life. 'Mother, it was so beautiful! I could dance to it all day. Can you hear it?'

I hugged Ada once more, barely hearing Hans murmur as he turned away, 'That's a fossegrim for you. No better enchanters I know of. Good luck to you both. I really must go now.'

'Enchanters? Fossegrim?' I trailed after Hans with Ada in tow. 'What do you mean — enchanters?'

Hans glanced over his shoulder. 'Fossegrim are from Norway like me. He must have come visiting. They use music to lure people into the forest and hold them captive. Your daughter was lucky.'

My breath caught. 'Do you think there may be other captives?'

'That's what I'm going to find out.'

The news at once terrified and thrilled me. I could already hear Governess Weatherby's stern monotone: *A man like Mortimer can take care of himself. Your place is with your daughter!* But I kept pressing on after Hans as he slid past reaching branches. I couldn't bear it. Mortimer could be in grave peril. And with her ears covered, Ada no longer seemed in immediate danger.

'This isn't the sort of place anyone should go exploring. And that's saying a lot, coming from me!' Hans warned.

'You must understand, my husband has been missing for three weeks. If there's even the slightest chance that he's under this creature's enchantment, I must know.'

Hans didn't answer, but neither did he stop us from following. So, on we went deeper into the heart of the woods, further than I had ever been. The trees drew closer together, casting a preternatural twilight. Still the cold wind blew fiercely against us. And all the while, the music grew louder. Something beyond my control longed to surrender to its rhythmic lilt.

But my purpose kept me anchored. Now and then, Ada's face went slack, and she would try to sway and spin. But I kept her by my side.

'Most humans would be jigging their socks off by now,' Hans said. 'You must have a strong will.'

'And you?' I returned.

'That, and I'm not a fan of fiddles. Too wild for me,' he said with a bit of a smirk, his good humour having apparently returned.

He motioned for silence as he crept towards a rocky outcropping. It overlooked a valley clearing with a little waterfall trickling down into a pool. I drew up alongside him with Ada close beside me.

'Oh my,' I murmured.

More than a dozen people ambled around the clearing, shuffling between torches planted in the turf. Their heads lolled from side to side as their arms swayed, like marionettes on strings. There was no sign of Mortimer among them.

I squeezed Ada a little tighter. What kind of mother was I? Bringing my daughter all this way with nothing but a fool's hope that her father awaited us.

I was about to tell Hans we were leaving when my eyes returned to the clearing and to Lily, Jem and Sukie's mother, who most townsfolk assumed had run away months ago. How could I leave her and all the rest if it was in my power to help?

'Where is this fossegrim?' I whispered.

Hans pointed to a withered tree beside the pool that swayed in time with the wind. 'Time to introduce myself.' Hans popped up. 'You two staying here?'

Not fully understanding why, I rose to my feet, heading after the little troll as he strode down the steep hillside into the clearing.

He made straight for the stunted tree. 'Hey, Fossy! It's me, Hans! You might not know me, but I bet your friends do!'

Keeping Ada close, I stopped behind Hans, glancing around at the entranced figures. We had walked right past Lily without so much as a flicker of recognition in her distant eyes.

'What do you here?' came a voice from the tree, like the cracking of wood in a gale. I peered closer and could vaguely make out thin knobby arms grasping what looked like a fiddle. A shabby suit coat made of seaweed clothed the thing's shoulders.

'You know, this really isn't your kind of place.' Hans perched on a stone next to the creature. 'Wouldn't you be much happier at the bottom of a nice crusty bog, serenading mud-nymphs in Vanaheim?'

The fossegrim scowled at Hans, its crimson eyes glowing under brows rimed with moss. All the while, its fingers never stopped dancing along the fiddle's strings, stirring an ever-stronger desire in me to surrender to its siren song. 'I will not away till you pay a fair price: five dappled she-goats presented in the light of the moon upon Thor's day.'

Hans glanced my way. 'What do you think?'

'I beg your pardon?'

'You wanted to help and you know these parts. Can we scrounge up 'five dappled she-goats' by Thursday?'

I could feel the heat of the fossegrim's eyes now bearing on me. 'I'm afraid not. Our only goat herd has gone missing.'

'Fossy, is that true?' Hans feigned surprise.

The fossegrim's eyes finally shifted from me to the pool beside it, lingering on its reflection until a cold smile crept across its lips. 'Here is my price, troll. Three pigs never kissed by the sun, dipped twice in the nearest stream, collared in mistletoe swaths. And you must not bring any others to my abode.'

Hans glanced at me. 'Pigs never kissed by the sun?' It was strange, to be sure, but what choice did we have? I gave a weak nod.

'Fossy, you got a deal!' Hans shot to his feet, so triumphant he almost embraced the slimy creature. 'We'll be back in no time with your non-sun-kissed piggies.'

'Twice dipped in a stream. Do not misplace the mistletoe swaths,' the fossegrim reminded. 'And no other visitors.'

'Of course,' Hans waved Ada and me past the huddle of townsfolk still cavorting to the fossegrim's fiddle.

'Well, that went about as good as you'd expect,' Hans said, back in the shelter of the trees. 'Guess we'd better scrounge up some pigs. Which way?'

I pointed weakly towards town, filled at once with foreboding and a vague sense of just how colossally strange this whole affair was.

•◊•◊•◊•◊•◊•◊•◊•◊•◊•

Meeting the fossegrim's demands proved challenging. After much haggling with Farmer Ramsden—and some threats from Hans to turn the man into a turnip—we returned with the three pigs to the fossegrim's valley, catching glimpses of even more poor souls wandering through the trees. None of them were Mortimer, that I could see.

Hans brought the trio of mistletoe-collared, twice-river-dipped hogs before the fossegrim. Ada and I stayed well clear of the creature. 'Hey, Fossy, here are your pigs,' Hans waved. 'And no, we didn't bring anybody with us. We know how you are about 'guests.' Now, would you be so good as to clear off?'

The fossegrim, fixated on its reflection, pursing its lips and tilting its head, made no answer for some time. All the while its fingers glided across the fiddle strings, setting its captives off in a capering waltz. There were even more of them now.

A dry bark of laughter interrupted my observations. 'The pigs have sunspots all over them. The bargain is void.'

My heart sank. Hans interjected, 'A walk now and then out in the sun surely wouldn't spoil the flavour.'

'No.' The fossegrim returned to admiring itself in the pond's reflection.

At the fossegrim's cold reply, a fire kindled in my breast. I could almost see Mortimer striding up to the vain creature, willing it to strike a deal. And then suddenly, I found myself withdrawing his pistol from my jacket, levelling it straight at the fossegrim. 'You will free these people,' I said as calmly as I could.

The fossegrim's restless fingers went still. It glowered at me before bursting into laughter and maniacally sawing at the fiddle.

The pistol in my hand began to twist and turn. Before I could stop it, it dropped out of my grip, skipping round the clearing along with the enchanted dancers. Soon half a dozen stones and saplings had uprooted themselves and joined the frantic dance.

I was speechless.

'Great Aunt Nelly's knickers,' Ada whispered.

'Be gone before I make slaves of you all,' said the fossegrim.

I glanced between Hans and Ada. The troll was gripping his cane tightly, more like a cudgel, whilst my daughter glanced around at the eerie faces. There had to be something —

'Father?' Ada pulled on my sleeve. 'Look, it's Father!'

My gaze shot across the clearing, taking in those familiar broad shoulders and long wavy hair and olive skin. I raced over to him. 'Mortimer?'

His eyes were unblinking, his hair tousled, his clothes spattered with mud. I wrapped my arms around him. It felt like hugging a lamppost.

'I said begone!' The fossegrim sliced its bow across the fiddle. Immediately, every person in the vale locked their gaze upon me. Still slack-jawed, they started marching closer, fingers extended like talons. Mortimer shoved me to the ground.

Hans and Ada rushed to help me. 'We have to go,' the troll said.

My heart sank even deeper. Mortimer was lost to me.

•◊•◊•◊•◊•◊•◊•◊•◊•

'Couldn't we wrap something around their ears?' Ada asked from her perch on the window seat.

Seated at the kitchen table, Hans shook his head whilst slicing off a third helping of my seed cake. 'No, that only worked on you because you hadn't fully fallen under the grim's enchantment.'

I sighed, pacing the parlour. 'There must be something we can do. Does the creature have any weaknesses?'

Another shake of the head from Hans. 'Not really. They hate crowds. And are just all around mean, crotchety, and no fun to deal with.'

'Not to mention vain,' I added.

'Huh?'

'You saw it, preening and primping over its reflection in the pond.'

96

'Oh, I suppose.'

'Heaven have mercy,' I mumbled as I sank down at my sewing table, absently fiddling with the satin from Lady Ylva.

If Governess Weatherby were here, she'd demand I leave it up to the constable. No, in fact, she would never have believed in something so outlandish as a fossegrim in the first place. Even my attempt at Mortimer's swashbuckling approach had availed nothing.

Still, I could think of nothing but my husband locked under the fossegrim's allure. Had he eaten at all these past three weeks? How long could the enchantment last?

A morose silence settled. Ada glanced out the window, brow furrowed. I continued toying with the satin. A dislike of crowds and a penchant for vanity... if only there were some way we could turn the fossegrim's—

Realisation struck like lightning. I glanced down at the satin then over to Hans and Ada as more bits of a plan fell into place. It was far bolder and slyer than I preferred. But what other choice was there? The lives of Mortimer and all the others hung in the balance.

•◇•◇•◇•◇•◇•◇•◇•◇•

The music was even more raucous than before, seeming to give life to the gale raking the treetops. I took a deep breath, adjusted the ribbon on the box I held, and set off down into the glen. Alone.

As I drew closer to the fossegrim, the impulse to yield to its melody redoubled. But the sight of Mortimer, his cheeks sunken and colourless, drove me onward.

When the fossegrim's gaze settled upon me, it brimmed over with cold venom. It made to summon its captives to attack again, but I hastily proffered the box. 'No, wait! I have a gift for you.'

The fossegrim threw its head back, its laughter as harsh as the crush of a rockslide. 'The troll has forsaken you! Leaving a poor witless mortal to barter with cheap trinkets for your mate's freedom!'

I bowed my head as meekly as I could manage. 'Please, it really is a fine gift. What would the loss of one dancer be to so great a minstrel as yourself?'

As forced and unnatural as the flattery was from my lips, the fossegrim took it with a smug grin. 'Perhaps. The gift must be fine indeed to win your mate's freedom.'

I edged closer, well aware that the lying creature would never make good on its word. I removed the wrappings and withdrew a navy suit coat I had made from Lady Ylva's finest satin and embroidered with intricate filigree along the cuffs.

Greed lit up the creature's face, but it affected a careless tone as it fingered the tatters of its seaweed coat. 'What need have I for such a worthless thing? I have a jacket already. Still, let us see how poorly it fits.'

My heart began to pound as I watched the fossegrim set down its fiddle and bow, turning around and extending its arms. I carefully drew closer, removed the fossegrim's scum-crusted jacket, and slipped on the new one. It let out a sigh of pleasure, beaming at its reflection in the pool. It was too caught up in itself to notice me unravel a band of leather from the back of the coat and loop it around the trunk of the nearest tree. Then I snatched up the fiddle and bow before backing away.

'Truly, this is a sight I have longed to see!' I couldn't stop the mockery pouring into my voice. The fossegrim turned. What an exquisite moment it was, seeing its look of pride curdle to gap-mouthed shock!

'How dare you?' it raged. It made to rip the fiddle out of my hands but was jerked to a halt by the leather band. It loosed a screech like a wounded gull, head whirling to see what held it back. Cursing, it turned once more towards me and lunged with all its might. The leather tore free from its jacket, and it landed just a yard away from me.

I backed away slowly, waiting for it to spring. Then its face took on a strange look. I turned to see, standing all around the valley's edge, children from Whitstead. Ada was in their midst, beaming proudly, having followed my instructions to the letter. All stared at the fossegrim with wonder mixed with fear.

The fossegrim snarled. 'Get out! Begone!' It pushed me over, wrenched the fiddle out of my hands, and started sawing at it. As one, its captives turned to face me and the children.

Seeing my plan falling into shambles, all I could do was cry out, 'Ada, go, all of you!'

None of them moved. The fossegrim's captives pressed closer with clawing fingers and hard stares. I closed my eyes. 'I tried, Mortimer, I truly did…'

All at once came a strange sound: laughter. 'Ha ha, don't be scared, mates! It's only an oversized frog with a snotty beard!'

I turned to see a strange boy with fiery red hair pointing at the fossegrim. 'Watch this!' He wove through the captives, skidding to a halt before the fossegrim. 'Here, Fossy, have some porridge!'

A flash of greyish substance splattered the fossegrim right in the face, and the boy — there was no doubt it was Hans disguised — darted out of the creature's clawing reach.

The other children's looks of horror melted first to chuckles then soon broke out in fits of laughter, rolling upon the ground. The porridge-clad fossegrim hissed at them like a half-drowned cat in bathwater, wilting in upon itself. With a final venomous snarl, it broke the fiddle over its knee before plunging headfirst into the pool.

Silence, true silence, fell over the clearing. All the fossegrim's captives stood stock still. My heart pounded with relief and lingering fear.

Ada reached Mortimer first, launching herself into his arms. A little unsteadily, he caught her, stumbling backward. 'Ada, w-what are you doing? I've had the strangest dream. There seemed to be music coming from this clearing. I came to investigate and…'

Seeing me, he trailed off and then caught sight of the horde of children and adults filling the valley. Hans, still disguised as the little boy, sidled up to Mortimer. 'Boy, if you thought that was weird, your wife sure has a story for you!'

'Esther?' Mortimer looked flummoxed.

'Mother saved you!' Ada grinned. 'You were enchanted by the fossegrim. But she outwitted him all on her own!'

'A fossegrim? I see.' Mortimer's eyebrows knitted together. 'It seems as though I am in your debt, my lady.' He bowed.

Governess Weatherby's lectures on being unobtrusive ran through my mind. I lowered my gaze. But, no, there was no need to fret over such things at a time of celebration like this. I met his eyes, full of affection and pride.

A smile spread across my face as I threw my arms around him. 'Surely, good husband,' I answered in a mock serious voice, 'you did not think you were the only adventurous one in the family!'

A Fitting End
by Dana Bell (fantasy/action/spiritual warfare)

Gliding across the darkening sky, Circe circled Wrekin, a hill with a long mythic history. Tucked into the trees, an ancient crumbling ruin poked fingers out, trying to remind the world of its former importance. Not that the fate of the once proud tribe by Roman hands concerned her.

She landed on her four paws, tucking her furred wings over her orange back, her black stripes helping her to blend in with the trees, bushes, and grasses. Her nose sniffed the air, smelling red harts nearby who shifted nervously as if sensing a predator. Rabbits, introduced by conquering Normans, ducked into their burrows. A white-headed goshawk soared overhead before landing in the top of a tree, its red eyes studying her. Not that she'd come to hunt rightful prey.

Circe's prey were far more dangerous.

Turning her head, she groomed a spot on her shoulder whilst she waited for the others. Limpet the great warrior always sharing his role in the battle against the Dark One. The other female Moutia, who had guarded the Creator's son at his birth, and Gabron, the one normally allowed to lead them. For this mission, she'd been selected.

Three other orange and black striped creatures landed near her, their matching wings folding against their massive and powerful bodies. Gabron came to stand next to her, his yellow-brown eyes seeing the land around them. He chuffed a greeting, turning his large head towards her, waiting for her command.

Opening her mouth, she tasted the scents. The animals she'd already scented she ignored. There was another she needed to find, which would be sweetly bitter and make her want to wash away the revolting flavour.

Creeping along the damp ground she found what she sought. Strong terror, mixed with the dirty bodies of humans and overpowering stench of decay. The last time she had battled these creatures had been long ago during dark sieges in Transylvania, under a cruel leader known for impaling heads.

'Vampires,' Gabron spat. He too must have smelled the decay.

'Rogues,' Circe corrected. She knew well these creatures. Once they had been human before the craving for coppery blood engulfed them, turning them into hunting beasts.

Moutia sniffed. 'Humans lie in wait for them.'

'Hunters.' Limpet snarled. 'No better than the ones they seek to destroy.'

Buried under all the conflicting aromas, another drifted. Sweet, delicate, and filled with fear, telling Circe human females were being used for bait. She snarled, her anger barely contained, not daring to release the growl known to freeze prey.

She held a soft spot for human females, often shadowing one on a late-night walk or protecting a child lost from wolf and bear-filled woods. Or scoundrels that might steal and sell them.

'We must hurry!' Circe sprang into the air, opening her wings, using all her strength to propel her towards what would soon be a blood-filled battlefield. Behind her she heard the others faintly as they followed.

They flew over the town of Whitstead, the tempting whiffs of baking bread and roasting meats reaching her nose. Dogs barked warnings and cats looked upward, their tails gently swaying back and forth. The smaller felines no doubt knew they had nothing to fear.

Passing the woods, they reached a field hidden between two brush-covered hillocks. Circe saw the hunters hunkered down in the mud, crossbows ready. Only one way lay open for the rogues' approach to the waiting bait.

What sickened her was the sight of young females chained to stakes driven into the ground. Most had their cloaks covering their heads as a light drizzle sprinkled the area. From the greying clouds, Circe knew they would be drenched soon, with no way to stay warm during the soggy cold night.

Choosing a spot behind a wet boulder, Circe landed, a low growl in her throat. Her three companions joined her, staying out of sight so none would see them.

'What is your plan?' Gabron inquired. He sat on his haunches, seeming oblivious to the squelching ground.

'Do they really think,' Limpet added, 'that the rogues will come that way?' He tossed his mighty head indicating the valley entrance.

Moutia placed her paws on the boulder, rising up on her hind legs, taking a closer look. 'The females are only cubs.'

'Older than cubs.' Not by much though. Circe wondered where the hunters had found them.

'Poor things.' Moutia retreated, knowing, as Circe did, the Creator's mighty ones could not be seen. They dared not instil fear into human hearts. Not when they'd come to help.

What am I supposed to do? Circe asked the Creator. *You wanted me to lead? These females will be terrified, and the hunters will try to kill us.*

You have allies, came the response.

Allies? What was the Creator talking about?

Her ears heard the rogues' howling cries and her green eyes followed their blurred movements as they loped on hands and feet, their fangs extended, ready to claim what they thought of as rightfully theirs.

101

Wood smoke caught her attention as well. No doubt the people in the village burnt their bonfire to keep away spirits and fairies. All it would do is lure the hungry vampires to them who would feast upon the unwarned villagers. That could not and would not happen!

The rogues split into three groups whilst still too far away for the hunters' weak human eyes to see them. Circe knew what they intended to do. Use the approaching group as a distraction whilst the others climbed the hillocks, taking the hunters by surprise and killing them.

Gabron shifted restlessly. 'Circe?' She knew he wanted to take action.

'Gabron, Limpet, each of you take a hillock. Moutia and I will engage the rogues before they reach the females.'

Limpet pushed upward, using the trees as cover. Gabron vanished into the bushes.

Moutia and Circe stalked the approaching vampires, hunkering down in the grasses, her belly covered in mud. She waited, ready to pounce and use her claws to slay the rogues. So many she had not expected. Hope stirred in her. The Creator had promised allies. She had only to wait on His timing.

The first of the undead reached the field and she jumped the one closest to her, sensing Moutia attack another. Taking the creatures' heads as they jumped into the fray, trying to prevent mortal death, only to hear terrified screams end suddenly.

No! Circe would not accept failure. Surely that was not why the Creator had sent them!

Growling loudly, her prey-freezing sound reached the approaching invaders, failing to stop them as it would have any rightful prey.

Horse whinnies reached her ears as mounted men and women joined the fight, using swords to kill the rogues. The leader, a fair-haired man was pulled from his saddle, landing with a squishy thud. Pushing to his feet, he fought back, using his sword to take the aggressor's head.

With a start, Circe recognised him.

A rogue hissed, trying to land on her back. She met him in the air, her claws sinking deep into flesh as her mouth took its head. How long the fight lasted, Circe couldn't be sure, hoping the noise would not attract the villagers. They needed to stay near the safety of their bonfire.

When the battle ended, the few surviving rogues fled, leaving in their wake a few dead hunters, several females, and a couple of mighty warriors. She watched as the others gently used heavy cloaks to cover them, slinging their bodies across the horses' backs.

Using a cloth to wipe blood from his face, the warrior Circe knew approached her, hands open. 'It has been a long time,' he said.

Two centuries, in fact, from what she recalled.

'I told you I would repay the debt.' He wiped his sword on the wet grass, placing it back in its jewelled scabbard. Rain plastered his pale hair to his head, trailing across his high cheekbones and dripping down his trimmed beard.

Rain never bothered him as she remembered, from the battle they'd fought together before, when they'd destroyed the last of the oldest known vampires.

Her fellow angels joined her, waiting for her orders. Rain pelted and cleaned their fur, leaving red puddles at their feet.

Go in peace, she told him.

'And the women?' His roughened hand indicated the few survivors.

Return them to their homes.

He bowed to her, giving orders in this native tongue. Several fighters hurried to obey, freeing the female captives, and carrying them to sit before them on their mounts.

'Tell the Creator I will always be there when he commands.' He bowed to her, taking one of the women, and placing her on his horse, taking a moment to make certain the female was properly covered, before swinging up his strong legs and settling in his saddle. 'Till we meet again.'

Circe watched him and his warriors ride away.

'So...' Gabron sounded intrigued. 'How do you know this undead?'

'Long story,' she replied. 'Let's just say I was sent to destroy him and when I discovered he worshipped the Creator, decided I'd let him live.' If he'd ever turned to the darkness, she would finish him. Thus had been her promise to him and the Son.

'At least the village is safe.' Moutia glanced towards where the bonfire had burnt. Heavy black smoke hovered distantly.

'Guess their superstition worked,' Limpet joked.

'Or could have caused their deaths.' Gabron groomed his shoulder.

'Our job is done.' Time to return to the Creator's throne room Circe decided. No doubt other tasks awaited them.

Limpet and Moutia sped upward, eager to go home, vanishing into the grey clouds.

Gabron waited for her. 'Who was he?'

'Just a warrior once turned by one of the evilest vampires.' She turned her head to look at Gabron.

'Ah.' Gabron pulled at his claws.

She knew he would not ask more questions. Gabron knew of whom she spoke.

'Let's go home.' Gabron launched, soaring through the rain, the heavy drops sliding off his back and wings.

Yes, definitely time to go home. She circled the field one final time before heading into the sky. The hunters would care for their wounded and dead, whilst the rogues' ashes would be buried deep in the soil, nourishing the plants.

A very fitting end for an ancient evil.

A Past to Bear
by Madisyn Carlin *(fantasy/action)*

Eltaen fisted his hand as he stared at the cluster of drooping plants. Sodden green leaves veined with purple lay limp against the grass. Stalks of the same colour and closed opaque petals sagged. If this rain continued, there'd be no gretha flowers to harvest. No chance to save his kin and people.

His joints popped as he stood. He was too old to live such a life, traipsing across this foreign countryside. How many summers had he watched thunder and lightning crack the heavens? How many winters had he stood guard, sword in hand, as shadows crept towards the unsuspecting Whitstead?

Eltaen grimaced as fine rain droplets peppered his face. At this rate, he'd soon be as waterlogged as the gretha.

'Only two days to go until harvest. Hold on till then,' he murmured.

Eltaen forced himself to return to the cabin. Staring at the gretha did naught but waste time. If they were to bloom, it wouldn't be by his doing.

Please, Lord, let them survive. Let me find a way to transport them home.

Raindrops dripped from deciduous leaves just brushed by autumn's first touch. He'd walked this path too many times to count, but a chill always climbed his spine. Not all of the woods surrounding Whitstead were unusual, but this part certainly was, with otherworldly power charging the air.

No birds trilled. Only pattering rain accompanied his footsteps.

Eltaen rolled his shoulders. Beneath the spiking adrenaline and urge to turn and run like the coward he was, the warning pulsed in his chest.

Something approached Whitstead, and it wasn't friendly.

Uncountable times evil desired to taint, destroy Whitstead. Uncountable times Eltaen repelled it. Pain still twinged in his right shoulder, a reminder of his most recent adversary.

Every time he sustained injury, it felt like it took him longer to recover.

Just another reminder of the archaic blood in his veins.

As Eltaen continued, a familiar, weighted portent sparked at the base of his spine.

He quieted his breathing. Save for the rain and bobbing branches, nothing moved. He closed his eyes and honed his hearing. There were benefits of being Kaltaran in a world where no one else possessed enhanced senses—even if the rain did dampen his attempts to use them.

A slight rustle, the whisper-snap of bending blades.

He drew his long knife and spun.

A lad and a silver dragon stood beyond arm's length. Though the lad said nothing, curiosity gleamed in his eyes. The dragon, larger than a minor yet significantly smaller than a grand, watched Eltaen with an intelligent gaze.

How a boy in 1845 Whitstead had a dragon for a companion, Eltaen couldn't fathom.

He inhaled. This was not the Kaltaran battlefield, not his first months on Earth. The dragon's presence meant the lad intended no harm, but Eltaen couldn't convince his fingers to release their death clench.

The dragon dipped his head in greeting.

Eltaen returned the gesture.

'You can see him?' The lad's voice pitched upward. Dark hair and the clothing of a working man gave him the appearance of a usual Whitsteader. Not quite Eltaen's height, he looked to be in his mid-teens, about ten years younger than Eltaen appeared.

If the boy was Kaltaran, he'd be preparing for his rites of passage.

Eltaen swallowed and willed his vocal cords to work. 'Why wouldn't I?'

The lad opened his mouth before shutting it with an audible click. He studied Eltaen a moment longer before speaking. 'You know what a dragon is.'

'Yes.'

'How?'

'Not your business, lad. What're you doing out here?'

'My name's Thomas, and we're taking a walk.'

See? Nothing to worry about.

The reassurance did little to reduce the adrenaline firing through Eltaen. 'Is he your companion?'

'You mean my pet? No, Silven is my sister Ava's, protector.'

Good. With what was coming, everyone could use extra protection.

Eltaen shifted away from Silven's intense gaze. 'Even with a dragon protector, take care where you go. You and your family are safest in town.'

Thomas' voice cracked, indicating his shift from youth to manhood. 'Are you from Whitstead? I've never seen you before.'

'I've lived here longer than you've been alive. I'll escort you to the treeline. From there, go straight home, understand?'

Thomas' calculating gaze exhibited more maturity than Eltaen usually saw in adults. 'Something's coming?'

'Yes.'

Thomas only nodded. Just what had this mere lad faced in life, that he'd be used to danger?

Eltaen inclined his head towards the trail. 'Let's go.'

Thomas soon broke the silence. 'How'd you come to Whitstead?'

Likely an innocent question, but so many had perished from evil shrouded as truth.

He's a threat. He'll destroy the gretha and all hope of saving your kin, a voice hissed. *You know what you need to do.*

Eltaen shook away the dark urges accompanying the thought. He had spilled innocent blood in the past, but he was no longer that man.

Or so he hoped. But God always ignored his pleas.

Images of burning buildings, lifeless bodies and crimson pools, and piles of valuables stolen from abbeys and cathedrals claimed his mind.

His chest tightened as his breaths wheezed.

No longer that man.

Thomas' merry chatting halted Eltaen's thoughts. 'I know because you don't dress like we do. You have a slight accent. And few carry weapons nowadays.'

Eltaen glanced at his clothes. He dressed like any respectable Kaltaran, wearing a worn leather jerkin over a comfortable shirt tucked into simple trousers lighter than his dark brown boots.

Ah, but you're no longer in Kaltara.

True, but being confined to Whitstead didn't mean he had to dress in their ridiculous fashions. The Lord be thanked, his clothing didn't wear out.

'I can fix your knife's hilt.'

'No, you can't.'

Mud squished beneath their feet. Only the dragon walked in silence. Something about the ethereal creature twisted a shard of longing in Eltaen's heart. He'd been scheduled to bond with his dragon companion the day after he was to return home.

That day never arrived, and the stunning black-and-teal grand dragon was long dead.

'I'm an experienced blacksmith.'

Eltaen grimaced. He felt antique just being near Thomas. 'The most experienced blacksmith on your world — even the most qualified weaponsmith — lacks the skill to mend it.'

He swallowed to ease his parched throat. It'd been months since he spoke this much.

'What caused the notch?'

What should he say? This inquisitive lad could go straight to the authorities and report Eltaen's existence. Or he could be frightened away by the truth. Maybe if he thought Eltaen insane, he'd leave him alone. 'I broke it fighting a man called the MidKnight.' Who'd given him a matching notch just below his right clavicle.

'Who?'

'Renifeer, also known as the MidKnight. He causes havoc by freezing time. Some caught in his evil never unfreeze.'

'What?' Colour drained from Thomas's face.

'They die.'

Thomas gaped before shuddering. 'How? And why is he called that?'

'I don't know exactly, just that Renifeer causes everyone to stop what they're doing—freezes them in place like human statues. He's called that because at midnight he's strongest. No, no more questions. I couldn't defeat him, but I was able to drive him out. Those not from this world are immune to his evil, and weapons not cast by human hands can be used to repel him.'

'What about Silven?' Thomas placed a hand on the dragon's shoulder. 'Can the MidKnight harm him?'

'I don't know, but he's not of this world, so probably not. It's likely he is immune or even able to somewhat repel the freeze.'

Eltaen halted as they reached the treeline. He fisted his hand before placing it on Thomas' shoulder. 'I pray you never face Renifeer, but, if you do, do not do so alone.' Why he said the words, he couldn't fathom, but they left him before he realised.

After sending Thomas and Silven on their way, Eltaen stared at Whitstead. Rooftops glistened with rain and small, human shapes hustled about. Whitstead looked like a normal town, but everything about it screamed unnatural.

His chest ached. Meeting Thomas seared his heart with a reminder he didn't need.

He'd never be a father. A husband. A confidant or mentor.

But there was nothing that could be done. He'd chosen his path when he accepted revenge's call. Every choice came with a consequence, and he'd be enduring the consequences of his actions for a long time.

•◇•◇•◇•◇•◇•◇•◇•◇•◇•

Petrichor hung in the air as Eltaen leaned against the cabin's doorframe. Fading embers cast a shifting glow in his periphery. Before him, the bit of light provided by the waning gibbous moon shone on wet bark and leaves. In the distance, mist crept over the hills.

Eltaen rubbed his eyes. Weariness weighted his limbs and fatigue slowed his senses. Despite his exhaustion, sleep eluded him. The cabin provided shelter, but too many memories lurked within its walls. How could something be both a haven and prison?

He exhaled. Another sleepless night. Might as well make the most of it.

Strapping on his favourite weapons, he made his way to the gretha cluster. Although not yet fully grown and bloomed, their sweet scent, similar to wildflowers, soothed his soul.

Moisture soaked through the knees of Eltaen's trousers when he knelt. In the moonlight, the glistening raindrops brought to mind a memory of Mither's dew-dotted roses.

Eltaen swallowed the emotion rising from the thought. Now wasn't the time to ruminate on what had been. What he would never again have.

He brushed off the petals. To think the one thing that could save his people grew in Whitstead's vicinity.

Perhaps God did remember his existence.

A shrieking hoot split the air.

Eltaen's muscles tensed and his knives cleared the sheaths before a wind gust slapped him.

An owl. It's just a tawny owl.

Eltaen rolled his neck. He shouldn't be so jumpy. Few entered this part of the woods, and even fewer travelled the paths leading into the sylvan heart.

He stood as the air pulsed and tingled, similar to what followed a nearby lightning strike. The hairs on his arms rose. The last time he experienced that particular feeling in the air, a portal appeared.

He stumbled back as thunder boomed and a force wave of energy crashed into him. Bright light flashed. A current cooler than the damp air chilled his skin.

A portal.

The light pulsed, piercing his eyelids like they were nothing. Ebbing from white to pale purple, it brought with it alternating currents of warmth and cold.

A lavender arc outlined the portal's arch and glimmered before cascading down the portal surface like a waterfall. The lingering glow bathed the gretha in a ghostly lilac glimmer.

Eltaen ground his teeth. His head throbbed from the intense luminosity, but the pain could not compare to the physical agony summer sickness caused. The flowers were the only remedy for the deadly illness. He could bear this if it meant saving his people by saving the gretha.

The surface rippled.

Eltaen's pulse danced as his breathing evened. His muscles tensed, preparing to utilize a fighting style he'd not used in a long time. None who entered Whitstead through portals ever intended good.

This wasn't only to protect Whitstead.

It was to protect his people.

Eltaen shifted into one of the classic fighting forms learnt when he was just a tot. Knees bent, feet staggered, and his left knife back and higher than the right. A solid starting position no matter how many intruders crossed the portal threshold.

The portal's middle darkened before a humanoid shape stumbled into Whitstead.

Eltaen sprang forward.

The man brought a knife up just in time to deflect his first blow.

Eltaen's blood froze as light illuminated the emblem emblazoned on the knife's cross guard. Heat fired through him, and he renewed his attack. Each deflection and collision reeled his mind from the fight until grey swarmed his vision.

His body kept fighting, a distant part of his brain supplying his muscles and limbs with movements and tactics. Externally he fought in a forest clearing. Internally, nothing but hazy fog surrounded him.

He failed his family. He hadn't returned, hadn't avenged Cela's death by bringing her murderer to justice, and his actions kept him from saving his family. The only way someone outside the clan would wield such a weapon was if every MacGredd perished.

Failure.

The taunt, burning but icy like snow, tunnelled into his consciousness. Feeling drained from him until he felt nothing more than a pinprick of pain and breathlessness.

Faces crowded his mind. His parents, siblings, other relatives. The baby bump of his first niece or nephew.

He failed them. Failed an unborn child.

The chains binding back his emotions cracked as fiery heat flared in his chest. Shadows and the impact of blade against blade replaced the grey.

Eltaen inhaled as he caught another glimpse of the emblem. Reality returned with a cold rush.

He sheathed a knife and caught the intruder's wrist in one fluid motion. The man cried out as Eltaen twisted his wrist. The stolen knife fell to the churned grass. With a quick move, Eltaen yanked the man to the ground and pinned him as he grabbed the man's hair and forced his head up, placing a blade to his throat.

'Where did you get the knife?' he hissed. 'Who are you?'

The man stilled when Eltaen nicked his throat. 'I —'

'Where. Did. You. Get. It?'

'It's a family heirloom.' His voice strained. 'My great-uncle's.'

Eltaen edged the blade deeper into the man's skin. 'Who are you?'

'Halar MacGredd.'

'Liar. Tell me your true identity and how you really came about that weapon, and I might let you return alive.'

The man lurched with a choked gasp. The portal's light did nothing for his pallor. 'I am. It was my great uncle's.'

'Who is your clan's founding patriarch?'

'Rolf MacGredd.'

'When did he die?'

'Over two hundred years ago.'

Eltaen released the man's head. How could this be? Portals existed in Kaltara. But save for the one he'd used all those decades ago, no other connected to Earth, let alone Whitstead.

He shook himself as Halar shifted. 'What are you doing here?'

'An herbalist said there'd be gretha flowers. She didn't mention the portal.'

'Why do you need gretha flowers?'

'The summer sickness. My little sister…'

Eltaen snatched the man's knife. 'Get up.'

The man did. Dark hair hung near his eyes, which the portal turned a sharp silver colour. 'Who are you?'

'None of your business. How much of Kaltara is ill?'

Halar recoiled. A thin trickle of blood dripped down his neck. 'How do you—'

'Answer me.'

'At least half of the area's population.' He raised his hands when Eltaen advanced. 'I've heard nothing about the rest. I promise.'

Silence descended. Eltaen stared at the man claiming to be his nephew. In the portal's fluctuating light, what little colour Halar's skin possessed faded.

Eltaen cursed as Halar swayed before toppling. A quick scan revealed a massive bloodstain spreading along Halar's right side.

He glanced at the gretha. More could follow Halar, cause unfixable trouble. Still, he was obligated to help the injured, even if the lad lied about being kin.

Lord, please protect the gretha.

Lightning flashed. Thunder cracked. Rain poured.

Grumbling, Eltaen tossed Halar over his shoulder and carried him to the cabin.

•◇•◇•◇•◇•◇•◇•◇•◇•

Awakening to a blade at one's throat was never pleasant. Awakening to find a burly, brutish lad demanding to know what Eltaen did to his cousin? Even more unpleasant.

'Half a second, Calan.' Halar's strained voice managed to pierce Calan's incessant threats. 'Kaine's men are to blame.'

Ice skittered up Eltaen's spine. He should have known that wretched fool Kaine wouldn't die when he needed to.

Eltaen pushed up from the wooden chair he'd fallen asleep in and withheld a groan as he pressed a hand to his back. He was too old for such things, and he'd needed to fix that accursed chair for decades.

'Who are you?'

'That doesn't matter right now.' He nodded to Halar. 'Did Kaine do this to you?'

Perhaps focusing on Halar would quell Calan's flood of questions.

Halar winced and eased back onto the bed. Though still pale, he no longer looked like he courted death. 'I'm not the only one looking for gretha. People were following me. I had to dissuade them.'

'And how did you manage that?'

'I fought them. Didn't notice the injury until you pinned me to the ground.'

Calan snorted. 'You didn't do a very good job. I had to introduce them to a Mikenzie blade. That scattered them well enough.'

Eltaen worked tension from his neck and shoulders. 'Why was Kaine chasing you?' The only way that yellow-bellied rat would still be alive was through becoming an Ancient.

Which was no pleasant process.

Calan snorted. 'Money and power. If he gets his hands on gretha, he can sell it for exorbitant prices. Only a select few will survive. That way he can whittle down the number of those resisting his attempts to gain more power and control over Kaltara.'

Typical Kaine.

'Again, who are you?' Calan's sword reappeared at Eltaen's throat.

Eltaen batted the blade away with one of his own before wresting it from Calan's grip. He ignored the growling lad as he opened the door and tossed it outside. He understood the concept of protecting kinfolk, but he'd not allow a sword at his throat in the closest thing he'd had to a home in over two hundred years.

Halar groaned as he stood. 'Eltaen Halar MacGredd. That's who you are, right? Our uncle?'

Eltaen froze.

'I saw the emblem on your short knife, the one missing from the family collection. Only MacGredds use that style. And you look like the paintings hanging in the family hall.'

Calan joined his cousin. Both lads shared dark hair and silver eyes, but Calan was shorter than Halar, and instead of Halar's athletic, yet leaner, build, Calan was stocky with broad shoulders and strength both natural and gained by hard work. With his particular facial expression and build, he looked like Lewys.

Eltaen's heart ached at the thought of his younger brother.

Something flickered in Calan's eyes. 'Is he right?'

'Yes.'

'Then you must be an Ancient.' Calan spit the title with as much venom as he pronounced Kaine's name. 'What did you do? The clan always thought you a hero who died for justice.'

Desired blood. Wanted vengeance. Murdered.

Which answer should he give?

Eltaen forced himself to meet their gazes. 'I let circumstances control me.' A short, bitter laugh scraped his throat. 'I'm not the hero you thought I was.'

'Why here? Something is unnatural about this place. I sensed it as I tracked Halar.'

Eltaen's mouth dried. Answers were never fun to provide, especially when they'd be relayed to those he failed. 'The reverend somehow knew of the binding and bound me to Whitstead. Said it'd need a protector.'

Some guardian he was. And it wasn't like he was the only one protecting Whitstead.

Halar gripped Calan's shoulder as Calan again opened his mouth. 'What day is it?'

'Twentieth September 1845.'

'So, the gretha will bloom tonight or early tomorrow?'

'Yes, provided the clouds dissipate long enough.'

Please, Lord, let it be so.

If it wasn't, innocent people would die.

•◊•◊•◊•◊•◊•◊•◊•◊•

Eltaen stood to the side as Halar and Calan inspected Whitstead through the cover of hills and woods. Why they wanted to was beyond him.

'These people are strange.'

'That's hilarious coming from you. You're the strangest person I've ever met.'

He stared at the lads as they continued bickering. In the few hours he'd seen the two together, Halar's dry sarcasm and Calan's wit collided, but a strong, unshakable bond tethered them together.

They'd need it.

His heart clenched at how Halar almost called him *uncle*. So close to again having a family, only for his past to drive them away.

You deserve it.

'Something's wrong with this place.'

'Could be the food shortage. This rain has all but destroyed crops.' Everyone was leaner than last year. Food, whilst still plentiful enough to prevent starvation, wasn't as abundant as past years.

Calan fisted his hands. 'They have no idea what they're protecting, do they?'

'No.'

Eltaen's breath caught as chilling pain arced through his spine and limbs. He stumbled, barely keeping from falling to his knees as he struggled to regain his breath.

The lads grabbed his arms, supporting him. 'What happened?'

'Something's coming.' His words wheezed around the lump in his throat.

Calan cursed. 'I bet it's Kaine.'

Eltaen drew a breath and straightened. As he stared at Whitstead, bustling despite the humid, chilly air, a forceful grip clenched his heart. If he sent the gretha with the lads, Kaine would hunt them down and potentially murder them. If he kept the flowers in Whitstead, Kaine would try demolishing the town or forcing it beneath his sadistic rule. Not to mention how many Kaltarans would suffer without the life-saving flower.

Lord, what do I do?

Half of him wanted to ensure his nephews' survival. The other half wanted to protect Whitstead, the town to which he was bound, for which he was made an Ancient.

He cringed. No matter his choice, he would fail.

•◇•◇•◇•◇•◇•◇•◇•◇•

'Are you sure this is the right time? I don't see the moon.'

'It's the first of autumn. Have faith.' Eltaen gripped his knife as they neared the clearing. The portal's light still shimmered. By God's grace alone, no one found it yesterday. Being unable to check on the gretha whilst he gave his nephews a tour and struggled answering their questions did little good for Eltaen's mental state.

He flinched as more pain twinged through his lower back. The threat neared.

The twenty-first of September. The second moonlight fell upon the gretha cluster, the flowers would bloom and be at full ability to heal.

In a corner unseen it grows, blossoming in autumn's first light. So said the chant every Kaltaran knew by heart and prayed would come to pass.

Eltaen exhaled. All ten flowers remained.

Thank You.

Time passed, silent save the occasional hoot of a tawny owl and brief crackling from the portal. Eltaen allowed himself to stare at his nephews. Chances were he'd never see them again. This brief-but-valuable time proved both a blessing and curse — and perhaps a sign of God's forgiveness.

'Look,' Halar whispered.

Eltaen's breath caught. A thin moonbeam rested upon the gretha. With graceful, fluid movements, the flowers grew a finger's length more before the first petals unfurled. Not a leaf stirred. No sound cut the air. After the silvery pistil of the last flower was revealed, the clouds moved in and the moonbeam vanished.

Ice stabbed his lower back and he grit his teeth to silence the pain. 'You need to leave. Kaine's coming.'

He helped them dig up the gretha, roots and all, and place them in the cotton bag Calan brought.

Halar toyed with his knife. 'We can't leave you to face Kaine alone.'

'I'll be fine. You need to leave. Now.'

As they moved to the portal, Calan grasped Eltaen's wrist in an old Kaltaran warrior greeting. Something flickered in the lad's eyes, respect Eltaen hadn't seen the nights before. With a short, decisive nod, Calan entered the portal.

Eltaen urged Halar along. 'I can't have you getting hurt.'

He refused to fail his family again.

'Take it.' Halar pushed a full gretha into Eltaen's hand. 'You won't escape this unscathed. No, no arguing, Uncle.' A ghost of a smile quirked his mouth. 'Now I see where Calan gets his stubbornness.'

The portal swallowed him, then disappeared.

Eltaen stared at the flower. Before he could fully comprehend Halar calling him *uncle*, agony rushed his body and his legs buckled, sending him to the ground.

Kaine was in Whitstead.

•◇•◇•◇•◇•◇•◇•◇•◇•◇•◇•

Eltaen ground his teeth, willing his body to push past the consuming pain as he hid the gretha and struggled to stay upright. Sunrise tinted the coming clouds, providing a hint of the light he lost when the portal disappeared.

He twitched as his senses detected approaching footsteps. Kaine entered the clearing a heartbeat later. Still arrogant, eyes still full of amused hatred, and still bearing that egotistical smirk.

'Eltaen MacGredd. Why am I not surprised? You've interfered with my plans since the beginning.' Kaine smirked and drew his sword. 'I suppose you know why I'm here. Looks like you'll die an Ancient.'

'Leave, Kaine. There're no more gretha.'

'Maybe not in this clearing, but I'll raze this pathetic town until I find more. Or maybe I'll even become its lord. Imagine the wealth a gretha farm would bring. But you won't know, since you'll be a rotting corpse.'

Eltaen drew his weapons. Despite his weakness, energy hummed through him. 'Leave, Kaine.'

Kaine bared his teeth. 'Make me. I know the old methods for killing Ancients. And when I'm through with you, I'll kill your stupid nephews.'

Eltaen initiated the fight. Thunder cracked in the distance. His muscles soon burnt, but with every blow, ice embedded deeper into his body.

He blocked Kaine's remise with his long knife and struck a quick blow with his short blade. Kaine cursed and launched a volley of strikes that numbed Eltaen's arms and shoulders.

Eltaen stumbled back after gouging Kaine along the shoulder. Were he and Kaine still evenly matched?

Their weapons again met with such ferocity sparks flew. Eltaen lost himself in the fight as rain blurred his vision and dulled his mind until he knew nothing save his aching muscles and the driving need to remove Kaine from Whitstead.

Burning along his cheek and side alerted him of upcoming blood loss.

But he couldn't give up. Couldn't give in.

Time passed without count, and still Kaine showed no sign of faltering.

Lord, please.

Rallying his fading strength, Eltaen ducked a sharp thrust, locked his short knife with Kaine's sword, and slammed his long knife's hilt into the underside of Kaine's jaw. Kaine dropped, sword falling from his limp fingers.

Eltaen sheathed his weapons, struggling to regain his breath and fight the darkness edging his vision. Kaine had arrived via another portal. Now to discover that portal's location.

By the time he found it on the other side of Whitstead, the clouds had cleared to reveal the afternoon sun. Kaine cursed through his gag and fought his bonds as Eltaen forced him to the portal.

Just before sending Kaine back to Kaltara, Eltaen whispered in his ear, 'I am an Ancient and Whitstead's protector. Come here again, and I will find a way to kill you.'

The portal flashed. Kaine disappeared.

Eltaen damaged the portal's foundational integrity. He'd return another day and fully deconstruct it, but, for now, it'd be rendered useless for quite a while.

He staggered to a hill overlooking Whitstead. Chatter filled the air as townsfolk continued their daily lives, oblivious to what just happened.

Groaning, Eltaen forced himself to stay upright. Blood soaked his clothes and sweat stung his injuries. He'd won, but barely. Kaine had been a sword's width away from dealing what would be a death blow for any non-Ancient.

His breaths heaved with the effort of staying conscious. Safe. Whitstead was safe. His nephews were safe. His people and land were safe.

Thank You, Lord.

With his remaining strength, Eltaen retrieved the gretha and planted it in a safe location. He felt all of his two hundred seventy-five years of life, but perhaps the inability to die was worthwhile if he could save innocent lives.

He again gazed at what he could see of Whitstead. His fingers flexed against his long knife's hilt. This tenuous peace would not last long, but for now, everything was as it should be.

116

At MidKnight
by E.J. Sobetski *(fantasy)*

My name is Thomas Winterhurst. I'm the blacksmith in the peaceful town of Whitstead, England.

Whitstead might have looked peaceful from the outside, but strange things happened almost every day. One being my youngest sister Ava, just nine, was sometimes called the dragon princess—though others thought she was a little mad. That was thanks to the invisible dragon Silven living amongst us. Silven is from Ava's imagination, but my father always said, 'If you believe in something hard enough, it will become'. I remember the night when I believed and saw the dragon myself. My mother and sister Emily saw it too, and after that Silven came everywhere with us.

It was October. In that time of year, the leaves turned colours and fell to the ground as the glorious smells of apple cider filled the crisp air.

On a day like any other, I lit the fire in the forge and prepared for the day's work. Villagers were out doing normal, and not so normal, things.

'Morning,' came a voice.

I jumped and whirled around with a hot metal rod.

Emily jumped back. 'What is it with you?'

'I'm sorry.' I cleared my throat, feeling awful.

My sister raised an eyebrow. 'For the last month you've been acting strange—everything seems to scare you.'

'Oh, yes,' I replied, 'just bad dreams.'

'Me too. I keep hearing fiddles in my mind.'

'Fiddles?'

'Yes, not sure why.'

'On your way to the bakery?' I asked.

Emily nodded, wiping her black hair from her face. 'Anything is better than the smell of smoke and burnt metal.' She laughed.

When Emily left, I sat in a chair as my thoughts ran.

'At darkness the MidKnight comes, to create havoc wherever he goes. Time will pause until his power is too strong.'

Or something like that.

Emily was right. Throughout the last month I had become increasingly anxious. Memories of the warrior Eltaen danced in my mind. He said something was coming.

Not being a warrior myself, I wondered if I would have to face such a threat. Every night I waited for something to happen. Eltaen said people would freeze in their tracks, as if standing still. If tonight really was the night, it would be during All Hallows' Eve. Eltaen said if I had to face Renifeer, not to do so alone. Why would he say that? I prayed every night for God to grant me courage and strength. But then again, I'd be frozen too, so how would I even face the MidKnight? Besides, I had no idea what Renifeer looked like. And what about the words Eltaen said of Silven? Could the dragon survive? Shaking my head, I told myself not to worry. If something happened, Eltaen would be there to save everyone. Yes, that was it, no need to—

'Thomas?'

I jumped again twirling around to see Ava. 'Oh, hi.'

'Are you all right?'

'Hmmm? Oh yes. How is your dragon today?'

Ava smiled. 'Good, he just yawned.'

I smiled. 'Yes, of course.'

There came a sudden thunderous sound like horse hooves. My heart was pounding at an alarming rate. Another sound like that and I could have a seizure!

A horse pulling a brown carriage-like box walked slowly into town. Ava followed me outside to where a man jumped to the ground.

'Come one, come all!' he called out. 'I am Master Fairbury the storyteller. I bring tales from faraway lands, even a few from over the waters to the east.'

Many gathered around as children sat on the ground. I sat in a chair with Ava on my knee.

Master Fairbury began: 'It happens that tonight is the thirty-first of October. A marvellous time of year that might be eerie to some. Now, have you heard of Renifeer?'

At the mention of the name, I gulped hard. My heart skipped a beat and felt like it lodged in my throat. Did he just mention the very name that had haunted my dreams for a month? No, no, of course not, I must have heard wrong.

'He is called… the MidKnight.'

'No, no,' I thought to myself; 'it can't be.'

Fairbury continued. 'He haunts towns at night. Anyone in his way is frozen in their tracks. Save for one brave soul. Legend has it one man, whom no one ever sees, is protecting these towns. His name is a mystery to all.'

'How does the MidKnight attack?' asked young Thaddeus.

'Ahh, it is said he can freeze an entire town in time. No one would ever know he was there. Renifeer carries many weapons, each night it is different. However, like I said, one man knows how to defeat the MidKnight.'

Ava laid backwards into me whilst her right hand stroked the air. Believing the dragon to be real, I saw her petting Silven's head. I had to wonder if the dragon could

118

remember things, like what Eltaen spoke of last month. But, even then, I pondered whether it was all a dream, and this storyteller's tale a coincidence.

When Master Fairbury's story was over, Ava turned to me. 'Do you think that's real?'

My thoughts broke at her voice. 'No, of course not. Like this man said… legend.'

That night, everything changed…

•◇•◇•◇•◇•◇•◇•◇•◇•

Mother, Emily, Ava, Silven, and I sat in our home as we could hear the guising begin. We would be joining the feast shortly. I munched on an apple whilst Ava sat next to me in front of a warm fire.

'Do you think Silven would want an apple?' I asked.

Ava nodded and smiled. 'He says yes.'

As I offered the apple to Silven, a strange wind blew through the house, knocking me over. I blinked several times as my head hurt.

'Is everyone all right?' I asked, looking up.

But to my surprise, no one answered. Noticing Silven's wing around me, I stood up and thanked the dragon for whatever he just did, instantly realizing no one else was moving. Emily stood behind us holding a tray of biscuits in one hand and a single biscuit to her mouth in the other. Ava sat by the fire, her hands towards the flames, which also did not move. I waved a hand in my sister's face; her blue eyes never blinked, but she held her kind smile. I gently touched her right hand. It was real. But what of the fireplace? The flames were still. Yes, that must be it—time had paused. But how would that be possible? I glanced at a clock on the mantle; it was stuck at the nine. I saw Mother in her chair, crocheting a blanket, but her fingers did not move. It was then I realised—Eltaen's warning: Renifeer was here. I gulped hard. I locked eyes with Silven, seeing he was still moving.

What should I do? I thought to myself, trying to remember everything Eltaen had told me. *Did Silven's wing protect me from the spell?*

I waved my hand through the flames without feeling burnt. Turning and coming to Emily, I gently took the biscuit from her hand. The flavour of cinnamon spice was delightful as I took a bite whilst thinking hard. Of course! The main thing Eltaen had said, in three hours Renifeer would be strongest. But would the so-called mysterious man of legend come to the rescue? What if I waited and he never came? And if clocks did not move, how could I tell what time had passed? I would be the only one alive. I could not let that happen, not to my family or the town.

Oh no, the town—was it the same?

'Silven,' I said quietly as the dragon nuzzled Ava's motionless fingers. 'She is frozen, everyone is. We must find the MidKnight and save the town.'

Silven looked from my family to me. Then he was by my side. I had no idea what to expect, what the town would look like, or even where to look for Renifeer.

Going outside, I saw everything and everyone was at a standstill.

Either I was dreaming or under a witch's spell. Shaking my head, I came to the bakery to see Jeremiah amidst taking a loaf of bread from the giant oven. As I continued, I saw four-year-old Margie by her home, her hands pressed against the outside wall. Her brother Robbie was somewhere, probably looking for her. Twelve-year-old Evelyn sat by a wooden fence under a torched light reading a book. I carefully removed the book from her hands, but she did not move or blink. Over the last year I had thought Evelyn to be rather pretty with her long brown hair.

I wanted to take her hand but told myself to focus on finding Renifeer. Carefully I placed the book into Evelyn's grasp, but upside down.

Quietly I said a quick prayer to God for strength.

Walking a bit more I spotted Thaddeus kneeling in the middle of the road near his home. I came closer seeing his right hand out to a grey dog. Neither moved.

It was then I heard footsteps and they were coming closer. I became still whilst looking out of the corner of my eye.

What I saw was the shadow, then the figure of a man in a cape coming towards us carrying a long staff. I pretended to be frozen whilst trying not to breathe with my own hand to the dog as the man walked past. My heart pounded as if it would leap from my chest. The figure disappeared in the opposite direction around a corner and out of sight. Who was he? I slowly got up and peeked around a building but saw no one. Just lanterns on corners and a dragon on a roof.

Wait—a dragon? Silven!

He seemed to be looking in the direction of the mysterious figure. I quickly ran across the road to the building where Silven was perched. Suddenly, he took off: I followed as best I could until I came to the edge of the wood. Renifeer stood in the middle of a field, not moving.

Suddenly he laughed. 'Two hours, Eltaen! You shall not stop me this time. No one will—at last my time has come. Midnight draws near.'

I felt fear crawling up my legs. *What should I do?*

Eltaen was not coming, I could feel it…

Behind me Silven remained quiet within the trees. I wanted to go home; until I heard Eltaen's voice in my head: 'At midnight, his power is too strong, and not everyone who freezes, unfreezes.'

The words trailed off like an echo, dropping my heart like a stone. I swallowed hard, took a deep breath, and stepped into the clearing.

At any sound of grass and leaves beneath my feet, Renifeer turned and stared right at me. He was covered in black armour with a cape and the face of a hawk on his breastplate. For what seemed like several minutes, neither of us said anything. I realised I had brought nothing with me—no weapon, no tools, just my hands. But what good were they against a powerful being with a staff who could freeze an entire town in their tracks?

'How?' was the first thing the knight said, his voice deep.

Trying to sound brave, I replied, 'How what?'

Renifeer took a step closer. 'Do not play games with me, boy. How are you moving?'

'Oh,' I replied. 'That… well… um.'

'Who are you?' the knight roared.

'T-Thomas. I'm a b-blacksmith.'

Renifeer laughed. 'So, did Eltaen send you to deal with me?'

How to answer that?

'No,' I answered. 'My family froze in place, and I was exploring to find out why.'

'Oh? I control everything that is time. Nothing moves unless I say so.' Renifeer stepped closer to me until he was a few inches from my face. 'So tell me, young Thomas, how are you still moving when time does not?'

Come on, Thomas, I told myself. *Be brave, have courage.*

I glanced at the knight. 'Perhaps you are not that strong.'

The MidKnight growled. 'You dare to insult me! Do you think time is everything?!'

I closed my eyes trying not to meet knight's gaze. But suddenly, a thought occurred. 'I do, I do know time is everything.' The words carried courage and determination with them. 'In fact, time is what I make in my life. And you have no power over that.'

Renifeer glared at me through his dark metal helmet. 'You know nothing of the power I have! With one strike on the ground with my staff, you will be still.'

I stepped back and held up a hand. 'Maybe, but if you're so powerful you can stop time for an entire village, then why do you not try again?'

Renifeer shrieked, slamming the staff on the ground again and again. I turned around, waiting for something to happen.

'Not possible,' he whispered. 'A mere boy cannot stop me. I'm a knight! You could not hope to fight me and win.'

A rustling sound in the trees caused my heart to leap as an idea spread on my face. Eltaen had said Silven could survive the time freeze, and he did, even shielding me with his wing to protect me. I realised how real the dragon was becoming and it brought a smile to my face.

'Why do you have that face? Do you not know what happens at midnight? Everyone you love will perish, and my power will be too strong for any man, even Eltaen.'

I nodded. 'You know, Renifeer, my sister Ava always said if you believe in something hard enough, it will become.'

Renifeer laughed. 'And tell me, what do you believe?'

I grinned. 'That even a dragon cannot be frozen in time. I believe with every ounce of my heart that Silven is more real than any nightmare such as this.'

The MidKnight's head cocked. 'What dragon?'

For the first time, I could hear thunderous steps. Turning to the forest, I could see a silver dragon emerging from the trees. No longer was he imaginary, for I could see teeth, the wings, the smoke pouring from the nostrils. I reached out and he put his nose on my hand. I could feel him.

Turning to the MidKnight, we saw him backing away slowly. I noticed Silven had not taken his eyes from the scared knight. Renifeer slammed his staff again and again, but the dragon slowly came towards him.

'Ever seen a dragon, Renifeer? Well, this is Silven. And he is a guardian of Whitstead.'

Renifeer turned and ran as fast as he could. But nothing could outrun the flames from Silven's mouth.

In a flash, the knight vanished into a puff of smoke.

I waited, but the villain did not return. Silven turned his head and looked at me. A thin line of smoke came from his nose. I slowly walked to where Renifeer had been, astonished to see his staff on the ground. The hooked handle had the carved head of a hawk. Picking it up, I heard a voice…

'Well done, lad.'

I spun around to see Eltaen leaning against a tree.

'Where were you?' I asked.

The warrior showed a grimacing smile. 'Is that so important at a moment like this?'

'I suppose not,' I answered.

'I've spent many weeks waiting for Renifeer and wondering if your dragon was the key to his defeat. And I saw you were the only one who could control the beast.'

'So you thought I would follow the MidKnight, and fight him?'

Eltaen nodded. 'I will not say what I thought exactly. But I know this, you have the power now to set things right.'

I looked down at the dark brown staff in my hand. Its hooked handle was a three ringed spiral whilst half of the shaft had black stripes down to the middle.

'Wait, if I use this, time will begin again?'

'And maybe more,' Eltaen answered as he turned to leave.

'Wait, will I see you again?'

The warrior turned and looked from me to Silven. 'I'll be around. Now, use that staff, boy.'

I gulped as I looked to the staff, raised it in the air, and slammed it into the ground. Suddenly, I was back in my house, with Ava, Emily, and our mother. And they moved! Silven rested by the fire as a nearby clock struck nine. I looked around me, but nothing froze.

'Are you going to give Silven the apple?'

I turned to Ava, who warmed her hands by the fire. 'What apple?'

Ava stared at me puzzled until I saw the apple in my own hand.

'Oh right, of course.'

The dragon lifted its head and ate the apple whole. I stared at him as he was back to his imaginary state.

'What happened?' I whispered.

I was not sure, but I could have sworn the dragon winked at me. Using the staff sent me back to before time froze — it worked! The town was safe. I felt a sigh of relief. But only Silven and I knew why.

Mother set down her crochet and stood to her feet. 'Who is ready for guising? We should join the festivities.'

'I'll supply the biscuits!' Emily announced, holding up the tray.

As we prepared to leave, Ava said, 'Thomas, there's something by the door that has your name on it.'

'What is it?' I asked, unsure who would send me anything.

Coming to where my sister stood, my eyes grew wide at the sight of Renifeer's staff.

'There's a note,' said Emily, pointing at the crooked handle.

My heart pounded as I read the letter…

Young Thomas, I found this in the fields and thought I should return it to you as it is rightfully yours now. Have fun tonight, and well done, young warrior. Your courage saved everyone, and I'm forever grateful for what you have done.

It was signed *Eltaen.*

The Harvest Field of Whitstead
by Erika Mathews *(historical/family)*

Her footsteps thudded up the lane, the dirt gently speckled with the browns, greens, and golds of early autumn, fallen in careless abandon. Ahead, greys floated and danced above the tree line, wisps of misty cloud-cover perhaps betokening an afternoon thunderstorm, perhaps not. Even the trees sat silent and still, as if waiting to sense which direction the weather would settle upon. Every fence post leaned perceptibly in the direction of the curve in the road, veterans of a thousand such afternoons in years past.

That summer had been filled with laughter, friends, chats at the gate, town festivals, and the primary and most recent highlights that arrested Evelyn's thoughts as she sauntered home: the tending of the home gardens and today's talk by the missionary from the London Missionary Society.

These events dominated her mind for good reason. In the first place, everything in the gardens seemed to need to be harvested at once, and there were only so many hours in a day. Already the potatoes seemed to be rotting in the ground, touched by some mysterious fungus. She and Mumsi had managed to get away for this afternoon's mission talk, but threatening storms meant they ought to hurry back to the waiting bounty.

In the second place, this hadn't been the first time a missionary had spoken at the church or the ladies' tea or at Miss Rossiter's, not by a long shot. Yet somehow the words of this one—a very young man this time—embedded themselves purposefully and irrefutably in her mind.

Pray ye therefore the Lord of the harvest, that he would send forth labourers into his harvest.

He'd spoken particularly of the many tiny islands whose names she'd never heard of before. She'd ask Eldon for his map when she got home—where *were* these islands? Why, the missionary had said that many of the peoples didn't even have a Bible in their language! The ache of that thought pierced her heart.

'What are you musing upon so soberly, my Evelyn?'

The gentle voice of her mother, for once taking a day away from her sewing to accompany Evelyn to the ladies' tea, settled like balm upon her heart.

'Why, only of what Mr Baker was saying, Mumsi. What *can* one think? Here we are with a perfect, whole family Bible of our very own, and yet so many people in the world don't have one. They don't know who Jesus was. And—' She paused, the solemnity and weight of the thought rushing from heart to face in a blush that echoed her depth of feeling as she quietly finished the sentence. 'And how *could* they live, never knowing Jesus?'

Mumsi nodded. 'I know what you mean.'

'But Mumsi, I can't help but wish I could do something!' Evelyn swung her handbag, unable to express all the longing enclosed in that one short sentence.

If only she could help! If only she could go! If only she could tell the truth of Jesus to those eager, spiritually hungry people who were, as Mr Baker described them, 'good soil, more than ready for the seed of the Word.' The desire, planted long ago, had slowly sprouted all summer, and now it burst forth into a blossom of overflowing yearning for a single object.

'Hello, Elfrida! Hello, Evelyn! A good day to you both.'

'Greetings, Norma.' Mumsi bowed her head courteously to the neighbour. 'How is Richard?'

'Improvin', I s'pose. I got more of those herbs Widow Larkin was givin' him.' She waved them expressively. 'And'—producing a white missive—'a letter from Harry, what do you think! He's safely over to that island with the mission society. Says people flock to him. He never imagined such excitement for what he preaches. Better than he expected—does me good to hear.' Mrs Norma Wilson's hand, letter and all, covered her heart.

Mumsi answered, but Evelyn didn't hear. Such excitement for what he had to preach! Why, it hadn't been even a year since Harry had left Whitstead, and now! He was doing something that mattered! He was making an eternal difference! What could she do in comparison? Why, *why* couldn't *she* do something that mattered?

And there was Christine Shepherd—no, Christine Liu now. She'd married and gone to China, and she'd written of the missions work there. Even Gwendolyn mentioned she'd be heading to India as a missionary… why did everyone else seem to be able to do something big for God, whilst she, Evelyn Weston, was stuck here in the town of Whitstead where nothing really important ever happened…

Can't I go?

Yet she couldn't. She blinked and watched as Mrs Wilson ambled on, then turned to find Mumsi regarding her compassionately.

'You look like some of those big feelings have gotten hold of you, dear.'

Mumsi knew, always. Evelyn nodded, savouring the way that they'd referred to such emotional moments ever since she'd been a young child. And Mumsi always knew how to make the 'big feelings' seem more manageable, even in the very hardest of times.

125

So, without hesitation, she spilled her longing to Mumsi, wincing as the yearnings tore at her heart afresh with the verbalizing of them.

She knew she couldn't go anywhere. She didn't need Mumsi's gentle reminder. She was young; she wasn't wealthy enough to travel; she had no one to travel with; she needed more education; she had to keep house for her family so that Mumsi and Eldon could earn their living as best they could; and she knew no other languages.

Silently the pair turned into the home garden. Fingers found cabbage and beetroot as imaginations travelled far, far away.

'It's like the garden, Mumsi.' Evelyn jerked a stubborn beetroot plant from clodded earth. 'Missionary Baker, and Harry Wilson, and Christine Liu, and I don't know how many others — they're in a white field. One overflowing with bounty, so much they can't even harvest it all themselves. And here I am, in this tiny little garden, where only rotten potatoes seem to grow. Or die.'

'Ah, it may *look* that way. But Evelyn, do you truly believe the God who loves you would put you in a harvest field with only death in it?'

Evelyn was silent.

'I'm thinking of Reverend Hollybrook, now,' Mumsi went on. 'He's a man doing the work of God, if anyone in town is. And look at how he's been here, doing so much good for all of us! This town just wouldn't be the same without him. And there's Miss Rossiter at the Charitable School — so many children right here in Whitstead owe their lives to her. Do you see? I *know* God has a harvest for you right where He's placed you. And I would challenge you to take the next month to find what that might be. Because I know you'll find it if you look.' Mumsi laid another head of cabbage in the wooden bucket.

A faint smile worked its way from Evelyn's heart to her face. 'Do you *really* think so? A mission here? A harvest here?'

Approaching footsteps jerked her gaze to the corner of the garden, where Grandpapa halted with two covered buckets dangling from his hands. ''Lift up your eyes unto the fields; for they are white already unto harvest.'' The honey harvest's here' — he swung his buckets — 'though it won't be nearly as big as usual, and whatever harvest you're looking for, Evy, I know you'll find it. Keep your eyes open.'

He winked at her, and she wanted to drop her beetroot and throw herself at him for a hug, dirt and all. But she only smiled. 'Oh, I will! I'll do *anything* if only I can find something lasting to spend my time on. Something to help someone — to change them in a way that matters.'

•◇•◇•◇•◇•◇•◇•◇•◇•

'Are you going to hear the missionary at the church tonight, Evelyn?' Eldon dropped a bag of dressmaking work on the table for his mother.

'I was planning on it.' Evelyn's skirts spun as she gave a final scrub to the last wrinkled potato from last year and then thrust potatoes one by one into the old oven. 'There! Now dinner's cooking, and I can see to the mending. Why—are you going?' A confiding tone lingered in her voice.

'Well… I saw Emily leaving the bakery just now, and she looked like she might have been crying. She almost never leaves this early.'

'Oh, shall I run over and check on her?' Evelyn dried her hands on her apron, then pulled it off.

Eldon's pause stretched a long moment. 'I *was* wondering… you know they lost their father two years ago this month. I guess I just…'

'Oh, I'll go right over! I haven't seen her for—well, too long, with all the garden work. I'll bring them that second apple tart I made—that girl needs a break from baking sometime! And perhaps some of the stew. I think there's enough left.' Evelyn flew hither and thither, briskly preparing.

'You know there won't be time to see the missionary.' Eldon's words were low and reluctant.

'No matter,' Evelyn threw over her shoulder, stifling the twinges of regret that threatened to crop up in her heart. 'If Emily needs me…'

A brisk shortcut over the dirt path along the river would bring her to the blacksmith and the Winterhurst home, but before she got half the distance, Emily herself appeared ahead of her.

'Emily! Emily!' Evelyn broke into a run, heedless of her basket and not stopping until she reached her friend.

Emily halted—not a very difficult feat when she'd only been travelling at a snail's pace. Evelyn scanned her up and down, noting the traces of tears, of exhaustion—perhaps of grief? 'Emily, are you all right? No—of course you aren't. What is it?'

Tears threatened to fill the dark eyes again, and Evelyn shook herself. 'No, what *am* I thinking? You don't need to answer. It's all right. Just—I'm here. I want to help, however I can. I brought you supper.' She dangled the basket at arm's length. 'You don't have to worry—but—oh, Emily! I'm so sorry. I don't know *what* to say. Here I am just babbling away, wanting to say the right thing, but probably saying nothing helpful.'

'No—just you being here is enough. And the supper—thank you. My mother— she will thank you. She has so much to do, and—with what happened two years ago…'

'Oh, I can't imagine how hard that must be! But do, please, let me bring you supper this week. I can cook for two families as well as not, and I so want to help if I can! And—what else weighs on you today?'

'The wash—it needs to be brought in, and I don't seem to have the strength for it tonight.'

Emily's sigh went straight to Evelyn's tender heart, prompting the immediate exclamation, 'Let me do it! I can, easy as anything.'

And so it was Evelyn, chatting all the while, who unpinned garment after garment from the long clothesline; and Evelyn, seeking to spread a ray of sunshine wherever she might, who carefully folded each item into the bureau drawers; and Evelyn, her eyes shining in sympathy for the widow Winterhurst, who set the table and heated the stew and apple tart.

And it was Evelyn, the joy of service radiating from her heart even as aches and tiredness radiated from her shoulder muscles, who tramped contentedly home to serve a late supper to her own loved ones, satisfied in leaving the Winterhursts a little more comfortable than she'd found them. Somehow, the twinge of regret at missing the missionary's talk tonight had lost its sting.

Surely this was part of God's harvest field for her.

●◇●◇●◇●◇●◇●◇●◇●◇●

'Let's go hunt for nuts in the forest today.' Evelyn scraped the last of the porridge from her bowl, then rose to wash up. 'We ought to gather some before it's too late in the season.'

'Can I come? I want to come!' little Edith piped up.

'You can come, if you promise to fill your bucket,' Evelyn assured her, drying her bowl on a towel.

'I will!' Edith's voice was confident. 'And Ellis? Can he come?'

'Yes, we certainly want Ellis. Someone might have to climb a tree and shake a branch!'

'I'll race you to the forest!' Ten-year-old Ellis crammed on his hat and scampered out the door.

'Come, Edith, let's catch him!'

Laughing and shrieking, the three children caught up buckets and dashed towards the forest, tagging and passing each other on the way.

'Maybe Jack will come with us,' Ellis said hopefully as the woods approached and the children's steps slowed to a walk. 'I've seen him here almost every time I've come this autumn!'

'The boy who moved into that old cottage?' Evelyn asked.

'That one. Yes. They had to move, Jack said. He ought to know where all the nuts are! Oh, there's his mother! Hello, Mrs Maggie! Is Jack out today?' Ellis called, waving his arm.

Evelyn's eyes jumped to the woman's face. Wisps of dark blonde hair danced about the sides of her countenance, and a worried look lingered about her eyes as she lugged a giant basket of laundry towards the cottage.

'Jack's ill,' the woman said quietly.

'Is it serious?' Compassion instantly flooded Evelyn's heart. Who cared that she didn't know this woman well? Her son suffered. She needed help.

'I—I don't know. He's feverish. Achy. Tired. Seems to have lost his energy.' The woman paused. 'I wish I knew what to do for him! My husband—he's away finding work.' She regarded the children more carefully. 'You live over down by the bakery, don't you?'

'Yes, we do,' Evelyn spoke up. 'I'm Evelyn Weston.'

'Of course. Elfrida's daughter. She's spoken to me.'

'Is there anything I can do? Get the healer? Something?'

Maggie shook her head. 'If there were anything more I knew to do for Jack, I'd have done it already. I just have to keep a roof over our heads until my husband returns. We—we couldn't keep our old place, and we simply must keep this one.'

'Oh—but your boy is ill…' Sudden determination seized Evelyn. 'You take in washing?'

'I do.'

'I'll come help with it. I can spare one morning a week. I'll ask Mumsi, but I'm sure she won't mind. And—' Evelyn broke off, suddenly shy, but with a firm resolve to continue. 'May I—may I come in and pray for Jack? I know God can heal him.'

'Come in,' Maggie murmured. 'Anything—anything to help him.'

As Evelyn crossed into the little cottage and laid a soft hand on the boy's head, a curious sense of wonder filled her heart. Here she'd been wishing for mission fields, and here God gave her an overworked mother and ill boy to minister to. 'Keep your eyes open,' Grandfather had said. Well! She scarcely felt she needed to keep them open, so apparent was the way before her in which God called her to walk.

Her prayer was low but sincere, faith radiating from every word. Surely—surely, God would heal Jack. Surely, He would see the struggles of the mother and let them keep this house. Surely, He would cause the father to find work. All this and more Evelyn poured out in her petition, and she rose to smile at Maggie.

'Thank you for letting me do that.'

'Oh, thank you. And—God bless you, dear child.'

Evelyn couldn't help the smile that bloomed whilst she skipped into the woods at last, her brother and sister flanking her. She'd come to harvest nuts, and nuts there were in abundance—but the greater harvest had begun right in that little cottage. God was there, and where God was, Evelyn meant to be too.

•◇•◇•◇•◇•◇•◇•◇•

''llo, Evelyn.'

'Hello, Augustus. How's your family been?' Evelyn stooped to gather an apronful of apples from the ground outside her home where two loaded apple trees flanked the road.

'All right, I s'pose. Mother's baby's come now, and she's 'most always in bed.'

'Oh, in bed, is she? Is she not well?'

'I dunno. I don't think she's very well, but I dunno. Me 'n' Shadrach are goin' fishin'. Trafford said he'd cook 'em if we caught 'em. So I'm goin'. Shad's comin'.'

Evelyn gathered both corners of her apron more securely in one hand and regarded him compassionately. If a seven-year-old thought Mrs Griffith wasn't well, surely, she mustn't be well.

Depositing the apples into a basket standing by the front step, she hiked two doors down to the dilapidated hut that the many Griffith children called home.

'Mrs Griffith?' As she knocked, she raised her voice to be heard over the clamour of young voices playing, fighting, wrestling, dancing—who knew what.

The door jerked open, and a pile of children tumbled at her feet. 'Evelyn!' they squealed, pulling at her skirt and dancing in delight.

She drew in a deep breath. No wonder their mother was abed. 'Hello, children. May I speak with your mother?'

'She's in the bedroom.' The tallest girl aimed a thumb at the one door, and Evelyn waded through the children towards it and let herself inside.

'Good day, Mrs Griffith. I hear you aren't well. Your baby is all right, isn't he?'

'Safe enough, I reckon, if only I'll be about soon. Don't know how much longer…' The feeble words trailed off in the commotion of the rest of the house.

Evelyn spoke up quickly. 'What can I do for you? Feed you? Feed them? Do the laundry?'

Mrs Griffith shook her head, cradling her newest child next to her in the bed. 'We've eaten. Just… the children. If only they could go somewhere else for a…'

'May I bring them to my house? They can play in the garden and by the river.'

A nod was the only answer, and Evelyn grinned. 'No fear. I'll take them for the rest of today. You rest up and get your energy back for your baby.'

'Thank you,' the woman whispered. 'You know, you're an angel, Evelyn. Never seen much proof of God on this earth—but you. Every time I see you, seems I see an angel.'

Ah, no wonder Evelyn's heart was full as she trooped back home again. Despite the noisy, chaotic crowd that surrounded her as her fingers flew through washing and preserving the apples, a peace flooded her heart. Mumsi was right. The harvest field was here. It was now. The people of Whitstead had needs too—needs she could fill. The Winterhursts, the Griffiths, Maggie and Jack—why, even her own family! For the first time, her eyes were opened to the multitude and sacredness of the many little everyday needs surrounding her. This was a holy calling. A smile wreathed her face as she lined the pantry with more jars of apple preserves. Despite appearances, God had granted their gardens a bountiful harvest, even without the potatoes. And despite appearances, God did have a spiritual harvest for little Evelyn to reap right here in Whitstead.

Father, help me be content, she prayed. *Content here at home, this quiet field to grow. Bless those labouring in fields elsewhere. And show me what else You have for me right here.*

Others might labour far abroad, but she'd strive to be faithful in her harvest field right in Whitstead.

Already she sensed that that harvest would be far greater than she'd ever imagined.

A Dance of the Good Fae
by R.J. Kingston (*fantasy*)

Maria breathed heavily as she raced through the woods on the west side of Abbey Farm looking for her daughter, Emma. The girl had taken off into the forest after something she had seen.

'Emma,' Maria shouted. 'I need you to come back to me now.'

Maria was concerned for her daughter's safety here in Whitstead. As a child of the area herself, she knew much of the tales and folklore surrounding the town. Tales of ghosts and fairies, some of which were too dreadful to think of.

Her mother had often told her the story of how a great fae took the life of her father. After that wretched thing happened, her mother couldn't bear to raise her in the place where her husband was murdered. She took her outside of Whitstead and raised her in Wales, away from the stories and creatures she feared. There Maria found a handsome man to marry and gave birth to her daughter, Emma.

Oh, Henry. Maria stopped for a minute in the bleak, wet woods.

Henry was a banker and a good one too. He was going to provide for her and her family for life, or so she had thought. Instead, he died of consumption. Maria didn't know what to do. Times were hard across Great Britain, and she couldn't find it in herself to marry another man, so she took her daughter, and moved back to her hometown of Whitstead to hope for the best.

She was still very much aware of the horrors that happened here when she was a child, including the death of her father; but she had also heard tales of great miracles. She needed a miracle in her life now as a widow raising her fatherless child.

Maria scurried on through the woods as the sun began to set, creating a hue of purple and orange in the western sky. She would have to find Emma soon, otherwise the child would be lost to the bitter cold darkness of the night. Leaves fell from the trees as the evening wind shook them. Harvest was near its end and the forest was growing bare.

The desperate mother searched everywhere, calling out to her daughter. 'Emma,' she shouted.

No answer.

Fear filled Maria's veins as she thought of the state of her daughter. Perhaps a wild animal would find Emma as its prey or maybe a ghoul would capture her, and Maria would never see her again. Maria's blood boiled at the thought of it.

Night crept over the trees as the sky darkened. The tips of the trees were the only thing left that revealed the last of the daylight. Soon, the light would not be able to aid her in the search for her daughter.

'Emma,' she shouted once more. One last cry within her to call out to her daughter and…

She heard a sweet voice singing in the wind.

The voice was not far from her. It was not Emma's, but perhaps this person singing had seen where her daughter went. Maria ran up a hill in the woods and behind it lay an open field in the late harvest. The field was damp with rain, and it looked as though it yielded no harvest this year. Shrivelled pumpkins and crops lay across the entire field.

As Maria ran across the field to see what the singing revealed, she caught a glimpse of Emma dancing with what appeared to be a glowing ball of light. Her heart pounded against her chest as she approached slowly. Her daughter had no expression of fear on her face. Emma only looked at the strange light with curious eyes and a hopeful smile.

Maria then examined the ball of light closely. As her eyes adjusted to its eerie blue glow, she saw the shape of a faerie within. The faerie reached out its hand to hold Emma's.

'Emma, no,' Maria shouted.

But Emma did not hesitate to reach out and grab the faerie's hand.

As the faerie held on, Maria reached for her daughter. The faerie flew into the air with Emma and hovered above Maria's head. When the faerie stopped singing, Maria thought that her daughter was doomed, and the creature had come to take Emma's life.

Maria fell to her knees, weeping. 'Please spare my daughter, o great fae.' She didn't know what else to do. Her father's life was taken by such a creature, her husband's by illness. Now her daughter's life hung in the balance. She had no other choice but to beg. 'Please, she's all I have.'

The faerie smiled and began to sing again. The words sounded like some ancient language, but the voice was sweet and soothing. The song echoed across the wasted land and the blue light shone brighter. The faerie danced in the night still holding onto Emma whilst singing its sweet song.

Maria watched with glistening eyes as her daughter flew with this great spectral sight. She began to make sense of the faerie's words.

> Ooo-oo-ooo, sing for the mother who cries,
> Ooo-oo-ooo, sing for the widow who sighs,
> Ooo-oo-ooo, sing for the mother who loves her child,
> Sing for the mother who won't let her die.

These were the only words she heard from the fae that she could understand. The song calmed the mother's heart and reassured her. Her daughter would be safe in this faerie's hands.

The fae sensed when the mother was calm and came down upon her with Emma. As soon as Emma reached the ground, she left the faerie's hands and ran to her mother. Maria embraced her daughter and hugged her tightly. Her heart filled with gratitude, she thanked the Fae for returning Emma safely to her arms.

'Go, live in peace and be blessed,' the Fae said. The faerie then shone even brighter than before and flew into the night sky, singing as it went.

Maybe things will be different now that I have returned, Maria thought as she held her daughter's hand. *Maybe I was meant to come home and things will be better again.* She smiled and for the first time in many years, felt peace within her. She began to hope again for the days ahead for her and Emma.

The Hand Mirror
by Sarah Earlene Shere (*fantasy/gothic/romance/time travel*)

oung Lord Terence Melville stood on the balcony of the tallest turret of his newly inherited estate, Caisteal Manor. The rain was letting up. Reluctantly, he turned and re-entered the house.

Terence hurried down the broad staircase. The light from the day's setting sun coming through the long windows was his only guide. He glanced up as he passed his father's portrait hanging in the hall. Those cold eyes seemed to look down upon him with disapproval even in death. Terence thought of how he agreed with his father, this once, as he went to work putting on his cloak and pulling on his gloves. All Hallows' Eve parties were a childish waste, even if they were dressed up in the guise of a costume ball. Still, he had promised his friends he would be there, although he insisted upon dressing from his current wardrobe, rather than taking part in the masquerade. His friends! Indeed, they felt closer than family; they were pieces of himself. This reason, alone, hastened his preparations.

Terence had introduced Lady Elaine Fentiman to his childhood friend, Lord Sterling St. Giles, Viscount Lindon, at a social event just over two years ago. It had been Terence's father's hope that the lady would become his bride, joining the Fentiman and Melville families. But neither Terence nor Elaine were able to feel more than mutual respect. Terence's instincts that she was better suited for his friend were quite accurate; the two were married within a year's time and had only last autumn welcomed their first child.

Terence set his top hat into place and picked up his umbrella, along with the drawing pencils he had promised to bring Cordelia, the youngest Lady Fentiman. Placing the latter inside his cloak pocket, he ventured out into the cold. He had chosen to not take his ostentatious carriage, causing another reason for his haste. He much preferred to walk. He kept his umbrella closed, using it more as a walking stick; he would have avoided bringing it altogether, but had no desire to enter the home of his friends as a soaking mess, should the rain begin again. The biting wind, along with the icy moisture in the air, invigorated him, and, at the same time, numbed him to the painful thoughts that tortured his mind.

•◇•◇•◇•◇•◇•◇•◇•◇•

Laughter erupted as Sarah Crawford plopped down, her black skirts rising like a cloud around her as she joined her friends on the floor. She responded with a smile and mock defence. 'All right, scoff if you will. But I was told this was a Victorian-themed party, and here I am, the only one who wore a petticoat!'

Sarah's university friends laughed even harder. Brittany lunged at the mobile phone in Sarah's hand and snatched it away. Dropping it into a wicker basket, she passed it around the circle, demanding the others to follow suit with their own phones. 'Okay, ladies, time to say goodbye to our current year of 2015. Let's go one hundred and seventy years back in time, to Halloween at Whitstead, 1845!'

Joby looked around furtively. 'Wow, Melody, you sure know how to pick the perfect location for a Halloween party. I'm expecting Dracula to step out from behind a dark corner of this old estate any minute now.'

Melody shook her head. 'Uh-uh. Dracula wasn't written yet.'

Brittany leaned towards Joby and spoke with wide eyes, in a hypnotized kind of voice. 'Just because his story wasn't written till 1897, doesn't mean he didn't exist in 1845!'

Sarah laughed. 'Why would you know when Dracula was written?'

Brittany threw a pinch of popcorn at her. 'Oh, this coming from the one being swallowed up by her petticoats!'

Melody threw a handful of popcorn at the two of them. 'Ladies, please! Remember, we are representing proper Victorian women. Let's begin to act like it!'

•◇•◇•◇•◇•◇•◇•◇•◇•◇•

Sarah looked down at the floral design on the ornate brass hand mirror in her left hand; Melody shoved a candlestick into her other. Sarah looked up at her with a questioning expression. 'Why do I have to do this, again?'

'Because you lost, and this is the consequence you randomly drew.'

Joby smiled. 'And, hey, don't think of it as a punishment. If this little trick works, you'll see the reflection of your future true love.'

Sarah looked back at the basement door behind her. 'Walking backward down the stairs, with a candlestick, while looking into a hand mirror? The next face I see will be the face of a doctor.'

Brittany opened the door, allowing a stray black cat to hurry into the darkness. Melody lit the candle. Positioning herself at the top of the basement stairs, Sarah gave a smile to her three friends. 'Well, here goes!'

•◇•◇•◇•◇•◇•◇•◇•◇•◇•

Terence gulped the last of his punch and firmly set the small glass down on the flat top of the end of the banister. He glanced up the stairs at the sound of laughter erupting from behind the closed door and rolled his eyes. The dark basement was hardly the place to spend a holiday evening, but he had to get away from the noisy crowd of partygoers. The path to all other exits being blocked, the basement was his only way out. With the light of the waxing gibbous moon every now and again peeking through the slowly moving clouds streaming through the small, high window, he had just enough light to not trip over anything in the dark.

He didn't think he could take one more flirtation thrown his way from the silly young females of Whitstead. Ever since he inherited his father's estate, two years ago in the autumn of 1843, young Lord Melville found himself the most eligible bachelor in the region. The ridiculous, superstitious games played at these All Hallows' Eve parties, trying to predict romantic futures, only heightened the ambitions of the girls who set their hopes on him. No, not on him. On his wealth and title. He knew marriage was expected of one in his position. But how would he find a wife who really loved him, for himself, someone with whom he could have a happy, peaceful marriage?

Suddenly, an eerie bluish light caught his eye, about halfway up the stairs. He thought, perhaps, it was a beam of moonlight reflecting off the brass knob of the door. But no. The light grew, till it was a circle almost as tall as himself. Soon, a black cat emerged from one side of it, hurrying past him with a 'me-ow'. Terence scowled after it but was quickly drawn back to the light as he saw a dark form begin to take shape at the centre and slowly become larger as it drew closer to him. It was the back of a young woman. The light from the candle in her right hand caused him to clearly see his reflection in the hand mirror she held in her left hand. When his face appeared over her shoulder, she jumped and cried out. Spinning around, she lost her footing. Dropping the candle and mirror, she fell into the arms of Lord Terence Melville.

•◇•◇•◇•◇•◇•◇•◇•◇•◇•

Sarah stared up into blue eyes under dark, furrowed brows. The pale, chiselled face was framed by unruly strands of dark-brown hair. The gentleman's firmly set lips parted, as if to speak, but no words came. Sarah felt his strong arms bracing her up and holding her close. Realizing the awkwardness of the moment, she wriggled free of his grasp. 'I'm all right, now. Thank you.' Then, laughing nervously, 'Melody sure went all out with this game! Wherever did she find you? How did you get down here without us seeing? Have you been here all night?'

Terence shook his head. 'I'm afraid you have me at a disadvantage. I know of no one called Melody.'

Sarah looked at the stranger, quizzically, then nodded. 'Oh, I see. Staying in character. Well done. Let's go back to the others.'

The young lord impulsively caught her wrist as she turned towards the door. 'Please, wait!' Terence was surprised at himself for this sudden action and sincere plea. Something intrigued him about the seemingly magical appearance of this lovely creature, and the fact that she was ready to leave his presence so quickly; this was a stark contrast to the giggling girls who crowded him at every turn.

Sarah stood there a moment, silent, as she studied his earnest expression by the moonlight; she saw a sadness and a gentle longing that pulled at her heart. A maternal instinct arose in her to reach down and care for the boy she saw behind the pain in those sapphire eyes, though she estimated he was a few years older than herself. She summoned a smile to mask the emotion she felt rising. 'All right. We can probably sit and talk for a while before my friends come hunting for us.'

Together, Sarah and Terence sat down on the stairs. Terence began the conversation by asking who her friends were.

'Brittany, Joby and Melody. Melody is kind of our appointed leader. I'm Sarah. We're foreign exchange students from America, graduating next year. We're all cosplayers. You know, we make our own costumes and stuff. We're totally into the whole Victorian era, so Melody had this great idea, that we have a Victorian themed Halloween party! She did all the research and planning. She found this perfect village frozen in time. Whitstead, they call it? Did you take a look around this place? They've kept it up really well. Most of the buildings are still intact, and even still furnished! Oh, I could explore this town forever!'

Sarah's mood turned from wistful to almost frightened at the look she saw on her companion's face. He stared at her intently, a scowl on his brow. She gave a nervous laugh. 'Did I say something wrong?'

Terence shook his head. 'No. Please pardon my expression. It's only — I'm at a loss for how to respond. I'm afraid I hardly understand a word you just said.'

Sarah laughed, relaxing. 'Oh, no problem. I have a habit of talking too much and too fast. There. I'm done. Tell me about yourself.'

Terence hesitated. 'You really have no idea who I am?'

Sarah looked at him a moment before answering. 'Should I?'

He gave a rare smile, showing a bit of relief. 'No. I suppose not. My name's Terence. This is my friends' home. I live not far from here.'

'And can you usually be found hiding in your friends' basements? Or is that just on special occasions, and to frighten unsuspecting partygoers?'

He laughed. 'No. I usually can be quite civil at parties. But I do prefer more peaceful surroundings, by myself.'

Sarah nodded as she looked around. 'You can't get much more alone in a peaceful surrounding than a basement, I suppose.'

Terence was seized by a sudden impulse to trust his new companion with a secret. 'I say! There is a better spot, a place I like to go and think. Would you like to see it?'

Sarah hesitated. 'But, my friends —'

'Your friends haven't come looking for you yet. They're doubtless preoccupied with a game.'

'But how will we escape without being seen?'

Just then, a golden glow appeared, low to the ground, on a wall of the basement. The glow began to grow, removing the wall with it, making an open access to the outside. A young boy on the other side called out, 'Margie!' The wall began to close. Terence grabbed Sarah's hand and whispered, 'Hurry!' The two squeezed through the opening as it closed behind them. Looking down the road, they saw a little boy running, pulling a smaller, golden-haired girl behind him.

Terence was quickly learning to not question the magical things he had seen take place on this night, especially since they were bringing him good fortune. He smiled as he turned towards Sarah but found her countenance in opposition to his own. Sarah's eyes were wide, and her mouth hung open as she looked around. She shook her head. 'I don't understand. Where are we? Where's the car park? Where's the sign for the hotel?' In a daze, she walked towards the windows of the house and stared blankly at the guests inside. 'Where did all those people come from? Where are my friends?'

Terence's heart ached at the sound of panic and fear in Sarah's voice. Instinctively, he reached out to touch her arm in comfort.

Sarah pulled away and spun around. 'No! Who are you? What's going on?'

Terence felt he needed to tell her everything and anything that might put her mind at ease. 'I'm Lord Terence Melville. You're in Whitstead. It's All Hallows' Eve, 1845.'

Sarah shook her head. 'No. It's 2015. I'm staying the night with my university friends at this hotel.' She pointed to the lively house.

'This is Whitmore Park, the estate of my friends, the Fentimans. They're hosting an All Hallows' Eve masquerade. I was in the basement when I saw a blue light suddenly appear on the stairs, down which you came, walking backward, holding a candle in one hand and a small mirror in the other. When you saw my reflection over your shoulder, you lost your footing and dropped what you were holding. Just before you came through the light, a black cat preceded you.'

Sarah looked down and spoke thoughtfully. 'The hand mirror game. I walked backwards. Too far back? Is that even possible? But that golden glow in the wall, our escape. That was real. I don't understand it, but it was real.'

Terence stepped close to Sarah and resisted the impulse to slip his arms around this otherworldly creature and draw her close. He steadied his voice to speak to her gently. 'Sarah, I don't know how you are here, or whence you've come, but let us not question how delightful company has come to be. May we not enjoy a little more time in each other's presence?'

Sarah felt inexplicably drawn to this stranger with sapphire eyes, but shook her head and replied, 'I have to get back. I don't belong here.'

Terence released a breathless laugh as he offered her his hand. 'Neither do I.'

•◇•◇•◇•◇•◇•◇•◇•◇•◇•

Sarah listened to the rain outside as she lay on the soft rug in front of the ample fireplace. She was grateful for the warmth of the fire, and that she and Terence had made it safely inside his house before the rain had soaked completely through her layers of skirts. 'It's so peaceful here. So quiet. And yet, sometimes I think I can hear a kind of ethereal music somewhere in the distance. I'm not sure where it's coming from.'

Terence, sitting near her, looked over his shoulder, away from his pocket-sized pad and pencil, towards a long window. 'It's coming from out there, within the forest.' Sarah rolled over onto her stomach, leaning on her elbows, to look in the direction of his gaze. Terence continued, 'I've heard that music all my life. As a small boy, I once ventured out to find its source. But when I approached a certain point, it came to an abrupt stop.'

Sarah looked up at him with a smile. 'I would've liked to see you as a child. Tell me, what kind of a boy were you? Were you very grave and serious, the way you looked when I first saw you? Or were you full of energy and fun?'

Going back to his work with the pad and pencil, he responded, 'The former, I'm afraid. Father was very strict and had firm convictions on exactly how a 'little gentleman' ought to behave. I felt much more at ease with my mother.'

'What was your mother like?'

Terence was silent a moment before he answered, his voice becoming soft. 'She was beautiful, patient, and kind. She was the perfect, submissive wife. An ideal ornament for my father, his title, and his estate. I always had the impression that she felt as trapped in my father's world as I did. The only time I ever remember her eyes truly coming to life and shining is when she would come home from a trip she and Father had taken. She'd always bring back a new piece of artwork, a painting, a sculpture, or something of that nature. Then she would sit with me and talk to me about the item, telling me where she got it and about the person who created it. With each trip she would bring some sort of artistic implements home to me. That was the only defiance of my father that I ever saw in my mother: her encouragement of my love for art. It was as if she felt imprisoned in my father's world and was determined to provide me the keys by which I might escape. But it hasn't proved so easy. I've discovered that my prison extends far beyond the walls of my father's estate; it stretches to every corner of high society.' Sarah noted the tightening of Terence's jaw and of his grip on the pencil in his hand as he continued, 'I'm repulsed by conventionalism!'

'So, why not be unconventional?'

He smiled. 'You almost make me think I could.' Then, referring to his friend's teenage sisters, 'Why is it that Cordelia may paint and Beatrice can spend her time frolicking out of doors, whilst I must manfully set my drawing aside?'

'Maybe you need to stop seeing your wealth and title as a curse. You could come up with clever ways to use it for others and, at the same time, do what you love.'

'You make it sound so simple.'

'Maybe it is.'

He sighed. 'I am my father's only child, and a son. With no brothers, I am the only one to carry on the Melville name. Society is watching me closely. How often I have wanted to tear down my father's portrait in the great hall, but his judgmental eyes forbade me. I can feel them watching me from every point of that room.'

Sarah placed her hand on his. 'But they are not watching you. He's not there. Don't allow a ghost to intimidate you.'

Terence turned towards her and smiled. 'I wish it were your green eyes I always saw watching me. Then I do believe I would have the courage to stand against anything!'

Sarah's heart was stirred deeply as she felt held in the softness of his gaze. 'Then I hope you always see me watching you, cheering you on and encouraging your endeavours.'

Terence looked down at the drawing in his hand and passed it to Sarah. She took it and admired the pencil strokes. 'It's beautiful! But wait. Is this supposed to be me? I'm afraid you're no good, after all. This girl is far too lovely!'

Terence gently brushed back some strands of Sarah's long, black hair that she had taken down from their confines an hour or so ago, declaring that its length and fullness would help keep her warm. 'When I first saw you, I thought you were a witch. You may be yet, for the way you have bewitched my heart.'

•◊•◊•◊•◊•◊•◊•◊•◊•

Terence sat in his green velvet, high-back armchair, staring into the flames that danced in the fireplace; he rolled the handle of an ornate brass hand mirror with his thumb in his right hand. A black cat was curled up, asleep, on the hearth. The skies outside had cleared, adding crystal starlight to the moonlight coming through the windows of Caisteal Manor. But Terence was blind to the visible, aware only of a vision etched into his memory of the smooth complexion of a pale-ivory face—green eyes shining up at him, a smile playing across delicate, pink lips —all framed by full, black, silken hair. He seemed to see the girlish lady now, walking barefoot atop a low stone wall, trying to keep her balance, carrying her shoes and stockings in one hand and gripping her skirts in the other, as she carefully watched her feet make their way along. He thought, even now, he heard her laugh with an exclamation of triumph as she came to the end of the wall and hopped down.

The chiming of the one o'clock hour from the French-porcelain hand-painted clock on the mantel woke Terence from his trance. An hour exactly since the midnight hour that brought with it a blinding, blueish light that quickly vanished, taking Sarah away

141

with it. Looking up, he caught sight of his mother's portrait hanging above the clock. Her kind face seemed to look down upon him softly. He flickered a smile and spoke aloud, 'You would have been quite fond of her, Mama. She reminded me of you. Or what you might have been, if allowed to be.'

With the lingering memory of the enchantress who had entered and exited his life far too quickly, and the comfort of his mother's smile looking down upon him, Terence fell asleep. His hands relaxed, sending the mirror falling gently onto the soft rug beneath his chair.

• ◊ • ◊ • ◊ • ◊ • ◊ • ◊ • ◊ • ◊ • ◊ • ◊ •

Crunching fallen leaves under her feet that had blown into the abandoned estate through long-ago-broken windows and open doors, Sarah bent down and picked up the brass hand mirror on the floor beside the high-back armchair. She studied the ornate object as she sat down on the dusty, worn, green velvet chair.

Such magic had taken place over the last few hours. She thought it had finally come to an end upon her re-entry into her present day at the stroke of midnight. Back among her friends, she suddenly felt out of place. Her heart ached to be back with Terence. With him she had felt the joy of being needed. For the first time in her life, she had discovered the longing to give of herself, with no concern as to a return. Still, she was certain he did return her feelings of love. In his world and time, she had felt the belonging she lacked now; she had felt home.

Sarah looked up in surprise at the chiming from the French-porcelain, hand-painted clock on the mantel. The clock and the mantel appeared to be one, for all the dust and cobwebs that had accumulated there. Who kept the clock in working order? Sarah rose and stepped towards it. Thoughtfully, she ran her finger around the clock's face. Finding the latch, she opened back the glass. The face of the clock, having been sheltered from the years behind its glass door, looked as clean and fresh as the day it was painted and set into place. Sarah dusted her finger off on her dress before tracing the hands and embossed numbers of the clock. She wondered if this night could hold a little more magic.

Sarah lifted the hand mirror in her left hand, holding it facing over her left shoulder. Staring into the dark reflection of the empty chair behind her, she began to gently turn the hands on the clock backward. She kept steadily at her work till she felt a warmth coming from the fireplace before her. She heard a cat purring at her feet. Light from the fireplace lit the reflection in the mirror. She snatched her fingers away when she saw the sleeping form of Lord Terence Melville appear in the chair.

Sarah quickly turned and went to her knees before Terence in his chair. Looking up at his bowed head, she tenderly caressed the rebellious strands of dark-brown hair from his white brow. Her heartbeat quickened as his eyelashes fluttered open.

• ◊ • ◊ • ◊ • ◊ • ◊ • ◊ • ◊ • ◊ • ◊ • ◊ •

142

For a moment, Terence stared blankly at the young woman before him, as if he expected her to be an illusion from his dreams that would disappear at any moment. Then he saw her smile. He felt her fingers running through his hair and heard her gentle voice say, 'Hello'.

Terence's eyes filled with tears as he suddenly reached down and pulled the small, willing frame into his lap. He buried his face against her soft, white neck, moistening it with his tears and tender kisses. Sarah nestled against his broad chest like a wounded woodland creature finding shelter in a storm. At the same time, she cradled him and cooed over him like a mother with her new-born babe.

Finally, Terence looked earnestly into her face. 'How can you be here?'

Sarah smiled and repeated the words he had spoken to her earlier that evening, 'Let us not question how delightful company has come to be. May we not enjoy a little more time in each other's presence?'

He lowered his head. 'Yes, 'a little more time'. For I cannot be selfish and keep you forever. I know you must go back to your own world.'

Sarah gently lifted his face in her hands and looked deeply into his large, blue eyes. 'You are my world! You are my home. You are the beat of my heart, and without you I have no wish to live, at any point in time!'

Terence softly breathed her name as he caressed her face and brought it close to his, reverently receiving her lips against his own.

•◇•◇•◇•◇•◇•◇•◇•◇•

Three female university friends stood in the great hall of Caisteal Manor, studying a painting of a beautiful, raven-haired woman with laughing green eyes, walking atop a low stone wall. In one hand she held her shoes and stockings; in the other hand she held her skirts high, out of the way of her bare feet.

One of the girls shook her head. 'I know the tour guide said this painting was nearly one hundred and seventy years old, but it looks nothing like the style of the mid-1800s.'

Another answered, 'I read that Lord Terence Melville was a little eccentric. He took after his great-great-grandfather in that way.'

The third friend chimed in, with eyes shining. 'Oh, but his and Sarah's love story was so romantic and mysterious! No one's ever really known how they met or where she came from. But all accounts agree that they were so much in love!'

The second friend nodded. 'I know. But theirs isn't the only story in Whitstead that claims magical events happening regularly. Did you look at this book from the gift shop? The stories in here are unbelievable!'

The first, more sceptical friend agreed. 'Whitstead is a beautiful tourist trap. But they can't honestly expect us to believe all these fantastic stories.'

Just then, a fourth voice entered the conversation. 'Aye, yet 'faith be th' substance o' things hoped for, th' evidence o' things not seen,' so th' Holy Scripture says.'

The three girls turned to see a short, round, elderly woman standing with them. The hazel eyes beneath a floppy hat fixed themselves on the first friend. The strangely dressed woman reached into her apron pocket and pulled something out. Taking the girl's right hand, she quickly transferred the contents of her own and closed the girl's fingers around them. With a smile, the mysterious woman spoke softly to the younger, ''Blessed are they that have not seen and yet have believed.''

The friends all looked down to see what lay in their companion's palm. 'Lovely, little white flowers.'

Lifting their heads, they saw the woman stepping out of the house into the sunlight. They watched in awe as a small bird flew straight towards her and comfortably perched upon her shoulder. The silver-haired lady paused only a moment to pet a black cat curled up beside a small brass hand mirror.

Take Two
by Lauren H Salisbury *(science fiction)*

yuch and Harsci emerged from hyperspace twenty thousand cubits from planet #2319-42a, indigenous designation: Earth.

Turning to her pilot, Syuch suffused her body with maroon, letting him read her seriousness. 'Are you certain you left your palm pad behind? Could it not be somewhere onboard?' She glanced around, half expecting the missing device to appear behind a console. 'Unless you did it on purpose.'

'I promised not to lie to you again, and I never break my word. It must have fallen out of my pocket on the way back to the ship. I distinctly remember stowing it there before we left the domicile that last time because it dug into my side when I picked up the pudding bowl.' He lowered his head. 'I am sorry, Syuch.'

No trace of guilty orange showed beneath his translucent skin, only the same flicker of embarrassed puce as when he had first informed her of the problem.

'Fine. But if we cannot find it, we will have to inform the Directorate, and the closest you will ever get to data collection in the future will be viewing it from inside a processing cubicle.'

They dived into the planet's atmosphere and scanned the surface for the location of their previous visit. A layer of thick vapours shrouded the target area, but they were through it in a few moments, visibility restored. Water gave way to rugged terrain, followed by undulating countryside and evidence of settlements.

Syuch stared. 'Where is the snow?'

'What?' Harsci looked up from his display panel. 'Oh.'

'Indeed.' What had previously been a vast blanket of white was now muddy brown, the skeletal plants covering the landscape merging with their surroundings rather than standing in relief. How long had they been gone? 'I told you time dilation would be a problem going through the Kepel bridge. We should have returned via the Pyricon nebula.'

Harsci rounded his pilot's console and approached the forward viewer, his inner hue turning ruddy. 'It looks completely different.'

'Well, we are here now. Let us just hope none of the peoples found your pad whilst we were gone.'

They landed in the same spot as before and secured the ship, Syuch checking the cloaking device twice for glitches. Then they shifted into their people forms, donned the clothing Harsci retrieved from the storage bay, and stepped out onto a thick layer of plant matter in various stages of decay.

Syuch activated her palm pad's tracking programme and swung it slowly from side to side. If Harsci had dropped his pad nearby, she would soon pick up the signal. Maybe they could be back in orbit and on their way to Zomidia II before anyone even realised they were here.

Harsci's hesitant throat-clearing crushed that hope like a Cethi giant stepping on a bug. She lowered her pad and looked over at him. 'What now?'

'Um.' He glanced away, rubbing the back of his head under the tall hat he wore. 'If as much time has passed here as I suspect, the pad's battery will be empty.'

She narrowed her eyes, then tilted her head to the side and blew out through her nose. 'Why in the name of the universe do I put up with you?'

'Because I helped you regain your natural curiosity and encourage you to try new things?'

Without another word, Syuch set off in the direction of the domicile they had used previously. The route was easier to navigate without the snow slowing her progress, and though the air threw a constant drizzle over the area, it was not as cold either.

Something crunched behind her, and a moment later, she caught sight of Harsci in her periphery. Wisely, he followed her lead and walked in silence, searching the ground for a flash of white polymer amidst the muted oranges and browns.

When they reached the domicile, she strode for the door, wanting nothing more than to get out of the worsening rain. Harsci could search outside whilst she dried off and —

She froze just inside the entrance, gripping the doorknob hard enough to cause it to creak. Before her, backlit by a flickering fire on the stone plinth, stood a diminutive female ladling something from a steaming pot into a cup. Warmth washed over Syuch, bringing with it the scent of cooked onions and herbs she remembered from their previous visit. The female turned, and their eyes met, the female's widening as her mouth dropped open.

'What are you doing here?' Syuch blurted.

'I-I'm sorry.' Fine tremors shook the female's hands as she backed away. 'They said this place was empty, and we had nowhere else to go.'

'Be at ease, my good woman.' Harsci squeezed past Syuch and held his arms out in a soothing gesture. 'My name is Arthur Cobbett, and this is my sister, Elizabeth. Please excuse her barging in like that. We did not know the building was occupied.'

'Margaret Pettleston — Maggie.' The female — woman — Maggie — offered a tremulous smile, bobbing her body down and up and brushing wisps of hair away from her face. 'What can I do for you, sir?'

Harsci removed his hat. 'We stayed here the last time we passed through the area and accidentally left my — something behind. We are here to collect it.'

Maggie slid the cup onto the table, her eyes bouncing between them. 'There was nothing here when we arrived. Honestly, sir. We would've set it aside if there were.'

Syuch slumped. It was to be expected – she had cleared the domicile herself before their departure – but she had hoped to find the pad quickly and quietly.

'Might I ask what you left behind? Maybe I missed it.'

'You would not have,' Syuch said. She held up her hands a span apart. 'It is a white rectangle this size with a black scr-top.'

'The puzzle box?'

The weak voice came from the shadows beside the left-hand wall. Syuch jerked her head towards the sound, her gaze piercing the dimness to find a small boy lying on a sleeping mat under a thin blanket. No wonder she had missed him. His skin had a grey, sickly pallor, his cheeks sunken, and damp hair stuck to his forehead. A wracking cough convulsed him, confirming her assessment of his grave condition.

Maggie knelt beside him when the coughing continued and, holding him upright, rubbed his back.

Syuch glanced around the rest of the domicile in case there were more peoples hidden in the recesses. A container of woven plant material holding a mountain of fabric sat along the opposite wall. Beside it was a metal tub with a long, ridged piece propped against the rim.

Otherwise, the small room was almost as empty as they had left it. No hint of a palm pad in sight. She returned her attention to the intruders – peoples.

When the boy's coughing finally eased and his head flopped back against Maggie's arm, she reached for the cup behind her and held it to his lips. The liquid trickled down his chin.

She lowered him back down, then stood and faced Syuch and Harsci again, moisture edging her eyes. 'He's been sick for a month. Came on so quick, I –' She sucked in a breath and raised her chin. 'A puzzle box, you say?'

'Er, yes, that is it. A puzzle box.' Harsci flashed her a smile before addressing the boy. 'Where is it now?'

Glazed eyes opened in their general direction, but the slurred mumble the boy emitted was incomprehensible. Syuch and Harsci turned as one to his mother.

Her lips pursed as she looked down at her son, a deep vee pulling her brows together. 'He did say something about a puzzle box when we first arrived, but I was so worried about everything else, I wasn't really listening.'

'Do you know where he stowed it?' Syuch asked.

Maggie looked up, panic written across her expression as she shook her head. 'I'm sorry. It's probably hidden somewhere with his other treasures.'

Syuch only blinked, a lifetime of exemplary service crumbling around the edges of her vision.

The woman rambled on. 'We lost our farm when the harvest failed, and the landlord took everything we owned when he evicted us, said it would take every scrap to pay off the overdue rent. So Jack hides his things outside now, or he did, before he got sick.

'Was it expensive, the puzzle box? We don't have any way to replace it right now, but my husband's out looking for work, and…'

Syuch's entire body pulled taut. An indigenous lifeform had discovered their advanced technology. They needed to get it back before it influenced the development of the species. 'We will leave now and look for it ourselves.' She spun to the door, then stopped and turned back, recalling Harsci's instructions on leave-taking. 'Thank you for a pleasant evening.'

With that, she strode outside into the drizzle and headed for the swathe of tall plants to the left, kicking through mounds of decaying plant matter with the toe of her boot.

'We should heal the boy,' Harsci said from behind her a few moments later. 'Then he can show us where he hid it.'

'Have you lost your senses as well as your equipment?' She sniffed. 'We can find it on our own. A puzzle box? He might not have even meant the palm pad.'

Harsci gave her an incredulous look, which she studiously ignored. A droplet of cold water slid down her neck, and she suppressed a shudder, hunching into the collar of her clothing. The climate was utterly miserable. How did it not break the peoples' will to survive?

The rain stopped sometime after they entered the woods, as Harsci called the array of tall plants. They continued to search, digging through sodden mulch and overturning every loose stone they came across, until the sun disappeared below the horizon and the lights of the settlement dwindled to pinpricks. Only when it became too dark to see beyond their outstretched arms did they retreat to the ship for the night.

Harsci tried to raise the notion of healing the boy again, but Syuch gave him a quelling look, her body flaring scarlet. Bad enough he had put them in this situation without adding to their list of infractions. She had no wish to be confined to the home world, stripped of her rank and all previous achievements.

•◇•◇•◇•◇•◇•◇•◇•◇•◇•

They set out again the next morning with a new strategy—focus on the settlement itself. There were plenty of places among the buildings for a small boy to hide things. Harsci started at the far end whilst Syuch began with the dwellings nearest the domicile—cottage. Blast his insistence on learning more of the language. Hopefully, when they met in the middle that afternoon, the palm pad would be in their possession and they could leave this place forever.

She studied the immediate area, eyes narrowed as she considered the options. Where would a small boy place his valued belongings? A bird flying out of a box attached to the nearest cottage caught her attention, but it was too high for the boy to reach, so she lowered her gaze to more likely locations at ground level.

She was investigating a hole in the wall between two larger cottages some time later when light footsteps splashed towards her.

'Penny for the guy?'

Syuch glanced up. Before her stood two small peoples carrying what appeared to be a straw-stuffed bag covered in a threadbare set of male clothing. A crooked line and two spots had been crudely marked onto the section of bag that poked up from the collar, and a worn hat perched on top.

She dragged her eyes from the lumpy mess to the boy on its left, then the slightly taller girl on its right and back again. The clothing hanging from their thin frames was little better than the rags on the thing they held between them.

'Penny for the guy,' the boy repeated, holding the thing out as if for closer inspection.

They wanted her to buy it?

Syuch pulled one of the metal disks Harsci had forced her to carry around from her pocket. She had no idea what she would do with whatever it was, but if the sale would satisfy the gleam of expectation in their eyes, she would oblige. Tossing the disk to the girl, she leaned down and hoisted the guy into her arms. It smelled like the wrong end of a hinosat, and she wrinkled her nose.

The peoples stared, open mouthed as she walked past them. Was the metal disk worth significantly more than the amount they had specified? It mattered not.

Apparently, it did. The peoples spoke from behind her at the same time.

'Oi, wha'cher doin'?'

'Hey, tha's ours.'

Syuch spun back to them, brows raised. Had they not requested she buy the prickly monstrosity now tucked under her arm? They glowered at her, little hands balled into fists at their sides.

She was saved from having to admit she had no idea of the value of the disk she had given them by Harsci appearing at her side. He took the sagging bag and handed it back to the little girl, causing Syuch's lower jaw to drop. Before she could reprimand him, he said, 'I apologise. My sister does not understand the tradition. We are not from here.'

The girl hefted the bag of straw, eyeing Syuch. 'Figured that when she took our guy.'

Harsci grinned and lifted his hat, then gripped Syuch's elbow and turned her in the opposite direction, walking away fast enough that she had to lift her clothing to ensure she did not trip over it.

'What did you do that for?' she whispered.

'You are supposed to give them money for looking at their creation, not buy it.'

She gaped at him. 'Are you sure? That makes no sense whatsoever.'

'It is part of a custom called Guy Forks Day. The man on crutches over there' — he pointed across the street to a man surrounded by children — 'is quite affable and has been telling me all about it.'

Syuch bit back her reminder that the last time Harsci had encountered a local custom, they had only realised the extent of his translation errors after their departure. 'And?'

'I think it is a celebration of some sort of ancient hero.'

•◊•◊•◊•◊•◊•◊•◊•◊•◊•

Back on the ship, Syuch shed her people form and flexed her muscles. It felt good to be in her own shape again, especially after a long day of fruitless searching culminating in that bizarre encounter with the peoples. She made her way into the galley and straight over to the replicator, where she chose her favourite meal.

When it was ready, she relaxed into a recliner with the steaming bowl of dawaha on her lap. The spicy aroma eased the last of her tension, and she scooped up a large portion. At the first ingested cube, the colour beneath her skin rippled, oscillating from yellow to mauve to deep aramide and back again at the familiar burst of flavour.

'Enjoying a taste of home?' Harsci flopped down beside her, also in his true form, and reached for a cube. His body thrummed with contented violet as he closed his eyes.

When he opened them again, his colour settled into a solid, serious red. 'We need to heal the boy. Our chances of finding the palm pad on our own are negligible. We both know this by now. And it will be discovered at some point — if not by the boy when he recovers then by another people in the future. We cannot allow that to happen.'

The dawaha soured, and Syuch set it aside, then eased over to the replicator. She barely registered the selection she made, her mind awhirl with questions for which she had no answers. At least, no satisfactory ones.

Intervene in the fate of an indigenous lifeform or leave the species exposed to technology beyond their comprehension? Either went against everything she had been trained to uphold. She sipped from her cup, pleasantly surprised to discover it contained hot fressil gar.

It came down to which option had the least impact, which appeared clear. Only... 'To heal him would be a deliberate act.'

She turned back to Harsci. 'Losing the palm pad was an accident. You are asking me to choose in which manner we will break the first rule of data collection.'

'I am sorry, Syuch.' His hue mottled, guilty orange mingling with shamed brown. 'I thought being a data collector would be the greatest adventure, and all I have done is bring you woe on woe.'

Silently, Syuch agreed. How had it come to this? First in her class, highest ranked of the collectors, her record was unblemished—even after the unfortunate incident her late partner had caused on Dracon. A breach of this magnitude could ruin her. She sucked in a breath to tell him so.

Not all close quarters data collection is straightforward. The age-gravelled voice of her instructor back at the training core floated across her memory, making her pause. *Occasionally, a species will surprise you, and you must be prepared to act decisively at a moment's notice.*

Her early years of active duty had been littered with such thrilling encounters, until her rise through the ranks had brought about a more cautious approach. One borne—it struck her now—not of experience but of the desire to protect her prestigious position. Decades of increasingly remote techniques had smothered the last of her passion into nought but cool detachment. Was that the legacy she would pass to Harsci?

She straightened and glided over to him. 'Data collecting *is* the greatest adventure. But it is not always as simple as the training programme would have us believe. Sometimes, difficult decisions have to be made in the field.'

He looked up at her, hopeful teal tingeing his expression. 'So what should we do?'

She met his eyes and attempted a smile. 'What we must.'

The next morning, Syuch trudged behind Harsci along the path to their old cottage. The weather echoed her mood, sheets of grey rain blurring the plants around them into indistinct, twisted shapes and turning the ground into a squelching river of mud. So many ways their plan could go wrong. So many ways they could be punished if it did.

By the time they stepped inside, the door held open for them by a wide-eyed Maggie, Syuch was on the uncomfortable side of damp. She walked over to the fire and held her hands out to its warmth.

'Oh, my. What has you out and about in this weather?' Maggie asked, taking Harsci's dripping outer clothing and draping it over the back of a chair.

'We have come to see if we can help your boy,' Harsci replied.

She clasped her hands together. 'Oh, sir. Do you think you can?'

'Maybe. Elizabeth has a new treatment for this type of disease that is not yet known among your local healers. Now tell me, how long has he been...'

Whilst Harsci distracted Maggie, Syuch knelt next to the boy's sleeping mat. His skin was clammy, his breath shallow and wheezing, and his head lolled listlessly to the side. He would die within days without treatment. She scanned his body, finding a bacterial infection centred around his lungs. Such a simple thing to fix.

With a quick glance over her shoulder to ensure Harsci still held Maggie's attention, Syuch pulled a healing module from her pocket and held it over the boy's chest. It activated immediately, the power it contained seeking out and destroying the disease, repairing damaged cells as it flooded his system.

Syuch focused on the module, watching the energy blaze to life, the colours shifting as it worked. Warmth seeped into her hand and with it a sense of peace she had not realised how much she had missed. She let it take her back to the home world, to her pod-mates and the training core where she –

The boy gasped, his wide-eyed gaze riveted to her hand, where the energy from the module cast a white glow over her skin. Finished. Syuch cursed and pulled back, tucking the module into a fold of her clothing.

'Are you an angel?' he whispered.

She blinked. 'No.'

His brows scrunched. 'You sure?'

'Quite. You should feel better now.'

He cautiously, almost experimentally, sucked in a lungful of air. Then he sat up and tried again. 'Mum! I can breathe!' he yelled, his thin face beaming.

Maggie spun and took in her son, her mouth opening. Her eyes filled with water, and a soft moan escaped her lips. Then she was flying across the small space, throwing herself to her knees, and wrapping her arms around the boy. 'Oh, Jack! Oh, my Jack! Thank you, Lord, thank you!'

Syuch stood and edged out of their way, pocketing the module as she gave Harsci a confirming nod.

A hand shot out and grasped her empty one, bringing her eyes back down. 'Thank you,' Maggie said. 'I don't know what I would've done if –' She swallowed, brushed a trail of water from her face. 'Just thank you.'

Squeezing her son again, she kissed the top of his head, then pushed up to her feet, facing Syuch and Harsci. 'How can I ever repay you?'

Harsci spread his hands. 'It was nothing.' He glanced at Syuch. 'But, perhaps now, Jack can help us find our puzzle box?'

Maggie looked down at the boy and back at them. 'Of course. As soon as he is well enough to –'

'I can take 'em now.' The boy scrambled to his feet and stared at Syuch as if she were one of the Prime Directors themselves.

'I'm not sure you're ready to go out yet. Maybe in a few days.'

His face fell, and he kicked at the floor with one foot. 'But I feel fine, Mum.'

Maggie turned questioning eyes to them.

'Our medicine is fast-working,' Harsci said. 'He should be fully recovered by –'

Syuch cleared her throat. Much as they needed to recover the palm pad, talk of miracle cures would do them no favours. It still paid to use some caution.

'By the morning,' Harsci finished with a smile.

'That was medicine?' The boy peered up at Syuch, head cocked, forehead puckered. 'I never seen anything work on the 'sum'shun before.'

'We have much experience with curing diseases where I am from. But please, do not mention it to anyone. We cannot heal anyone else.'

His eyes flicked to her pocket and back, then he nodded, biting his lip. 'You ran out. Don't worry, Miss. I can keep a secret. Just… Thank you for savin' me.'

He threw himself at her, wrapping his arms around her middle and squeezing. She stared down at him, her own arms raised high above his head, then slowly lowered them and awkwardly patted his back until he let go.

'It was nothing,' she said, her insides warming despite her best efforts.

'Let the lady go, Jack,' Maggie tugged the boy back and gave Syuch an apologetic smile. 'You'll make a mess of her fine gown.'

They managed to extricate themselves from the cottage, after much unnecessary fussing from Maggie, and as soon as they were outside, Harsci excused himself with the flimsiest reason for heading into the settlement that Syuch had ever heard. Nevertheless, she let him go. She needed the solitude to process what she had just done.

Because *she* had done it, not Harsci. She had used their advanced technology to heal a lifeform that should otherwise have died. She had broken the first rule of data collection—changed the fates of those whom she observed.

What implications would her actions have? What future events would occur because she had intervened? She had chosen the optimum course, all things considered. But the questions remained, shadows of repercussions drifting in her periphery as she traversed the woods towards their ship.

'Tomorrow,' she assured herself. Tomorrow, they would retrieve the palm pad, and the risk she had taken would be rewarded. Or her days as a data collector were numbered.

●◇●◇●◇●◇●◇●◇●◇●◇●

'That is where you hide your things? Up there?'

Jack shrugged. 'There's some big holes in these trees.' He frowned, little fists bunching. 'An' no landlord'll think to search 'em!'

Syuch eyed the thick, tall plant with a dubious frown. 'And you can get up there without assistance?'

'O'course. I been climbing trees since I were small. This one's easy.' A grin flashed across his grubby face, and he set off for the plant—tree—at a run.

She stood dumbfounded as he scrambled up it as easily as he had walked along the path. It had never occurred to her that peoples would climb trees. All evidence pointed to them making their homes at ground level. Why had they not considered it earlier?

Pieces of plant matter, dislodged from his ascent, rained down on her and Harsci. She blinked against the fragments seeking her eyes and stepped out of range, but Harsci merely brushed some debris from his shoulder, his gaze fixed on the small boy now approximately three lengths above their heads.

She tapped her foot against the damp undergrowth whilst she waited for him to recover the palm pad. To think it had been safely hidden away in the hole of a tree all this time. Jack was certainly a fascinating people. The warmth of his thin arms lingered where he had touched her the day before, tugging at the corners of her lips. She flattened them with a quick sideways glance at Harsci.

'You like him,' he said.

Blast him for noticing. She lifted her chin. 'He is retrieving your palm pad. I am grateful we will not need to report the loss to the Directorate.'

Harsci winced, but a shout from above saved him from having to reply.

'I've got it.'

There was no further movement for a few moments, and Syuch twisted her fingers together. What if Jack had been mistaken about his 'puzzle box' and the palm pad was elsewhere? Had all this been in vain?

Something rustled above, and he half climbed half slid back down the tree, landing at its base with a soft thud. He lofted the palm pad in one hand, then examined it, his forehead puckering.

'I don't think the rain got to it. How's it work, anyway? I can't see any hinges, and it's a strange shape for a puzzle box.'

Syuch stepped forwards and slid it from his unresisting grasp. Relief swept through her as her fingers closed over the cool polymer, the tension in her gut finally unspooling. She cast Harsci a look before returning her attention to Jack. 'It is a special design that only we know how to open.'

'Oh,' Jack said.

His eyes gleamed with interest, so she stowed the palm pad in the pocket of her clothing. 'Thank you for returning this to us. We are in your debt.'

'Not half as much as I am. I thought I was goin' to die.'

Water welled in his eyes, and he gripped her around the middle again. She raised one brow at Harsci, who shrugged, and squeezed Jack back. The action came more naturally this time, and she could not decide what that said about her as a data collector.

After a few moments, she disengaged and gave him a bright smile. 'It was a pleasure to meet you. Goodbye, Jack.'

She motioned to Harsci and turned in the direction of their ship, but Jack spoke before she took her first step.

'You're not stayin' for the bonfire?'

She shook her head. 'We have a long journey ahead of us and we must be on our way.'

Harsci coughed beside her. 'Um, about that…'

Slowly, she twisted to face him, suspicion tightening her muscles. He refused to meet her eyes as he said, 'I might have agreed to provide assistance at the celebration.'

'You did what?'

'Mr Mattie needed someone to help with the fireworks, and I gave my word. I cannot go back on it now.'

She gave him a look that promised there would be much he would not be able to do when she had finished with him. 'Fine,' she gritted. 'We will stay for the celebration of Guy Forks.'

'Yes!' Jack leaped into the air, reminding her of his presence. He set off for the settlement at a run, calling over his shoulder, 'I'll tell Mum you're stayin'.'

When he was out of hearing, Harsci stepped closer to Syuch. 'There is only one problem left. What are we going to tell the Directorate?'

She considered letting him suffer for a few rotations, but the deep crease between his brows and the way he bit his lip softened her resolve. 'I have been giving that some thought,' she said, following Jack's progress through the trees. 'And I think I have a plan.'

Harsci grinned from ear to ear. 'Yes, sir.'

Autumnus Triumphant
by Ari Lewis (*ghost story*)

At last, she had escaped from her nephew's first birthday celebration. Stealing away to her room to paint, she heard a rise of voices from the end of the corridor, so Cordelia Fentiman, youngest daughter of the earl of Morestead, dove into an empty guest room and hid behind the door. The voices came and went. About to release a sigh, she heard an unmistakable tap along the passage—her grandmother's walking stick. The tapping stopped just on the other side of the door. Then her grandmother's imperious tone rang out.

'What do you think you are doing in that corner?'

Instinctively straightening, she prayed that her grandmother's question had been directed at someone else.

'Do not deceive yourself that I cannot see you just because I must use eye-glasses on occasion. Come out this instant.'

The sigh finally fled, and with a bowed head, Cordelia came away from her hiding place. 'Grandmama, it was not at all because…' she began, raising her head, but faltered.

Her grandmother had her back to Cordelia. The object of her injunction, to Cordelia's amazement and accelerating horror, was the apparition of a man in his thirties hovering sheepishly behind a portrait of a long-deceased ancestor. She could feel a scream forming in the depths of her mind and making its way to her mouth.

'Uncle Leo,' the dowager Lady Fentiman sighed, 'do come down from there.'

'But Eleanor, I really cannot work in these conditions,' the ghost complained as he continued to hover the portrait. 'There are too many people, and the atmosphere is not conducive for the muse to descend.'

The scream was now in Cordelia's throat.

'My dear fellow,' sighed the dowager, 'you are dead because you waited beside an open window through a thunderstorm for a muse that would not come. Now that you are what you are, you must make the best of it and get to work.'

At last, the scream escaped between Cordelia's lips in a sharp shrill before she could clamp her hands over her mouth. The two others turned to her. Uncle Leo darted back behind the portrait.

On seeing her youngest granddaughter, Lady Eleanor smiled. Cordelia started to draw back, but her grandmother stretched out a hand towards her. 'Your appearance is most serendipitous, my dear. Providential, likely as not.'

Cordelia tried to protest, but her voice seemed to flee each time her eyes darted up to the spectre. Instead, she was insistently drawn forwards in the way that only frail old women can to healthy younger generations.

'Cordelia, may I present Leopold Henry Updike Elmsworth, your grandfather's maternal great uncle. He is quite harmless if a bit self-important.' She then directed her voice to the portrait. 'Uncle Leo, this is my granddaughter, Cordelia.'

Nothing appeared or moved from the area around the portrait. Each silent second seemed like a passing age to Cordelia. Her grandmother's foot began to tap. 'Uncle Leo, has death robbed you not only of breath but also your good manners?'

The apparition reappeared and floated down to the ground. Cordelia fought between the urge to squeeze her eyes shut and the sense that her eyes were trying to pop out of her head. In her terror, she fixated on his costume. Whilst quite out of the modern fashion, his clothes were neat and well-tailored. Atop his head, he wore a wide-brimmed hat with a plume. She tried not to notice how she could almost see through him to the other side of the room.

A few steps from her, he swept the hat from his head in a stately bow. Cordelia dropped a curtsy that would have been a full collapse if not for her grandmother's steady hand beneath her elbow. 'Forgive me, dear Cordelia,' Leopold apologised. 'It is a pleasure to make your acquaintance.'

'The pleasure is mine,' Cordelia rasped.

Leopold's face fell, and he took several steps back and into the air. 'You see, Eleanor. I am unfit to meet any living creature in this unholy state.' He began to float back to his haunt around the painting when Lady Eleanor's voice arrested his ascent.

'Then what am I? A wraith?'

'You know perfectly well, Eleanor, that you are different and thus cannot be counted with the rest of creation.'

'Tish tosh. Your vanity is merely wounded because this pretty young girl is afraid of you instead of being at her ease.'

To Cordelia, the apparition seemed to sulk. In that moment, she saw in him her brothers and male friends who had had their vanity wounded. She could not suppress the giggle that danced up her throat and finally into her mouth. Her grandmother gave her a surprised look and then proceeded to laugh with her. Leopold, glancing over his shoulder, gave his two relations a withering look.

'Dear Uncle Leo, you must understand how absurd you look, acting like a child unjustly put in the corner,' Lady Eleanor said between fits of laughter. 'Come now, be friends. You must show Cordelia your masterpiece. She too is an artist.'

At this, the apparition visibly brightened and became more animated. 'Would you indeed like to see my work, Cordelia? Would it interest you?'

'But of course, Uncle Leopold,' she answered. 'Is it one of the ones in the gallery?'

Disappointment flitted across Leopold's face before he could collect himself. 'No, it is my private masterpiece,' he finally said.

'Meaning it is unfinished,' further explained Lady Eleanor, 'and thus has been for his eyes only.'

Leopold threw up his hands dramatically and tried to fall languidly into one of the chairs but instead fell halfway through it. Appealing to Cordelia from amidst the chair, he said, 'Surely, as a fellow artist, you understand the need to protect one's artistic child from the harsh eyes of others before it is ready to bear such weights, what irreparable harm may come from an untimely word on one's artistic outlay.'

Cordelia did her best to keep her composure despite the undignified state of her relation. 'Perhaps, but I know that Terence, our neighbour, has often been of immense help because he can see what I have overlooked or what I could do to improve it.'

With apparent effort, Leopold once more regained his feet. 'Perhaps you are right. I have kept my child to myself for almost fifty years. I suppose it may be time to allow someone else to see it.'

'Again, I suppose my visits do not count within those fifty years,' Lady Eleanor chided as they followed the apparition out into the corridor.

'I only include your very first visit, dearest Eleanor,' Leopold said over his shoulder. 'Though I should say calling it a 'visit' is incredibly generous. 'Laying siege' would be a better description.'

Lady Eleanor only huffed, and Cordelia smiled to herself. No story that she and her friends had shared had ever featured ghosts such as the one she had just met. Of course, there had been knee-knocking terror on first seeing him, but now he seemed almost like any other person. Perhaps it was Grandmama's ordinary way of treating him, as if he were just another wayward grandchild rather than something out of nightmares or novels.

As they walked, Cordelia recognised where they were going, and her steps started to slow. 'Grandmama, is this not a dangerous part of the house?' she asked nervously. 'Father said that it is in desperate need of repair.'

Lady Eleanor patted her granddaughter's hand. 'There is nothing more dangerous than me in this part of the house. Those like Uncle Leo tend to create an atmosphere that pushes away those who do not understand. But now you shall be able to do a great amount of good. I have tried my best, but his need is just not within my expertise. You are exactly what he needs.'

Cordelia did not quite follow all of this, but her grandmother's easy confidence allayed her present fears. Finally, they stood before the door to an unused guest room. Whilst Leopold slipped through the door, Lady Eleanor pulled out a set of keys and put one in the lock. With a bit of noise, it turned and opened. Inside, moonlight provided the only illumination and threw the room into shades of black and silver. Uncle Leopold was standing near a settee behind which lay something large beneath a sheet.

Cordelia walked to him. 'Is that your masterpiece?' she asked, pointing to the sheet.

'Yes,' he answered in an almost reverential whisper.

Lady Eleanor pulled out a box of matches from a hidden pocket and asked, 'Do you want more light for your great unveiling or does the moon do?'

'The moon shall suffice,' Leopold answered.

Replacing the matches from whence they came, the dowager lady strode forwards and, with Cordelia's aid, managed to get the large canvas leaning against the settee in full moonlight. Leopold had his large hat between his hands and was scootching it between thumbs and forefingers in undisguised agitation. With a sparkling glance from Leopold to Cordelia, Lady Eleanor whisked away the sheet.

'I call it *Autumnus Triumphant*,' the artist explained as Cordelia let her eyes feast upon what she saw. Against a vibrant sunset over a rolling countryside, a bronzed young man, crowned with autumn leaves and vegetable vines, sat enthroned on a veritable mountain of autumn harvest. Orange pumpkins, green squashes, purple grapes, red apples, golden wheat - all intermingled in a glory of colour beneath the young man, Autumnus. In contrast, he wore a subdued ensemble; burgundies, dark greens, and browns were most pronounced. What drew Cordelia's eye, though, was Autumnus' face.

'He's perfect,' she said aloud.

Behind her, Leopold visibly relaxed at her words. Lady Eleanor, who had moved to lean against the windowsill, looked out at the moon with a satisfied smile.

'You captured that balance of joy and melancholy that fills the autumn season,' Cordelia explained, still entranced by the painting. 'The brilliance of the harvest, the dying colours of his clothes—marvellous.'

A sniff caught her ear, so Cordelia turned to see Leopold with his face in his hat. 'Oh, Uncle Leo, forgive me. I did not mean to upset you.'

'Dearest Cordelia, you could not have said anything that would have given me greater pleasure,' the apparition assured her. 'There are others I could mention who have not your eye to recognise genius when they see it.'

'Just because I saw what needed doing over what had been done does not mean that I am oblivious to beauty,' Lady Eleanor responded to the thinly veiled accusation. 'I believe I quite babbled over it the first time I saw it.'

Leopold gave a haughty sniff.

'But, my dear,' continued Lady Eleanor, coming to stand next to her granddaughter, 'what else do you notice about this piece?'

Cordelia closed her eyes and then opened them. She looked from Autumnus's face to his throne to the countryside of his domain to the sun in its heaven. Stillness held the room for several minutes. Finally, Cordelia spoke. 'Why is he triumphant?' she asked.

Leopold groaned. Lady Eleanor tapped the tip of Cordelia's nose affectionately with her forefinger. 'Precisely, darling. That is what has kept poor Uncle Leo here rather than passing on like all good souls should.'

'I would have gone,' Leopold interjected, 'but as I heard the call towards eternity, I felt that this work must be done before I could enter everlasting happiness.'

'Do not all wayward souls tell themselves such sweet things in order to justify remaining in a place that is not theirs?' countered Lady Eleanor.

Leopold tossed his head. 'Please, cousin, as if finishing a rare piece of beauty could at all be considered the same as trifling jealousies or injustices that keep lesser spirits.'

The dowager only shook her head.

'Then how is your work to be finished, Uncle Leo?' Cordelia asked.

'Well,' began the ghost, striking a dramatic thinking pose. 'I have had many ideas over the years, but none seemed quite sufficient. However, I am confident that I may finally have the one I need. Give me a moment to decide how best to convey it.'

Leopold's face scrunched in intense concentration. Then, with a sudden burst, he flew into the air, his head disappearing into the ceiling of the room. His voice in excited tones came muffled down to them.

Raising her cane, the dowager tapped on the ceiling near the apparition. 'Uncle Leo, only the mice and brownies are hearing your idea.'

Leopold floated down muttering, '...stuck in the middle of furniture or carpentry and looking a complete fool.' He brushed at his hat and shoulders.

Cordelia suppressed a rising giggle as her grandmother gave a chuckle.

The apparition glared reproachfully at the old woman before starting again. 'Triumph denotes conquest and thus something must be defeated. So what, my fair relations, does Autumnus conquer?'

Leopold looked down eagerly at the ladies below him, but as the moments ticked by, he grew visibly impatient. 'Come now, ladies, the answer should be obvious.'

'Himself?' Cordelia ventured. 'Because even as he gathers bounty, the producers of those bounties die?'

'My dear Cordelia, how morbid!' chided the deceased artist. 'Whilst I appreciate the drama and truth of your vision, it is hardly what leaps to the eye. Cousin Eleanor, you understand my meaning surely.'

'Uncle Leo, I believe you would burst if you had to wait any more.'

'You are a poor sport,' sulked the ghost, but his minor melancholy did not last long. 'It is Æstas—summer!' Leopold threw his arms out wide. 'Autumn conquers summer as it takes its place in the sequence of the seasons. So here is my idea:

Autumnus enthroned as he is but with a triumphant look rather than his current generous melancholy. And at his feet lies the bright form of Æstas, defeated and consumed by the produce of the throne.'

Cordelia gasped. Lady Eleanor let out a long sigh.

'Uncle Leo, how dreadful,' said Cordelia, 'and utterly unfitting for Autumnus. He would never slay someone and consume them. He is much too gentle.'

'I do not understand where you are getting the idea that Autumnus is gentle,' answered the ghost with a touch of spirit. 'Does not autumn come with its cold winds and sudden frosts? Is he not the harbinger of winter?'

'But…' Cordelia trailed off as she looked back at the painting, back at the face of Autumnus. 'That is not all of autumn either. It gives bounty and beauty and reasons to gather close with family and friends.' She pulled back her shoulders and stood up as straight as she could, fixing an unflinching gaze on the spectre. 'I do not and cannot agree with your idea.'

The dowager placed a hand on Cordelia's shoulder and gave it a light squeeze.

'Well said, my girl.'

Leopold looked utterly affronted. 'If that is the kind of criticism with which my brilliance is to be met, then I shall keep all further ideas to myself.'

He made to float away through the wall, but Lady Eleanor called him back. 'No, Uncle Leo, we will have no more tantrums. You and Cordelia are going to finish this painting, and you will finally enter the rest you should have taken decades ago.'

With a huff, the ghost slowly drifted back to the ground.

'Cordelia, please go get what you need,' the dowager said, gently pushing her towards the door. 'I will make sure that your collaborator is ready for you.'

With a nod, Cordelia left, relieved to be out of the sudden tension that had fallen. As quickly as she could, she went to her bedroom and gathered up her painting and sketching tools, placing them in a small satchel. Under one arm, she carried one of her larger easels and a sketchpad. All her things gathered, she began to make her way back. Fortunately, most of the guests had either left or were dancing so the hallways were blessedly clear.

As she neared the room, she strained to hear any voices, but nothing reached her ears. With tentative steps, she moved to the doorway. Whatever conversation had happened in her absence seemed to be concluded. Her grandmother sat on the settee to one side of the painting, both hands laid over the top of her cane. Leopold hovered in a corner, obviously still brooding.

'Grandmama, where should I set my things?'

The dowager patted the seat beside her. Cordelia came to the settee, set her bag of artist's tools on the seat, and set up the easel. The ghost muttered something to himself which Cordelia could not catch, but the dowager tutted.

'There is no need or place for such language,' she reprimanded. She looked back at Cordelia. 'I will help you with the painting, dear.'

As Cordelia reached for the painting, the ghost cried out. She stopped and looked back at him, watching as his face moved from distress to resignation. He closed his eyes. 'Just,' he sighed, 'be careful.'

'Of course, Uncle Leo,' said Cordelia as kindly as she could.

With Lady Eleanor's help, she got the painting onto the easel. Throughout, Leopold hovered like a mother bird over her chicks, giving tiny directions as to how to carry the painting or reprimanding if it was jostled too much. Once the painting was in place, Cordelia sat.

'I believe my work is done here for the time being,' stated the dowager. 'I shall be by later with refreshments.' Crooking her finger under her granddaughter's chin, Lady Eleanor tilted Cordelia's face up so she could look her full in the eyes. 'You are going to be fine, my dear. Have courage.' She placed a light kiss on Cordelia's head.

With that, the old lady exited the room leaving Cordelia alone with the ghost. A minute went by in silence, Cordelia waiting on Leopold for what to do next. He did not move, so she arranged her tools to her liking. She turned back to the ghost. He still had not moved. She busied herself by looking out the window. Just as she was beginning to trace the face of the man in the moon, the apparition spoke.

'I suppose you have another idea as to how to make Autumnus triumphant since you so vehemently denounced mine?'

Cordelia's head snapped to look at her relative. He was still not looking at her but at the face of the young man in the painting. Grabbing her sketchbook and a pencil, Cordelia began tracing some rough outlines.

'What if we have him standing beside the bounty of the season as if he has just collected all these things himself?' She held out to him a rough sketch of the vegetative dais on which Autumnus currently sat but now with a figure beside it holding a hoe.

Leopold looked it over and shook his head. 'I think we would be moving away from the majesty of the season by associating him with menial work,' he said with a sniff.

'Menial work, as you put it,' Cordelia responded with her own sniff, 'is what has supported our family for generations.'

The ghost's only response was a clearing of the throat. She felt her point taken so she did not press him further. Returning to the sketchpad, she began trying out a new idea.

For the next few hours, the two went back and forth proposing ideas and then finding fault with and discarding each. With every rejected idea, Cordelia grew more agitated and frustrated with her deceased relation. For someone who had spent so much time trying to find the way to complete his painting, he seemed much too ready to criticize and reject ideas.

'What if we give Autumnus more movement? Commanding the change of colours and the growth of produce perhaps.' On yet another sheet, she made a rough sketch of a figure with one arm upraised towards a grove of trees and the other extended to low lying foliage.

'It is not a bad idea,' he began, 'but I do not think it strong enough. Any passing nymph might be able to do the same, but his triumph must be something worthy of a season.'

With a vicious rip, she tore the sheet from her sketchpad to lie with the others on the floor. 'Uncle Leo, since it is your passing on to eternity at stake, let us take your original idea of Æstas slain at Autumnus's feet.'

She began furiously sketching, eventually holding out the image of two figures, one on the ground with its arms thrown outwards and over its head and the other seated on a raised dais with a scythe in one hand above the downed figure. The ghost gazed at it, giving it the most attention that any of her sketches had garnered yet. Cordelia began to breathe out a relieved sigh.

'Now that you have captured my idea, I do believe that you were right in your initial pronouncement. This is not what I want for Autumnus.'

That was the final straw. Snapping the sketchbook closed, she began gathering up the failed attempts that littered the floor. 'I do not know how to help you, uncle,' she said sharply. 'I have tried my best, but apparently you are determined to remain a spectre and to leave your masterpiece unfinished.'

Leopold drew himself up, rising a foot into the air. 'If you do not have the stamina to thoroughly pursue the muse wherever it may lead and through what difficulties it will, perhaps you are not the artist who can help me.'

Angry tears welled in Cordelia's eyes as she stuffed the pages and artist's tools into her satchel. Despite her best attempts to help and advise, it galled her that he would blame her for their lack of progress. Storming from the room, she almost collided with her grandmother bearing a basket of fruit in the hallway.

'My child, what is the matter?' asked Lady Eleanor.

The kindness of her grandmother's tone undid her. Cordelia flung her arms around her and sobbed. Lady Eleanor wrapped her arms around the girl and held her. It was a safety and security that Cordelia had forgotten from early childhood days, the reassurance of weathered skin and gentle pressure.

Eventually, her sobs subsided, and she regained her composure. When she pulled away, Lady Eleanor already had a handkerchief ready for her. Cordelia took it gratefully. Whilst she dabbed her eyes and blew her nose, her grandmother just stroked her hair without saying a word. Somehow, Cordelia felt she knew.

'Better?' asked Lady Eleanor once Cordelia had finished.

'Thank you, Grandmama.'

The old lady took Cordelia's hand and pressed it tightly. 'I see that Uncle Leo has been more trying than I had anticipated. Please forgive me for not staying with you.'

'Of course, Grandmama,' Cordelia said, squeezing back.

'Now,' Lady Eleanor began, looking past Cordelia to the room beyond. 'I do believe it is time for Uncle Leo to face what he really wants.' Her green eyes flashed.

Handing the basket to Cordelia, the dowager linked their arms and began walking purposefully back to the artist's room. Cordelia found herself having to walk briskly to keep in step. At the doorway, they saw the ghost talking to his painting.

'I shall give you a proper send-off. I promise. I just have yet to find the perfect...'

'I believe we shall have done with 'perfect',' interrupted Lady Eleanor.

The ghost turned shocked eyes on them and briefly floated up a few inches. Just as quickly though, his manner returned to haughty disdain.

'That is hardly for you to say, Cousin Eleanor. It is my painting after all.'

The dowager left Cordelia in the doorway and strode into the room. The ghost floated back. His eyes darted to the door and then to the sides of the room.

'Leopold Henry Updike Elmsworth, look at me,' commanded the old lady.

His eyes snapped to Lady Eleanor, and she held his gaze with unrelenting intensity. 'Why is it so hard for you to finish your painting?'

He opened his mouth, but the dowager raised a hand. 'No, it is not that you do not have a suitable assistant or conducive atmosphere or a compelling idea. In Cordelia and this room, you have had all those things. Be honest now.'

Leopold closed his mouth and then his eyes. Several beats later, he opened his eyes. 'I do not want to finish my painting.'

Cordelia gasped. Lady Eleanor did not move.

'I do not want to finish my painting,' repeated the ghost, 'because I do not want to be done creating.'

Lady Eleanor's whole demeanour relaxed. Cordelia came to stand behind her grandmother. Leopold looked deflated at his own confession.

'Oh, Uncle Leo,' said the dowager in much the same tone she had used with Cordelia only moments earlier. 'Do you think that the Creator of the universe would not have a place for your creativity in His blessed repose?'

'It is not that, Eleanor,' said the ghost, pulling his hat into his hands. His eyes went back to his painting. 'I do not want to be done with this painting. I had such dreams for it when I was alive that have only grown since my death. Making even the most minute changes to it brings me more joy than I have ever known. To have that taken away with its completion, I feel that I would break.'

Leopold turned such mournful, hopeless eyes to them that Cordelia felt her own eyes well with tears. But in that moment, an idea struck her. 'Grandmama, Uncle Leo, will you give me some time with Autumnus?'

The ghost made to protest, but he was cut short by Lady Eleanor. She gave Cordelia a knowing smile. 'You'll find us back where we first met,' said the dowager.

With much cajoling, she and Leopold made their exit. Retaking her seat on the settee, Cordelia laid out her tools once more. After taking a slow breath, she picked up her palette and knife and began laying on paint. As she worked, she let Leopold's words float around her mind. Each brushstroke clarified the vision until at last she was done. She smiled at her handiwork. Yes, Uncle Leo would approve this; she was sure of it.

She made her way back to the first room in which she had seen Leopold. At the doorway, she called to them, 'It's ready.'

Leopold flew through the walls of the rooms, immediately disappearing. Lady Eleanor walked more sedately, and Cordelia could hear her chuckling. Taking her granddaughter's arm, she said, 'Much like a child at Christmas, is he not?'

Together, the ladies made their way back. When they got there, Cordelia hesitated in the doorway. Leopold was staring at her work. Lady Eleanor patted her hand and gently ushered her into the room. All three of them then stood before the painting. Autumnus still sat upon his throne of bounty, but now he was bent towards a figure in the foreground. In Autumnus's outstretched hands was a bouquet of sunflowers and on his face was a gentle smile. The figure in the foreground was Leopold.

'Uncle Leo… what do you think?' asked Lady Eleanor.

The ghost continued to gape at the image before him. Cordelia's hold on her grandmother's arm tightened slightly as the moments ticked by. 'It's perfect,' came the barely audible whisper.

Cordelia's face broke into a smile. 'I thought you would approve.' She moved past her grandmother to stand beside the ghost.

'I thought what better way to show how much Autumnus has been to you than to have you receive his bounty.'

Phantasmal tears streaked Leopold's face. Turning to his relatives, he beamed upon them, and in his eyes shone a golden light. 'Thank you, my dear ladies,' he said through slight hiccoughing breaths. 'Eleanor, I do believe I am ready at last.'

'Godspeed and blessed rest to you,' the old lady answered, placing her hands on Cordelia's shoulders.

'Farewell, Uncle Leo,' said Cordelia.

As they watched, the light that had shone in Leopold's eyes expanded and enveloped him. Just as quickly as it happened, it was gone to be replaced by the familiar moonlight, leaving Cordelia alone with her grandmother and Autumnus.

Of Witches and Angels
by Ellie West (*fantasy*)

A large bay horse stopped outside the livery and stared at Flora Cooper as she passed by. She was tempted to greet it, but the surly old man guiding it into the stable didn't appear to be in the mood to have a stranger interrupt.

Flora gave the horse a nod and continued. A man across the street stared at her with wide eyes, and she sighed. Why had she acknowledged the horse without checking to see who might be watching?

She was supposed to remain inconspicuous in this village, not attract attention. She was also supposed to stay with her travelling companion and protector, but she'd wanted a bit of freedom from Molly's watchful eye. Isaac, her betrothed, wasn't there to protect her. Until he arrived tomorrow, she had to ensure she didn't do anything to make the locals suspect her.

Lord, give me the strength to handle whatever comes my way and the courage to do Your will, no matter what that may entail.

She drew in a deep breath and slowly released it with her prayer. God would take care of her the same way He always had.

Flora left the village proper and realised a cat followed her. The small black feline seemed perfectly content walking at her side. She stopped, not surprised when the cat stopped with her and looked up.

'Do you plan to follow me for my entire stroll?' Flora leaned down to pet the friendly feline.

It meowed and rubbed its head against her hand.

'Right, then. Let's carry on.'

Men worked in a nearby field, scything wheat. Several boys followed, gathering stalks and laying them out to be bound. Flora watched for a moment then continued with the cat trotting alongside.

A shout from the wheat field halted her. Everyone was rushing towards a central point, near a boy who looked far too young to use the scythe he held. A burly man yanked the scythe from the boy's hands and said something that sent him running towards the road.

Flora intercepted him. Tears streamed down his face, and the poor child was so pale she feared he might be ill.

She laid a hand on his shoulder. 'What's wrong?'

'I've cut off his leg! I know I have!' He sobbed and shook his head. 'I didn't mean to!'

Flora felt the nudge in her heart that always told her what to do. 'Why don't we go see if I can help him?'

The boy shook off her hand and backed away. 'I can't go back there!' He ran down the road towards the village.

Flora whispered a prayer for him as she faced the field again. The men had gathered, presumably around the injured man. She'd never heard of a limb being removed by a scythe, and she doubted a child of nine or ten would have the strength to cleave bone. Still, the nudge in her heart said she should help.

She whispered a prayer for courage and protection as she entered the field. Even though her gifts came from God, she'd been driven from more than one place after someone saw her healing ability and assumed it was witchcraft.

One of the men stepped away from the group and stopped her. 'You'd best not go any closer, miss. Poor John's got quite the leg wound.'

'I'm a healer.' Flora hoped he would let her pass. 'The boy told me he cut the man's leg off, but I doubt that's accurate.'

'No, miss, John's leg is still firmly attached. He just has a deep cut.' He studied her for a moment. 'You're a healer, you say?'

'Yes, and I would be happy to help.'

'I hope you don't mind the sight of blood.' He sounded sceptical but led her to the others. 'John, this young lady says she's a healer.'

The man on the ground grimaced as she knelt beside him. 'If you can do anything for this leg of mine, I'd be grateful.'

'You'll soon be whole.' Flora offered a smile and turned her attention to the blood-soaked cloth around his left calf. 'You may feel some warmth, but don't be alarmed. It's part of the healing process.'

She ignored the murmurs of the men surrounding them as she laid her hands on John's leg, one above the wound and one below it. Then she bowed her head and whispered a prayer.

'Thank You, Father, for giving me the gift of healing. Please use me to heal this man's leg and make him whole once more.'

She continued whispering prayers as she felt the familiar warmth of her healing gift flow through her hands and into John's leg. He shifted, almost dislodging her hands.

'What are you doing to me?' His worried voice interrupted her concentration.

'Healing your wound.' She offered another smile. 'It will only take a moment longer.'

She closed her eyes and concentrated on mending the cut on his leg as she whispered another prayer of thanks for God working through her. The flow of warmth slowed, letting her know the process was almost complete. Then she lifted her hands from his leg and sat back with a sigh. 'Thank You, Father,' she whispered. Then she looked at John, who stared back with wide eyes. 'How does your leg feel?'

'Like nothing ever happened to it.' He unwound the cloth from his leg. Blood still soaked his trousers, but the skin showing through the torn fabric was unscathed. He lifted his gaze to her as the murmurs around them increased. 'How'd you do that?'

'I have the gift of healing.' A soft bump to her arm brought her gaze down, and she met the brilliant green eyes of her feline companion. 'Well, hello again.'

The cat meowed, and silence fell over the group.

Flora saw the suspicion in the men around her and said a silent prayer for protection as she stood. 'I'll take my leave now. Have a blessed day.'

She turned towards the road, and the cat followed her. Before she left the field, she heard the rustle of an approaching person.

'Wait, miss!' John called.

She stopped and turned around, praying this conversation wasn't a mistake.

'We weren't properly introduced. My name is John Moore.'

'It's a pleasure to meet you, Mr Moore. I'm Miss Flora Cooper.'

'Pleased to meet you, Miss Cooper. I want to thank you for what you've done for me.' He shook his head and looked away for a moment. 'If you hadn't come along, I don't know what might have happened. I have a daughter, and I feared I wouldn't be able to provide for her.'

'There's no need to thank me.' She offered another smile, grateful he wasn't misjudging her ability. 'God did the healing. I'm just the vessel He chose to use for it.'

'You can be sure I'll be thanking Him as well.' John studied her for a moment. 'I'd still like to do something for you, though. Would you allow me and my daughter to provide supper for you this evening?'

'I'm honoured, but I have a companion travelling with me. She'll be upset if I leave her behind for the second time today.'

He chuckled. 'She's invited too. We want to keep things proper, after all.'

'Then I will gladly accept your invitation.'

'Good!' He gave her directions to his cottage. 'Clara and I look forwards to seeing you and your companion this evening, Miss Cooper.'

'We'll be there at the appointed time. Have a good day, Mr Moore.'

•◇•◇•◇•◇•◇•◇•◇•◇•

'How am I supposed to protect you if I don't know where to find you?' Molly Thatcher fumed as she tied a shawl around her shoulders. 'And then to accept a supper invitation from a widower right after showing your gift to a crowd? Flora, you're supposed to be cautious!'

'I tried.' She straightened her own shawl as they prepared to leave the inn. 'But I couldn't leave that man to suffer with such an injury. You know I follow God's leading. It wasn't a coincidence that I was there at the right moment. God arranged it as surely as He gave me the gift of healing.'

'You're right. I know. But I wish you would have taken me with you.'

'I needed some time alone. It's a rare commodity.'

'The baseless accusations against you are precisely why you're supposed to stay with me.' Molly sighed and moved to the door. 'There are already whispers around town. Please stay with me until we leave Whitstead so that I can fulfil my vows to the Order and protect you.'

'I will, Molly, I promise.' Flora followed her into the corridor and hoped the whispers wouldn't grow into threats as they had in the past.

As a descendant of the Renowned, her life wasn't easy. Too many thought that the gifts passed down to her through the generations were evidence of witchcraft, rather than evidence of angelic ancestors.

Thankfully, the Divine Order of Renowned Protectors existed to help those with Renowned blood. Molly had been with Flora for two years and helped her escape danger countless times. They were currently on their way to a village associated with the Order in the south of England. Not only would Flora find safety there, she and Isaac, also a Renowned descendant, would be able to live free from the worry of being driven away by those who misunderstood the origin of their gifts.

As Flora and Molly walked through town, glances and whispers followed them with disconcerting familiarity. Flora tried to ignore them, but it was difficult—especially when every animal she passed tried to come to her.

'I don't suppose you could let all the animals in the area know you want them to ignore you,' Molly said as they passed a horse trying to walk over to them despite its rider's best efforts.

'Not unless you want me to speak with every animal in the area, and even then, they might not listen to me.' Flora sighed as a man hurried his wife past her.

'I thought that might be the case, but it was worth asking.'

They followed the curve of the road past the churchyard. A familiar meow near the walkway leading to the church itself made Flora pause her steps. Sure enough, the black cat that had followed her earlier sat by the side of the road.

'You again?' Flora leaned down to pet the cat.

'I see you made a friend whilst you were gone this afternoon,' Molly said.

Flora straightened and shrugged. 'It kept me company on my walk.'

They went on, and Molly laughed softly. 'It appears your friend wants to keep you company again.'

Flora looked down and spotted the cat trotting alongside. As she lifted her gaze, movement at one of the windows in the house they were passing caught her attention.

'I hope Isaac arrives early tomorrow. I fear we may have to leave before afternoon.'

'Why is that?' Molly sounded concerned.

'Someone was watching us, which means they likely saw me interacting with this cat.' Tears stung Flora's eyes. 'If they didn't already believe I was a witch, they now have even more evidence against me.'

Molly hooked her arm through Flora's. 'If people would listen to the truth, they would realise how wrong their assumptions are.'

'Yes, but few have listened yet.'

'We'll pray nothing comes of it. A few whispers here and there can be ignored.'

'It still hurts.'

'I know.' Molly gave her arm a gentle squeeze, providing comfort and support in an otherwise unbearable situation.

They crossed the bridge over the river and went between the rows of small houses sheltering Whitstead's poor families. She hated feeling as if the occupants of every house they passed watched her with fear and suspicion.

A wedge of light shone from one of the doorways ahead. Molly let go of Flora's arm and became more alert. With all the whispers going around, it wouldn't surprise Flora if someone came out of that house and tried to run her out of town.

The small, pale face peering around the door relieved her apprehension. It was the boy who'd thought he cut off John Moore's leg. Flora smiled at him, but she didn't have a chance to speak. His eyes widened, and he slammed the door.

Molly glanced at her. 'That boy seemed more frightened than he should.'

'He's the one responsible for the incident earlier. I'd hoped to tell him Mr Moore is fine, but I guess he'll have to hear it from someone else.'

The cat darted over to the boy's house and stared at the door for a moment before trotting around the side of the building.

'At least I won't have to explain my feline friend to Moore and his daughter,' Flora said.

•◇•◇•◇•◇•◇•◇•◇•◇•

They arrived at the Moore cottage without further incident. A wide-eyed girl in a well-worn dress answered Flora's knock.

'Are you the one that healed my papa?'

'Yes, I am.' Flora smiled, happy to see no fear in the curious child.

'Let them in, Clara,' John said from somewhere behind the girl.

'Oh! Sorry.' Clara blushed and stepped back to allow them to enter. 'Please, do come in.'

'Thank you.' Flora entered the one-room cottage with Molly close behind.

A steaming pot hung over the fire in the fireplace. Whatever it contained smelled delicious.

John smiled as his daughter moved to his side. 'Welcome to our home, Miss Cooper. This is my daughter, Clara.'

'It's a pleasure to meet you, Clara.' Flora lifted a hand towards Molly. 'This is my companion, Miss Molly Thatcher.'

Molly nodded to their hosts. 'I'm happy to meet you, Mr Moore, Clara.'

'Won't you please sit down?' John indicated the four chairs around the table.

The square table offered no clues to the head and foot of it, and Flora didn't want to risk sitting in the wrong spot.

Clara saved her by pulling out one of the chairs. 'You sit here, Miss Cooper.'

'Thank you.'

Clara hurried around the table and pulled out the chair across from Flora. 'Miss Thatcher, you sit here.'

'Thank you, Clara.' Molly sat in the offered seat.

John brought the pot over from the fireplace. 'I hope fish stew is all right. I'm sorry I can't offer you anything nicer.'

'Fish stew sounds lovely,' Molly said.

'Yes, it does.' Before Flora could thank him again for inviting them to supper, an animal rubbed against her leg. 'I didn't realise you had a cat.'

She leaned back, hoping to catch a glimpse of the animal, but she didn't see anything.

'We don't have a cat,' John said as he ladled stew into the bowls.

'Then what—' Flora gasped as a brilliant green, cat-sized dragon leaped into her lap and curled up. 'Oh! You're definitely not a cat, are you?'

The dragon looked up at her with bright golden eyes and purred.

'Ember!' Clara said, looking at the dragon. 'You're not supposed to sit on people during meals.'

The dragon spared a glance at the girl before laying her head down and purring louder.

John sighed as he set the pot back on the fire. 'Clara, I told you to make sure she was outside.'

'I did! She must have sneaked back in.' The girl looked at Flora with tears in her eyes. 'I'm sorry, miss. Ember can be stubborn, but she's quite nice.'

'It's all right.' Flora risked her fingers and stroked the dragon's smooth scales. Ember sighed contentedly and closed her eyes. 'I love animals, and they love me.'

Molly smothered a laugh. 'Yes, you do have a way with them.'

'Clara,' John said, taking his seat. 'Why don't you take Ember and put her outside?'

'I don't know if she'll let me.' Clara peered at the dragon. 'She looks happy where she is.'

'Try anyway.'

Clara slid off her chair and reached for Ember. The dragon lifted her head and growled, then settled back down with another purr.

Flora laughed. 'I think it would be safer to leave her where she is.'

'If you're sure you don't mind...' John said, his expression doubtful.

'It's quite all right.' She petted the dragon again and spoke to her. 'You just have to promise to leave my supper alone.'

Ember stopped purring and gave her an insulted look.

Flora fought back a laugh. 'I apologise, Ember. I'm sure your behaviour will be perfect.'

That seemed to placate the dragon, and she started purring softly once more.

Midway through the meal, John turned to Flora. 'I'm afraid I can't contain my curiosity a moment longer.'

'Oh?' She braced herself for whatever he planned to ask.

'This afternoon, you said God healed my leg through you.'

'That's right...'

'How? I've seen people pray over someone, and it still takes days or weeks for them to heal completely. How did you do it in minutes?'

Flora exchanged a glance with Molly. If she told him the truth, he might be able to clear up some of the rumours surrounding her. Then again, he might not believe her.

The nudge in her heart let her know she had to tell the truth. 'Have you ever heard the verse in the Bible that says, '...when the sons of God came in unto the daughters of men, and they bare children to them, the same became mighty men which were of old, men of renown'?'

'It sounds familiar.'

'Well, I'm a descendant of the Renowned.'

John studied her for a moment. 'What does that mean?'

'I have a touch of angel blood in me.'

'Bless my soul!' Clara stared at her with wide eyes. 'You're an angel?'

'Only a very tiny part of me.' Flora smiled at her before focusing on John again. 'But that tiny part is what enabled me to heal you so quickly.'

He leaned back in his chair. 'Allow me to quote my daughter. Bless my soul.'

Flora laughed. 'That's a common reaction when people find out the truth about me.'

Clara leaned forward. 'Are you a part angel too, Miss Thatcher?'

'Me? No.' Molly shook her head. 'I'm as fully human as you are. But I do have a very important job.'

'What's that?'

'My job is to protect Miss Cooper and others like her.'

'That's amazing!'

John studied Flora. 'Are there many like you, Miss Cooper?'

172

'Few. My father was one, and my betrothed is, but I've met very few others.'

She answered more questions about her heritage and abilities, and then Molly shifted the conversation away from her. Flora breathed a little easier as they discussed the unusually cool and wet weather the area had been experiencing.

Talking about her angelic ancestry always made her a little nervous. People tended to either think she was lying or fawn over her because she was an angel. Thankfully, the Moores did neither. Although clearly fascinated, they continued to treat her the same way they did Molly.

●◇●◇●◇●◇●◇●◇●◇●◇●

A knock sounded as Flora and Molly prepared to leave the Moore cottage. Ember scurried behind the mattress leaning against the back wall as John went to open the door.

A distraught woman stood there wringing her hands. A taller, burly man Flora recognised from the wheat field stood behind her with an expression somewhere between worry and reluctance.

'What can I do for you, William, Agnes?' John asked, his tone friendly.

'It's not you we've come to see.' Agnes peered past him. 'It's the miss over there.'

Flora exchanged a glance with Molly, seeing her confusion mirrored. She took a step towards the couple. 'May I ask why you've come to see me?'

'It's my boy, Thomas.' She clasped her hands together and studiously avoided Flora's gaze. 'He's taken ill.'

'Refused his supper, he did,' William said. 'Not like the boy to refuse a meal.'

'What does that have to do with Miss Cooper?' John asked. 'Thomas is probably suffering from guilt, nothing more.'

'He was fine until the miss and her companion passed by.' Agnes shivered and held her hands tighter. 'She left her cat to bewitch him.'

'Black cat it is, too,' William added.

'So, please, miss,' Agnes said, her eyes filled with tears. 'Would you take the spell off him? We don't have much, but we'll give you whatever you want that we do have.'

'I don't want anything.' Flora fought to keep her composure. 'I'm not a witch, and I didn't put a spell on your son.'

'Well,' William said, shifting uncomfortably, 'whatever you call yourself, could you please undo whatever you've done to him?'

Flora closed her eyes and sighed. They clearly weren't going to leave her alone until she agreed to help, even though she didn't know what she could do. Healing illnesses was different from healing injuries, and she wasn't nearly as gifted at it.

A hand touched her shoulder, and she opened her eyes to find Molly close to her side.

'Maybe you should talk to the boy,' Molly whispered, her gaze on the frightened couple. 'If it's something you can heal, that might be enough to keep peace until we leave Whitstead.'

Flora nodded and focused on the couple. 'I'll come see your son.'

'Oh, thank you, miss!' Agnes's expression held both fear and gratitude. 'That's ever so kind of you.'

Flora turned to John. 'Thank you, Mr Moore, for a lovely evening.'

'Would you like me to escort you back to the inn?' Concern shone in his eyes.

'Thank you for the offer, but we'll be all right.'

After bidding Clara farewell, Flora and Molly left the cottage and followed William and Agnes to their house. As William opened the door, Flora spotted several of their neighbours watching and whispering. She made a quick decision that might repair her reputation in this village. Or it could go horribly wrong and make things worse.

She turned to Agnes. 'Please bring Thomas out to me.'

The poor woman's eyes widened far enough to be concerning. 'In view of the neighbours?'

'I have nothing to be ashamed of.'

Agnes and William both disappeared inside. Molly kept a wary eye on the growing crowd as she leaned closer to Flora. 'Are you sure about this?'

'No, but it's the best idea I have.' She heard a familiar meow and sighed. 'The source of this current trouble has decided to appear.'

The black cat sauntered over and rubbed against her skirts.

Flora looked down, inadvertently meeting the cat's gaze. 'You've caused enough trouble for one day. Away with you!'

The cat flicked its tail and ran off. Unfortunately, it only caused more frantic whispers among the gathered villagers.

Agnes and William returned with their son. He trembled as he stood in front of Flora.

She offered a friendly smile. 'Are you Thomas?'

'Yes, miss,' he whispered, his eyes on the ground.

'I'm pleased to meet you. My name is Miss Cooper.' She waited in vain for him to respond. 'I hear you refused to eat your supper.'

'Yes, miss.'

'Is it because you're feeling poorly?'

He nodded and swiped at his eyes.

'I see.' Flora glanced at the gathered crowd and prayed her next question wasn't a mistake. 'Did I do anything to make you feel poorly?'

'N-no, miss.' He sniffled and finally looked up at her. 'I didn't mean to hurt him! I swear I didn't!'

'I know you didn't, Thomas.' She laid her hands on his shoulders and smiled. 'I made Mr Moore's leg well again. It's as if nothing ever happened to it.'

'My father said that, but… are you a witch, miss?'

'No. My abilities come from God, not the devil.'

'And Mr Moore is truly healed?'

'He is.' She turned him towards the end of the lane. 'Why don't you go see for yourself? I'm sure that will bring your appetite back.'

He looked towards his parents, and his father nodded. Thomas hurried down the lane, and Flora turned to William and Agnes.

'There's nothing wrong with your son that making amends with Mr Moore won't cure. Lingering guilt is what made him ill.'

'Oh, thank you, miss, for making my boy well!' Agnes cried, leaving Flora to wonder if the woman had heard what she'd said.

'It was a pleasure to speak with him. We'll take our leave now.'

Once they were away from the crowd, Molly sighed. 'I know you meant to show those people your innocence, but I fear it didn't work.'

'Yes, I'm afraid they now may be more convinced than ever that I'm a witch.' Flora groaned as they crossed the bridge. 'Why did I have to touch him? Why couldn't any of those people have listened to what I said?'

'There's no way to know. We can only trust that God is in control of the situation and will somehow use it for good.' Molly hooked her arm through Flora's. 'For now, let's hurry back to the inn and hope things remain peaceful until your Isaac arrives tomorrow.'

They picked up their pace, and Flora prayed for safety.

At the bend in the road, near the path leading to the church, three or four boys ambushed them. Flora raised her arms to fend off the rocks and sticks thrown at her.

Molly pushed her into the churchyard. 'Hurry! If we can make it to the vicarage, we might find safety.'

Flora only ran a few steps before she heard Molly cry out behind her. Whirling around, she spotted her companion sitting on the ground with her hand to her forehead.

'Molly!' Flora rushed back to her despite the advancing youngsters yelling at her to leave. She knelt beside her companion. 'Are you well?'

Molly shook her head and groaned. When she pulled her hand away, Flora spotted the darkness of blood. Her temper rose and, despite her better judgment, she looked at the children preparing to hurl more rocks at her.

'You've harmed an innocent woman with your ignorance!' Tears pricked her eyes as she put an arm around Molly and pulled her close. 'I'm no witch. Would I be in a churchyard if I were?'

She didn't bother to wait for a response. Laying a hand on Molly's head, she closed her eyes and whispered prayers for her friend's healing.

'Flora...' Molly grasped her arm.

'Be still and let me help you.' She kept praying as the warmth flowed from her. As the process reached its end, she realised silence had fallen over the churchyard.

She opened her eyes to a familiar blue glow emanating from the man before her. Isaac Hill stood between her and their attackers. His angel luminescence illuminated the area around him, and the blade of the sword in his hand glowed the same shade.

'Isaac!' Tears slid down her cheeks as she rose and helped Molly to her feet.

He glanced back, righteous anger shining in his eyes along with concern. 'Are you all right?'

She nodded and looked past him. The slack-jawed boys had empty hands as they stared at Isaac.

'What are you?' the smallest boy asked, his tone somewhere between awe and fear.

'I am a descendant of angels.' Isaac's deep voice carried easily in the night air. 'As is this woman you've accused of being a witch. Her gifts come from the one true God.'

'But everyone said —'

'They were wrong.' Isaac slid his sword into the sheath strapped to his back, and his luminescence began to dim. 'Now, I suggest you all apologise to these two women you've frightened, and then go home and tell your parents what you've seen this night.'

Each child muttered an apology and walked away. Flora's heart lifted a little with each one. Perhaps when all those families heard what the children had witnessed, they would realise their error.

Once the last of the children had gone, Isaac turned to Flora. 'I'm sorry I didn't arrive sooner.'

'I'm only happy you're here.' She held out her hands, and he took them. 'How did you know where to find us?'

'I heard some people discuss you passing this way. From the tone of their conversation, I was concerned enough to come looking for you.'

'I'm glad you did.' She looked at Molly, who stood back smiling. 'How is your head?'

'As whole and hard as ever.' She blew out a breath. 'Shall we head back to the inn? This has been a long day.'

Isaac tucked Flora's hand in his elbow. 'The tale those children will tell should keep us from having any more excitement until we leave Whitstead.'

'Let's pray we encounter no worse during the rest of our journey.'

The Dragon's Chosen
by Erudessa Gentian (*fantasy*)

'Is Athalulf absolutely sure?' Kara 'Draco' Drake asked, peering down the road at a sleepy little village. Weeks of exhausting travel had brought them here?

Her friend, Ylva 'Blood Wolfe' Wulfsige, nodded while looking around. 'Whitstead. I certainly wouldn't have expected to find Dragons around a place like this.'

'Precisely what I was thinking,' Kara said, tone biting.

She had been terrified of Athalulf when she had first met the huge, rust-coloured Wolfe, but was now comfortable enough to glare at him without fear of being eaten. She wasn't stupid enough to do more than throw dirty looks and an occasional verbal barb at the mystical prince of the Blood Wolfe Pack. A single magical Wolfe was far more dangerous than an entire pack of regular wolves.

'Draco, I don't feel comfortable leaving you alone.' The crusty voice of her most trusted General, Arthur Bering, broke into Kara's thoughts.

'You're not leaving me alone.' She dismissed his worries with a wave of her black-gloved hand. 'Even if you weren't leaving two of your men with us, Ylva, Athalulf and I would be perfectly safe. Vincent's bloody fist hasn't reached this far yet.'

Ylva stiffened at the mention of her traitorous cousin.

'I need the Dragons' help if I want to reclaim the throne,' Kara reminded Arthur. 'As skilled as you are, you can't help me with that. Go meet Admiral Edmund.'

Arthur hesitated only a moment before giving her a deep bow. 'I will be back for you in a week.' Spinning on the two soldiers currently disguised as menservants, he barked, 'Guard your Queen with your lives!'

Kara sighed as Arthur made his way back to their airship. He could be so overprotective, especially considering she was the Dragon's Chosen; blessed with magical flames and enhanced physical abilities. Still, she understood his remorse at being unable to save her family during the coup. After all, she was never meant to be Queen. Until Ylva's cousin slaughtered her entire family, Kara was merely one of the princesses on the outside. Only a chosen few knew her alter ego: Draco, mysterious gentleman and secret assassin for the crown.

Once they recruited a real, live Dragon, Ylva's cousin wouldn't hold onto the throne for long.

Straightening her cravat, she turned to her companions. The two disguised manservants carrying a couple carpetbags trailed behind Ylva, who minced forwards in her layers of petticoats and fabric. But anyone who underestimated the short, slightly plump, red-headed Duke's daughter was in for a fatal surprise. Not only did she have at least half a dozen blades hidden on her person, she was the Wolfe Pack's Chosen. Athalulf would tear apart anyone who wished to harm her.

Kara offered her arm to Ylva and lowered her naturally husky voice. 'Shall we, sister dear?'

●◇●◇●◇●◇●◇●◇●◇●◇●

Ylva was grateful entering the quaint town of Whitstead went smoothly. The innkeepers, noting their luxurious garments and aristocratic speech, happily showed them to the best rooms. Kara allowed her two soldiers to indulge themselves in the tavern below. Athalulf, who everyone had either fawned or fainted over, waited outside to lead them to the hidden Dragon's cave. But Kara's plan for their exit from the inn was just... well, as a proper lady, she couldn't be as free with her language as 'Draco.'

Ylva gaped at Kara. 'You expect me to wear what?' She sputtered at the men's clothes Kara held out to her.

'Surely you weren't planning on searching for hidden magical portals in that ridiculous outfit?' Kara laughed. 'What if we need to climb something? Or swim?'

Ylva sniffed with indignation. The 'ridiculous outfit' she currently wore was a respectable walking habit. The hardy skirt wasn't hampered by a dozen petticoats and gave her legs plenty of freedom to move. 'I am a lady!' she cried. 'How am I supposed to get to the woods without being seen? I would expire from mortification.'

Kara ignored all her protests, eventually coaxing Ylva to hide the scandalous clothing under her thick, floor-length cloak. At least the current drizzle made the wrap natural.

'No one will suspect a thing,' Kara assured her.

Clutching the cloak together in a white-knuckled grip, Ylva crept down the stairs. Just as they neared the bottom step, slurred shouts from the tavern had everyone's attention.

''At's enough for you, Jedediah Micklewright. You've 'ad more'n enough for today.' Grunts and punches followed the shrill voice.

Before the fight could block their way, Ylva, Kara and Athalulf swept out the front door.

Torn between the urge to get out of sight and the lady-like pace instilled in her, Ylva walked with stiff legs. She could feel Athalulf's laugh inside her head. She rarely regretted their telepathic connection, but there were times the big Wolfe just couldn't sympathize with her delicate female emotions.

Ylva kept her gaze down, fervently praying no one took notice of her. Alas, her worst fears came to pass.

'Hello, big boy,' a cheerful voice sounded from in front of the trio.

Ylva's head snapped up to see a tall man in front of them, his gaze fastened on Athalulf. Despite his crutches, the man's back was straight as a ramrod. Perhaps military training was in his past?

He gave a friendly smile then introduced himself. 'I'm Mattie Rossiter. Your pup is magnificent! Not even the sheep dogs I've seen compare.'

Sheep dogs, indeed!

Athalulf snorted derisively. Now it was Ylva's turn to chuckle internally.

'You folks staying in town?' Mattie asked.

'My sister and I are here for a restful week in the countryside.' Kara smiled back at him.

'Then you should come out for bonfire night! There's going to be a grand time for all.'

Ylva, still petrified of being discovered in men's clothing, hardly tracked the friendly conversation between Draco and Mattie, politely nodding and humming noncommittal answers when needed. She didn't breathe easy until they were deep into the neighbouring forest. Even then, she kept a tight grip on her cloak.

Athalulf led the two women to a babbling brook, immediately heading upstream. Before too long, Ylva smelled the air.

Lilac and roses? Isn't it a little late in the season for –

She stepped past a tree and the cold, rainy autumn they had been trudging through melted away into sunny springtide.

Ylva and Kara stopped to gawk at the peculiar sight, while an unimpressed Athalulf kept moving. Where had the dreary cloud cover gone? The bright, warm air hung heavy with the strong scents of the blooming garden ahead. Towering amidst it, a giant oak spread welcoming branches.

'Is that a green door in the tree's trunk?' Kara asked. 'Why is there a door in a tree? What is this place?'

Magical phenomena tend to gravitate towards each other. Athalulf explained telepathically. *A woman named Maisie Bloom lives here. Come, we still have a long way to go.*

The women followed, reluctant especially as they re-entered the cold autumn drizzle. The trio continued upstream until a dark, foreboding cave yawned before them. Ylva tried her best to suppress a shiver.

'Are you sure this is the place?' Kara whispered.

'Athalulf says he smells dragons from that cave,' Ylva muttered back, then caught sight of Kara's pale face. 'Are you all right?'

'A little worried that I'll be burned to death before I even reach the cave's entrance,' Kara admitted.

No. Athalulf's voice rumbled in Ylva's head. *She is blessed with the Dragon's Breath. They will not harm her, nor will they touch you. Our races agreed long ago never to harm the Chosen.*

'Athalulf says it's safe for all of us,' Ylva said.

Even with the reassurance, Ylva didn't blame Kara for her hesitation. Dragons were even more mysterious than Wolves. But Kara was going to need their power to reclaim her throne.

Procrastinating, Kara straightened her sword belt while Ylva fingered her fan. The familiar, lady-like implement calmed her nerves.

When Athalulf impatiently loped towards the cave, they finally stumbled after him.

Kara brought a small ball of flaming Dragon's Breath to rest in her palm before following Athalulf into the yawning black hole. The firelight helped their human eyes enough to not stumble along the cave's passages, but the misshapen, dancing shadows seemed to hide danger beyond every footstep.

Out of the drizzle, they began to dry off. Ylva fiddled with the decorative pin that hid a poison-tipped dagger nestled in her hair. She eventually gave up trying to tame the blood-red curls.

Finally, the three found themselves at the entrance of a monstrous cavern. Kara's light revealed a huge lake. The sound of running water came from the inky blackness beyond the light's reach. Kara held the flame up, probably trying to pinpoint the source. Perhaps it was a small waterfall or swiftly flowing river?

'Why — isn't *this* unusual?' an unfamiliar, seductive voice floated on the air around them.

Kara froze mid-step, the Dragon's Breath wavering in her palm.

'Wolves and Dragons have not sought out counsel with each other for many years.' The silky voice seemed to wrap itself around both Kara and Ylva.

Athalulf sat, unruffled. A soft light grew from the far side of the cavern, revealing a shadowy waterfall that began to part in the middle.

'What brings the future Alpha and your Chosen to our door?'

The giant monstrosity that appeared through the curtain of water could have stepped out of legend.

The gold and violet scales reflected every tiny bit of light, making it seem as if they glowed by themselves. Its long neck had a black mane that swished with every slight movement. As the Dragon leisurely swam towards the trio, Ylva realized the head alone had to be about six feet long.

'Welcome, Athalulf and the Wolves' Chosen.'

Ylva's heart skipped a beat as the Dragon's giant head came down to study her.

That voice! The hypnotic, velvety smoothness drew her in. Made her want to touch…

Athalulf curled protectively around her, the low growl growing in Ylva's head rumbled in his huge frame.

She's ours! Athalulf snarled.

The Dragon's silky laugh filled the cavern. 'You know we would not steal your Chosen, Wolfe. That doesn't mean I can't be a gracious host. You came all this way, after all.'

'You can hear Athalulf?' Ylva drew back the hand she'd unconsciously reached out. Pet a Dragon? What had she been thinking? Out of habit, she snapped open her fan and tried to smile demurely. Despite the fact she was sopping wet and wearing trousers, she was a lady and would act like it!

'Indeed.' The Dragon chuckled, amused by her airs. 'Dragons can speak both verbally and telepathically.'

Ylva gasped as she studied the Dragon. 'Kara, look! Its eyes are the same shade of violet as yours!'

Kara's breath hitched as the Dragon's gaze flicked to Kara.

'Draco,' the Dragon breathed the one word coldly before turning back to Ylva and ignoring Kara. 'Blood Wolf, what brings you and the Pack here?'

Both Ylva and Kara stood stunned.

'W-we came…' The stammer betrayed how bewildered Ylva was. But she regained her wits and gave Kara the best curtsy she could muster in trousers. Then she looked back and forth between everyone, frowning as the Dragon continued to ignore Kara. 'We came for our Queen.'

Kara stepped in front of the Dragon, flames engulfing both hands. 'I am Kara Drake, heir to the dragon throne. And Draco, the Dragon's Chosen!'

'So?' The Dragon remained unimpressed.

Kara blinked. 'But, I'm your Chosen…'

'So?' The Dragon now sounded bored, edging on annoyance.

'Don't you want to know for what reason she's come?' Ylva asked as Athalulf herded her a short distance away from the lake.

'I already know why she is here.' The Dragon's silky voice now held an undertone of anger. 'She wants more power. She wants us to do something more for her, just like every other human blessed with the Dragon's Breath.'

Ylva opened her mouth to snap back.

Leave them be. Athalulf curled up comfortably.

But – she started to argue.

Dragons and Wolves are different, Blood Wolf. Athalulf shook his head. *Dragon Tribes are not as tight knit as Wolfe Packs. Wolves decide our Chosen together because instead of power, you get the protection and help of the entire pack. The Dragon's Breath is a power passed from generation to generation, so the Dragons don't have to be personally involved. But we both want our Chosen to prove their worth. We chose you because you bled for us. Now Draco must convince the Dragons to choose her. We all resent being used.*

•◇•◇•◇•◇•◇•◇•◇•◇•

Kara's thoughts were in upheaval. When the Dragon first appeared, excitement and hope had bloomed in her chest. Anger at being ignored replaced those emotions. And now she was just flabbergasted.

Why weren't things going according to plan? They were supposed to help take back her kingdom from Ylva's cousin. With the backing of a real Dragon, not just their flames, no one would ever —

'You always come, demanding allegiance or servitude, as if our gift weren't enough. As if we should bow down to a little human king. Or queen,' the Dragon added scornfully. 'Why should we trouble ourselves with the lives of humans?'

'You made a pact with my family!'

'We agreed to let one member in a generation of your people have the use of Dragon's Breath and enhanced physical abilities. Anything beyond that is up to the personal preference of the Dragons. We have stayed sequestered from your kind for many years. Why should that change now?'

Kara blinked. She hadn't been prepared to defend her position. She was the rightful heir to the throne. She was the Dragon's Chosen. How could they not help recover her birthright?

She realized with a wave of shame that her family had indeed looked upon the Dragons as a tool, as something to rule and command. No wonder the creatures made themselves nigh impossible to find.

Kara's head drooped, and the Dragon's Breath all but extinguished in her guilt.

The Dragon snorted dismissively, then swam towards the waterfall.

'I'm sorry.' Kara's soft voice arrested the Dragon's departure.

Kara was pretty sure she hadn't had to apologize to anyone since she was a little girl. She was, after all, the princess of a powerful kingdom.

The Dragon turned back to look at her curiously.

'I cannot apologize for the actions of my ancestors. But I, myself, have behaved dishonorably towards the Dragons. You are not mine to command.' Kara looked up at it with a clear, strong gaze. 'My needs remain the same, but my wish is for the Dragons to be an ally and friend. Like Ylva and the Wolves. Will you help me reclaim the throne for the Drake Family?'

Kara drew her sword, sending flames licking down the blade. Resting the sword's tip on the ground, she lowered herself to one knee in a regal bow. The two small humans held their breath as the Dragon pondered Kara's words.

'I will present your case to the Tribe. If any choose to stand with you, they will offer their help.' The Dragon's voice was back to silky smooth. 'Wait here, Draco.'

The Dragon turned and noiselessly went back through the parted waterfall before the liquid curtain closed.

Kara breathed deeply, attempting to slow her racing heart. Then she settled in beside Ylva and Athalulf to await the Dragon's decision.

•◇•◇•◇•◇•◇•◇•◇•◇•◇•

'Draco finally found us, eh?' An elderly white Dragon wrinkled her nose in displeasure. 'This time, I thought we hid our entrance pretty well.'

The influential members of the Dragon Tribe were gathered in their official council field. Nestled in a deep valley, it was surrounded by thick woods on one side and rocky cliffs on another. A cool stream flowed through the middle, giving anyone who needed it a drink or respite from a hot sun.

'Someone helped her,' the large, gold and violet Dragon said in a velvety voice.

'It's a she this time?' a red and silver Dragon asked curiously. 'How long has it been since we checked on the human realm?'

'Maybe twenty years?' the white Dragon guessed.

'It's been fifty,' a green Dragon corrected. 'It doesn't matter how many Dracos have come and gone. How did this one find us?'

'The Wolfe Pack heir brought their Chosen and Draco to the waterfall,' the gold Dragon said.

'Why would Athalulf betray us like that?' a black Dragon snarled.

'That was no betrayal.' The gold Dragon smacked the smaller Dragon on the head with its tail. 'He merely brought her to the entrance. He did not show her how to enter our realm.'

'But why did he?' a silver Dragon asked.

'It seems Draco and the Blood Wolfe pack's Chosen are friends,' the gold Dragon answered.

'Of course, they are,' the white Dragon scoffed. 'The Wulfsige family have long been the royal Drake family's most loyal subjects. The surprising fact is that the Wolfe Pack actually has a Chosen. Tell me more about them. I missed the meeting with the Wolfe Pack.'

'Ylva Wulfsige.' The gold Dragon gave a silky chuckle. 'She is entertaining. I see why Athalulf is so protective of her.'

The Dragons, always fond of entertaining things, barraged the gold Dragon with questions about the long-awaited Wolfe Pack Chosen, until a little pink Dragon seemed to remember why they were there in the first place.

'Why did Draco come to us?' she asked.

'Why do they ever try to find us?' The black Dragon snorted dismissively. 'They want something, of course.'

Grumbles of agreement.

'True,' the gold Dragon admitted. 'But, Kara seems different.'

Everyone looked at him.

'Different how?' the black Dragon asked suspiciously.

'She acknowledged we are not hers to command.'

Gasps of surprise and murmurs of disbelief. The last person to acknowledge their partnership as at least equal was Athelstan Drake, the first Draco.

'She comes with a request, not a demand,' the gold Dragon continued, silencing the buzz. 'She wishes for us to ally with the Wolves and help reclaim her throne.'

'She was overthrown?' The white Dragon shook her head. 'Why should we help someone who can't keep their birth right, even with our gifts?'

That started a whole round of arguments that lasted nearly half an hour.

Finally, a powerful voice silenced them all. 'What were Draco's words?'

'"My wish is for the Dragons to be an ally and friend. Like Ylva and the Wolves. Will you help me reclaim the throne for the Drake Family?"' the gold Dragon repeated.

A long, thoughtful silence stretched between them. This was new. Most of Athelstan's descendants had been disappointing. This Kara Drake just might be worth their interest.

•◊•◊•◊•◊•◊•◊•◊•◊•◊•

Kara paced the cave's lake edges anxiously. How long had it been since the huge, gold Dragon had left, saying they would present her case to the Tribe? Her nerves were taut as a bow string.

She glared at her friend. How could Ylva nap at a time like this? Of course, the gigantic, rust colored Wolfe she used for both warmth and a pillow probably helped.

Athalulf slowly blinked his amber eyes before lifting his lip in a toothy smile, making fun of Kara.

'Your entire future isn't hanging in the balance,' Kara muttered.

She couldn't speak telepathically with the giant Wolfe like Ylva, but Kara could swear he laughed at her.

Ignoring Athalulf, Kara swept her gaze around the small area her ball of Dragon's Breath lit. They still waited by the giant lake deep underground. The rush of distant water was the only hint of the waterfall that lay beyond.

Kara returned to sit beside Athalulf. Ylva snored softly, and Kara smiled to herself. Every inch an aristocratic lady, Ylva would be horrified to learn she could make such a sound.

To entertain herself, Kara played with her Dragon's Breath, gathering energy in her hands to form balls of fire.

Athalulf finally lifted his head and looked out over the lake.

Ylva startled awake as Kara jumped up, running to the water's edge.

'Are they coming?' Ylva tried to suppress a yawn.

'Yes, look!' Kara pointed to where a small speck of light grew in the darkness.

It soon revealed the waterfall, which parted to let the gold Dragon through.

Ylva stood beside Kara as they waited for the swimming Dragon.

Athalulf took his time stretching before sauntering over. The Dragon stopped in front of them, its huge body again dwarfing the humans and Wolfe.

'Draco,' the Dragon's voice wrapped around the women. 'We have made our decision.'

The friends held their breaths.

'A Dragon has decided to accompany you on your travels,' the gold Dragon declared.

Kara almost slumped in relief. Finally! She looked expectantly at the Dragon with glittering eyes.

'Who is it?'

'Me,' a small voice echoed throughout the cave.

Kara and Ylva looked around, then at each other in confusion. Where had that voice come from?

'I'm up here, Draco,' the voice said.

Kara saw movement on the gold Dragon's shoulder.

What on Earth?

The tiny speck jumped from the gold Dragon and flew right towards the friends.

Startled, Kara instinctively jumped back, right hand pulling out her sword, left hand raised, with the Dragon's Breath flickering around her fingers.

Perhaps because she was more used to legendary, powerful creatures, Ylva flinched—but then held out her hand when she saw it clearly.

'Oh, Kara, it's such a darling!' she cooed, the Dragon drifting onto Ylva's palm.

Kara extinguished the flames and sheathed her sword before coming up to see the 'oh-so-powerful' creature that was supposed to help her reclaim the throne.

The tiny Dragon was barely the size of Ylva's pale, delicate hand. Deep purple scales appeared to glow from the inside, and the silver mane looked soft and silky.

'Hello.' Ylva brought her hand up to smile at the Dragon.

'You are interesting, Blood Wolfe!' The purple Dragon laughed.

Athalulf gave a warning growl.

'I know, I know, Wolfe. Relax,' the creature huffed.

Athalulf kept an eye on the Dragon but didn't protest as it jumped to Ylva's shoulder.

It stared at Kara with the same violet eyes every member of the Drake family was born with.

Is that where we got it from? Proof we are the Dragon's chosen family?

'Well?' The purple Dragon tilted its head at Kara.

'Um...' Kara was at a loss.

Ylva caught her gaze and mouthed, 'thank you'.

'Ah, thank you,' Kara said. 'I'm happy to have your... help.'

What was this lizard supposed to do? It was adorable, not intimidating.

'I agreed to come with you, not assist.' The purple Dragon sniffed imperiously. 'Not yet.'

Kara felt her chest tighten. What was the point of coming here if the Dragons weren't actually going to do anything? She needed allies, not spectators.

'I shall take my leave.' The gold Dragon turned to Athalulf. 'Please, give our greetings to your father. Be safe, all of you.'

The golden glow disappeared behind the waterfall, causing the light in the cave to grow much dimmer. But a soft purple light came from the remaining Dragon, still residing on Ylva's shoulder.

'We should be off as well,' the Dragon said, nestling against Ylva's neck. 'It has been many years since I visited the human realm.'

Athalulf led the way back through the maze of tunnels, Ylva chatting amiably with the Dragon.

'What is your name?' Ylva asked.

'You have not earned my name.' The Dragon puffed up with self-importance.

Kara rolled her eyes behind Ylva's back.

Dragon names are powerful. They are not given out easily.

When Ylva relayed Athalulf's explanation, Kara felt guilty about the eyeroll. 'But we need to call you something,' she pointed out.

'Fine,' the Dragon huffed, as if Kara's completely logical point was a pain in its tail. 'Call me Silver.'

It felt like they were being given a great privilege.

Kara continued towards the exit, wondering just what on Earth she had gotten herself into.

Falling Through
by Faith Tilley Johnson *(fantasy/time travel)*

The overwhelming feeling of being underwater and falling at the same time. It disturbed the senses. Letting the darkness take over and no longer fighting the pull, I fell asleep.

It was the nudging that finally woke me. I hoped it would leave me alone if I did not respond. Keeping my eyes closed, I sucked in a deep breath slowly. And then, just one more nudge.

I yelled, jumping up. The child ran screaming into the woods. It took a few minutes to gather my senses as I looked around. I was in a wooded area that had a strong spiritual, or supernatural, connection. As foreign as the woods were, there was a familiar comfort.

Accepting that I had travelled somewhere I had never been, I took a deep breath and gathered myself up. A smile came as I saw my rucksack on the ground by my feet. I quickly took inventory. There was an earth-tone cloak and a pewter brooch, a Ziploc bag of granola, and two large red apples. I pulled the cloak out and started to wrap it around my shoulders but paused to remove my fancy shawl and fold it gently, tucking it away in the bag. Securing the cloak around me, I dusted off debris from the forest floor. As I secured my bag, I heard voices.

'Fergus, nobody lives out here. There is no reason a woman would be here.'

The child grumbled. 'I know what I saw, Cait-Mai. There was a woman dressed in a purple silk dress lying on the ground. I thought she was dead!'

I swept the cloak over my dress. Carefully, I stepped into the brush. The child burst through the trees and pointed where I had been lying not that long ago.

The look on his face was broken. 'I *know* there was a woman here!'

The woman with him looked around and shook her head. Her appearance caught my attention; she looked familiar, though I was sure I had never met her before. As I watched, I must have made a noise because she abruptly turned my way and made eye contact.

Fergus followed her stare and started jumping up and down when he saw me. 'It's her! Cait-Mai! It's her!'

'Calm down.' She placed her hand on his shoulder to still him. 'Are you a faerie?'

I laughed. The simple question told me I was in an area of Celtic influence. At least, the woman in front of me had been influenced. 'No, I'm not a faerie. I am merely a traveller.'

'Well then, traveller, let us take you to the manse and get you something to eat. I am humbled to be at your service.'

The boy offered to take my rucksack and I graciously accepted. There was no sign of danger, only the unknown. The three of us walked through the woods until we reached a clearing just short of a roadbed. The compressed dirt of the bed was smooth, indicating it was a well-established lane. Not much further on, we came upon a large hedge of privet. My hostess ducked under a cut out in the hedge to allow passage and motioned for me to follow. Stepping through it we entered an enchanting garden with chrysanthemums and echinacea in bloom.

'Welcome to Hedges. Home of Lord Augustus and Lady Mamie Twickenham.' She nodded to the boy. 'And son Fergus Twickenham. I am Cait-Mai, the housekeeper.'

'I am Chenoa Damshóir, a traveller. I thank you for your hospitality.' I gave a proper curtsy to the two of them.

Cait-Mai nodded and shooed off Fergus. 'Make sure the chickens and pig are fed.'

Fergus ran off around the side of the manse and busily got to work. Cait-Mai motioned to the door to the summer kitchen just off the house.

'Damshóir? Are you Celt?' Realizing she was harshly blunt, she blushed. 'It's not a common name here.'

We went inside the kitchen and Cait-Mai began making breakfast. She pointed to a stool by the butcherblock counter that had loaves on it. Then reached for the hanging sausages and pulled them down to her by the woodstove.

'My family, whilst sparse, is widespread. I believe there is Celtic influence. It's not a common name in general.' I smiled trying to get her to relax. 'Can I help?'

Cait-Mai looked at the bread, 'Can I trust you with a knife?'

I looked at her with a smirk, thinking she must be joking. She was not. 'Yes. I can be trusted.'

The two of us prepared breakfast for the family as I learnt about where I was. The Twickenhams were peculiar people that lived just outside of Whitstead in their stone manse. The compound was lovingly called Hedges for the rows of hedges that Mamie had installed when they first bought the property a good ten years prior. Cait-Mai was hired on as the housekeeper by Mamie's mother whilst they were in Rollingsford not long ago. Mamie had her hands full caring for Augustus, whose health was waning.

'I've told you about us, what about you?' Cait-Mai asked with a pointed expression.

I nodded. I knew this was coming. The problem was, I was unsure of what I could safely tell her. 'Well, I am a traveller.'

'You are a Romani?'

I stopped for a moment. 'No, I am not Romani. I am not originally from this country.'

'We are too far from port for you to have been travellin' by sea. Where you from?'

I took a deep breath and smiled. 'Would you believe if I told you I were an *auld one*?'

The face that Cait-Mai made told me there was shock, but not disbelief. After a moment, she shook her head. 'I believe you could be connected to them, but I do not believe you are one.'

Cait-Mai looked me over and nodded. Not much was said as she finished preparing the sausage and slicing the cheese. As she prepared the breakfast platter, she hummed a song that rang familiar, but I was unable to place it. There was a lot about her that seemed familiar.

'So, you are not of this time.'

The statement caught me off guard. I had never been asked about being time displaced. I knew I had to be careful with my answer, but I could not lie. Was it possible that I met another of the Kamama? In the Damshóir clan there are those of us that have unique gifts called the Kamama. We are all dancers, and it is truly magical when we perform the Kamama dance. If Cait-Mai is one of my people, it would be quite uplifting right now.

'Chenoa?'

I blinked. 'I am unsure what you mean.'

'The speech you have is different. Whilst that could be simply because you are not from this area, I believe there is more to it. The dress you wear is not one that would be seen in this region either. Nor even the northern villages.' She paused. 'You have an energy about you. It is unique. As if you have been touched by magic or something.'

'What do you mean by magic? Could it not just be that I was in the woodland? There is a powerful sense of magic where you had found me.'

She stared at me. 'Your aura does not match Maisie's. Maisie is the guardian of the wood. As I said, you be unique.'

'I see.' I put the knife down, finished slicing the bread. Looking straight at Cait-Mai, I quietly answered. 'I am not from this time; I am not from this land. I was born in Appalachia. Although I am not sure what year exactly. My people are descendants of the *Auld Ones*.'

She wiped her hands on her apron and leaned back against the sink. 'I am familiar with the legends. Do you have control of your travel?' Seeing the confusion on my face she gathered the answer. 'I can teach you if you be willing. There is only one problem, you cannot stay here long.'

I took in what she said. I had no idea that travel could be controlled. Irma had never said anything about it. I blinked and started, 'How are you familiar? Are you an *Auld One*?'

Cait-Mai laughed. Then she gathered up the breakfast platter and took it through the door and into the dining room. Once the breakfast was served, Cait-Mai offered one of her dresses for me to wear so I would be more comfortable. After I changed, she pointed to a platter on the butcher block counter. 'Have a seat. Let us talk whilst we eat.'

We spent the morning talking about the Kamama. Cait-Mai was not of the Damshóir clan, but she was familiar with those with the Kamama blessing. As we talked and shared about ourselves, I learnt that she was not from the region either and her awareness of the Damshóir and Kamama was because of a woman she met when she was a child. Her family was what many referred to as black Scots, and she was aware of many of the legends of the auld ones. Whilst she knew most of the legends were elaborate stories, some rang true. One being of the Damshóir and their slànachadh women, the healers that were often called witches. The Damshóir clan was an old clan with mixed Scotch-Irish heritage that many believed to have been decimated when William the Conqueror invaded the isles. The stories that have been passed down include the slànachadh making it to the New World and becoming the Kamama women.

'The whole thing is speculation. That's not what matters though since you are here and have a connection to the slànachadh.' Cait-Mai smiled. 'The question is why?'

I thought for a moment. 'I cannot answer that. My travelling has always been unexpected, often involving a catastrophe.'

'Cait-Mai!' The shout came from the sitting room. It was the lady of the house, Mamie. 'Come. Help.' The voice was panicked, and we both jumped up and went into the room. The sight before us was horrifying.

'Mamie! What has happened?' Cait-Mai saw the same as I. Lord Twickenham was on passed out the floor. He looked as if he fallen from his chair.

'Augustus collapsed. He was sitting there chastising Fergus about his dirty shirt and then fell. He was not shouting. It was like he got a case of the vapours.' Mamie covered her mouth as she referred to the vapours. I immediately checked his pulse. It was nice and strong. I checked his pupils, and the light response was good.

'Do you by chance have any smelling salts?' I asked. 'And Fergus, can you run into the village and get a doctor or a healer?'

Both Mamie and Fergus looked at me as if I had grown a second head. Fergus was the first to respond. 'Papa would not want me to do that. He thinks Widow Larkin is a crazy old hag that pretends to be a witch.'

'Fergus!' Mamie and Cait-Mai in unison chastised him for speaking ill of her.

'Ma-ma! It's what Papa said.'

Cait-Mai offered smelling salts to me. 'Here are the smelling salts. Do you believe it is a case of the vapours?'

I nodded as I took the smelling salts. 'I believe so.'

Waving the ammonia bottle under Lord Twickenham's nose I was relieved to see him come around quickly. I helped the man up carefully; without a doctor, caution was best. 'Cait-Mai, can you get some cool water for Lord Twickenham? And a cool cloth.'

Twickenham slowly regained his bearings. He sat on the floor with me supporting him. Lady Twickenham was nearby in one of the table chairs. 'Oh Auggie. I was so worried!'

I looked at Cait-Mai as she returned with the cloth and a glass of water. I offered the water for him to drink and placed the cool cloth on the back of his neck. It was not until Lord Twickenham was cognizant of the situation that he took a good look at me and demanded, 'Just who are you and what are you doing in my home?'

Mamie looked at me and then at Cait-Mai. She then looked at me again. In the excitement she had not realised I was there. 'Cait-Mai? Is this a friend of yours? I do not recall being informed of a visitor to our manse.'

'Lady Twickenham, I do apologise. I was going to inform you of the arrival as soon as breakfast was complete.' Cait-Mai looked at me. 'This is Ch — Charletta. She lived in the same children's home I did in Rollingsford before coming here. She decided to come through Whitstead before going to port and travelling to the new world where she has been hired.'

'Charletta? You do not look as though you are German. Or is it French?' Twickenham pressed. The older man tensed. He was a man used to knowing everything and did not like the situation.

'One of the housemothers at the children's home named me. I was told I was left on the step in the night as a newborn. I do not know the origin of the name, only the meaning is freedom.' I turned away from the man and took a deep breath. In that breath I prayed and thanked God for knowledge. 'As Cait-Mai said, I am travelling through to get to port so I can journey to America. I have been hired by a Master William Alexander Grey in Virginia.'

Twickenham got up from the floor stiffly. He flopped into the chair that he had fallen out of minutes earlier. 'I see. I suppose I should thank you for assistance.'

Lady Twickenham threw herself across him, 'Oh Auggie! I was so worried. I did not know what to do. You had this blank look on your face and then your eyes rolled backwards, and you just fell to the floor. It is nothing but a miracle she was here.'

Lord Twickenham laughed off the situation. 'Mamie, it was just the vapours. I am sure the excitement of your news got to me. I certainly was not expecting it.' He turned towards me. 'Thank you, Charletta.'

Cait-Mai looked to Mamie. 'My Lady, there is news?'

Mamie smiled. 'Oh yes! So exciting! My sister will be having her baby soon and my mother has requested Auggie and I to come and visit. I told her we would be there on the fifth. We will leave Fergus here with you.'

'Of course, my Lady.' Cait-Mai looked at the child. 'Fergus will be no problem at all.'

As if on cue, the young boy ran out the door to the kitchen. Cait-Mai followed him.

Lady Twickenham turned to me. 'Charletta? It was lovely to meet you. It is a shame I will not get to know you; we are leaving in the morning to make sure we have time to be with my sister.'

I graciously nodded. 'I understand. I am certain that I will have left by the time you and Lord Twickenham return. I pray you have a safe journey to Rollingsford.'

The Twickenhams excused themselves and left to busy themselves with packing for their trip. Once we were alone, Cait-Mai could talk freely about what she knew and how to help me.

The rest of the day went smoothly whilst the Twickenhams packed and dinner was prepared. Cait-Mai made extra bread and packed away some cheese for their trip. At dinner Fergus insisted that Lord Twickenham read Scripture. Cait-Mai explained that the boy would have nightmares and psalms calmed him.

'Because he hath set his love upon me, therefore will I deliver him: I will set him on high, because he hath known my name. He shall call upon me, and I will answer him: I will be with him in trouble; I will deliver him, and honour him. With long life will I satisfy him, and shew him my salvation.' As Lord Twickenham finished, a sense of peace filled the room. As I thought about what the Scripture said, I was interrupted when Fergus gave me a hug goodnight and followed his parents off to bed.

I sat quietly for a moment and then looked Cait-Mai. 'Why Charletta?'

She laughed. 'Of all the questions.'

I looked at her and shook my head. 'Seriously, why Charletta?'

'You look exotic enough. An uncommon but recognizable name along with an established friendship keeps questions limited.'

'That makes sense. Right now, I need sleep — we will talk tomorrow.'

Sleep came quickly as I laid my head on the pillow. I slept through breakfast and the Twickenhams' departure. When I made my way to the kitchen, Cait-Mai had out a platter of bread and cheese whilst she busied herself with her tasks.

'Do you remember the Scripture from last night?' she asked when she saw me.

I nodded as I poured some tea and sat. 'It was about how God will protect and bless those that acknowledge Him. Those that love Him.'

'Do you love God?'

I took a deep breath. 'My relationship with God is difficult to explain. I acknowledge who He is, but I often feel like a punching bag that has been left out in the rain.'

'That is an interesting way to express it. I suspect that your life has been difficult. Especially if your travel has been associated with catastrophes or unexpected. That is why you need to know how to control it. I believe I can help you.'

'Well, Irma was my only teacher. So, how do we proceed?'

'Who is Irma?'

'Irma is *ulisi*, grandmother. She teaches all Kamama. She has taken on the role of matriarch. We do not all travel. There are different gifts.'

Cait-Mai nodded. 'Well, then. To be in control is to let go. I asked if you loved God. If you can let go and trust Him. Let His peace fill you.' She jumped up and grabbed my hand pulling me outside to the garden. 'The Kamama dance is one that starts with grief. The butterfly had to let go of her sadness. Only then was she able to gain peace and find joy.'

I looked at her. 'I understand you, but that is an oversimplification of the process of grief.' I took a deep breath. 'You are saying I have to let go of what I have lost and find that peace within me. The peace that God gives — and He will bless me.'

Nodding again, Cait-Mai grabbed a bodhran from near the door and slowly tapped it giving a beat like the native drums I was used to. My feet started tapping to the beat and I began to dance. Looking down at the ground with my arms behind me. The beat sped up as did my dance. As I danced, I thought of what Cait-Mai had said about God. Life could be hard and there were trials, but that did not give me reason to believe I was abandoned. Not by family, or by God. I continued dancing as my spirit calmed. I began to feel joy.

I am not sure how long I danced, but when I finished, I felt energized. The grief the butterfly danced through to find restoration—I was there now. Cait-Mai and I spoke over household tasks, and she encouraged me to do my dance at the bonfire. I was not sure how appropriate that would be around a Guy Fawkes bonfire, but after the last few days, it felt right.

Whilst the Kamama dance was about loss and restoration, the purpose of the bonfires was a focus on coming together. Through talks with Cait-Mai, I felt like a part of me that I did not know was missing had finally been restored. Cait-Mai suggested I wait until after the festivities began and then make my way to the bonfires to dance. That way, if anybody did notice me it would not draw as much attention. It was common for young people to celebrate around the fires.

I hoped what Cait-Mai taught me would allow me to return to my home and people.

Fergus kept us busy throughout the day. We decided once we had the chores done, we would go into the village and see the festivities.

Getting ready was harder than I expected. Putting my Kamama dress on surrounded me with memories of the last bonfire where I danced. I missed my family so much it was overwhelming. Tonight more than ever, the Kamama dance would be from my heart. I was grateful for Cait-Mai helping me dress and braiding my hair up. She gingerly placed silver pins to hold the loose wisps around my face. Fergus walked in as I was pulling on my moccasins. His eyes were wide.

'You *are* a faerie!'

I laughed. It was a good, soul filling laugh. 'Not quite, love.'

I wrapped my cloak around me and secured it with the pewter brooch, noticing the design. It was a simple, Celtic design with the knots woven in the melt cast. *Irma always knows.* I glanced to Cait-Mai who was wrapping her own cloak around her. 'Are we ready?'

She looked over to Fergus as he was grabbing another roll from the pantry cabinet. 'We best be going before he eats all the food for tomorrow!'

We all laughed as we walked out the door. Outside a cart was waiting. Cait-Mai and I looked at each other and then Fergus tugged on both of our cloaks. 'I got the cart ready, so we didn't have to walk all the way into town. Did I do good?'

'Yes, you did wonderful.' Cait-Mai climbed into the cart and grabbed the reins, making sure to leave room for me on the seat. As I climbed up, Fergus made his way to the back of the cart and sat on the lip. We all secured ourselves and off we went.

The evening was enjoyable. The village people were pleasant. As the festivities progressed, the throng of people moved down towards St. Nicholas Church where the effigy of Guy Fawkes was standing, and the wood stacked for the bonfires. The caretaker was preparing to light the large bonfire as we arrived at the church grounds. The energy in the air was captivating. I suspected there was more going on than the typical bonfire night. The area surrounding the village was strong in energies.

I smiled and relaxed. I prayed. *Abba, Father, thank you. I know I do not always see why I am on the journey that I am, but I know you always have a purpose. Thank you for bringing me to Cait-Mai. I know she is somebody special and I feel I will see her again. Most of all, Abba, please honour the request of my heart. I need to return home. I need to be with my family.*

As I ended my prayer, the bonfire flared up, vibrant as the flames caught to the wood. I slipped off my cloak and folded it into my rucksack. I carefully hung the sack across my body and tightened it so it would not get in the way. I then adjusted the fancy shawl so that it had free movement. The purple satin looked like a river of silk enhanced with silver embroidery. The underside of the shawl was a silver satin with deep purple embroidery. The dress was a matching purple with silver embroidery and my moccasins were white leather.

Cait-Mai smiled at me. The flicker of light danced on the fabric. 'You know, Fergus is right. You do look like a faerie.'

'Well, let's see if this faerie can fly.'

We walked closer to the bonfire as the crowd grew. There was an underlying rhythm as the excitement mounted. I tried to focus on my dance movements, but the atmosphere was too chaotic. 'Cait-Mai, I'm going to go off a little distance so that I can focus. If this works, thank you. Make sure to let Fergus know I'm all right.'

When I got away from the crowd, I heard a cheer go up. I turned to look and saw the effigy of Guy burn hot and bright. I did not really understand the meaning of the burning, but I knew that the Kamama dance was best with a bonfire. Turning away again, I found my centre. *Thank you, Abba.*

The dance started slow. One step then another. With each step I purposefully thought of home and my loved ones. As I found peace in the movements, I raised my arms and let the fancy shawl spread like wings. As the dance sped up, I saw bright lights in the sky that reminded me of fireworks. It was beautiful. And then, it was dark.

The Unfortunate Pie
by Valerie Yeva Shaw (fantasy/misadventure)

'This is a good plan,' Kirot repeated to himself for the third time.

The young gnome, his blond beard just coming in, was crouching beneath a pile of embroidery set casually on a table. Its owner was nowhere in sight.

His eyes were fixed on the thimble, lying on its side next to the sewing. It glittered appealingly in the flitting afternoon sunlight, scrolls of embossed flowers dancing around its delicate sides.

It would win him Flana Buttonstead's heart, he was sure of it.

Across the room, his friend Ifin waved his arms, trying to catch Kirot's attention, but the gnome ignored him.

Ifin wasn't a bold gnome.

Ifin wasn't trying to win the heart of the loveliest gnome in the gathering, either. That white-bearded Draff Horseknot was after Flana too, and Kirot needed to make sure that he, not Draff, was the one she was thinking of. He wanted to ask for her hand amongst the squash vines - her favourite place in Whitstead, for some reason, something to do with the striped, squeaking beetles that lived in the garden - and there wasn't much time left. Already, the leaves were blazing into colour, and the cold rains were beginning to return. Soon the vines would become sodden, the beetles would burrow, and the harvest season would be over. She'd said nothing about winterfrost being her favourite.

Bold moves yield bold rewards, Kirot told himself. His feet didn't seem to agree. They seemed impossibly heavy. There was a reason things like this were best done at night. He swallowed. Maybe he should have waited, like Ifin had advised.

No. His plan was a good one. This Tall One always packed her things up neatly before bed. He might never have a chance at this beautiful thimble again.

Darting another glance at the door, Kirot whispered one last prayer, then forced himself to run.

The gnome scampered across the table and scooped up his prize, neatly leaving a token of gratitude behind. The polished acorn cap spun and tottered like a top where the thimble had been.

He ran as if his life depended on it.

Kirot was young. He was healthy and fit. He weighed as much as a light mouse, and now his feet were quick as heartbeats.

He fairly flew through the Tall One's home, vaguely aware that Ifin was running too, somewhere behind him. They were doing great! He could envision Flana's overjoyed face. Maybe she would kiss his cheek!

He ran into the kitchen and hiked up onto the counter. Now he was breathing rather hard; the thimble didn't fit into his backpack, so he had to hold it under his arm and do everything one-handed. That made climbing very difficult. He jogged around a huge pie cooling on the board and went 'round a mess of apples.

Up to the windowsill, huzzah, hooray! It was still cracked open just the littlest bit, as they'd left it before. Tall One hadn't even noticed. Nearly there!

And then, disaster.

The cold Autumn wind gusted strongly, slamming the windowpane shut just as Kirot sprang for it. He hit the closed window with a grunt, then staggered backward, his nose stinging.

The stunned gnome lost his balance. He teetered, tottered, and then fell, head over-tea-kettle, into the giant pie below.

The warmth of it hit him first. Thank goodness it had been out of the oven for a while, or he might have been cooked within. As it was, it was like falling into a hot bath. A hot bath tasting of pumpkin and spices and weighing each and every one of his limbs down like the thickest of mud. It filled the thimble, it oozed into his clothing, it stuck to his eyelids and went up his nose. Kirot tried to jump, he tried to run, but all he could manage was a miserable slow wallow.

Across the room, halfway across a shelf on the wall, Ifin skidded to a stop and slammed his hands over his mouth, his eyes wide with horror.

His expression grew even more terrified as the Tall One re-entered the room. She was humming, her footsteps loud on the floorboards.

Kirot froze, his eyes rising to lock with Ifin's.

No Tall One was to ever see a gnome.

He swallowed.

They weren't supposed to eat one, either.

●◇●◇●◇●◇●◇●◇●◇●◇●

Kirot stayed very still, his mind racing. He could plead. She might spare him, if he sounded sweet enough. He'd never heard of a Tall One intentionally hurting a gnome. But would she even hear his voice? Across the room, he could see Ifin running about, dodging and ducking around the tins on the shelf. He had no idea what his friend was doing. Panicking, most likely.

The Tall One might be angry that he'd borrowed her thimble. Had she seen the beautiful bowl he'd given her in return? Or would she assume he was a common thief, like the pixies?

What if she thought he was a pixie? She might eat him for spite!

Now Ifin was making his way slowly among the shelves, heading for Kirot. His friend's arms were full of something, something that looked like black string, perhaps.

Kirot held his breath. Was Ifin intending to throw him a line?

The Tall One was washing dishes, her humming filling the room. Kirot's fear made the ordinarily pleasant sound into something threatening.

Ifin made it to the ledge above the pie, then opened his arms.

A flurry of spiders, their legs outstretched in alarm, rained down. They stuck immediately onto the surface of the pie, hissing in protest.

Kirot blinked in surprise. This was Ifin's plan? Spiders? How could this possibly help? There was no method by which they could supply web, mired in the goop just as he was. He shied away from a particularly large one as it lunged viciously at his leg.

The Tall One turned in his direction, and Kirot held his breath and sank into the filling, disappearing from sight.

The scream was muffled by the pumpkin in his ears.

The woman took one look at her pie, the top jumbly-tumbly, speckled with a dozen struggling spiders, and threw open the window. In one motion, punctuated with shrieks, she whisked the horrifying pie off her counter, and flung it outside, dish and all.

The sensation of soaring through the air was not a pleasant one. Kirot clung to the precious thimble, praying mightily as he flew. Thankfully, the pie hit a garden post and flipped, coming to splat sideways in the chicken yard. Kirot tumbled from the mess, dazed but unhurt.

The chickens descended upon the feast.

Normally, Kirot was not afraid of the huge birds. He had never encountered them whilst covered in delicious pumpkin pie before, though.

He yelped and dodged as the chickens pecked at him. Kirot tried to sing the soothing song, but the stupid birds had lost their minds in their hunger and forgot to listen.

Suddenly, heavy boots sounded in the yard.

Another Tall One!

Kirot had a split second to react. Hugging the thimble to his chest with his left arm, with his right he grabbed the feathers of the mighty rooster beside him and hauled himself up. He tucked himself beneath one of the great wings, cringing in the moist heat of the rooster's body.

This was also a disaster.

What Kirot hadn't known was that tonight was an evening for a special dinner, and this particular rooster had chased the Master's wife one too many times. The jig was up for the cockerel.

In one fell swoop, the Tall One snagged the brash bird by the legs, swinging it upside down. Kirot clung with all his might as the giant wings beat mercilessly in protest, buffeting him heartily. The bird went horizontal, but the shadow of the tall one loomed. Kirot cowered in the stinky feathers. Just as he thought that he would faint, or fall off, or perhaps lose his hearing from all the battering his poor noggin was taking, there was a mighty, horrible, THWACK!

The deed was done.

The world suddenly whooshed upside down again, and Kirot barely caught the thimble with one hand as it threatened to fall from his grasp.

Whistling, the Tall One set down the axe and went into the shed.

Kirot knew what came next. The big pot of boiling water, that was what.

The problem was, he was now suspended man-height in the air, bobbing on the laundry line. Below him, the hard stone and packed dirt of the yard promised an unfortunate landing.

Kirot climbed through the feathers, coming to stand on top of the bird. Could he balance on the line? Maybe, but there was no ladder down, no extra rope to swing on. He'd left his at home, in his rush to get going. For the tenth time, he regretted his impatience.

A movement across the yard caught his eye.

A cat.

Kirot froze.

If there was one beast that gnomes were frightened of, it was the cat. Cats never listened to the soothing song. They couldn't resist a scampering gnome. Drawn no doubt by the scent of the slain bird, the cat approached swiftly.

Its eyes widened, sighting him.

This was no good, no good at all. That thing could easily jump and swat him off. He'd be but two bites in its needle-sharp maw. The wind blew hard, nearly knocking his hat off his head. A rainstorm was coming, no doubt of it. He looked down, dazzled by the height. There was no sign of Ifin at all. Kirot was on his own. How to escape? Gnomes did not fly. He didn't have feathers like this bird; big, plank-like feathers, wide enough to… to…

Kirot threw off his hat and thrust the hard metal thimble onto his head. Then he frantically began to pluck. One feather. Two. Three. Fourfivesix.

The cat below wiggled its rear, watching him with eyes that had enlarged to black holes. It would leap any second.

What he was about to do was ridiculous, and he knew it. He could see no other choice.

Kirot tucked the feathers, three on each side, beneath his arms, and just as the cat sprang, he jumped.

In what had to be a gift of divine intervention, the Autumn wind gusted hard, carrying the gnome with it.

Kirot glided. He rode the wind, whooping with joy, as it carried him over the frustrated cat, over the dying garden, over the chicken yard. Shifting this way and that, mingling with the falling leaves and the splattering raindrops, Kirot glided into the edge of the forest. He bumped into a tree, grasped a branch with his feet, and pulled himself into the safety of its arms. Then, swift as a squirrel, he made his way down, and it was a quick zoop into the nearest mouse hole.

He gave himself a minute to get his heart under control.

Maybe two or three minutes.

'Kirot?'

A familiar shape filled the entry of the tunnel.

Ifin's face, worried and pale, loomed large.

In response, Kirot raised the thimble in victory.

'I will win 'er 'eart like I won this prize!' he exclaimed.

•◇•◇•◇•◇•◇•◇•◇•◇•◇•

'No, Papa,' Sush giggled and snuggled in closer to her father's chest. 'You didn't say that! That's not what you tol' us last time.'

'I did!' said Kirot, his eyes twinkling. Sush was the littlest of his three children, blessed with the same doe eyes as her mother.

'No, you didn't,' insisted Killy, his middle child. 'You said, 'I 'ave defeated the pie, vanquished the cat, an' avoided the axe! The beautiful Flana shall be mine!'

Across the room, Pittar rolled his eyes. 'The girls always make it so flowery. Let's hear the bit about the rooster again, an' the cat.'

Kirot looked to Flana, who was putting a loaf of fresh baked acorn bread on the table, next to a pumpkin pie and a sliced apple. In the centre, the thimble sat, stuffed with fresh moss and the prettiest leaves the children could find. His house, right next door to Ifin's, smelled of baking and spices, warmth, and food.

'What do you say, wife? Didn't I tell the story well?'

Flana grinned, pulling a jug of cider from the shelf. 'You did, love. You just left one wee bit out.'

He looked puzzled. 'What was that, then?'

She straightened the leaves in the thimble. 'The way Ifin tells it, a certain brave gnome was resting after his flight, an' the mouse which owned that hole came home. He tells me you screamed loud enough t' frighten the entire village, Buttonstead an' all.'

Kirot's eyes widened, whilst his children began to giggle.

'Well,' he said, rubbing his neck and smiling sheepishly, 'I wasn't expectin' the grey fellow.'

His children laughed, whilst Flana wrapped her arms around his neck.

'You know, it wasn't the thimble itself that won my heart.'

Kirot looked up at her, through the jostling of his children. 'No? What was it then?'

She smiled down at him. 'You think fast on your feet. You make do with what you 'ave. An'…' Her smile warmed further. 'You remembered that I loved the autumn beetles.'

Kirot grinned at her. 'How could I forget such a thing? No one else has a 'eart for those beasties.' He kissed his wife, then rubbed his hands, looking towards the small table. 'So, is that a pie I'm smellin', darlin' one?'

'It is, and it's pumpkin, too.'

Pittar held up a finger. 'Without the spiders.'

An All Hallows' Toast
by Hillari DeSchane *(mystery/suspense/supernatural)*

I opened the door to admit the doctor, along with a swirl of yellow and red leaves borne on the late October wind. 'Come in, Craddock, and get out of the weather! I've built up the fire in my study.' I gestured towards the back of the house.

'Evening, vicar.' Craddock glanced towards the staircase. 'You didn't call me here for Gwendolyn, did you? You have been administering the medicine as I directed?'

I waved my hands. 'No trouble there. She seems to be improving with every dose I give her. Fever's broken, heart's no longer beating out of her chest, and the headaches are not nearly as piercing.'

Craddock gave me a quick, assessing look. 'Is that so? I'd best go up and check.'

I caught his elbow. 'I looked in on her just before you arrived. She's sleeping peacefully.'

'I'll see her in the morning, then, just to be sure.'

I waved him to the chair facing the fire. The firelight caught the brandy in the crystal decanter, turning it to liquid fire as I poured into his upraised glass.

Craddock held his hand over his glass. 'Enough. I need to keep my wits about me. No telling what mischief the lads of Whitstead will get up to in honour of Hallowe'en, and what injuries I'll have to patch up. I've never seen such a place for observing the old traditions. Even your own household.' He tipped his glass to the carved turnip lanterns my housekeeper had set as decorations on either end of the mantel. 'Since you haven't called me to see your niece, and I don't see the chessboard laid out, you must have a perplexing case to discuss.'

From nearly the first week Craddock had arrived in Whitstead, some seven years ago, he and I had met frequently to discuss the more challenging cases presented by those under our care. The doctor was a 'new man,' a scientist and an agnostic. I had tried to woo him for our Lord. In seven years, he came to assent intellectually to my philosophy, just as I came to appreciate his science. Yet Craddock's heart remained unmoved by matters beyond what he could touch and measure. So it was with some trepidation that I said, 'I want to tell you a ghost story.'

Craddock's brows rose. 'Appropriate for the night. Won't lose your dog collar if this gets out, though, will you?'

The doctor was not always an easy man, but he was always good company. 'I'm retired so there's not much danger of my being defrocked,' I said. 'I'm expected to be eccentric. But this one is difficult to pass off as mere superstition. There's as much fact as fiction involved. Most intriguing of all, the ending remains to be written.'

'And you think I can help supply one? I'm honoured, Buell.'

'I believe this calls for a toast.' I raised my glass. "May faithful friends surround us, faithless ones depart, God grant us the wisdom to see the difference, and His justice to act when we daren't."

Craddock raised his own glass, grimacing at the sting of the strong spirits. I couldn't be sure the burning in my own throat was from my overlarge swallow from my glass, the answer to my prayer, or a foretaste of punishment.

I stifled a little gasp and began: 'You see, the ghosts in this matter are still alive.'

•◇•◇•◇•◇•◇•◇•◇•◇•◇•

It was a Monday morning a month earlier, and I was hurrying towards the coach stop, grateful my pink cheeks would be credited to my haste. None of the villagers I passed would suspect I was meeting the woman I loved most in the world.

I was an established bachelor—to be more accurate, at my present age of seventy, I was a confirmed one. In my university days I had fallen in love with a young woman named Margaret. But she chose another, my best friend Charles. He was a good man, certainly a better husband for her. This had been no tragedy beyond the commonplace one of an inarticulate young man who couldn't bring himself to speak the words a young woman needs to hear.

We remained friends, the three of us. Being an orphan, I cherished their adoption of me into their new family. We exchanged letters at holidays and upon all the important occasions—Margaret's first child, and my first pulpit. Charles' rise in county politics, and my preferment to a prosperous and comfortable midlands city. And at long last, Charles a baronet and their last child, the long-hoped-for girl. They honoured me by naming her 'Gwendolyn' after my fanciful suggestion.

It wasn't all grim sacrifice on my part. I drew closer to God than I could otherwise, turning a practical vocation into a sincere one. If some of my flock were surprised over the years by my sympathetic counsel in their own romantic travails, then that redeemed my pain.

For the truth and the shame is, I had found a new love. Before you call me faithless, let me explain that the new object of my affection was a saint, and ten centuries dead. The perfect woman for an ageing cleric, you might say. But pursuing her had become an obsession, one I feared to confess even to God.

In the years after losing Margaret to Charles, I'd cultivated a taste for archaeology. Long bachelor nights and holidays need something to fill them. I see now, it was my first major discovery nearly three decades ago in a half-ruined Denbighshire vault that set my feet on the path to a Whitstead hearth rug on that blustery All Hallows' night.

The illuminations in the fragile old manuscript had crumbled to gold and lapis dust, but the letters written in ox gall ink remained clear. As I read, I fell in love with the tenth century Welsh princess Winefride, lovely as the moon and as chaste, who had dedicated her life and her body to serving God. Caradoc, warrior chieftain, enraged when Winefride refused him, declared if he could not have her, neither would that interloper, Jesus the Christ. Caradoc seized his great sword and cut off her head, but Winefride's uncle, sainted Bono, restored her head and her life. The old saint cursed Caradoc to be swallowed up by the earth for his impiety. When Winefride eventually died, a healing spring rose from the place her body was laid, not far outside the village that would come to be known as Whitstead, and a well was built round the spring and became a pilgrimage site. But on the fate of Caradoc, that manuscript and all the books I sought out over the years were silent.

My shiver on that long ago morning had nothing to do with the chill of the vault. I recognised the names in the tale, anglicized though they were. 'Bono' had transformed over the centuries into my last name, Buell. 'Winefride' was the medieval English attempt at the Welsh 'Gwenffrewi.' The name was pronounced Gwendolyn nowadays.

I can still hear the ghostly sound that made me throw up my head and stare about me when my lips formed the name, as if a heavy iron-bound door had just been slammed shut. Even then I recognised the sound of my destiny being sealed, echoing down the corridors of time. I didn't know, then, that it knelled the destiny of two other souls as well.

◆◇◆◇◆◇◆◇◆◇◆◇◆◇◆

My right hand curled into a fist in my pocket and brushed against the black-bordered envelope, pulling me back to the Monday morning coaching inn. Addressed in Charles's hand, plain and unpretentious, the announcement was just as plain. 'My old friend John. You will have guessed by the stationery that Margaret has died.'

Charles had begged me, as a kindness to them both, to give Gwendolyn a change of scenery and of occupation. I'd recently taken a bit of a tumble-down whilst digging around Saint Winefride's well, and the ensuing congestion of the lungs from a long slow hobble home in a soaking rain had been slow to pass off. Now Gwendolyn was coming to Whitstead to care for 'Uncle' John. Charles also laid a charge on me. Out of love for Margaret, he asked me to counsel Gwendolyn and give her a last chance to reconsider a choice she'd made.

When a twelve-year-old Gwennie had announced she wished to become a foreign missionary, Margaret and Charles put it down to a charming if slightly misguided tribute to 'dear old Uncle John.' When she turned fourteen and had determined it was to India she would carry the Light of the World, Gwendolyn's alarmed parents curtailed her summer visits to me and packed her off to a ladies' academy.

Seven years' time, Gwendolyn's steady insistence on her calling, and now Margaret's death, had worn down Charles. His letter asked only that I speak to Gwendolyn as honestly as possible about the reality of what she proposed. 'Be as open with her about your sacrifices,' he wrote, 'as you've been humble about your fulfilment. Speak to her of loneliness.'

The composed young woman in mourning black took me aback. It was if a ghost had stepped down from the coach, some amalgam of Margaret and Winefride. An icy bead of sweat traced my spine. *Two women I've loved and lost. Are you warning me, Lord, that you are going to take this woman from me too?*

Gwendolyn pressed my hand. 'Don't look so sad, Uncle John. I promise I'll help you get well and strong. Then you'll have the energy to try to talk sense into me before I leave.' Her expression was mischievous. 'I know all about my father's request. To set me straight on the harsh realities of missionary life for young women.'

'You're not upset?'

'Of course not. It is just what I should do if I had a daughter proposing to go off to a remote and hostile nation. The mission field is no place for romantics. No matter their sex.'

Drawing her arm through mine for the slow amble home, I pushed her ominous 'before I leave' into a far corner of my mind.

I wasn't the only man beguiled by Gwendolyn that morning. Dr Craddock was still holding his hat aloft with a poll-axed expression even after I followed Gwendolyn through the coach house gate.

He returned to the present with a little start. 'A relation of yours?'

He had never met her, I reminded myself. Craddock had moved to Whitstead only after Gwendolyn had gone off to school. I squelched the little spurt of unworthy emotion. 'Gwendolyn is the daughter of my oldest friend and his wife.'

'Ahhh.' The single syllable was freighted with meaning. 'She's staying with you?'

'Yes.'

'That reminds me. I should take a last look at you before I pronounce you fit in wind and limb. Tonight be convenient?'

My 'Convenient enough' was grudging, but I needn't have worried about insulting him. I was speaking to Craddock's back as he strode off after Gwendolyn. She was directing the footman and barely glanced at him. I took no small satisfaction in her disinterest.

•◇•◇•◇•◇•◇•◇•◇•◇•

Whatever Craddock expected, Gwendolyn remained unimpressed by his advances over the next two weeks. She had given her heart to another, and He would not be supplanted by earthly suitors. As I write this account years later, I still wonder. How could Craddock not see how his arguments — his insistence on making her his —

only set the seal on Gwendolyn's resolve? Or was he aware but helpless to stop himself? Perhaps that explains his desperation, and what it led him to do.

Tuesday fortnight, Craddock was helping Gwendolyn pass the after-dinner coffee in a demonstration of domestic agreeableness. I found myself studying him. Craddock was years younger than I, certainly young enough to consider marriage and begetting a family. He'd had a good career in the army, came of an old county family of similar rank and wealth to Gwendolyn's own, and lived on the family estate he'd inherited within easy riding distance of Whitstead. His practice was busy, and he was respected in the neighbourhood. He was highly eligible.

Craddock set down Gwendolyn's cup with enough force to make the porcelain ring. They had resumed the argument that had been their sole topic of conversation since the day they'd met. 'The heat, the mosquitoes, the typhoid, or smallpox, they'll kill you in a year,' he said. 'Or you'll catch the eye of some princeling and be forced into his har—er...' Craddock had the grace to blush. 'Well, better to die of the typhoid than that, if you see what I mean,' he finished.

Gwendolyn's cheeks were nearly as red as Craddock's, but her hands continued composedly with her needlework. 'All the more reason for me to remain unmarried. I shall not be neglecting children or a husband. I shall not even be alone. The Society for Promoting Female Education in the East is sending me as part of a team.'

Craddock took up his coffee and drank. 'There's nothing wrong with a woman being religious. All I'm saying is let her do that here in England, where she can make a home for her husband and raise her children in safety.'

Gwendolyn's smile was pointed. 'The Society tells me they never have enough doctors.'

Craddock snorted. 'I did my service. Nearly thirty years, most of them in India.'

Gwendolyn responded with aplomb that hinted at the steel within. 'You should consider joining us, Doctor. Uncle John told me you never married.'

I frowned a warning at her. Craddock was in love with her and she must not tease him. It was the difference between the reed and the oak. The young reed could bend under the rush of emotions, be bruised but recover. The mature oak would withstand the buffeting until suddenly it broke and was destroyed.

'You misquote me, my dear,' I interjected into the taut silence. 'I said Dr Craddock has not married yet.'

'My apologies, Doctor,' Gwendolyn murmured.

Craddock propped his fists on the mantel and stood looking down into the embers. 'I am sorry you will not listen to reason, Gwendolyn.'

Gwendolyn's eyes widened. This was a different Craddock, quiet and grave rather than blustering.

'India offers a hundred ways for a woman to die...I've seen them all. But if you won't accept the facts, I offer you the words of your God.' The guttering candle painted Craddock's profile with lurid tones. 'Did not God create a wife for Adam because it was not good the man should be alone?' he said. 'Did He not then command them to be fruitful and multiply?' Craddock pushed away from the hearth. 'It is a woman's duty to marry a strong man and bear his children, if she truly fears God as you claim you –'

'I do not deny,' Gwendolyn interrupted him, 'that it is many women's joy to marry and bear children. But some of us have been called to serve God in a different way.' Her outspread hands appealed for his understanding. 'You are correct, Doctor. I do fear God, and I will serve Him on the mission field with all that I have, body, mind, and soul. Because I love Him.'

The two figures swam in my vision as if a wavering curtain of gauze had dropped between us. I caught barbaric gleams from a crimson cloak, a woman's hair plaited with gold in a mode ten centuries out of date, and a great sword with a jewelled hilt. It was as if I was looking at Gwendolyn and Craddock through the wrong end of a telescope, seeing them not over a distance but back through time.

I blinked hard, the veil of my tears dissolved, and the present returned. For the cloak there was a crimson shawl tossed over the back of Craddock's chair; the glittering plaits were no more than the thread Gwendolyn held up to the light as she prepared her needle. And the sword – nothing more than a fireplace poker with enamelled handle.

Craddock nodded curtly. 'As you will, my lady.'

Anguish gripped me. *Surely not that, Lord? Have you not said you desire mercy, not sacrifice?*

Gwendolyn fell ill that night.

•◇•◇•◇•◇•◇•◇•◇•◇•

'The diagnosing physician is well advised to commit to memory the following rhyme: *Blind as a bat, red as a beet, hot as a hare, and the heart runs alone.*'

Gwendolyn's symptoms had puzzled me since the night her illness began. Ten days of Craddock's care and prescriptions brought no improvement. In my dreams, a dim memory uncurled of a rare and deadly lore, an ancient ritual reawakened. In my waking hours, I scoured my library.

Now I reread the rhyme to be sure, then shoved the medical textbook aside. With trembling hands, I dumped out an envelope of yellowed newspaper clippings. Bold-point headlines swirled as I stirred the brittle newsprint with my finger. 'Thuggees Revenge? Rash of Poison Deaths.' 'Suspect All Servants Police Warn.' 'More Deaths, Detectives Mystified.' The piece I wanted was just a scrap, torn rather than cut from the 'Letters to the Editor' page of the Madras Times.

There! I scanned it. '…phenomenon of organised *thuggee* was always greater by rumour than by confirmed… current rash of murders depends on the administration of a decoction of the native plant *datura,* commonly known as 'devil's trumpet…' argues for administration by someone known or close to the vic…'

The rest of the piece was missing, but I now knew or suspected enough to complete it myself. I glanced at my desk calendar. The twenty-fifth day of October. There was much for me to do, and not much time.

•◊•◊•◊•◊•◊•◊•◊•◊•

'…why I said the ghosts in this matter are still alive,' I concluded my tale that All Hallows' Eve, six nights later.

'Neatly told.' Craddock's smile was thin as a knife. 'Even the not-so-subtle hint that justice has yet to be done. That toast, you made it up yourself, didn't you? Bit on the nose, old chap.'

I shrugged. 'I'm a priest, not a poet.'

'Well, you promised me I should have a part in creating the ending of this little drama of yours. Let us be certain all of our characters have taken the stage.'

Brandy splattered the carpet as he gestured towards me with his glass. 'First, we have good old Saint Bono, played in the present by elderly vicar John Buell. I imagine you see the old saint as the hero, though to my taste he fulfils the role of buffoon.'

'Yes, I can see how you'd feel that way.'

He began to pace. 'Then there is the villain of the piece, the warrior prince Caradoc of ten centuries ago. Did you know his clan held most of the land in this area? Including a certain spring.'

Craddock laughed, an odd sound almost like a giggle. 'Don't look so shocked, Vicar. You're not the only one who can use a library. I was curious about the thunderclap that struck me that day I first saw Gwendolyn. You should be gratified to know I've come to believe your little fable that we three are destined to resolve the old business. Only this time, Morris Craddock will do Prince Caradoc one better. I intend to come out the winner.'

'Do you, now?' My mild reply disguised my confusion. Craddock should be nearly comatose by now, not prowling the room like a caged tiger. How had I miscalculated so badly?

As if reading my thoughts, he said, 'Calculating datura's dosage correctly for slow poison rather than the quick kill is most demanding. Why do you think I was constantly bringing over new formulations for Gwendolyn? I had no desire to kill my bride, just make her more compliant. As for your attempt on me tonight, I take it you planned to render me unconscious so you could truss me up then turn me over to the magistrate.' His shrug was condescending. 'Datura is extremely bitter. Even brandy cannot hide the taste from someone who is as intimately familiar with the drug as I am. Whilst you were pouring your own glass, I spat out my mouthful.'

That was it, then. My last chance to bring about a justice denied across ten centuries and two continents. *Have I misunderstood you, Lord? Is it true, I'm only an old fool beguiled by the past? If not, then you must make a way. I cannot do it myself.*

'There is one last player who has yet to make her appearance. Yet wait—' Craddock held a hand to his ear as a creak sounded from the stairs. 'Here she comes, right on cue.'

Gwendolyn's voice reached us first. 'Uncle John, I need to ask you about this medicine. What you've been giving me this past week tastes different than what Dr Craddock sent over originally. Surely my suspicions are just fever dreams, but...' Gwendolyn's voice trailed off as Craddock met her in the entryway.

He plucked the brown bottle from her hand and ushered her into the room. 'Enter our heroine, and future martyr. Oh, I beg your pardon. Future saint.' He turned the bottle to read the label, squinting as if his eyes hurt him. 'A good forgery, Vicar, but not perfect.' He tossed the bottle into the hearth.

Craddock's voice took on a dreamy note. 'It used to puzzle me... Why did those women have to die?' He rubbed his forehead absently. 'You can't imagine the pressure to marry, once I arrived in India... Widows, spinsters, lonely do-gooders... four unattached women for every man, each one grasping for a man, any man. But I had to keep myself free to seize my destiny when she was delivered to me.' His hand brushed aside pestering insects only he could see. 'I killed them so I could be ready when I found you.'

'And now you say you belong to another.' With a motion as quick as a striking cobra, Craddock seized Gwendolyn's wrist and pulled her against him.

I saw with horror that his eyes were mad, the pupils like black holes.

Gwendolyn gasped in his grip, but her face remained calm. 'I know the old legend too, doctor. I will never be yours, no matter what you do to my body.'

Craddock's face contorted. 'Then you know how this must end. If God wants you for Himself, let Him plumb the depths and pry you out of my arms!' He seized the fireplace poker and swung it high.

I threw myself forward, but my old knees gave way. Searing pain cracked across the base of my skull, the room spun, then the darkness swallowed me up.

•◇•◇•◇•◇•◇•◇•◇•◇•

I returned to consciousness as if struggling upwards through dark water. I was alive, but alone. Where was Gwennie? Where had Craddock taken her? My vision still wavered, and the burnt-out turnip lanterns looked down on me like faces spied dimly through the depths.

Through the depths, they mocked me, through the depths...

I pitched one of the ugly things into the fire and wiped my hand in disgust. Then I realised the voice had been Craddock's, and I knew where he had taken Gwendolyn.

I heard Saint Winefride's spring before I saw it. It had swollen from the recent storms and overrun its channel, only to be dammed into a swirling lake by the remains of the old well. Two figures grappled at the water's edge. Orange and yellow pinpoints of light needled them from the votive lanterns some superstitious soul had hung from the arms of the listing granite cross.

Ten centuries of erosion had widened the original holy spring into a deep chasm and undermined the foundation of the old well structure. One day earlier this summer I had prevailed upon Craddock to visit the site with me whilst he still could. I'd told him this winter's rains would doubtless see the remains of the ancient structure slide into the bottomless opening. I remembered Craddock's enthrallment as he'd peered over the edge, listening over long seconds for the tiny splash of the pebble he'd dropped to reach the water below.

Now I had to shout to be heard over the seething water. 'Craddock! You don't need to do this. You can still choose your own destiny!'

His grin was a jack-o-lantern's rictus, and his eyes started in their sockets. There could be no reasoning with Craddock. The sane part of him had fled.

Then I heard a 'crack' and Craddock reeled backwards. That was my girl! She must have landed a facer on Craddock, the benefit of growing up the little sister to three boys. Craddock flailed his arms, caught hold of Gwendolyn — then both tumbled into the whirlpool and were swept into the chasm and out of sight.

I threw myself flat on my belly and levered my upper body over the edge. Two faces like pale moons stared up at me out of the darkness, blinking against the spray. 'Take my hands, Gwennie. I'll pull you up.'

'That won't work, Uncle John.' Gwendolyn's voice was low, as if taking a larger breath would upset the delicate equilibrium that prevented both from plunging the rest of the way.

'She's right, Buell,' Craddock said. 'You don't have the leverage to pull her up, and you're not strong enough. You'd just overbalance and come down on top of us.'

There was a strained tone to his voice. Sanity had returned, but for how long? 'What do you suggest?' I asked.

'My legs are caught in a root. That's what's holding us. For how long, I don't know, especially with this runoff.'

The spring pulsed below us, alternately throwing up gouts of muddy water, then sucking them away again. And with each rise and fall, it tore away at the confining earth. Inches from my hand, a chunk of the edge broke loose, tumbling into the abyss. Craddock was right. Their perch could not last long.

'I'll push Gwennie up as far as I can,' Craddock said. 'If she can get purchase with her elbows, you can pull her the rest of the way.'

The wind rose to a shriek then suddenly dropped. There was a breathless silence. What Craddock suggested would put both of us in his power.

Craddock's wolfish smile flashed. 'I know what you're thinking. But none of those women who died in India were my patients. Both of you are, and I've never killed a patient. At least not deliberately. Not yet.' He made that odd giggle I'd heard earlier tonight. 'Time to climb up, Gwendolyn. Doctor's orders.' And with a mighty shove, Craddock pushed Gwendolyn several feet upwards.

She anchored one elbow in the mud whilst I seized her other wrist with both hands. I started to pull, but Gwendolyn twisted back around. 'Morris, there's still a chance,' she urged. 'Even this late, there must still be people about for All Hallows'. We can get help. You can still be saved. I promise you.'

Craddock pushed himself up far enough to touch Gwendolyn's fingertips with his own. 'That's the only time you've called me by my name. I waited an eternity for you. But He won. Your God.'

The spring roared. A plume of water cascaded over Craddock's upturned face, seeming to wash away the features we knew, eroding them into a fiercer, younger face, a face of uncivilised passions. He—whoever he was—rolled blind eyes towards me.

'Your toast was wrong, priest. Whatever else I've been, I've never been faithless. But I see now, His justice may come slowly, but it cannot be denied.' He bowed his head. 'I accept.'

He released his grip on Gwendolyn. Instinct made me reach for his hand, but with some superhuman reserve of strength, Craddock bent my restraining fingers backwards and released himself into the depths.

•◇•◇•◇•◇•◇•◇•◇•◇•

I bear the twisted fingers to this day, fitting reminder of my sin in delaying so long in acting. I had long suspected Dr Craddock of those deaths in a country halfway around the globe. Missionary friends had sent me the clippings, passed on reliable accounts. But my fear of scandal, nay, my moral cowardice, kept me silent.

Gwendolyn has little memory of that night or the preceding weeks, courtesy, Whitstead's new young doctor says, of the low doses of poison Craddock administered daily before I intervened. God was merciful to her, and she went off to India without a shadow of guilt.

As for the Lord righting an injustice in the past through those living in the present, I have written down the entire account as I witnessed it. There are none living who can confirm the truth of it. When this is read after my death, let it be taken as either the ramblings of an old man wandering in his wits at the end of his life, or as his attempt to spin a thrilling All Hallows' ghost story.

I care not which, for I am certain three redeemed souls passed through His crucible that night.

The Guardian and the Golden Gathering
by Abigail Falanga (*fantasy/action*)

faerie is strongest at the season of her birth.' Mistress Maeve spoke soft and low as wind in grass. 'Anorah is nearly seven years, an important age for all faeries. Keep a special watch on her. Be wary when she is not. See that she doesn't wander far.' The old faerie cupped Rence's face in her worn hand. 'Of all the forest animals, my daughter chose you as her companion and guardian, so this is your responsibility.'

Rence gently nibbled her thumb in assent. Words were still hard for him, but he'd found she understood this form of communication.

He was special, of course, growing up much slower than ordinary fawns to keep the faerie child he guarded company as she matured.

Mistress Maeve bent to kiss his head, murmuring words of encouragement and blessing, then gathered her basket of garden produce and went in.

She'd left a few of the tastier fruits for him, and he munched thoughtfully on a plum.

Anorah *had* been different lately.

She seemed to glow with golden abundance. A faerie-child of sunshine and the scent of warm grasses, as the long days of summer eased towards harvest time, she was merrier and more generous than ever.

Her magic coming?

He'd watch. But what good could a little fawn do?

•◇•◇•◇•◇•◇•◇•◇•◇•◇•

The smells of the forest were complex and rich. Late-summer trees and ferns mixed with damp old leaves. A soft, musty scent, blending with the tingly grey smell of mushrooms. Moss softened the rain-rich air, berries added a sweet tang, nuts sent out an appealing deliciousness.

Rence nudged aside a new drift of leaves and uncovered a cluster of acorns, perfectly ripe. He flicked one up with his tongue, cracked the shell, and munched happily, keeping a wary eye and nose on the forest. Because sometimes quiet is dangerous —

A new odour.

Rence's nose twitched and he lifted his head, trying to identify it, pin down the source…

Decay. Not musty mouldering leaves, but like rotting flesh. Like sometimes came from the graveyard near the church if a body hadn't been buried properly. There was vegetable rot, too, like gourds left too long on the vine.

He looked around—and lost it. A gust of wind carried away the faint stench, though he was certain whatever-it-was was still out there.

Rence grumbled and licked up another acorn.

Before he could start really worrying, a joyful call interrupted the birdsong.

Anorah skipped through the trees towards him, wearing a plain homespun dress, smelling of sun-drenched grasses and wildflowers.

Rence leapt over to greet her. 'Where have you been?'

'Mam said I must dress neatly to play with the human children,' Anorah laughed. 'They're picking blackberries, and everyone will get very dirty, so I don't see why. Are you coming?'

Rence bounded after her as she ran towards Whitstead. 'To pick blackberries?'

''Course, silly! They won't notice you in the brambles. You can eat as much as you like.'

The human children were almost as happy to see her as she was to play with them. Normally, humans from the village thought creatures from the forest strange and beneath them—even of their own kind, which was odd. But everyone liked Anorah. She was too merry not to like.

'Is there a race?' she asked. 'You're all picking quick as a gale!'

'Aye!' one boy said. 'Mr Barrows is paying a penny a bushel for blackberries, so we're filling buckets swift as may be.'

'What fun!' Anorah cried, plunging into the brambles regardless of scratching thorns, and picking until her flying hands turned midnight blue.

She'd already filled one basket, despite eating enough to fill another, when a girl walked by on the path near the bramble patch. Her garments were neat and of fine quality, but she looked too distracted to be happy.

'Nell!' the children cried joyously, and some crashed down around her.

'Careful, chickens!' she cried, good-naturedly. 'Don't stain my frock, or Miss Rossiter will be cross.'

'Come pick with us, Nell,' pleaded the boy.

'Can't, love.' She sighed, pushing back her bonnet with a distracted hand. 'I'm meant to call on Miss Rossiter with a letter from my uncle and then on Reverend Hollybrook, and he will most likely send me to Mr Needsworth, and I simply can't muss my frock. Or stay and talk!'

The other children groaned. But Nell shook her head and began walking on—

Until she caught sight of Anorah. She stopped, with a puzzled expression.

'Norah,' she said after a moment of opening and closing her mouth. 'There's something… different about you.'

'It's almost my birthday!' the faerie-child announced, for truth was always first in her mouth. 'I'm going to be seven, and—'

Rence risked being seen to butt into her leg before she could go on.

Nell shrugged and walked on towards Whitstead, and Rence breathed a sigh of relief.

•◇•◇•◇•◇•◇•◇•◇•◇•◇•

'Nell used to be fun,' Anorah complained as they returned later. 'Even when she was busy working, she'd still play when she could. But ever since she found that stupid treasure, she's always away or can't do anything.'

'What's treasure?' Rence asked, wrinkling his nose. 'Sounds nasty.'

'The way humans talk of it, I think 'treasure' is their strongest magic.' Anorah sighed. 'Very dull, though treasures seem to be precious things. Why would precious things be dreary?'

'Precious things—like blackberries?'

'Blackberries are precious. I think I've had too many today, however.'

'Maybe having too much makes them dreary.' Rence stopped to lick a scratch on his leg. 'And because they're scratchy and difficult.'

Anorah agreed, but the next moment said, 'Wouldn't it be splendid to find a real treasure? Like Nell did?'

'No, it wouldn't. Because she got boring after.'

'That was a human treasure.' She skipped down a path deeper into the woods. 'Human treasures are dreary. We'll find a real one—precious and magical. Come on!'

Rence kept close to Anorah until late-afternoon mists curled from the ground. She talked the whole time, about what treasure they might find, poking into hollows and greeting pixies and wild gnomes, who forgave her intrusion as soon as they realised she meant no harm.

'We've gone too far,' Rence said finally.

'You can find the way back!'

'Yes, of course. But it's getting late and—'

'Look, look!' Anorah leapt forwards into a small hollow.

The underbrush was thick and mist thicker, laced with something—some smell—familiar, but—

Every worry from earlier returned to Rence all at once. He kept close beside the faerie-girl, and they reached the source of the soft golden glow at the same time.

It was a tiny acorn.

A blue tape tied its stem and it glowed softly, like sun on mist.

Rence was both surprised and suspicious. He sniffed at it, expecting the usual oaky sweetness.

The odour of decay and death from earlier hit him stronger than ever. But before he could move, Anorah reached towards the acorn, her eyes huge and glowing golden, her magic so strong he could nearly taste it.

The acorn shivered, broke, rooted, and began to grow, shimmering in the golden magic from the little faerie. Her magic—emerging before she was old enough to control it!

Rence glanced at her face and saw it going pale.

Something evil was doing this—had tricked her!

The sapling was now a distorted young tree, twisting as it grew. Mist poured from its branches; not the bright, golden mist—a dark, dense fog with a horrible stench like graves too near a river.

Enough!

Rence knocked against Anorah, sending her tumbling to the ground.

She coughed and blinked. 'What—happened?'

'Can you run?' He nudged himself under her arm. 'We have to get away.'

Anorah staggered a few steps, glancing over her shoulder at the still-growing tree. Then she found her feet and ran after Rence straight for her mother's cottage.

•◇•◇•◇•◇•◇•◇•◇•◇•◇•◇•◇•

Mist followed them home, colder than late summer ought to be.

Anorah was nearly dropping from exhaustion. Her mother, tutting gently, washed and put her snugly to bed. She allowed Rence to nestle at her feet, for he would not leave. He was horribly worried.

Dismal rain pattered through the night, and stray drops hissed and sputtered down the chimney into the embers.

All next day, Anorah kept to her bed, tossing, turning, and feverish.

And the next day.

And the next.

Rence tried to explain what had happened, but Mistress Maeve only nodded without understanding.

Rence wandered in and out of the cottage to check on Anorah. Sometimes, Mistress Maeve sent him to fetch herbs or other ingredients from the forest. She didn't seem too anxious.

And indeed, Anorah's fever abated and within a few days she was sitting up and chattering again. Not quite her old self. She seemed dimmer and weaker, and snuggled with Rence for hours on end—which normally he would have objected to, but he was so relieved that he didn't mind.

Still it rained.

'I'd let you sit in the garden, but it's mud-soup, Anorah dear,' she said, 'and the only creature it would do any good to is a frog.'

•◇•◇•◇•◇•◇•◇•◇•◇•

Some weeks later, Rence found Mistress Maeve standing on her flooded garden path, frowning up at the sky.

'I don't like it,' she muttered to herself. 'I don't like it one bit. 'Tisn't natural.'

She caught sight of Rence and her face eased. 'You've noticed it, haven't you, little one? All this chill rain, so early in the year… It's unnatural, and what's more — it's evil! There's ill a-brewing, isn't there?'

Rence nodded vigorously.

Mistress Maeve shook herself decisively. 'It's a Devior, or I'm a goblin. Something must be done about it. At once!'

She bustled about the cottage getting ready for a journey, packing books and her most powerful lichens and berries.

'You're doing well enough now,' she said to Anorah, who was knitting in the corner by the fire. 'I must be gone a few days — a week at most — to see to this ill-weather business. But you're getting better and stronger by the day and will be well on your own here!'

'What ill weather?' Anorah wrapped her shapeless blob of yarn around Rence's head before he realised what was happening and could pull away.

'It's been raining days on end, just when the harvest ought to be coming in. The village folk must be having it very ill, though I haven't been to see, poor dears.'

'It does seem very chilly.'

'A faerie ought always to know what the skies are about.'

'I can't know,' Anorah pouted. 'You haven't let me outside in days and days and days!'

'Well, stay in a few days longer, whilst I'm away. You're missing nothing besides mud.'

'I like mud.'

Mistress Maeve laughed, gave her some dough to play with from the evening's loaf, and then took herself off the moment the sun set.

•◇•◇•◇•◇•◇•◇•◇•◇•

Some days later, the rains stopped long enough for a fine morning. Rence expected Mistress Maeve back and triumphant at any moment.

Anorah seemed so much better that Rence didn't stop her when she went out into the garden for fresh air. After all, for a faerie there was no better medicine in the world.

Autumn painted the trees a rich gold, deepening into brown as leaves drifted down. Pixies were out hunting, along with small animals gathering the last nuts and berries.

Only a trace weather of mist and sudden chill winds remained.

Rence munched at the last vegetation in the garden and Anorah chattered to the birds, herself, and even the pixies (who weren't too happy about it).

He finally uprooted a particularly tasty old squash vine—and noticed silence.

No sign of Anorah anywhere in the garden.

He sniffed at the air and finally caught a whiff of her, in the direction of the village, and set off quick as his legs would take him. Quicker than she could walk or even run, so he caught up with her before he'd gotten far down the soggy path.

'Don't run off without me!' he chided. 'Where are you going to, anyway? Your mother said—'

'She said the village folk must be having a hard time with all the rain.' Anorah frowned. 'So I'm checking on them.'

'But you must stay near the cottage!'

'Whitstead isn't far.'

'You're supposed to—'

'You're no fun.' She glared.

'I am too!'

'Then come on! We will be back before noontime. Race you!'

'I always beat you.'

'Not this time!'

Anorah took off, feet flying over moss and mud and leaf-drifts. Rence gave her a fair start, especially since she'd been ill, then bounded after her. He covered the ground with joyful ease. It was all going to be all right. There was nothing to worry about.

'Ha!' he shouted, passing her.

'No fair!' Anorah panted and laughed at the same time.

He rounded a corner in the path, bringing him in sight of Whitstead, and that horrid, corrupt odour slammed into him.

Anorah shrieked behind him.

Rence turned and sprinted back up the path, round the corner just in time to see black fog cover the trees again—and no Anorah. She was only a few steps behind him! Where—?

Something else moved through the fog—a huge wolf, almost as tall as a tree, black as night. It snarled at him and Rence cowered. Then it turned and vanished into the forest.

Heart pounding, Rence plunged this way and that among the trees, trying to see through the rising mist, trying to smell past the horrible stench. Where was his faerie?

'Anorah!' he called when everything else failed. No answer. 'Anorah, where are you? Anorah!'

'Norah?'

Another voice not far away. Mistress Maeve?

'I can't find her!' he called, words clear as he could manage, hoping against hope she would understand. 'Something took her. Wolf — mist — magic —'

'I'm nearly there,' the other voice said.

The form solidified as it neared through the trees. And it wasn't Mistress Maeve. It was Nell.

She froze the moment she saw him, and he froze too, staring at her.

'Oh,' she laughed uncertainly. 'I thought — I didn't mean to startle you. Where's your mother? You seem awfully small to —'

Rence made up his mind. 'We have to find Anorah,' he said. 'Something took her, and there's no time to waste.'

Nell's mouth fell open. 'You spoke!'

'You can understand me!' He nodded vigorously. 'I'm Anorah's guardian. Or — but — I let the *Something* take her, and now I can't even find her scent. Please help me!'

'Norah is… is a faerie, isn't she?'

'Of course!'

'Ah. I knew there was something different about her.' Nell blinked a few times, pushing her bonnet back absentmindedly. 'It's so strange ever since the snowman-faeries at Christmastime, and now this. Oh, well…' She looked at him. 'No one's seen her since that day picking blackberries.'

'She was sick. The Something took her magic and made the fog, and now it's taken her. Mistress Maeve said it was a Devior and went off to do something about it, but now this!'

'Devior?'

'I think that's what she said. Mistress Maeve doesn't often understand me. You're the first person to really know what I'm saying, besides Anorah.'

'Because I'm still a child, most likely.' Nell screwed up her face into a concentrating frown. 'Now, do hush so I can think!'

Rence was quiet, but he couldn't be still. He nosed among the leaves at the side of the path and sniffed with dying hope at the air. There was no sign of Anorah anywhere.

'That's it!' Nell slapped her hands together. 'I saw something about Devior in one of Mr Needsworth's books. Come on — we'll go look!'

'Humans have books about Devior?' Rence followed as she sped towards Whitstead.

'Mr Needsworth has some very odd books, and don't mind me looking at them; I'm staying with him, since the roads are bad and — and I don't want to go back to my uncle's house.'

'Why is that?' Rence asked, completely confused.

Nell was silent for a moment, slowing as they reached the edge of the forest. 'My uncle drinks too much,' she said in a sudden rush. 'And he's not happy since Mr

Needsworth and the other executors made sure that he can't access the treasure-money. He's not kind. I don't want to stay with him. I don't care that he's all the family I have!'

'My family is gone, too. I haven't seen them much since I became Anorah's guardian.'

'Oh. I'm sorry.'

'It's all right. I love Anorah, and I've the gift of speech.'

Nell smiled. 'What's your name?'

'Rence.' He stopped. The churchyard was ahead, and people were somewhere near beyond that to tell by the smell. 'I can't go on. Someone will notice.'

'I can carry you under my cloak, but you have to promise not to squirm.'

He promised and she lifted him gently, pulling the cloak close around both of them until he could see nothing but grass and then the cobbles of the street.

Nell went quickly and Rence only caught a few words from the people they passed. The harvest was bad, again. Fields flooded. Fowl off laying. No sign of the weather turning. They shouldn't have hoped…

Must be this Devior. It must have taken Anorah to use her magic for this ill purpose!

Rence had to do something—it was his fault; he was supposed to keep her safe!

Nell held him tighter. 'Shh! We're almost there.'

She went around a corner into a quieter area, stuffy from the enclosing walls with dirt, shifted her hold of him, and opened a door with a soft metallic click. A pause as darkness and smells of cooking grease and old flour engulfed them. Then the girl released a long breath and set him down.

'No one about! Mrs Mallory must be out still—Mr Needsworth is at his office, and we only need to avoid Dickon. Come on, Rence; the library is along here.'

Rence followed through dark rooms smelling of dust, tallow, rodents, and dry herbs, first flagstones and then thick carpeting feeling strange under his hooves. The place was full of echoes that set him on edge. It was the first time he'd been in a dwelling larger than Mistress Maeve's cottage, and he felt lost in the succession of room after room.

Nell chose a door with as much assurance as he could find the hollow where the best mushrooms grew, and they entered a place lined with so many books that Rence stood gaping at them for a long minute.

'Can you read?' Nell said, crouching at one bookshelf with a finger running along the spines. 'I suppose you don't. I mean—do they teach you to read when you learn to speak, or…?'

Rence shook his head.

'Never mind—there are pictures.' She seized a large volume with a musty, crumbly cover. 'Here it is! We'll have to sit down to look at it. If you *can* sit?'

'If you're sure the house-master doesn't mind,' Rence said, hopping up onto the velvety cushion of a chair near the desk.

'I'll clean up after,' Nell replied cheerfully. 'I'm good at cleaning. Now, let's see...'

She opened the book and began turning pages slowly, examining curious lines of dark scribbles on each before going to the next. There *were* pictures, but of the strange human sort. It would have been much more sensible to mark pages with different scents, but humans never seemed to think of these things.

Silence fell for so long that a steady rain began to beat against the windowpanes.

'Here it is,' she said at last.

She pointed at a page with a curious drawing of a figure standing at the top of steps with a too-large head but a human shape, wearing a robe. Its arms were raised and it had a cruel smile. On either side seemed to be trees, withered and twisted.

'The Devior,' Nell read.

She went on, droning over stilted words that Rence had never heard before.

'I don't understand,' he interrupted, hopping up so that he could nudge the picture with his nose. 'Is that the Devior? What is it?'

Nell had gone paler than the chilly room could account for. 'Devior are witches,' she said in a whisper. 'Humans, who try to steal power from fairies and other magical things, so they can get into the faerie world and live on and on forever.'

'That's what got Anorah,' Rence said, collapsing back. 'They took her and her magic, and that's why.'

'This says that whole countries could be stripped of their magic and turned into wastelands.'

'And so this poor harvest-tide...'

'Do you think that's part of it?'

Rence nodded, misery settling. 'The fog started because Anorah was tricked into giving it her magic. And now it's getting worse again, after the Devior took her.'

'Then we have to get her back!'

'Can we?'

Nell nodded, bending over the book again. 'The Devior must have taken Norah into the faerie world, and we can follow him there and find her. Or you can at least— I don't think I'll be able.' She pointed to a line of scribbles. 'Yes! Here it says they have their havens in Faerie, built out of stolen corrupt magic. Can you find that?'

'If it's the awful-smelling stuff, it should be easy!' Rence's ears perked up. 'But how do I get in?'

Nell looked a little shy. 'Well, you could wait until All Hallows' Eve, when the veils are thinner between worlds, like my mum used to say.'

'But when's that?'

'A few weeks' time.'

Rence shook his head vigorously.

'Too long to wait!' Nell agreed. 'Mr Needsworth says there are doors into Faerie in this house, so mayhap—'

'Where?'

'Down in the dining room—at least according to the story he told me about last Christmas. But—Wait!'

Rence was already clattering into the corridor. But once out, he remembered how confusing the house was and hesitated, panic clawing under his fur.

'Follow me,' said Nell, rushing past.

She led towards a brighter part of the house and a faint smell of human food. At last, she opened a door on a larger room than any other with a long table lit by windows.

In the wall at the far side of the table was a faint shimmer like golden sunlight slanting through trees.

'There it is!' Rence cried, springing towards it.

'Where?' Nell stopped by the table. 'I can't see anything. That means I probably can't come. I'm sorry. Good luck, Rence. I hope you find Norah!'

'Thank you!' he said and bounded through the shimmer.

•◇•◇•◇•◇•◇•◇•◇•◇•

The country on the other side of the door was as big and empty as the town and the house had been enclosed. Mist like smoke clouded the air, and for a moment Rence nearly panicked—he could see nothing no matter how hard he blinked.

But he could still *smell*, and that was what counted.

The horrid odour was clearer, though still faint. He set out towards it, cautious but trusting to his nose.

Every step it grew stronger, and it didn't seem long before Rence could make out a form in the strange mistiness.

It was like a structure made of pillars, but not solid—it wavered like black smoke. The stench was so strong that Rence nearly staggered back on his haunches. But he kept on, for at the centre of the structure, like an ember in ashes, something glowed warm and golden. And he knew that glow:

Anorah.

A dark, human figure moved within the structure, with a huge head and long robes, rhythmically circling the glow.

Rence would get her out. He had to.

Something came sideways out of the haze, so suddenly he couldn't react. It knocked into him, throwing him aside, and stood snarling.

The wolf!

Rence caught the breath knocked out of him, then stumbled to his feet. He was so near the smoke-structure now that he could see Anorah's face within. She seemed asleep, but uneasy and twisted with pain; suspended in midair, the goldenness being drawn from her.

With an eye on the wolf, Rence edged towards her.

'Kill it!' The Devior faced him, still within his refuge, malevolence emanating off him as strong as his foul magic stench.

The wolf jumped and landed between Rence and the structure, teeth bared in an empty snarl.

Empty?

Rence looked closer. The wolf seemed more like a shell than a beast — hollow and hazy, except for white teeth and red eyes. But he recognised in it the same marks of enchantment he had. It was like himself — but emptied.

'You don't have to serve the Devior!' Rence shouted desperately. 'It took your magic. You don't owe it anything.'

The wolf still snarled, but its ear quirked.

Rence took his chance and charged, lowering his head and butting it against the wolf's snout. To his great surprise, he connected with a shuddering clunk and drew back ready for another charge. The wolf yelped and recoiled, blood on its snout and dripping from Rence's... antlers?

When had he gotten antlers?

It must be the magic of this place.

'Please,' he panted. 'Let me help her, as you weren't able to help whatever you guarded.'

'Kill it!' the Devior commanded again.

The wolf snarled at him, but then turned on Rence. Rence bellowed and charged again with all the strength he still wasn't sure how to use. His antlers connected with the wolf's flank and with a mighty heave he threw it aside.

He bounded past the smell of blood straight into the smoke-structure. Anorah stirred and moaned as he neared, but the Devior didn't flinch.

'You can't stop me, Guardian,' he sneered. 'I have summoned the cold fogs. I have drawn dark and foul invaders to strengthen me — the locusts, the hunters, the MidKnight, the ghosts. All with your faerie's magic. And once begun, I take magic until my power is manifest.'

'Then take mine,' Rence said, moving between him and Anorah.

The glow drawn from her flickered and faded as he intercepted it. The Devior hesitated, and then laughed cruelly.

'Very well,' he said: 'You've brought this on yourself, Guardian — and now, you will have neither power nor understanding to save your little faerie or her Whitstead...!'

Rence flinched and stumbled, words jumbling in his mind as if pulled out of him. But he would help her still.

He would carry her out.

He must.

The path back.

The door.

Save… Anorah…

A shriek — a stench of rotting and death!

'Rence — quick! Get away!' a new voice called.

Rence shook himself, scrambled words falling back into place, and tried to take in what was happening.

The structure was crumbling around him. Anorah lay on the ground, motionless but breathing, the golden glow coiling back into her. The wolf crouched, snarling and tearing, over the broken form of the Devior, which struggled to no avail.

Nell rushed up beside Rence and lay a hand on his neck. 'Are you all right? Please — '

'Yes.' He choked a little on sorcery that still muddled him. 'You were just in time. How?'

'It's All Hallows' Eve.' Nell lifted Anorah, smiling with relief. 'You hadn't come back — I was so anxious. Miss Rossiter wouldn't give me leave from my lessons, but I had to try. Then it seemed she'd been turned to stone, so I slipped away and found the door, and do hurry!'

'I'll carry her — I'm strong enough.' He followed her past the collapsing structure and the tearing wolf. 'How is it All Hallows' Eve already?'

'They say time's different in Faerie,' said Nell, placing the sleeping Anorah on his back.

They went some distance — it was hard to tell how far. Then, they came to a place that shimmered and shone. They scrambled through —

Out into the soft light of early dawn in the forest. The air was bonfire-scented and chill — free of darkness and the horrid stench of sorcery.

And Mistress Maeve awaited them, keeping open the door for them in the roots of an old tree that had grown over a long-fallen wall.

'At last!' she cried, tears streaking her face as she gathered Anorah into her arms. 'We drove the Devior back, but we couldn't defeat him. Then, when I returned to worse fogs and rains than ever — I thought I'd lost my daughter!'

She turned to Nell, who was blinking in the sunlight. 'Thank you, my dear.'

'I didn't do much, Mistress Maeve.' Nell dropped a curtsy. 'But Rence nearly gave up everything to save Anorah!'

Rence, very shaky and back to fawn-size, collapsed into a comfortable pile of leaves and couldn't say anything from sheer exhaustion.

'I know,' said the old faerie softly, and stroked his head.

Anorah was already asleep—content and healing. The damage was done, her magic taken and misused. But now the darkness was ridden from the land, and wholeness would be restored—though it might take time.

What Once Was Lost
by Laura Nelson Selinsky *(historical/ghost story)*

er family's monument was ice cold beneath Agnes's fingers. She knelt to place a new bouquet at the foot of the obelisk in memory of her beloved grandmother. A moment's prayer, and she would start the long walk to Whitwillow Farm, the home her grandmother had left her.

A sharp-edged voice sliced through her meditation. 'Imagine the gall of that Agnes Collins. Surely, Reverend Hollybrook, you must agree that a proper young lady has no business housing common thieves. Let alone those twins. Why one of them is mad!'

Agnes wanted to march up to that miserable creature and set her straight. Jem and Sukie were no thieves…at least, no more thieves than any other starving children. But Reverend Hollybrook would think her an eavesdropper.

The rector took a conciliatory tone. 'I admire Miss Collins's charitable spirit. Who else will spare the time to prepare indigents for farm work or household service? She's even taught them to read and write.'

'Wasted effort. Those vagrants should go straight to the workhouse. Get them out of Whitstead. I shall speak to the trustees before Agnes's ridiculous dinner.' Miss Rossiter's belligerent voice rose to a spiteful screech. 'I'll tell them — Take those urchins away from that — that — that — *girl pirate*.'

'There was no piracy. Captain Collins sailed a successful merchantman,' said Reverend Hollybrook. Agnes peeped around a tombstone to see him guiding Miss Rossiter towards the graveyard gate. 'After her father's death, Miss Collins herself captained his ship from India to England. I believe she can manage a few unfortunate youths who are without parents.'

Miss Rossiter snarled and slammed the gate, leaving Reverend Hollybrook looking after her in dismay.

Agnes felt her heart pounding; dread formed a lump in her throat. I must get home. Everything has to be perfect. I can't lose Jem and Sukie.

• ◇ • ◇ • ◇ • ◇ • ◇ • ◇ • ◇ • ◇ •

Sukie flitted, light as a will-o-wisp, to each window, door, and gate. Tap, tap, tap. Three knocks on the barndoor, propped so the drover could see to feed the team. Tap, tap, tap on the buttery window. Tap, tap, tap — the henhouse door. Tap, tap, tap — the pasture gate.

No wonder they call her mad. I must set her to work, not let her persist in fantasy. But Agnes lingered, grateful for the mug of tea that warmed her after her hurried walk from the village. She must bundle up again and haul Sukie in to help with the cooking.

Two coats hung by the door, her grandmother's and her father's. Her dead father's greatcoat was so tempting. He was a decisive leader, even a bit of a tyrant. Beside his coat hung her grandmother's faded one, the hem bright from being let down to cover Agnes' long legs. Wasn't the captain who she must be especially tonight when the stakes were so high! *So why do I hesitate?* Because last Christmas Eve, she had imitated her grandmother's kindness, not her father's ferocity, and saved Jem and Sukie from starving on the street.

Agnes opened the scullery window and peered into the twilight. In her sternest voice, she called, 'Get to w —' But Jem and Sukie were already hard at work. Each had a broom and was sweeping scraps of straw and wood chips across the cobbles towards the dung heap. Two buckets of late apples waited beside the steps, one picked by each twin. Agnes banged the window shut.

With a sigh, she turned to the press where lay two matching piles of newly polished silverplate beside two stacks of crisp linens. She gave a little growl of frustration. There were supposed to be strict roles on Agnes' farm, just as there had been strict roles aboard ship. Sweeping the cobbles was Jem's job. Polishing the silver was Sukie's. Apples — Jem. Linens — Sukie. Everything shipshape. But from the day the twins arrived, Jem and Sukie did every task together. Always. She brushed back the curtain to gaze into the dusk again.

Just then Molly, her housekeeper, bustled past on her way to the buttery. She carried a tiny stoneware bowl. 'No use staring, Miss Agnes,' she called. 'You know our Sukie is not coming in until she and her brother finish sweeping the stable-yard.'

'I had hoped that tonight…' Agnes hesitated, searching for exactly the right words. 'That tonight they might make a good impression. These guests must seriously consider my ideas.'

'In exchange for an excellent dinner,' added Molly. 'And them trustees will get their fine meal, Miss Agnes. Never you worry.'

'I went to place autumn flowers on my grandmother's grave this afternoon.'

'Yes, ma'am. Like every Friday.' Molly nodded anxious agreement.

'By accident, I overheard Miss Rossiter speak of me to Reverend Hollybrook. I wasn't eavesdropping. I was kneeling, arranging the flowers. They mustn't have seen me.'

Molly gave a relieved, 'Humph, Miss Rossiter! Her tittle-tattle is nay worth your notice, beggin' your pardon. She has never a kind word for —'

Agnes held up a hand, halting her chatter. 'It's not her regular unkindness or even her opposition to my plan. She's not content to keep me from taking in others. No.

She told Reverend Hollybrook that he and the trustees should make me surrender the twins.'

Even in the twilight, Agnes saw Molly's cheeks pale. One workworn hand flew to her mouth in dismay. Her voice came small and unsure. 'What did he say?'

Agnes gave a weary smile. 'He told her no.'

'Well, she's put in her place. No need to fear.'

'Perhaps she'll change his mind. Change all the trustees' minds. Jem and Sukie would be separated. Can you imagine Sukie in an orphanage? Jem in a factory?'

Molly shook her head.

'Tonight must be perfect. That woman does not give up easily.'

'Neither do you, ma'am.' Molly offered a tentative smile. 'I'm back to work.' She picked up a tray and returned to the buttery.

To herself, Agnes murmured, 'But how will I keep Jem and Sukie safe? If the guests tonight choose to take Miss Rossiter's side?'

Her view of the stable yard was fading into shadow. Now the twins were sweeping the last of the refuse in perfect tandem. In eerie lockstep, they stowed the brooms and hefted the buckets of apples. 'Do you think all twins are like them? Doing and speaking always together?'

'One family in my village had three sets of twins,' called Molly from the adjoining room. Melancholy touched her voice.

Agnes could hear the hollow thump as Molly set the lid of the apple barrel on the floor. *Her abandoned village back in Ireland. Every able-bodied soul fled*, Agnes thought. *Doubt any twins remain. All gone abroad for work, as Molly did.*

Molly returned with the little bowl, brimming with milk. 'Them twins I knew come in matched pairs, but they was different as any six wee'uns. I think Jem and Sukie are something else.' She crossed herself and threw an anxious glance to the window. She pushed it open and set the dish of milk on the outer ledge. 'I think that Jem don't dare to leave Sukie alone. Piskies will carry her off to Tír na nÓg.'

'She does seem halfway between here and some other place,' Agnes equivocated. *Though I don't think pixies have aught to do with Sukie's odd behaviour. If I did, I'd be putting out milk for the pixies, too.*

Tap, tap, tap.

Agnes sighed in exasperation. Jem said his sister's tapping kept the Otherworld from opening a way into the farm. *Utter codswallop.* Seafarers were inclined to useless superstition, but the captain had taught Agnes to suppress their timewasting tripe. Yet she'd never forced Sukie to stop tapping—it was the only action she did independent of her twin.

The scullery door slammed open on a gust. 'Sorry, miss,' called Jem. 'Wind caught the door from me as we carried in the apples.'

'Apples, apples,' murmured Sukie. Then she reached back and tapped the door three more times.

Agnes flinched. Time to speak up. No one was going to entrust young labourers to her supervision if Sukie made a spectacle of herself. Even Jem and Sukie would be taken.

Seeing his benefactor's discomfort, Jem said, 'Tapping keeps your farm safe. It's moon-dark and All Hallows' Eve, Miss Agnes. The walls between worlds is mighty thin tonight.'

Sukie's echo, 'Tonight, tonight.'

Agnes rubbed her temples. *Such a long day, and the evening will be longer still.* She knew her proposal was bold, especially from an unmarried lady. But she had trained many a young sailor. Tonight's dinner had to convince the trustees that youths would benefit from training at Whitwillow Farm. Surely, she offered a better future than the blacking factories. 'Take those apples to the buttery to be washed. Then Sukie, peel apples for pies. Jem, you stock the hearths throughout the house. We'll have warm fires for my guests.'

Jem shook his head, a gesture so automatic that Agnes doubted he knew he was doing it. She frowned, nonetheless. 'We'll get those apples peeled quick whilst Miss Molly rolls pie crust. Then she can bake them whilst we ready the fires.'

'Fires, fires.' Sukie's voice ghosted through the dim kitchen.

Of course, you'll do them together, thought Agnes. *Why would tonight be any different?* 'That is exactly the kind of disobedience that tonight's guests abhor. Get to work and be quick about it.' She handed Sukie a paring knife. Sukie drew in a fearful breath and gazed at the knife as if it were a viper.

'Jem's made a sensible suggestion, ma'am,' said Molly, rolling her eyes. 'Let's get those apples ready, my dears. Only two hours 'til high and mighty folk come to dine.' She grasped the twins' shoulders and steered them across the scullery.

Agnes took up the cutlery and headed for the shadowed dining room. A single taper flickered in anticipation of lighting the hearth and an array of candles. When the guests arrived, candlelight would sparkle across crystal and reflect from the costly mirror. As Agnes laid out the silver, she admired her grandmother's fine porcelain, which graced the handsome rosewood table. Slender stalks of late-blooming betony and yellow devil's bit glowed in crystal vases. Though the wildflowers Molly gathered were lovely, Agnes regretted not being able to afford glasshouse blossoms. *Will my little display be enough to convince the trustees of my idea's worth?* She pulled a clean hanky from her pocket and gave the mirror a final polish.

Tap, tap, tap.

Startled, Agnes spun round to see Sukie with tinder in one arm and the other free to knock. Jem followed, burdened with split logs for the grand fireplace. Agnes clapped her hands for attention, then waited until both twins met her eyes. 'You must both display the proper behaviour.' Jem nodded. 'Sukie. You must not irritate my guests with your rapping. We must impress this evening.'

'Evening, evening,' whispered Sukie, as she set the firewood on the hearth. She edged to a bank of windows and raised her hand. Tap, tap, tap. Her anxious gaze skittered to Agnes, but she sidled to the next window. Tap, tap, tap.

Agnes groaned and thumped her palm on the table. 'Sukie, desist. You must listen carefully.'

'Carefully, carefully.' More a breath than a voice.

Jem set down his load of firewood, then plopped himself on the floor before the cold hearth. 'You prepared right wonderful, Miss Agnes. Now, she's preparing, too.' He nodded towards his sister; she tapped the fourth window, then the fifth. He looked more pensive than the lively young sailors Agnes had supervised. 'Last year, my sister and Mam and me—unprepared.'

'Un'pared, un'pared.' Tap, tap, tap.

The last window, thank goodness. The mantle clock chimed five, but Agnes forced herself not to glare at it. 'Unprepared?'

Jem nodded. 'So, a year tonight, our mam was lost.'

'Lost, lost,' murmured a voice light as mist. 'Lost' echoed through the house, a breath of grief drifting through empty rooms.

'But you prepared, Miss Agnes. All these candles and fires against moon-dark. Your flowers: betony to repel spirits and Devil's bit to fright...' Jem raised a finger to his lips and whispered, 'to fright the Devil.'

'Devil, devil.'

'Molly picked the flowers, not I.' Hmm. Had Molly simply picked whatever autumn blooms remained, or was this another of her superstitious charms, like milk for pixies?

'She's wise, Molly is.' Jem nodded. 'Last year, we weren't ready. No money for candles, no time to pick flowers.'

'Flowers, flowers.' Tap, tap, tap.

From Whitstead's rumours, Agnes had pieced together the tale from the previous winter. Before their mother Lily vanished, they had been harvesting late potatoes for that wretch Farmer Booth. Cold muddy work from dawn to dark, seven days a week. Then Lily was gone, and the twins were outcast. Avoiding authorities who would send a boy one way and a girl the other way, no matter how close they were. Until Agnes had impulsively offered the twins a few coins to carry her Christmas parcels to the farm.

Jem had continued whilst she'd been wool gathering. '...Mam started to hear bespelled music. Fiddle music. Silent to us, but that music called her to that devil's dance. I said, 'Jest hang on 'til dawn. Come sunrise, all be well.' I begged her, and whenever I begged...'

'...Sukie begged,' Agnes finished, imagining Jem's desperation echoed in Sukie's whisper.

'Begged, begged.' Usually, Sukie's words were hushed reproductions of Jem's, but 'begged' exuded her own sorrow.

Tap, tap, tap.

But she already tapped all the windows. Dark glass panes reflected Sukie's silent tears, as she continued a new round of tapping. Agnes felt a wave of sympathy. Does the poor thing believe performing her ritual well would have saved her mother? Perhaps she's making doubly sure that whatever stole her mother spares us.

'Mam tried to stay with us when the music claimed her. She'd cling to the doorframe, dig her nails into the wood 'til splinters lifted and her blood ran. Sukie'd clutch her waist, and I'd salve her hands.' In the window's dark reflection, Agnes saw Sukie swallow a sob. Jem continued, 'Hour after hour, Mam wailed for the fiddler to wait for her. She swore to him she'd come.'

'Come, come.' Sukie calling her broken mother back.

Agnes stiffened. *Why would anyone leave her own children?* 'Your poor mother. Perhaps she was going mad. Had she often entertained delusions?'

Jem's snort of contempt drowned out Sukie's 'delusions, delusions.' He rose and stamped in anger. 'No dee-illusions. Real music. Real black magic. Dark as tonight, Miss Agnes. I don't know whether 'twas the devil hisself played my Mam away. Tales says he favors the fiddle. Or maybe 'twas Fiddler Fossegrim who the North folk left here long back. But Mam heard real music. She lasted three nights — it callin' her away, us callin' her back. Three nights of torment. Us so tired from watchin' over her.'

Sukie gave a little sob, sharing Jem's misery.

'One day, we fell asleep when we should have been loading potatoes. Old Booth hit me and Sukie with his carriage whip.'

'No. No, no, no.' Sukie's despair. 'No, no.'

Agnes' gasped, heart aching that Sukie's one word was a desperate 'no.'

'She said 'no' then, too,' Jam said, his voice too old for a boy of twelve. 'Any other word from her would've been a miracle.' He paused, and silence smothered them all. When he finally continued, resignation coloured his voice. 'But work or starve, so we worked. Didn't matter. Farmer fired us anyway after Mam... After.'

Jem reached for the flowers, running his fingers over the betony. 'Maybe if we'd got this, Mam would've been safe when we fell asleep. But 'twas All Hallows' Eve, and the Otherworld was as close to our world as hand in hand.' He pressed his palms together. Agnes shuddered to think of that Otherworld clasping Whitstead in its lethal grip. 'That third night, Sukie tied her wrist to Mam's, and I coaxed them to lie down for a bit. We fell asleep. Mam didn't. Music woke us, awful screeching music. When it played, me and Sukie couldn't move. Mam had untied the ribbon. Music dragged her through the door into the greenwood. She didn't look back. Then the fiddling stopped. I could move again, too late.'

Jem crushed his fists against his eyes, as if he could erase what he had seen. By the solitary flame, Agnes could see guilt twisting his features. 'I fell asleep, so she was lost.' He slumped to the floor and crouched there, weeping.

'Lost, lost.' Sukie crept closer.

Without looking up, Jem continued, 'I grabbed her cloak for she'd not taken it. Sukie built up our fire and propped the door wide to show the way home. We searched. Tripped on roots and fell in streams. Wandered 'til we could scarce see our fire's glow. The greenwood swallowed her, and it would swallow us. We had to turn back. Had to.'

'Had to. Had to.' Sukie laid her hand on his. She knelt beside him.

'Dawn came. Mam didn't. Noon. Dusk and dark. Still no Mam. The second day, we went back to Farmer Booth for we had no more bread. But he run us off his place for skipping a day's labour. After that, it was all dark.' Tears glistened in his dark eyes.

'Dark, dark,' whispered Sukie before giving his hand a squeeze and releasing it. She rose and went to the fireplace. Rising to her tiptoes, she lifted the glowing taper from the mantle, and smiled into its light. Turning, she extended the tiny flame towards Agnes with an inquiring look. Tendrils of shining hair had slipped from her braids, and there was a smudge on her cheek. With one small hand, she gestured to the unlit candles on the table. She did not speak. But her plea for light was clear and irresistible.

Agnes bit her lip. *Beeswax tapers are expensive. Guests won't arrive for an hour. The burnt down candles will show me to be profligate. Those pinchpenny trustees will never understand. But what is that compared to a bit of comfort for Jem and Sukie whose mother is lost in the dark?*

'Light them all!' Agnes said, kindling a second taper and handing it to Jem.

'All, all, all, all, all, all.' Hope threaded Sukie's chant as she hurried to light all the manor's candles. Agnes saw her pass and repass the dining room door as she skipped from room to room. 'All, all, all,' became a song. Jem circled the dining room, laying flame to each wick on the table and sideboard. He pulled off his shoes, scrambled onto the table, and lit the dusty tapers in the chandelier. When he blew out his taper and hopped to the floor, the dining room was aglow.

Jem mopped his tears with his sleeve and donned his shoes. He raked his fingers though his black locks and smiled at Agnes. 'If a devil carried off Mum, well, then an angel saved us. Last Christmas when you handed us those packages and the peppermints. Our angel.'

Blushing, Agnes stammered, 'Less than an angel, I think, much less. But if the trustees believe that bilgewater, then we'll have a future together.' Agnes snatched a blossom from the vase on the table. She tucked the flower into Jem's buttonhole. 'There, you look like a gentleman.'

'Betony. I'm ready for what trouble comes,' said Jem. He grinned through the last of his tears.

'Let's hope the worst demon we'll face tonight is that dreadful matron from the charitable house.' Their shared laughter was brighter because the night was dark. Agnes plucked the rest of the blooms from the vase. She began to twine the stems into a circlet, as her grandmother had taught her.

A few minutes later, Tap, tap, tap, Sukie trotted into the room, still carolling 'All, all, all.'

Agnes crowned Sukie's tousled hair with the flower wreath. 'You'll do,' she said, smoothing Sukie's pinafore. *Please Lord, let me keep this faerie girl and her brother safe.*

An almighty clang echoed down the lane from the farm's gate. *The bell. They're here.*

•◇•◇•◇•◇•◇•◇•◇•◇•

Two Weeks Later...

Molly knocked on the study door and let herself in. At the library table, Agnes was wedged between the twins. All three were glaring at *Introduction to English Grammar*.

'Please, Miss Agnes, can't we go help Molly scrub the hearths? This is so dull.'

Sukie's chin rested on her folded hands, but she rolled her eyes and intoned, 'Dull, duuuullll.'

'As soon as we finish prepositional phrases, we shall read another chapter of *The Swiss Family Robinson*.' Agnes's voice sounded a little desperate. 'I'll even tell you about a shipwreck my father, the captain, once endured.'

'Beggin' your pardon, ma'am. I think there's something more important to be read.' Molly slapped the letter onto the open book. Her eyes met Agnes's, and she murmured, 'God willing.'

Both twins turned anxious faces to Agnes. She let out a long, slow breath, and pulled her paper knife from a drawer. Then she slit the envelope and dropped the knife back into its place.

'For luck,' Agnes said and tapped the table three times, earning a nervous giggle from Sukie. Agnes cleared her throat and began reading.

'Dear Miss Collins,

'On behalf of my fellow trustees and our benevolent matron, I must thank you for your recent lovely dinner. I admit that we were doubtful that a young woman could operate Whitwillow Farm after years at sea, but the delicious produce served at your table put that worry to rest. (Please, require your housekeeper to send mine the pie receipt.)

'We had two significant concerns. First, you are an unlikely caretaker for vagrant and orphaned youth. Second, children of doubtful parentage rarely succeed in polite company. However, the behaviour of your charges was above reproach. How charming that the girl knocks whenever she enters a room. The boy's reference to you as "our angel," in regard to your rescuing them last Christmas, speaks to admirable, if unorthodox, faith. Surely, your frequent church attendance will correct any petty heresy soon enough.

'You have succeeded both in keeping Whitwillow Farm prosperous and in training two lowly youth for useful service. Therefore, we are willing that other fatherless youth between the ages of eleven and fifteen years join your household, as an alternative to sending them to the less salubrious factories.

'You will hear from us further in the new year.

'Respectfully submitted,

Milford Featherworthy'

'Worthy, worthy, worthy,' Sukie chanted.

Worthy, indeed. Falling tears blurred the ink and puddled on the stationery. Agnes fumbled for her handkerchief. Sukie pressed her own crumpled hankie into her hand.

'Well, Miss Agnes, what have you got us into?' laughed Molly. 'We'll soon be neck deep in useless mouths to feed. No escaping now.'

'To celebrate, we should skip prepositions,' said Jem. 'Go straight to *The Swiss Family Robinson* with tea and cake.'

'Cake, cake, cake!'

'I'm after getting the tea. Come along and carry for me, Sukie,' said Molly, slipping towards the study door. 'We'll be setting out a wee drop of cream to thank the piskies.' Sukie scurried after her, quickly tapping the doorframe as she passed.

Agnes dabbed her tears from her cheeks, then slapped shut the grammar book.

'Chapter Seventeen,' announced Jem, opening *The Swiss Family Robinson* and sliding it in front of her.

The afternoon was dark, but on Whitwillow Farm, all hearts were light.

Locusts and Lanterns
by John K. Patterson (*fantasy/thriller/action/spiritual warfare*)

28 October 1845

Johann Schneider buried himself alone in the emptiest corner of the Fentiman Arms. He did his best to ignore sore joints and focus on the pocket watch he was repairing for the Twickenhams, when a young woman entered the tavern. To say she walked may not have been the right word; 'glide' or 'drift' would be closer to the mark. A traveller for certain. She did not carry herself like a Whitsteader.

Dying flames in the hearth leapt an inch higher. He was not sure it was the wind that had stoked them. Reinvigorated embers poured golden light across her dark green cloak, which shimmered and flowed like liquid. For a moment the edges of her garment seemed to ebb in and out of visibility. Johann blinked and set his tools down, making sure his cup of ale was only half-empty. Still, he pushed the cup away. It would not do for a tinkerer to blunt his senses and hinder his work.

Keeping her hood up, she looked around at the other guests, who trickled in as suppertime drew near. Johann glanced at them and felt a familiar ache. A little companionship would do his heart some good. He and Mila had enjoyed many meetings here.

But the Twickenhams would be pleased if their watch returned ahead of schedule, he decided. Besides, he wanted to keep an eye on this woman. At least he was out of the house and around people, not wasting away in the dark.

She approached him. Her eyes seemed black, until they caught the firelight. The irises flashed deep violet, like a clear sky well into dusk but not yet ready to show the stars. Johann had never seen such eyes. They fastened his attention, and he could sense a litany of intense, urgent thoughts behind them.

It took him a moment to notice the rest of her face: firmly holding the quality of youth, but with high cheekbones and the weathered look of a lady who spent her days out of doors. Without being sure why, he felt she was quite older than his initial impression.

She was pretty enough. But was that a faint scar on the bridge of her nose? And another on her temple? What had happened to her?

'Johann Schneider,' she said.

Her sharp voice and lack of formality caught him unawares before he remembered to stand. His chair loudly scraped back as he hurried to his feet. His knees complained, and he suppressed a groan. 'A pleasant evening to you, my dear. Can I repair something for you?'

That was why everyone came to him these days. He pointed to his tools, most of them awaiting use in a leather roll-up bag, spread beside the watch. 'I am occupied, but I would be happy to assist you once—'

She took the chair opposite him with hardly a sound. 'Mister Schneider, your life is in peril.'

Johann no longer heard the din of conversation. There was only the slow crackle of the embers, someone chewing loudly behind him, and a strange emptiness where his thoughts normally droned. He straightened his waistcoat and sat back down. 'I beg your pardon?'

'Your life, sir. There are forces at work against you as we speak.'

'Well, time works against all of us,' he said, trying not to sound too curt as he indicated the timepiece. 'If the orphanage children have put you up to some practical joke, it is in poor taste, and I'd rather continue my work.'

'I normally do not speak to hu—' Her lips snapped closed, then she cleared her throat. 'To *people* in my travels. Especially not strangers.' She seemed to relax, but he noted the tension knotted in her neck. The cloak allowed him to see little else. She had not even removed her hood.

She spoke more gently, glancing to the floor. 'Forgive me, sir. I am aware of the impropriety of this talk, and that others might take notice of it.'

'It seems they already have,' he said. Stares came their way from several other patrons, and the women huddled over their drinks or meals and whispered to each other. Village gossip would likely say that he and this stranger were sparking a romance.

After Mila, a few women had decided to play matchmaker and tried setting Johann up, without asking his permission. He was forty-five. Wasn't their time better spent pestering younger bachelors? Some broken things could not be fixed. And tombs were not in the habit of opening.

'I don't even know your name,' he said, 'nor where you're from.'

She delivered both in haste. 'Velith Nightlock, of Yorkshire.'

'That does not sound like a Yorkshire name or accent, Miss Nightlock. Perhaps North London.' Johann pocketed the watch and rolled up his tool bag.

'Well, Schneider is a strange name in Whitstead.'

A half-smile crossed his face. He rubbed at the stubble along his jaw. 'My wife Mila and I settled here some years ago.'

'Wife?'

He could only blame himself for bringing it up. 'God rest her soul, I fear. It's been some years.' Her violet eyes softened. Johann decided to change the subject before she could express condolences. 'Do you really believe I am in danger?'

Her unseen arms rustled inside the cloak. She produced a metal object and placed it on the table. Johann leaned forward. It resembled a metal tankard with a brass handle, converted into a lantern with a curved glass window on its side. Filigree patterns of trees and flowers flowed from base to rim. It glimmered more like silver than pewter, and a mild blue light shone inside. He couldn't tell what was glowing, but it was no flame.

Velith turned a small knob on the handle's top corner. The glow brightened, then dimmed. 'I can adjust it like so. This is a gift from… friends of mine. Any being caught in its glow will show its true nature. And I fear we will need to use it before the night is out.'

'True nature?'

She leaned over the table, speaking nearly in whispers. 'We both know this village has more than a trace of the supernatural, Mister Schneider, and creatures from another realm threaten your life.'

She was right about Whitstead, that much was certain. She might have picked up gossip of gnomes or fairies, or the floating carriage which had captured the village's attention last winter. But what could this stranger know about him?

Before he could ask her, he took note of a scent that charged the air like static. Lilacs. *Lilacs in autumn?* The familiar bouquet thickened the air and provoked a sudden lump in Johann's throat.

'Is there some manner of perfume you are wearing?' he asked.

Velith shook her head. She raised her head slightly and sniffed. 'There are two or three other ladies in this tavern with some fragrance. But not I.'

The air almost stung with lilac perfume. Mila's perfume. She had loved it enough to wear it year-round. It came from every direction, invaded his brain, made his eyes water. He kept looking out through the windows and towards the entrance to Fentiman Arms, as if Mila had exited her grave and would join him for supper.

'Angels guard this village and its people most zealously,' Velith said, 'but they attend most readily to incorporeal threats. The creatures I spoke of are inclined to bewitch their target's mind, and then attack the body. They feed on those who are isolated. Withdrawn.'

His attention dwindled the more she spoke. 'I smell my late bride's perfume,' he said, possibly to no one but himself.

Velith's eyes widened. Her right hand darted below the table and reached to grip something by her waist. 'They have come sooner than I thought. I urge you to stay indoors and in view of others, Mister Schneider. These creatures isolate their prey and strike in the dark. I'll need to reconnoitre, but I will return.'

She rose from her seat and snatched up the lantern, hiding it in her cloak. She slid to the door, vanished before he could see which direction she had gone.

236

As the door closed, a voice came singing from outside. They were not words, but the tones Mila had so enjoyed, the rising and falling notes she could hold as softly as a bird in her hand.

His breath caught. It was Mila's voice.

The memory of why he was here, and with whom he had shared his table, faded until it was nearly lost. Johann pushed his chair back and stood. Somehow his knees no longer ached. Moving felt light and effortless. He pushed the door open and entered the cool evening.

Outside, there could be no mistaking it. The singing voice was that of his wife, four years departed and yet fresh as the day before she had fallen ill with fever. Her lilac perfume no longer stung his eyes or nose. It became a balm to his lonely soul. A few other villagers conversed or strolled or entered shops, seemingly oblivious to her voice. Couldn't they hear it?

Perhaps not. Except when they sang together in church, she cherished her voice as a private gift, for his ears alone. As if from a great distance, he also heard Velith— wait, who was Velith?—calling his name, faint but insistent, like a stain that had been scrubbed many times but never quite disappeared. What was she so worried about, again?

It didn't matter. His wife was here. Somehow. The conviction sprang from nowhere yet felt as certain as his knowledge of how to replace cartwheels and door locks. Whitstead had thin places, where the spirit world could meet his own. It was almost All Hallows' Eve when thin places might dissolve altogether.

Could the living and the dead truly reunite, if only for a while? It was not the first time Johann had contemplated it. Yearned for it. Prayed for it with tears, begging God to bring her back and fill the cavern in his heart.

The voice came from behind the Fentiman Arms. The sun's last light lingered on the horizon, and stars emerged from the dark, accompanied by the slim grin of a crescent moon. Would Mila be a ghost? Had a miracle occurred, whereupon she emerged from her grave like Lazarus? If any tombs could open, surely they would be in Whitstead.

He rounded the building, passing a cart heavy with wine barrels. His wife's singing faded. Johann looked around, heartbeat and worry rising in concert. If only he could hold her once more and forget laying her to rest. He had not even attended service at St. Nicholas since she had been buried, despite the pleading of Reverend Hollybrook to return. How could the reverend, and God Himself, expect Johann to walk past her gravestone every Sunday, feeling that loss over and over?

But now… perhaps now he wouldn't have to.

A grassy meadow lay behind the Fentiman Arms, across which awaited his house. Their house. The homes to either side already had their windows aglow from lamp and hearth.

Johann hardly took note, focusing on a figure in a white dress that glowed like moonlight.

Was it Mila? Spirits could take so many forms. He broke into a sprint.

Behind Johann, a female voice interrupted the rapturous melodies. 'Johann!' the cry came, 'they're setting a trap for you!'

That woman who met him in the Fentiman Arms. What was her name? The memory, so recent, felt a lifetime ago.

Johann slowed his sprint. There was the cultured poise, the coy eyes that could convey her thoughts from across a room, the dark red curls shining like bronze.

Mila had returned. He stumbled forward. The crushing burden of the last four years lifted away from his heart. 'Mila. Mila, you're here.'

'I have missed you so,' she said, her words carrying a music of their own though she did not sing them.

'Johann,' whispered a half-remembered voice behind him, accompanied by rustling grass. 'Your wife is gone. This is an illusion to lure you in. Do not listen to her!'

He never broke eye contact with Mila, who gave no sign of noticing anyone other than him. A hundred thoughts and questions clamoured to be spoken.

'I am truly sorry, Johann,' the whisper spoke again, cracked with regret. 'For your sake, I must show you.'

Next to him, he should have seen whoever had spoken, but found only the grass, lit silver by Mila's glow. Something rustled like fabric, nearly unseen, until a woman's hand appeared mid-air. A hand holding a tall silver vessel, with a curious blue light shining from its glass door. The lantern. Its glow strengthened to surpass even that of a full moon.

Johann blinked, too confused to react. He stared into the light, and all the memories of a few minutes ago spilled back in. He shook his head, frantic to sort things out.

'You must see what deceives you,' Velith's voice said. 'Look.'

The unearthly beam fell on Mila. The glow from her dress disappeared. Johann felt he had a boulder rather than a head atop his shoulders, turning ponderously. He saw something enormous, something dark, glistening in the lantern light.

Johann slowly realised he saw a ghastly face, skin stretched over its skull. There was a dull glow inside the pupils, like sullen coals wrapped in thick darkness. Black hair draped from the head, as threads of algae clinging to something pulled from a watery grave, and out of the hair rose a circle of glinting golden spines like the points of a crown.

He quelled a scream.

The thing's lips snagged on long teeth— the fangs of a tiger or wolf. It stared at him with baleful eyes, pupils flaring bright, and he couldn't tell if its expression was a greedy smile or the grimace of pain.

'What is the matter, darling?' it said. It still spoke in Mila's voice, sensuous and gentle. 'Don't you want to sing? Our voices made such beauty together.'

Did the horror know it had been exposed? Or was it revelling in his reaction to its true form? Hearing her voice coming from that creature... it pushed bile into his mouth. Revulsion and anger twisted in his gut.

Johann's legs gave out. He fell on his backside, unable to tear his gaze away, even as Velith's cloak flashed back into visibility next to him. She held the lantern higher, revealing more of the creature.

The form behind that abomination of a face belonged to nothing human. A long body, slung low to the ground, supported by two pairs of crooked legs, armoured like those of an insect. To either side rose a third set of legs, edged with spines and bent at an angle like the jumping legs of a locust.

A locust the size of a Clydesdale.

'Back!' Velith commanded. 'You will not have him!'

'My business lies with you as well, Velith Nightlock,' hissed the monstrosity. It had abandoned Mila's voice, sounding bestial and broken. Its fangs shimmered with oily drool. 'You speared my sister on this very field, last winter.'

'And I'll gladly reunite you,' Velith snarled.

Another noise cut the night air, something rhythmic and metallic like iron wings beating the sky into submission. Darkness itself seemed to close in, and marshal to the monster's aid.

The demonic locust cackled, sounding like it laughed through a slit throat. 'I brought reinforcements, Velith.' Its smile gave Johann's fear a jagged edge. 'Kill one hornet, and you draw the colony's ire.'

Johann regarded the creature with growing contempt. It had stolen Mila's image and tried to manipulate him. Now it came after the woman who had forced him to see the truth and had pulled him back from a precipice of self-delusion.

All he had for a weapon was a small knife to carve meat, and no doubt it would never finish off a creature this size. Even so, Johann took a half-step forward, already brandishing the blade. He did not remember drawing it but held it firm and stared into those infernal eyes.

'Whatever you are,' he said, hearing the quaver in his voice, 'you're not welcome in Whitstead. By God and by all the angels, leave this place and do not come back.'

The locust's rattling laugh resumed, and Johann felt his marrow freeze. 'A bold invocation, from a sad man of weak faith. A man who avoids the sanctuary of the church, not wanting to see his wife's grave.'

Johann's sight turned crimson. His body filled with heat, fingers gripping the knife so tight he heard the joints crack.

Something dark lifted behind the creature. A strong hand jerked Johann back with astonishing strength, and he found himself sliding back through the grass. The creature's tail stabbed forward, pierced the ground where he had stood. It ripped free. A giant scorpion's tail, the stinger bigger than his knife and dripping with sizzling venom.

Velith flashed into action next to him, the cloak sweeping out like wings as she sprang, landing between him and the monster. The lantern clattered to the ground, throwing its light across the field. Velith brandished a pair of rods or spears, lengthy and pale. Where had those come from?

She held one out in front of her like a quarterstaff and threw the other to Johann. It landed in the grass next to him. She parried a blow from the scorpion tail, another from one of the locust's front legs. It knocked her aside, then descended over her, stinger poised to strike.

A sound of impact. The creature let out a grating scream that sliced into Johann's ears. A wooden javelin stuck out of its neck, lodged between plates of chitinous armour.

Velith got back to her feet, still clutching her own weapon, and pushed her words through gritted teeth. 'I didn't come alone, either.'

Johann gaped as four other forms coalesced into being next to her — more cloaked women. Three held spears of their own. The one without a weapon, a redhead in a cloak like blue midnight, reached into a pocket and drew out what looked for all the world like a hazelnut. She cracked it between her fingers, and out of it grew another spear. It could not possibly have fit inside the nut's shell. Johann blinked, not sure of what he had just witnessed.

Magic. It had to be.

The injured locust hissed, lashed its tail in wide sweeps. All five women approached Johann to form a defensive barrier around him, each one aiming her gaze skywards.

'It would have been safer indoors,' Velith said as she picked up the lantern. 'Stay with us and keep low.'

This was his fault. Johann had wandered out of safety. Hands fumbling, he picked up the spear she had tossed him. It was a heavy wood, the grain spiralling around to a needle-sharp point like a narwhal tusk.

When he looked at Velith, she jabbed her spear upwards. 'Focus on them. We'll protect you.'

He watched the darkening sky, looking for any shapes that blocked the emerging stars. Johann wanted to ask what the creatures were, what they wanted of him, who the women were. Anything that might help him gain a shred of understanding. 'I'm so sorry,' he managed.

'Don't be,' one of the other women said. 'They can bewitch the best of us.'

The sound of rattling wings filled his ears. Three other locusts slammed into the grassy earth, their spined legs scratching deep furrows as they folded bladelike wings against their backs. Two closed in protectively around their injured comrade. The largest one crawled forward, scorpion tail swinging over its head. Its stinger was as long as Johann's forearm. It glared at the women, snarling something in a language Johann could not identify.

From behind the light, a flutter of huge wings from behind drew his attention. The creature that had imitated Mila still whimpered behind its comrades, but his wife's image beckoned again. Another monster.

White dress aglow, her form was now rotted and grey, bones showing through gaps in the flesh. The eyes were gone from their sockets. Lips had rotted, exposing grey teeth. And behind the illusion, Johann heard the clicking of insect jaws and a hellish cackle.

It was evil enough that they used her likeness at all. To desecrate it like this…

He pushed past the women and screamed his rage.

'Johann, no!' cried Velith.

He threw the spear, but the weapon went wide and stuck in the earth.

The locust burst forth from the illusion, pupils burning and claws extended. Johann had no time to react. He saw the stinger shoot forward, rake across his chest. Lightning shot to every nerve, and he dropped to the ground writhing. Cold sweat beaded on his skin. A deep shaking took hold of him. He could barely keep watching the locust. Its face twisted in a triumphant leer.

He turned and dragged himself away, nearly getting stepped on as the redhead backed up towards him and held off the largest of the locusts. A sickening cry came from its throat as her spear pierced one of its blazing eyes. The other women stabbed and slashed at the other creatures, darting back to avoid their stings and then lunging forwards for the kill.

Johann felt his stomach drop as a spined insect leg pressed down on his back. The one he had thrown his spear at.

Velith ran behind the creature, striking out with a curved sword. The raised tail dropped to the ground, convulsing like a dying snake. Another wooden spear shot through the creature's body, pinning it to the earth next to Johann. It screamed.

Velith came forward. The blade of her sword was marred with violet blood. The giant insect struggled in vain against the javelin.

Johann pressed a hand to his stinger wound. The burning grew, and his breath came in short gasps. It took all his effort to stay conscious.

Velith drove her sword between the armour plates on the creature's neck.

Johann saw lights of every colour dance in his vision, not sure if it was because of the pain. But the locust seemed to lose its colour. Then its body broke into ashen fragments, clouds of dust billowing as its form disintegrated. The javelin crumbled with it.

Suddenly his pain subsided. The wound was still there, throbbing and bleeding, but it no longer felt as if someone had stabbed him with a lightning bolt. Had the venom ceased to act when the creature that gave it was dead? He cautiously regained his feet and stood next to Velith.

The other women stood among piles of ash. Only one of the locusts was still alive. The original one, who had first stolen Mila's likeness. It writhed on the ground, watched over by one of the women, a tall blonde in a red cloak.

'Your courage is commendable,' Velith said. She breathed hard, gripped her sword with white knuckles. Johann noticed faint scars running across her fingers.

'If you want,' she said, 'this one is all yours.'

Johann nodded. He found the spear he had thrown, pulling it out of the earth. His wound would need tending, but it was shallow.

He stalked over to the wounded locust, its tail and jumping legs severed. It snapped at him, then opened its mouth to speak.

Johann thrust the javelin forwards, denying it any last words.

After its ashes had fallen in a loose heap, he turned around to thank the women.

Velith stood there, hood drawn back and showing curls of mahogany-coloured hair. She held the strange lantern, its light still brilliant enough to hurt his vision.

Her companions had all vanished.

'My sisters do not care to be seen,' she explained. 'Not when they can help it. If they find any other locusts, they will despatch them.' She stepped forward. 'Well done and thank you for your effort. You did not need to do that.'

'Yes, I did. You came to my defence.' He lifted his gaze, looking at the crescent moon. 'Lady warriors. Whitstead does attract the most peculiar sorts. Are you the Amazons of old? Valkyries?'

'The Greeks called us Dryads,' Velith said. 'Most of us tend trees and forests, unseen by humans. But some of us have different callings.'

'And what manner of creatures attacked us? What do they want with me?'

Velith's face darkened. 'Shapeshifters. Fallen angels who rely on illusion to draw their prey. They can spend years tormenting the grieving and the lonely, to drive them to despair. The more despondent you become, the more it whets their appetite.'

The thought made his lips pull back in disgust. 'Fallen angels,' he repeated.

'One variety, yes. The Scriptures mention them in the ninth chapter of Revelation. Servants of Abaddon the Destroyer, one of the devil's strongest knights.'

He shuddered, even as fatigue began to take hold. 'And I thought the grasshoppers in my garden were troublemakers.' Johann pointed to the unearthly lantern. 'What of that device? You said it shows the true form of things.'

She seemed to weigh her thoughts before she spoke. 'A token of thanks from the Fae. I rescued one of their own from that locust's sister last Christmas. In your household, as it happens.'

Johann looked pointedly at her. 'Were you the one who broke my kitchen window?'

Velith's head dipped apologetically. 'To save my own life, yes. I hope the gold I left was sufficient to cover the expense.'

He gave a weary smile. 'More than sufficient. It was a strange burglary. Mila and I have never been robbed out here before.' He clamped his lips shut. Did he have to keep mentioning her as if she still lived?

He got back to his feet, looked down at the shallow wound. It hardly even bled now.

'I will make every effort to avoid burglary in the future,' she said. She started to walk away, past the nearest mound of ashes, and he feared she might vanish like the other Dryads.

'Wait.'

She turned.

'How can I repay you?' he said.

Velith wiped her sword across the grass and resheathed it. 'There is no need. But I will counsel you in something difficult.'

'Anything.'

Her expression turned sombre. 'Allow yourself to feel pain. Even the loss of your dear bride. That is the way of healing.'

The words felt like a fist to his stomach. But Johann would stay true to his word.

She lifted her hood, standing there against the stars. 'The Dryads of the Yorkshire Unseen will watch over Whitstead. Especially those who are lonely and who grieve.' She smiled, came back to put her hand on his shoulder. 'I do not believe you have seen the last of us, Johann Schneider.'

She turned, her fluid cloak sweeping along with her. The Dryad walked a dozen steps, vanishing all the while. Johann could see the grass depressed where she stepped on it, until her path took her into the trees, and she was gone.

'Mila,' he whispered. This time, he welcomed his tears.

Ollie and the Saints

by Melinda K. Busch *(fantasy/ghost story/spiritual warfare)*

Ollie Dobbins watched by the flickering light of his turnip lantern as his brother Frank held a dusty wooden jar out of Davey Micklewright's reach. Frank was taller than Davey by a couple heads, and he raised the jar high in one hand whilst holding Davey back with the other.

Davey didn't want that jar opened. He said it came down to him from his mam, who got it from her da, and she said something terrible would happen if the stopper was pulled. Frank told Davey to stop his whinging, 'cause Lyddie Micklewright was dead and would never know, and nothing terrible could come of opening an old jar, anyway. Ollie wasn't so sure.

When Davey's eyes turned to him, silently pleading for support, Ollie looked away. He sympathised with Davey. Ollie still remembered the ache he got in his chest when his mam died the previous year. Moreover, everyone knew Jedediah Micklewright spent all his coin on drink, then went home and knocked Davey about. George Dobbins hadn't had much to give his sons when he was living, but at least he'd never struck them.

'Give it back!' Tears shone on Davey's cheeks, but Frank ignored them and shoved Davey against the tree trunk.

Ollie's gut churned. He regretted telling his brother about Davey's hidey hole in the hollow of the oak tree behind the Micklewright cottage. Davey didn't keep much there—just a carved wooden box and the jar. Now the box was crushed, a victim to Frank's heel; at Frank's word, a silver cross pendant that had been inside it was now in Ollie's pocket.

'If you want the cross, let me open the jar,' Frank growled. At once, Davey stopped struggling and stood staring, his lower lip quivering.

'He's nought but a cowardy custard, eh, Ollie?' Frank jeered.

Ollie forced a laugh. At ten years old, he was not brave enough to gainsay Frank, three years his elder. 'Aye. It's proper hen-hearted he is!' he chirped. But Ollie knew the truth—he was the real 'cowardy custard.' He wished he'd stayed at the Charitable School instead of sneaking out with Frank tonight.

Davey straightened, rubbing away his tears with a sleeve. 'Go on, then! You'll see... curiosity killed the cat, Mam said... killed it dead as a doornail.'

Ollie winced. Many of the ghost stories he'd heard involved an evil spirit trapped in a jar, but Frank insisted such tales were nonsense.

Davey stood back and watched Frank tug at the stopper. After a few seconds of vain effort, Frank swore and flexed his hand, then tried again. Ollie instinctively turned away, squeezing his eyes shut. A second later, he heard a loud 'pop,' and a freezing blast of wind nearly toppled him. Then the air grew still. Ollie opened his eyes a sliver just in time to see a shadow flit away around the cottage and disappear.

When Ollie turned back, he stood saucer eyed. Frank and Davey were frozen in place, eyes blank, jaws slack. Ollie held up his lantern for a closer look and watched a patch of grey spread from their feet upward. By the time he realised what that patch was, it had reached their knees. Before his very eyes, his brother and Davey were turning to stone, as sure as if they'd laid eyes on that Medusa creature from Uncle Mattie's tales.

Summoning his courage, Ollie leapt forwards and tugged at his brother's hand in a vain effort to pull him free. Frank did not budge. By the time Ollie let go and stepped back, the grey stone had crept to Frank's shoulders and was inching down his arms. Soon, all that remained of flesh on either boy was from the neck upward. Ollie turned and fled, howling in terror.

•◊•◊•◊•◊•◊•◊•◊•◊•

Ollie paid no heed to the path he took. Deeper into the dark woods he plunged, bawling as he ran, his bare feet churning through the muck and tears blinding his eyes. Suddenly, he ran straight into ample arms that pulled him close. A warbling voice clucked over him, wrapping round him like a warm blanket. 'Ollie, lad! Tell me, what has you so afraid that you come bargin' into my home, makin' a noise like the Hag o' the Mist?'

Startled into silence, Ollie rubbed the tears from his eyes, then found himself looking into the round, wrinkled face of none other than Maisie Bloom. He'd heard tales about the old woman and always kept a respectful distance when she came padding through Whitstead. Frank said she was 'nought but an old bat,' but Maisie frightened Ollie. She was a small woman by height, only a few inches taller than he, with a tangle of silver hair. The other children said she lived in the woods and turned into a bird when she wasn't around people. If she could become a bird, that meant she was a witch, didn't it? Fear-stricken, he clapped his hands over his eyes. 'Please, Maisie Bloom, don't turn me into a hoptoad!'

'There now, lad,' she soothed. 'I'll do no such thing.'

She released him, and he cast a wary eye about him, uncertain whether he should stay or flee. Of a sudden, Ollie perceived that he had entered a strange and wonderful place here in the heart of the woods. Outside Maisie's glade, it was a cold, wet night, but here it was broad day, with trees all a-blossom. Soft, sun-warmed grass was thawing his frozen feet. Close by stood a cherry tree laden with fruit, and all around, a riot of birdsong sounded louder even than a church choir. Honeysuckle and lilacs filled the air with sweet perfume. Somehow, Ollie had stumbled into the midst of springtide!

In the middle of Maisie's glade, an oak stretched out many-fingered branches dripping with yellow catkins. Set in the trunk at ground level was a great green door. Ollie had never seen such a thing! Almost forgetting the terror from which he had fled, he turned about, his jaw slung low. ''Tis the proper Garden of Eden!' he breathed out in awestruck wonder.

'Eden? Nay, lad. But 'tis hallowed ground no less, my own cathedral.' The old woman's steady voice chased away the last of Ollie's fears. A witch wouldn't live in a place of such beauty. She would prefer a gloomy place crawling with spiders. Besides, no one looking long into Maisie Bloom's eyes could think her anything but good.

'Aye, Ollie, me lad, 'tis the true King I serve, not the dark prince!' Maisie laughed, a laugh like wind playing amongst the trees. Ollie wondered that she knew his thoughts, but he almost found it a comfort. Surely it would help her believe his odd tale. The memory of what he had seen sent a shiver through him.

Maisie lay a hand on his shoulder and gave a light squeeze. 'Fear not, lad. 'Tis in the hands of the King we are.' She ran a hand through his curls. 'Tell your odd tale. What fearsome sight sent a brave lad such as yourself runnin' like a skittish hare?'

'My brother… and Davey Micklewright… they…' Ollie gulped. Had he really seen it? In this peaceful place, it seemed impossible. Sucking in a breath, he continued. 'Frank made Davey open a jar and a Medusa comed out and… and… turned 'em both to stone! And the Medusa's loose and it'll turn everyone to stone!'

As he finished his speech, he was certain Maisie would laugh, for he was aware what a wild tale it was, and Miss Rossiter had more than once told it around town that Oliver Dobbins was the most outrageous liar she ever knew.

But Maisie did not laugh. She gasped a little, then looked Ollie right in the eyes, her own hazel eyes glistening. 'Trust in the King, young Ollie. As the saint said, "All manner of things shall be well."'

Consternation stirred in Ollie's gut. Why did Maisie keep jawing about a king, when everyone knew a queen sat on England's throne?

Suddenly Maisie's eyes did a merry dance, and she did laugh, but it was joyful, with no mockery behind it. 'I speak of no mortal king, lad! Victoria reigns in Britain, aye, but a King there is what rules o'er earth and heaven! Why, 'tis right there in the hymn, you know!'

Ollie did not know, but he nodded. Maisie's confidence was catching, and his heart grew bolder with each word she spoke.

She smiled, her hand resting lightly on his arm. 'Ollie, lad, 'tis your own courage you must find and not be restin' on mine.' Her eyes still danced, but her tone grew quite sombre. 'When all is dark, boyo, then must you call upon the King. 'Tis His light what chases away shadows and turns night to day.'

Ollie wasn't sure what she meant, but she must be right, for here in her domain it was day, even though beyond this glade the night was dark and deep. He would do as she said.

Maisie plucked a flower from a hawthorn shrub and tucked it in his pocket. 'There you go... hawthorn for hope. Now, let us go see what the King has for us.' She took his hand and led him towards the edge of the glade. The further they got from the tree with the door, the darker it grew; soon they marched through the dark forest, with dripping branches overhead and sodden leaves underfoot.

•◇•◇•◇•◇•◇•◇•◇•◇•

Maisie led the way. Ollie was glad because he could not have found Davey's oak by himself. As she tramped amidst the trees, Ollie's hand tightly gripped in her own, she began to sing. It was no hymn Ollie recognised. Granted, he rarely heeded the words of church hymns, but he was sure this song was Maisie's own.

> In the pow'r of the Father,
> Strength I procure,
> In His loving arms
> I stand secure,
> My victory
> In Him is sure.
>
> Kyrie eleison.
>
> In the name of the Son
> Is my spirit healed,
> At the word of the Son
> My foe is felled,
> In His nail-pierced hands
> I am upheld.
>
> Christe eleison.
>
> By the Holy Ghost
> I am consoled,
> On the Holy Ghost,
> I stake my soul,
> With His hand to guide,
> I step forth bold.

Kyrie Eleison.

In the Father I trust,
To the Son I call,
By the Spirit led,
Three in One,
At Your feet I fall.

Gloria Patri et Filio
Et Spiritu Sancto
In Saecula Saeculorum.

A grand song it was. It stirred Ollie's blood and made his heart thrum. He felt like a warrior of olden days instead of a timid boy led through a dark wood by a silver-haired woman in a patched skirt. When she sang it a second time and then a third, his high soprano voice joined Maisie's deep alto, though he stumbled over the strange words.

Soon they reached the oak, where the stone Frank and Davey still stood. Maisie sighed over the silent statues, then dropped Ollie's hand and stooped to pick up the wooden jar. Standing straight again, she lifted her face to the heavens, raised her hands, and closed her eyes. When she opened them a minute later, Ollie thought he saw a ghost of a smile flit across her features. She reached for his hand. 'Come along, Ollie.'

'But...' Ollie felt like he'd swallowed a rock. Were Frank and Davey beyond hope? Why wasn't Maisie doing something?

Maisie patted the hawthorn blossom that stuck slightly out of his pocket. 'Hope we always have, Ollie, and a task we have as well. We must find the spirit that was loosed from this jar. Then we shall fight a battle.'

'A battle?' Ollie's heart sank. He wanted to run away and hide in a corner, but he had to see this through. 'Will they be put right again after we fight the ghost?'

'I don't know, lad. But God knows, and I trust Him. All shall be well.' Maisie smiled and squeezed his hand, and together they marched towards the village square. As they turned the corner onto the High Road, two new statues met his eyes: the first, a cow — it had to be the Widow Sutcliffe's — and not ten strides past it, Miss Rossiter herself! Maisie strode past them without comment, so Ollie did the same.

As they walked on, she began to talk, the musical cadence of her speech comforting and emboldening Ollie. 'This night, 'tis no ghost that is our enemy, lad. A kind soul was Caitrin Lloyd. From Oswestry she came, and all the men from miles around longed to court her. Many were the women what looked upon sweet Caitrin with envy. Most jealous of all was a witch with a silver tongue and a heart of stone. She served the dark prince, and from him, she gained terrible powers. Aye, lad, sometimes in this world, evil is allowed to think it holds sway, but the King is only waitin' for the time He has decreed. His is the victory.'

Weaving her tale, Maisie led the boy through the streets of Whitstead to the churchyard. When they stepped through the eastern gate, Ollie heard a sound of weeping, though he saw not a soul in that mournful place. He shivered, but not from cold. Like the fragrance of spring, warmth clung to Maisie Bloom. It flowed from her too. Without her at his side, Ollie did not think he could have stepped into the churchyard that All Hallows' Eve. It was a place of sorrow for him, where he'd bid farewell first to Mam, then to Da six months past.

Maisie released his hand and lay an arm across his shoulders as they passed the elder Dobbins' gravestones. 'You'll see 'em again, lad, if you pledge yourself to the King,' she soothed.

Onwards they strode, towards the western edge of the churchyard. The closer they got to the western wall, the louder the weeping grew. Just beyond that wall stood an old statue. Ollie had seen it many times. The statue had stood longer than anyone in Whitstead had been living.

''Tis Caitrin weepin',' Maisie said. 'Two hundred years ago this night, a few days ere she was to wed Alton Fletcher, the witch lured her from Oswestry. In the woods near Whitstead, they heard the bells of St. Nicholas ring, wakin' Caitrin from the spell that lay upon her. She broke free and ran for the protection of the church, but alas, there was no gate in the western wall in those days, and she could not gain entrance. Ere she could find a way, the witch sang out a new spell, and, in that instant, a stone figure stood by the churchyard wall.

'Neither livin' nor dead, Caitrin's soul was set to wander so long as her statue stands, with this curse upon it—that any being what looks upon her spirit's face will likewise turn to stone. She has no wish to do harm—she wants only to be set free from the stone so that her spirit might take flight homeward.'

Ollie wrinkled his brow. 'To Oswestry?'

Maisie chuckled. 'Nay, lad… to Glory. Because she never died, her spirit remained bound to this earth. Only the witch's defeat can free her.' They stood near the gate now, still in the churchyard, across the wall from the statue.

'What about the jar?' Ollie asked.

'Ah, the jar.' Maisie lifted the small, wooden container. 'After the cursin' of Caitrin Lloyd, three of Ebenezer Whitwillow's goats went missin'. He found 'em out in his field, turned to stone. You've seen 'em, haven't you? And then there was Malachy Carver's old hound, Steadfast.'

'Th' Houndstone, over behind the Charitable House!' Ollie felt the thrill of vindication. Frank had often teased him for believing the old stories, but Maisie had as much as said they were true, though again, he wondered how she knew.

'I know, Ollie, because I was there to see it, but you spoke aright, the Houndstone. Well, the townsfolk were sore afraid, and they asked the Reverend Gregory Lightheart what could be done. The good Reverend recognised the work of a cursed spirit, and he did the very thing I'll be doin'. He coaxed Caitrin's spirit into this jar and sealed it tight against the day she could be restored to her proper form. Look now — see the shadow at the base of the statue? 'Tis herself hidin' there. Fear not — you're safe here.'

Ollie squinted and peered into the night, but he could not see what Maisie saw. His turnip lantern had long since burnt out, and too many clouds in the moonless sky obscured any starlight that might have fallen upon the small meadow.

Maisie held the jar aloft and sang boldly. 'Come to me, Caitrin, soon shalt have thy rest. And the Good Lord be willin', I'll see thee home tonight.' A sudden blast of cold air, such as Ollie felt when Frank first opened the jar, rushed past, and the vessel seemed to jump a little in Maisie's hands. After popping the stopper in place, she slipped the jar into a pocket of her apron. 'There.' She patted the pocket and smiled. 'Now she'll be safe whilst we engage the foe.'

Ollie's stomach flipped. 'The foe?' he asked, near choking on the word, but his fingers went to the hawthorn flower. He took in a deep breath and straightened his shoulders. 'Hope we always have, right, Maisie Bloom?'

'Right you are, boyo. Hope in the King.' She smiled briefly, then narrowed her lips into a grim line. 'I feel it in my bones, the witch is comin'. She's thinkin' to claim this jar and force Caitrin to her service. Be ready, lad, and whatever else you may do, keep behind me.'

Barely had her warning faded when a dulcet voice rang through the darkness. 'Maisie Bloom, let these things be! Who art thou to strive with me?' The sound was sweet, but Ollie sensed dark magic in it. He scooted behind Maisie, peering around her ample frame as a vague form emerged from the line of trees behind the old church.

Soon, he perceived a noise of strumming, and the figure glowed ice blue. Ollie knew he should look away, but good sense gave way to curiosity. The glow captivated him. As the figure drew closer, he recognised it as a woman. Clad in a sapphire blue gown and a pale cloak, her skin was like porcelain. Her hair flowed in rippling waves down her back, shiny and black as a raven's wing, and she played on a lyre. Her blue eyes seemed to summon him. Maisie's firm hand held him in place, but his legs twitched with desire to run out and throw himself on the ground before her.

'We meet again, Ceridwen.' Maisie's voice did not waver. Ollie heard no fear in her steady tone, only deep sorrow and stern resolve. Quietly, for his ears alone, she offered reassurance. 'Here in the churchyard, lad, you're safe. She can tempt you, but she cannot touch you on this hallowed ground.'

Drawing alongside the statue, Ceridwen stopped. Her slender fingers stroked the statue's surface, which had grown rough after years of exposure. After a long moment, she locked eyes with Maisie. 'You have what is mine, Sister.' She extended her hand but did not reach over the wall. 'Give it here.' The command dripped like honey from Ceridwen's tongue, and Ollie wondered that Maisie did not hand over the jar and beg forgiveness then and there.

'You have no claim to Caitrin, Ceridwen.' Maisie's homespun speech seemed suddenly rough and rude, its former lilting music now a harsh grating in Ollie's ears. 'Though you cursed her to stone, she was never yours.'

'It was no more than she deserved,' Ceridwen spat, her voice suddenly knife sharp. 'For turning men's heads as she did. She fancied herself a beauty.'

Maisie stood firm, seemingly unruffled. 'Caitrin's truest beauty was in the kindness of her heart and the strength of her faith, and that is truer than a fair face and stronger than the magic of your lyre. For all your power, you never could conjure a true love or a trusty friend.'

Ceridwen did not answer. Instead, she added soft singing to her strumming. Ollie couldn't make out her words, and he felt a dire need to get closer so he could hear better. He tried to scoot out from behind his protector, but Maisie held him back. On the witch sang, ever louder. Her words seeped inside Ollie, thrumming in his head, making him dizzy. 'Come to me, boy. I've silver and gold. Come and I'll give thee riches untold.'

Maisie's sharp squeeze to his shoulder briefly stopped the spinning. 'Heed not her lies. She'll give naught but misery!'

But the temptation was too strong, or Ollie was too weak. He broke free of Maisie's grasp and darted forward, no longer able to resist. He had forgotten Frank and Davey — indeed, he cared for nothing but answering Ceridwen's call.

As the church bells began tolling the midnight hour, just before the boy could pass through the churchyard gate, he was stopped short. With startling agility for one of her age and girth, Maisie leapt forwards and threw herself in front of him, pushing him back so that she stepped through the gate instead of Ollie.

In that very moment, Ceridwen strummed her lyre and chanted in a strange tongue. When Ollie saw what her incantation accomplished, Ceridwen's bewitchment over him was broken, for Maisie stood frozen in place, no longer flesh and bone, but a statue herself. At last, Ollie understood. Ceridwen had meant to turn him to stone. Maisie had given herself to save him.

But to what purpose? He stood alone now, with nothing between him and this fearsome witch but a stone Maisie. She could no longer help him, and he was no match for Ceridwen. The witch had stopped playing her lyre. Instead, she was laughing, a bell-like laughter that made Ollie want to stuff his ears with cotton so he would not hear it. He dared not peer around the stone Maisie, for fear that he would fall again to temptation. He could never hope to slip through her net.

Hope we always have, Ollie. Maisie's words whispering in his heart, Ollie pressed his cheek against the cold grey stone that had been the old woman's soft, warm side. For the second time tonight, tears blinded him. He was cold and wet and miserable.

'I'm sorry, Maisie Bloom,' he mumbled. 'I didn't mean it. Please come back and tell me what to do!' Sniffling, he dragged his ragged sleeve across his nose and wet cheeks. Maisie couldn't come back, but he could remember her words. *She can tempt you, but she cannot touch you on this hallowed ground.* Here in the churchyard, he was safe. But Frank and Davey… dear Maisie Bloom… the widow's cow… even Miss Rossiter — he had to help them!

Maisie's words pulsed within him. *When all is dark, boyo, then must you call upon the King.* Ollie sent a silent prayer heavenward — a prayer of repentance and a plea for help. His hand found its way into his pocket and fastened on what he found there. Then he scrambled to his feet and lifted a stubborn fist towards the sky as he turned to face Ceridwen. Davey's silver cross flashed as a bolt of lightning split the air. 'I call 'pon the power of the comin' King,' he shouted, 'for I belong to Him! He will shine His light and… and chase your shadows out!'

No longer laughing, Ceridwen strummed her lyre again. Her voice was low and sweet. 'Such a wee boy, contriving to master me? What a vain conceit.' She shook her head, and her fingers plucked the strings. 'In the end, even my sister could not defeat me. She betrayed me, but now she is nothing. Cross the threshold, child, and come to me.'

Ollie ignored her; he would not be deceived again. He began to sing Maisie Bloom's song, timidly at first and barely above a whisper. As his courage blossomed into full flower, his chant grew stronger, louder, until it reached a grand fortissimo, drowning out Ceridwen and her lyre.

Gradually, Ollie perceived that he no longer sang alone. Many voices joined his, and he turned slowly to see a host of ghostly figures arrayed around him. They shone with a heavenly light that illuminated the whole churchyard, as sure as if it were day. A few hours ago, such a sight would have left him shaking with terror. Now it sent a thrill of victory through him. It was no longer All Hallows' Eve — it was All Saints' Day, and the saints themselves had joined him in battle! Angelic warriors stood nearby, blending their voices with the ghostly choir.

The saint nearest Ollie was a churchman, attired even now in the robes of his office, with a bald head and a salt-and-pepper beard. He drew close to Ollie's side and smiled down at him, and the boy felt the brush of a hand on his right shoulder. Another light touch to his left brought his head whipping around, and he saw Mam and Da standing beside and behind him, looking pleased and proud as they sang. When Ollie turned back to face Ceridwen, all the strings on her lyre snapped. Her glow faded and she sank to her knees. In a matter of seconds, she was nought but a heap of stone in the meadow.

In that instant, Maisie's flesh grew soft and pink and warm, and a smile bloomed across her face as she turned to enfold Ollie in her arms. 'Well done, boyo. Well done, indeed.'

The old statue outside the churchyard had also transformed. Where it once stood, there lay a woman, so very pale. She was every bit as ancient as her statue had been, but she was yet beautiful. Maisie knelt beside her and opened the jar. 'Thou art free, dear one,' she said softly. As Ollie watched, the shadow slipped out of the vessel and seemed to melt into the woman's form. She blinked open her eyes for a long moment, and Maisie grasped her hands. ''Tis time for thy homegoin', Caitrin. Of water wast thou born, now to wine shalt thou be made.'

Caitrin clutched at Maisie with frail hands, and a wan smile flitted across her lips as she nodded weakly. Then she closed her eyes and Ollie heard the same soft rattling he remembered from when Da gave up the ghost. He thought he saw a slight rippling of the air around Caitrin's body, and he wondered if it were her spirit flying homeward. Awestruck and exhausted, Ollie watched as Caitrin's empty shell crumbled to dust and drifted away in a gust of wind.

●◇●◇●◇●◇●◇●◇●◇●◇●

'Ollie!' Davey's voice broke through Ollie's stupor. Ollie felt as if he were waking from a dream. Maisie was gone; the churchyard was dark and quiet. The only sign that anything had happened here was that Caitrin's statue had vanished and in its place was a shapeless heap of stone that had not been there before.

'Davey! You're all right!' Ollie held out the cross. 'This is yours. I'm proper sorry for what I done. I won't do it again. Can you forgive me?'

Davey sniffled as he took the cross and pressed it close to his heart. 'It were Mam's.' He put the chain around his neck and tucked the pendant under his shirt. 'I forgive you, Ollie.'

Ollie nodded as he glanced around, suddenly anxious. 'Davey, where's Frank?'

'He left,' Davey said solemnly. 'He were proper angry when we awoke. Said he weren't stayin' here no more.'

'He… left?' Ollie blinked back tears. His heart ached to think his brother would abandon him, but even this bitter loss could not quench the hope Maisie Bloom had stirred to life within him. He didn't know where Frank had gone or when he'd see him again. But God knew, and that was enough. Ollie drew in a deep breath, then flung an arm around Davey's thin shoulders. 'Come on, Davey lad. I'll walk you home.'

The Battle is the Lord's
by Pam Halter *(spiritual warfare)*

26 October 1845

ophiel glided, invisible, through the graveyard by the church. Even though he was in his angelic form, the dreary, dank weather felt heavy to him. The residents of Whitstead were more affected. The crops sagged and mildewed, mostly wheat. And the newspaper headlines shouted that the Irish potato crop was failing.

Someone was in the shadows, moving from one poor house to another. Maisie Bloom. The good woman often left food for the poorest families. The Lord Almighty was pleased with her giving heart and her love for His people.

Zophiel nodded to his angelic guardians as he passed house after house. After checking on the children at the Charitable School, he made his way into the forest. Here the dryads tended the trees, as per the Almighty's order. He stopped by an English Oak, where Velith was plucking moth eggs from under the leaves.

'Greetings, Velith,' he said. 'I have an assignment for you.'

'What could I possibly do for an angel of the Most High?' she responded.

'Much,' he answered. 'The Almighty is sending you to the human, Johann Schneider, as he is in grave peril.'

Velith ran a hand over the silvery bark on the trunk. 'I already dispensed with the mirror in the human's house that had trapped a Sentinel Fae. And we killed a demon together.' She rubbed her arms, as if they ached. 'I'd rather not face another demon, especially alone.'

'An angelic army will be there to face it, along with four Dryad warriors of your choosing.'

This seemed to please Velith, for she gave a satisfied smile. 'Well then, I guess I can help you out.'

Zophiel nodded. He moved on in the direction of the church. After the battle last Christmas Eve, Aa'rin had gone off with his charge, Alice Adair, and the Almighty had given Zophiel charge of the village of Whitstead instead of another human. He felt pleased the Lord had trust in him. And he wanted to glorify Him by serving Him faithfully in this new task. Not quite an archangel, but Zophiel was pleased, nonetheless. His angelic brethren were one in spirit, all for the glory of God. No jealousy ran through any of them. They were all faithful to whatever they were called to do, loving the Lord with all their might. The fallen brethren, who had chosen to follow Lucifer eons ago, were now the enemy, and Zophiel wanted to defend the Lord's people with all the strength God gave him.

A lone candle burnt in the sanctuary. Zophiel went in and saw the reverend at the altar, deep in prayer. Saroniel, the reverend's guardian, had a hand on his shoulder, giving encouragement to his prayers. Zophiel slipped quietly out.

He flew to the outskirts of the town and perused the perimeter in its entirety. Even though the Almighty favoured Whitstead, it still had the problems of existing in a fallen world. Zophiel and the other guardians worked as they were allowed to ease the burden of a bad growing and harvest season. God used hardships to refine the peoples' faith, so he and the other angels assigned there did no more than they were told.

His rounds completed, Zophiel returned to the small cottage he still used. The one that used to belong to Aminta and her granddaughter, Ella Zoe. It now housed Rosco Smithwell, an 80-year-old wood carver. Rosco was an eccentric chap, so most people avoided him. But the children at the Charitable School loved the small toys he carved for them.

Zophiel worshipped the Almighty until sunrise when he left for his morning rounds.

•◇•◇•◇•◇•◇•◇•◇•◇•

28 October 1845, early morning

The morning started as dreary as the previous three. Rain started around three a.m. and by sunrise was still pouring down. Zophiel began his morning rounds in the cemetery. As he wove around the gravestones, his eye caught the name *Mila Schneider*. Even though she was no longer here, the coming battle would involve her and her widower husband, Johann.

The centre of town was nearly deserted. None of the shops had opened yet, except the bakery, and that wouldn't be open long, as the supply of wheat had dwindled to almost nothing.

Zophiel approached the edge of the only road into the town. He stopped and waited. Two angelic forms materialized to his left.

'Greetings, Valeon and Krio.' Zophiel bowed his head. 'What word do you bring from on High?'

Valeon put a hand over his heart. 'All praise to our God.'

'Glory to His holy name,' Zophiel responded.

'The enemy is sending the demon locust army this evening,' Valeon said. 'You are to engage and hold them in the forest.'

Zophiel nodded.

'All but five,' Krio added. 'It is the Lord's will for the man to be strengthened by the fight.'

Zophiel nodded again. 'His will be done!'

•◇•◇•◇•◇•◇•◇•◇•◇•

28 October 1845, late evening

As Zophiel patrolled the forest, more and more archangels arrived. The last to come was their captain, Michael. 'Position yourselves in the branches and shroud your glory-light,' he commanded. 'Await my signal. All to the glory of God!'

'To the glory of God!' they responded.

Zophiel approached Prince Michael. 'How can I serve the Lord tonight?'

'The Almighty has decreed for you to stand behind and strengthen the dryad, Velith.'

'His will be done,' Zophiel said.

Michael turned to Rylan, Johann Schneider's guardian. 'Do not leave your charge, but do not do the work for him.'

Rylan placed a hand on his chest. 'His will be done.'

'It is good to wait on the LORD,' Michael said before shrouding his own glory-light. 'For the battle belongs to Him!'

•◇•◇•◇•◇•◇•◇•◇•◇•

Two hours later

Zophiel and Rylan stood close behind their charges as the demon, disguised as Johann's dead wife, worked to deceive him. Even though Johann was in mortal danger, they waited, not daring to move as they had not received the Word to do so.

Velith appeared, although not visible to Johann for the moment. The demon continued to advance on Johann.

Now!

Zophiel moved behind Velith, ready to give whatever strength she needed. He sensed the other dryads waiting in the shadows. Then the demons who had been allowed through flew forward. The hidden dryads burst onto the scene, javelins in their hands. One threw hers and hit the demon who had impersonated Mila Schneider.

Rylan hadn't moved yet, clearly waiting, as the dryads and demons battled. Then, in a flash, he shot towards Johann, but not in time to prevent the demon from using the scorpion-like tail to sting him. Johann dropped to his knees, his body shaking, as Rylan, still invisible, supported him, lowering him to the ground.

Zophiel saw movement over Velith's shoulder and almost left her. Hundreds of demon locusts were soaring towards the clearing where the dryads fought for not only their own lives, but Johann Schneider's life. But before he could make a move, Prince Michael and his archangel army exploded out of hiding and engaged the demon army. Zophiel grinned and turned his attention back to his charge.

Velith and the dryads continued to fight, their strength increased as all the guardian angels of Whitstead also joined in the fray.

Almost as suddenly as it started, it was done. With the locust army defeated, the angel army vanished back into heaven, and the guardians of Whitstead returned to their charges as Velith gave Johann comfort and wisdom.

Zophiel saluted Rylan, who had his arms around Johann as Velith walked away. The poor man wept, but not alone. Peace returned to the night.

But it wouldn't last.

•◇•◇•◇•◇•◇•◇•◇•◇•

31 October 1845, almost midnight

Zophiel felt restless. He had heard Maisie Bloom singing earlier, which filled his whole being with praise for Almighty God. And part way through the hymn, a clear soprano voice—a young boy, Zophiel guessed— had joined in. But there was something else in the air. He had no Word from above, so he continued his rounds.

As he neared the west side of the church, he heard weeping, but not human. Nay, it had an ethereal sound, here and yet not. As he rounded the corner of the church, he saw the statue of Caitrin Lloyd, which had stood just outside the churchyard for two hundred years. And standing nearby was Maisie Bloom with the lad, Ollie Dobbins. Where was his brother, Frank? The two were rarely apart since their parents died.

Zophiel prayed for wisdom and immediately received an answer. He telepathed all the guardian angels. As they arrived, the archangel army came right behind. For the second time that week, Prince Michael gave the command for the angelic army to shield their glory-light and stand firm. No sooner had they gotten in place when an other-worldly creature appeared.

The witch, Ceridwen.

Michael repeated the command to stand firm. The church bells began to chime midnight. The angels watched as Ceridwen, after turning Maisie Bloom to stone, attempted to bring Ollie Dobbins to herself. Ollie's angel, Rohair, stood to the side, his face filled with rage, but he made no move.

Lord? Zophiel prayed. *Would You have us intervene?*

Stand firm. The battle is mine. I will direct you when the time is right.

Zophiel knelt in reverence as he heard his Lord's voice. *Yea, Lord. All glory be Yours alone.*

Ollie Dobbins was singing softly. The witch laughed and taunted him. He sang louder. It was Maisie Bloom's song. Then Ollie's voice was joined by others. Not the townspeople, the town's saints. All Saints' Day had begun. More and more saints awakened and joined in, their voices building, strong as when they lived on the Earth.

Sing! Michael commanded. *Sing with the saints! The battle is the Lord's!*

The angels lifted their voices, joining with the saints and Ollie Dobbins.

> In the Father I trust,
> To the Son I call,
> By the Spirit led,
> Three in One,
> At Your feet I fall.
>
> Gloria Patri et Filio
> Et Spiritu Sancto
> In Saecula Saeculorum.

The glory of the Lord filled the spirit realm and spilled into the earthen one, and the song of praise swelled in triumph. Ceridwen crumbled into stone as Maisie Bloom, the animals, Miss Rossiter, Ollie's brother Frank, and poor Davey Micklewright turned back to flesh. Caitrin's soul entered into glory.

A breeze blew away Ceridwen's dust. And Maisie Bloom returned to her glade in the woods.

The archangel army, their glory-light still hidden, flew back to heaven. Gennet, Frank's guardian, who had been instructed not to interfere in Frank's life for the last year, saluted as he flew past Zophiel. *All praise to our Mighty God for His great mercy! I'm away to watch over Frank Dobbins again!*

All glory be unto Him! Zophiel called as Gennet vanished into the woods. Then he turned and watched Ollie walk Davey back to the Charitable School. Rohair, Ollie's guardian, followed behind. He saw Zophiel and waved. *It is the Lord's will for Matthew Rossiter to take over the Charitable House in place of his sister soon. All praise to His mercy!*

Giving thanks to the Lord, Zophiel returned to the cottage. Satisfaction filled him as he lit the fire. He pulled out a box of wood pieces from a closet, sat down at the table and continued praising God as he whittled. He wanted to make sure every child in Whitstead had a toy from Rosco Smithwell to go along with whatever food basket Maisie Bloom could provide for them next week.

As he carved, the residents slept, unaware of the battle that had just been fought. It was God's mercy the people were unaware of most of the spiritual battles that went on in Whitstead this harvest season. Although, even if they had been awake, there was nothing they could have done.

Because, Zophiel reminded himself joyfully, *the battle is always the Lord's.*

Recipe ~ Soul Cakes
A Treat for the All Saints' Season

Ingredients:

100 g butter (a little less than a stick)

100 g caster sugar

2 eggs

250 g plain flour

Pinch saffron or turmeric (for colouring)

1 tsp clove

½ tsp mixed spice

1 tsp caraway seeds

2 tbs milk

Handful raisins

1/8 cup chopped candied ginger

Directions: Warm butter until slightly melted. Using an electric mixer, cream butter and sugar together in a medium-sized mixing bowl until light and fluffy. Whisk in eggs. Add flour and spices, adding enough milk to form a dough that holds together. Stir in raisins and candied ginger. Set oven to 360° F. Turn the dough out onto a floured surface and roll out to about 1 cm thick. Make cakes with 2-inch cookie cutter. Wipe a little milk over the cakes, slice thin crosses over the top, and sprinkle with sugar. Bake for about twenty minutes until golden and firm.

About the Authors

Abigail Falanga

Believing firmly in magic and merriment, valour and peace, Abigail Falanga is an author of fantasy and science fiction. She lives in New Mexico with family, books, too many hobbies, and many wild ambitions. Besides short stories published in various anthologies, she has released her first book, *A Time of Mourning and Dancing*, the beginning of a series of dark fantasy fairy-tale retellings.

Sarah Falanga

Sarah Falanga lives under the open skies of New Mexico, where she's growing her business of cosiness and enjoying simple pleasures. She started writing science-fiction stories when she became too old to 'make-believe' them. Her fiction is inspired by George MacDonald, C.S. Lewis, E. Nesbit, Ellis Peters, Doctor Who, Pixar movies, and Marvel movies. Besides writing, she loves to sketch, sew, bake, walk, and listen to music.

Joanna Bair

Joanna Bair has a BA in English and Theatre, having written and produced a handful of plays in the US and Malta. She's had short stories published in anthologies by Zimbell House Publishing, *Splickety, Spark,* and *Keys for Kids.* Her novella *Nightmare in Nice* is available on Amazon. A Connecticut native who has lived in England and Malta, Joanna now teaches in South Florida.

Sondra Bateman

Sondra Bateman has an undergraduate degree from the University of North Texas. She has read and studied history in all different time periods with great interest for many years and has found it quite engaging to bring different time periods to life with words for the avid reader.

Dana Bell

Owned by two cats, Taj and Esther, Dana Bell often uses felines in her tales. She is notorious for mixing genres and tying her various universes together. These include her Winter Trilogy, Five Systems/Borders and vampire cats. Currently she has three books released: *Bast's Chosen Ones, Winter Awakening* and *God's Gift.* She is an editor as well, with seven anthologies compiled and published. Belle Blukat is the pen name she uses for Paranormal Romances. Her first novel *Blood Bride* will be released soon. Hobbies include flower arranging, making candle holders, soap, and dollhouses.

Melinda K. Busch

In addition to her Whitstead stories, Melinda K. Busch has written four Arch Books and *The Maiden and the Toad*. She is currently co-writing a series of World War II novels with her wonderful husband, Andy. A book lover from her earliest days, Melinda's childhood imagination teemed with hobbits and dragons, talking beasts, and all manner of faerie. As a mother, a grandmother, and a writer, she hopes to inspire hearts and minds through her stories. She lives in Southern California with her husband and their three crazy mutts, and when she isn't writing, she keeps busy chasing the world's cutest grandbabies around the house.

Madisyn Carlin

Madisyn Carlin is a Christian, homeschool graduate, author, intern editor at AiG, and avid bookdragon. When not spending time with family and adding to her notebook hoard, she weaves tales of redemption, faith, and action.

Hillari DeSchane

Hillari DeSchane's 'Fatally Fun' family friendly cosy mysteries combine her four favourite things: The Regency Era of Jane Austen, mysteries, humour, and pets. *A Christmas Tail*, Hillari's debut novel, received a certificate of merit from the Cat Writers Association. When not traveling internationally to research her novels, Hillari enjoys training therapy dogs, volunteering with youth at her church, and serving on the board of her regional opera company. She lives in California with her 'Fur-rensics Team," Jocko the black Labrador and Ambrose the Siamese cat. Find Hillari's books including her latest pet cosy *Throw a Dog a Dead Man's Bone*, on Amazon in both digital and paperback formats. Follow her at hillarideschane.com or on Facebook and Instagram.

Sara Francis

Sara Francis is an author, media designer, and speaker. She has written/published the YA Dystopian/SciFi trilogy *The Terra Testimonies*, the children's series *Adventures of Wobot*, and the poetry collection *Stardust*. When she is not writing, she is designing for clients and assisting indie authors with social media marketing. Outside the professional realm, she loves a good mystery and playing games with friends. With everything she does, Sara Francis hopes to light a torch in the darkness with the desire that others will do the same and make the world bright again.

Erudessa Gentian

Erudessa Gentian is a firm believer that clean entertainment can be powerful. She strives to produce dynamic art that will spark imagination and touch souls. To learn more, visit www.erudessagentian.com

Ronnell Gibson

Ronnell surrounds herself with words and teenagers. She specializes in young adult contemporary with a sprinkling of the mysterious. She also writes youth and adult devotions and is one of the editors for HAVOK Publishing. Self-proclaimed coffee snob and Marvel movie addict, Ronnell has also titled herself a macaron padawan and a cupcake Jedi. High on her bucket list is to someday attend San Diego Comic Con. Ronnell lives in central Wisconsin, with her husband, two teenagers, and two Pomeranian puppies. Find out more about Ronnell at ronnellkaygibson.com.

Beka Gremikova

Beka Gremikova writes folkloric fantasy from her nook in the Ottawa Valley, Ontario, Canada. When she's not travelling, playing video games, or dabbling in art, she can be found curled up with a mystery novel. Her work is featured in Havok Publishing's anthologies Bingeworthy, Sensational, and Prismatic as well as the collections Moonlight and Claws, What Darkness Fears, Faces to the Sun, and A Kind of Death. Currently, she's plotting a plethora of dark fantasy fairy tales. To learn more about her various projects, you can follow her on Twitter, Facebook and Instagram, or sign up for her newsletter on her website, www.bekagremikova.com.

Pam Halter

Pam Halter is a children's picture book, middle grade, and YA fantasy author. She is also a freelance editor of picture books and the children's book editor for Fruitbearer Publishing. When she's not writing, Pam enjoys quilting, cooking, reading, playing the piano, and Bible study. Pam lives in South Jersey with her husband, special needs adult daughter, and three cats. You can learn more about her at www.pamhalter.com.

Faith Tilley Johnson

Faith Tilley Johnson is a multi-genre writer, recently published *Advent: A Journey of Preparation* and the fiction short story *Falling Through*. When not writing, she enjoys spending time with her family and hiking in her local state park.

Deborah Kelty

Abiding at a coastal town in North Wales with her family and three guinea pigs for company, Deborah Kelty immerses herself into writing imaginative tales inspired from Celtic folklore, ancient myths, and more. She has written short stories for writing competitions that include the BBC Young Writers Award, and currently completing her debut fantasy novel for a planned five-part series. Her interests consist of blogging, drawing, reading or binging films/TV shows, or exploring the nearby countryside. Website: www.writerlyobservance.com

R.J. Kingston

R.J. Kingston is an aspiring author who loves to write and sketch characters from his stories. He also enjoys painting and playing video games. His biggest goal is to publish his superhero stories one day

David W. Landrum

David W. Landrum teaches Literature at Grand Valley State University in Michigan. His fiction and poetry have appeared widely in journals in the US, UK, Canada, and Australia.

Sarah Levesque

Sarah Levesque loves stories, whether she is reading them, writing them or editing them. She is a high school teacher and the Editor in Chief of LogoSophia Magazine, as well as a freelance editor in her spare time. She loves the snows of her native New England and may be found curled up with her dogs near the Christmas tree with a Jane Austen book or her *Lord of the Rings* fanfiction.

Ari Lewis

Ari Lewis has always loved stories, especially fantasy and mysteries. Her love of stories drove her to study literature at the University of St. Katherine and then to pass on what she learned and loved to students as a high school English teacher. Her favourite authors include C.S. Lewis, G.K. Chesterton, Terry Pratchett, and Agatha Christie. Currently, she is living happily ever after with her husband in southern California.

Becky Ann Little

Becky Ann Little has been in missions for over thirty years, both in the states and Brazil. Which has given her a lot of fodder for the speculative stories she dreams up. When not writing, she enjoys spending time with her 10 grandchildren and her very bossy Cairn Terrier.

Erika Mathews

Erika Mathews writes Christian living books, both fiction and non-fiction, that demonstrate the power of God in the life of a believer, transforming daily life into His resting life. Her kingdom adventure novel series *Truth from Taerna* features spiritually challenging and refreshing adventure and unique Christian twists on cliched plots. Outside of writing, she spends time with her husband Josh, mothers her little ones, reads, edits, enjoys the great Minnesota outdoors, plays piano and violin, makes heroic ventures into minimalism, clean eating, and gardening, and uses the Oxford comma. You can connect with Erika at restinglife.com.

John K. Patterson

John K. Patterson is a lifelong lover of fantasy and science fiction. Fuelled mainly by coffee, Patterson is the author of the *Arrivers* series, and loves to challenge the word 'impossible' wherever it shows up. All the better that his stories can do so with aliens, dragons, dinosaurs, wizards, the undead, and on occasion all of the above. He lives at the roots of Pikes Peak in Colorado Springs, CO.

Nathan Peterson

Nathan is an aspiring novelist and artist. Growing up with a passion for all things Star Wars and Lord of the Rings, it's no surprise he loves weaving sci-fi, fantasy, and real life into his stories. When he's not drawing or writing, you can find him working out, eating 'rabbit food,' or watching movies. You can learn more about his new comic book series at vidarandhans.wordpress.com.

Lauren H. Salisbury

Lauren H. Salisbury is a lover of all things science fiction/fantasy, creative, and edible, but not always in that order. An English teacher for sixteen years, she now tutors part-time while trying to figure out how to use an MA in Education as an author. She lives in Yorkshire with her husband and a room full of books but likes to winter abroad, following the sunshine. Her favourite stories include faith, hope, and courage. Visit her website at laurenhsalisbury.com

Laura Nelson Selinksy

Laura Nelson Selinsky teaches British Literature, so she jumped at the chance to play with *A Christmas Carol* in Dickens' era Whitstead. She's published fiction and nonfiction in a variety of genres and is especially proud of her Christmas novella *Season of Hope* from Anaiah Press. If Laura can't travel the world with Barry, her beloved husband, and their family, then her favourite ways to have fun are teaching Chaucer, gardening, and leading second grade Sunday School.

Valerie Shaw

Valerie Shaw is a compulsive writer living in Upstate, NY, with her beloved husband and two tweenage kids. Valerie has written for the Upstate Gardener's Journal and blogged in women's ministry, but her real passion lies in writing fictional novels long past her bedtime. Valerie is a homeschool mom, an avid reader, and a staunch believer in both true love and second breakfast. You can find her on Twitter @ValerieYeva or on Facebook as VE Shaw.

Sarah Earlene Shere

Sarah Earlene Shere is an author, actress and cosplayer in her native home of Southern California. Sarah fell in love with storytelling at the age of eleven. As she's grown closer to God and fallen in love with Jesus, her stories have become biblical and allegorical, reflecting her favourite authors, John Bunyan and Hans Christian Andersen. Besides Amazon, Sarah's stories and writings can be found under Hosanna Heralds on Facebook and WordPress. Since 2018, Sarah has been acting with the Long Beach based Masquer Theatre Company. In 2017, she started volunteering with a local cosplay non-profit, Kids Can Cosplay.

E.J. Sobetski

Growing up, E.J. was usually outnumbered. Youngest of seven and the only boy, while an uncle of seventeen, Christmas can be very fun. (Or as he likes to call it, organised chaos.) E.J. loves fantasy with writers such as J. R. R. Tolkien, C. S. Lewis and Wayne Thomas Batson as inspiration. He has three books written with several more on the way. Find E.J. on Facebook and Amazon.

A.D. Uhlar

A.D. Uhlar's purpose is to unearth treasure as a wife, mother, writer, and teacher. Her treasure hunt has recently taken her to the University of Nebraska Omaha's MFA in Creative Writing program. Join her as her characters unearth treasure in all its forms. You may even unearth the treasure inside you! www.aduhlar.com

Ellie West

Ellie West is a sucker for happy endings. Tea and chocolate fuel her imagination. Her two dogs are her constant companions and have helped brainstorm more than one story, which could explain a lot. Ellie also writes contemporary fiction under the name E. A. West. Visit her website at ellie.eawestauthor.com.

Acknowledgements

The editors and compilers would like to extend deepest gratitude to…

Melinda Busch for proofreading and formatting, and conspiring Whitstead details with us. Her passion for this project almost equals our own, and without her Maisie Bloom wouldn't be here.

Sara Francis, for designing a beautiful cover yet again, perfectly capturing our vision and the essence of Whitstead adventures.

Hannah Falanga, for truly lovely paintings to grace the cover and inspire the authors.

Lauren Salisbury, for proofreading, being our long-suffering Genuine Brit, and catching our strange American foibles.

Joanna Bair, for proofreading with an eye for pesky Americanisms.

Chuck Heintzelman with PubShare, for being helpful and never more than an email away when we invariably run into problems.

Rodge, for giving up his afterlife for the sake of brevity.

To the authors for producing such amazing stories, and to all the others who couldn't write stories this time for their community, imagination, and support.

To our family and friends.

And to our Lord Jesus Christ, for inspiration, guidance, love, and most of all for being the true Light in the darkness.